MISSING IN MALMÖ

Torquil MacLeod

MᶜNIDDER & GRACE CRIME

To Corbyn. Always make sure you enjoy life.

Published by McNidder & Grace
21 Bridge Street
Carmarthen
SA31 3JS

www.mcnidderandgrace.co.uk

Original paperback first published in 2015
©Torquil MacLeod and Torquil MacLeod Books Ltd
www.torquilmacleodbooks.com

A catalogue record for this work is available from the British Library.

ISBN: 9780857161154

Designed by Obsidian Design

Printed and bound in the United Kingdom by
Short Run Press Ltd, Exeter, UK

ABOUT THE AUTHOR

Torquil MacLeod was born in Edinburgh. He now lives in Cumbria with his wife, Susan. He came up with the idea for the Malmö Mysteries after visiting his elder son in southern Sweden in 2000. He still goes to Malmö regularly to see his Swedish grandson.

Missing in Malmö is the third book in the series of best-selling crime mysteries featuring Inspector Anita Sundström. *Midnight in Malmö* is the fourth story.

ACKNOWLEDGEMENTS

This book wouldn't have been possible without the input of the following Swedes: Paula for all that jazz, Sigyn's views of living in Britain, Göran for running a Swedish eye over the novel, Eva for taking me to the Moderna Museet, and, of course, Karin for useful titbits on Swedish policing and much besides. Again, liberties taken with police procedure are entirely mine.

I'd also like to thank Vanessa for medical advice, Fraser for restraining my use of extraneous Swedish information, Nick at The Roundhouse for another great cover design, and Calum and Sarah for their usual support. Last, but not least, I would like to thank Susan for all the toil she's put in to make the novel work. It is far better now than when I first presented it to her.

I would also like to thank all those friends and readers who have encouraged me with their positive comments. It makes it all worthwhile.

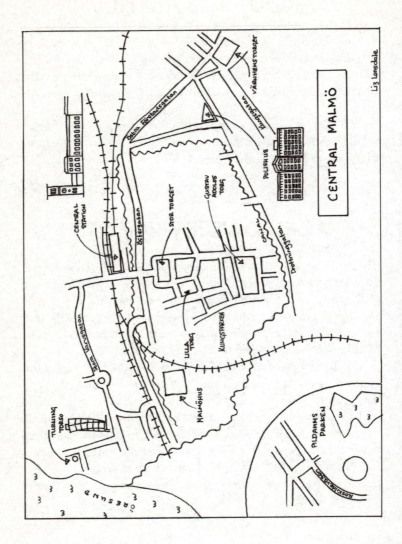

CENTRAL MALMÖ

Liz Lonsdale

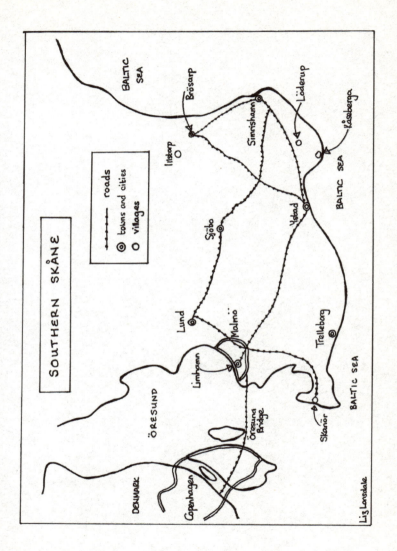

SOUTHERN SKÅNE

BALTIC SEA

Brösarp

Löderup

Simrishamn

Ilstorp

Kåseberga

BALTIC SEA

roads
towns and cities
villages

Sjöbo

Ystad

Lund

Malmö

Limhamn

ÖRESUND

Trelleborg

BALTIC SEA

Öresund Bridge

Skanör

DENMARK

Copenhagen

Liz Lonsdale

PROLOGUE

It was like an explosion in the still night air. The sound reverberated round the unused wharfs and shabby warehouses, which, by 1993, were devoid of the vibrancy which had characterised the River Tyne for centuries. To him, there was no mistaking the noise. The sawn-off shotgun had just pumped its deadly contents into something – or someone – down below on the quayside. Shit! That wasn't supposed to happen! He got a clear view through his night-vision binoculars. He could make out the horror on the face of the jeweller illuminated by the light above the gangway, but the rest of the scene was obscured by the security van. This couldn't go wrong. It mustn't.

His mind raced back to a brief half hour ago. Then, everything seemed to be working like clockwork. He had taken up his place on a deserted Ballast Hill Road. It gave him a perfect view of Commission Quay below. It was a clear night. The Tyne shimmered in the light of a striking half-moon. On the opposite bank, the lights of South Shields glowed in pockets among swathes of darkness. It was bright enough to make out the hulk of The Sentinel as it lay motionless at its berth. It was the only ship by the North Shields quay that night. The ferry terminal beyond was empty; its last occupant had left for Scandinavia a few hours earlier. In the other direction, he could see a cluster of small fishing boats bobbing on the incoming tide. Looming above them was the whitewashed tower of the Low Lights, which had once guided ships into the mouth of the Tyne.

He had known when the diamonds were to be taken off the ship – at a time of night long after the other British-bound cargo had been unloaded so as not to arouse any curiosity. The Sentinel had arrived from Holland that October afternoon. The consignment of diamonds was bound for a group of independent North East jewellers who had set up a consortium to buy directly from one of the top houses in Amsterdam. Combining their resources would guarantee a respectable discount on an otherwise inconceivable deal. And what a deal! He wasn't sure of the amount, but it was supposedly upwards of four million pounds.

That's why he had alerted Nicky Pew, one of the region's more specialist villains. Pew was known to the police, but they had never been able to pin any robberies on him. From his large house in Darras Hall, an upwardly mobile enclave just north of Newcastle, Pew planned robberies with panache. He was careful that his crew carried out jobs well away from their home turf. His rule had always been that they do the job, get away as fast as possible and keep their heads down in the safety of their own back yard, while whoever was investigating the crime would hassle their own felons. But this one had fallen into his lap. It was too good to ignore. And rules were there to be broken.

Nicky Pew was an interesting character. A smart boy from a small town near Liverpool, he had gone to a minor public school and then university, where he wasted his time playing his crazy shit jazz before dropping out. He could have turned his hand to anything, but crime, which he carried out with aplomb, was his chosen route to riches. Even the cops had a grudging admiration for him. He was charming, sophisticated and utterly ruthless. Not a person to cross. But Pew had never actually killed anyone on a job. That's why the shot was so alarming.

He didn't have an intimate knowledge of Pew's plan, but he knew the pick-up schedule. Two customs officers had arrived at ten and gone on board. Shortly afterwards, a white Mercedes belonging to the Newcastle jeweller, Quentin Myers, the consortium's contact, pulled up close to the gangway. This was followed by an Imerson Security Services van with a driver and two guards. The driver stayed in the van while all the others went onto The Sentinel. The police had been informed out of courtesy, but had not been asked to supply any support. This was a private business transaction.

The handover was to take place on the vessel. He assumed that Pew and his gang wouldn't carry out the robbery on the ship itself. Narrow corridors and umpteen cabins would make it a lottery. And once the diamonds were in the security van, the task would be even more difficult. The gangway was the weak point. He'd already heard the puttering of an outboard engine, so knew their escape route was across the river. They would then vanish into the wilderness of South Shields, where a getaway car would be waiting for them. By the time the police were alerted, they would be long gone. As he anxiously scanned the area, he had briefly caught sight of the inflatable dinghy, just before it disappeared under the lip of the quay wall, only a few yards from the ship. At the same time, what looked like a Ford Sierra had snaked down the incline and driven slowly past the Mercedes and security van, before turning back towards the parked vehicles. Then he had heard voices and turned his glasses onto the gangway. The two security officers had appeared first, one with a briefcase chained to his wrist. Behind him was Myers, the jeweller, and someone he hadn't seen before – presumably the representative from the Dutch diamond house. He heard muffled voices and hoarse laughter then three masked men had appeared from the Sierra. One had a shotgun – he knew that would be Pew. He couldn't see what happened next because of the van. Then came the explosive shot. His mind raced and he steeled himself to stay calm. Then he got the hell out.

CHAPTER 1

Greta Jansson twirled her glass of chardonnay. The light liquid lapped against the side before settling down. She checked her phone again; she was waiting for a call from Ulrika to tell her which bar she was in. Greta hadn't seen her since she had fled Uppsala, and now she wanted to put her old university friend straight about what had happened. Ulrika was down in Malmö for a meeting, and was fitting in a drink before she took a late flight back up to Stockholm.

This evening was important to Greta. It would be the first chance she had had to explain what she had done and, more importantly, why she had come south to restart her life. 2012 had been a bad year – the sooner she put it behind her the better. At first, the situation she had found herself in had become irritating. Then more alarming. Finally, she had actually felt in danger, and had had to get away. Yet in the two months she had been in Malmö, she hadn't been able to talk to anyone about it, other than the odd hint to colleagues. A fresh start meant that she was dealing with people who had no idea about her and her past. That was the attraction. They treated her on a blissfully superficial level because they weren't encumbered with the knowledge of the emotional baggage that she carried around with her every day. Yet the disadvantage was that she had no outlets for the feelings that she couldn't escape from, however hard she tried. Hence, her delight when

Ulrika called and said she was making a flying visit to Malmö, and could they hook up when her meeting was finished? Ulrika knew the background, and the man that was at the epicentre of her problems. She would understand and sympathise. And, hopefully, Ulrika would endorse her decision to escape. The thought made her feel better. She was more relaxed than she had been for some time. She hadn't even minded being chatted up by the young barman.

The place was filling up. Young professionals celebrating the end of the working week. A noisy group of men were laughing at one of their number. The joker. Her own life had been laughter-free for quite a while. But she liked her new colleagues at Kungsskolan, one of the city's secondary schools. The teaching was tough as most of the kids didn't understand why they had to learn English when many of them were struggling to get to grips with Swedish, the language of their newly adopted country. Not many of them would end up like the executives who were buying their expensive drinks in this Lilla Torg bar. Greta wasn't sure what a modern Sweden had to offer her students. They were mistrusted. Misunderstood. Certainly they were a challenge, but one that she was starting to enjoy in a rather masochistic way.

The group of young men spilled out into Lilla Torg, Malmö's trendiest square, and gathered round a couple of the tables. Though it was the end of September, the early evening was pleasant, and the gas heaters would keep them warm. Greta suddenly became aware of her mobile phone buzzing. She opened her bag and took it out. The name of the caller was illuminated. She tensed and stared at the screen for a few moments as the mobile continued to vibrate in her hand. Then she cut the connection. She left the phone on the wooden table top next to the glass of wine.

Ten minutes later, there was hardly room to stand, let alone sit. It was getting harder to keep a seat free for her friend.

Greta had nearly finished her wine and she glanced yet again at her watch. How much longer would she give her? Another fifteen minutes? She would nurse her drink until then. She had relied on Ulrika to pick up the tab. Her friend would probably put it on expenses. Greta's mobile buzzed again. This time Ulrika's name came up. 'Hi! Where are you?'

'Greta, I'm so sorry. The bloody meeting has overrun and I'm not going to have time to meet you, or I'll miss my flight.'

'Why not stay the night in my apartment and then go back to Stockholm tomorrow morning?'

'Oh, Greta, I wish I could, but I've got something on first thing tomorrow. I really wanted to see you and find out why you suddenly disappeared.'

'I really can't explain over the phone.'

Ulrika said she understood and that they'd have to catch up another time. Then she rang off.

Greta felt a sudden surge of disappointment engulf her. Tonight was going to be a release, a safety valve for her pent-up frustrations and disorientated emotions. She had even made the effort to look smart because she knew that Ulrika, now a successful businesswoman, would be immaculately turned out. As it was, it looked like it was going to be another early night. Then she heard a voice.

'Why don't I get you another one?'

CHAPTER 2

Fridolfs café. Graeme Todd bit into his cinnamon bun. This was so exciting! This was where Kurt Wallander came to get his pastries and cups of coffee. A place to give him sustenance when faced with yet another baffling – usually gruesome – case. All right, he was a fictional character – Graeme knew that – but Henning Mankell must have come here himself so he could situate his famous detective in real places. From his table, Todd surveyed the overcast, early-October scene through the large picture window. This was his first visit to the country, and Ystad was living up to all his expectations of a Swedish town. The first thing he'd done after leaving his train, hurrying along the seemingly endless platform and plunging into the bustling square, was to get a Wallander Trail leaflet from the tourist information office. The tall, blonde girl at the desk had smiled pleasantly, obviously used to the sparkling enthusiasm. He had followed the route religiously, only deviating once to take a quick look at the port, where an impressive, multi-decked ferry was about to leave for Poland. Todd was in heaven. As he made his way to Wallander's flat in Mariagatan, he soaked up the atmosphere like salt on spilt red wine. The town's quaint and colourful cottages nestled happily alongside modern structures, the latter not detracting from the pleasing aesthetics. Many of the streets were cobbled and had narrow pavements, and in some of the shop doorways candles spluttered, brightening the gloom. Though not much interested in architecture, Todd couldn't help but admire the Gothic Hansa Sankta Maria Kyrka (where Kurt had married Mona) and the neo-classical theatre with its pale-yellow columns and dark-maroon panels and pediments. But the highlight of the tour had to be the elegant Hotel Continental, where Wallander had gone when he had an occasion to celebrate. The patient receptionist, used to the constant procession of Wallander addicts wandering into the foyer, had been more than happy to take his photograph, while giving him a potted history of the hotel (apparently one of Sweden's oldest, opened in 1829). Moreover, she didn't even show any outward disappointment when he failed to go into the restaurant, leaving after his coffee. She simply inhaled slowly and promised herself, yet again, that she must get round to reading one of the bloody books.

It was the real, recognisable locations that fascinated Todd about the Wallander stories. He remembered his wife, Jennifer, dragging him off for a holiday in Dorset once to follow Thomas Hardy's novels. He'd never really liked Hardy. *Tess of the d'Urbervilles* had been enough for him – too much fatalism. Yet visiting the locations which Hardy had used had inspired him to read more. Now he was experiencing Kurt Wallander's world. Possibly not on the same plane as Hardy's, he had to admit, but he was comfortable with it.

Todd took a sip of his coffee. He winced slightly. It was strong. The coffee at the hotel, too, had been more robust than he was used to at home. Maybe it was a Swedish thing. The bun was tasty. He wiped away a crumb from his lip. He wasn't really that hungry, even though this was the first food he had had since an early breakfast that morning. The excitement of going round the Wallander sights had banished the nervousness he now felt. It wouldn't be long now. He wasn't sure how it was going to play out. The main reason he was sitting in this little café in a small town in the south of Sweden was the result of his own Wallander-like investigations. He had dug for information just as diligently as any detective. It had produced a cast of characters, involved interviewing many of them and had eventually led to the person he was after. What had pleased him most was that he had succeeded where others, with infinitely superior resources, had failed. He couldn't help a smug smile.

He toyed with the remains of his bun. He realised he couldn't finish it. In the next hour he would meet someone who was going to change his life. All the skills he had learned over the years, all the grafting and hours of mind-numbing research, the wasted leads, the paltry successes were now invested in this one moment. Everything that had gone before would mean nothing. This was the "jackpot". He had better not blow it.

He took another sip of his coffee. It did nothing to quell the tingling thrill of anxious anticipation. He glanced at his watch before pushing his cup away. 13.22. Graeme Todd stood up and left Fridolfs.

CHAPTER 3

Inspector Anita Sundström stared at her computer screen. She had just finished a report on the arrest of an arsonist that she and Hakim had eventually apprehended after two weeks of boring surveillance. They had caught the culprit red-handed as he was in the process of starting a potential conflagration at the site of a factory unit on the outskirts of Malmö. They had enough evidence for a conviction. Whether he would do much time inside was another matter. But that, she thought with a sigh, was the Swedish justice system.

She glanced across the compact office where Hakim was squeezed in behind his desk. Though the office was modern, this one wasn't designed for two members of staff. The young police trainee didn't bother to stifle a yawn. They hadn't had much sleep over the last three nights.

'Hakim, go home. Get your mamma to make you a nice meal, and then get some sleep.'

Hakim flashed Anita a grateful smile.

'Don't bother coming in until lunchtime tomorrow. Enjoy a lie in.'

'What about the chief inspector?' Khalid Hakim Mirza knew Chief Inspector Moberg's notorious temper only too well, having now been attached to the Skåne County Criminal Investigation Squad for over a year. The chief inspector wasn't the most tolerant or understanding of bosses.

She peered over the top of her spectacles. 'Don't worry about him. Now go!'

The tall, thin, swarthy young man with jet black hair quickly extricated himself from behind his desk. He turned his engaging smile on again as he left.

She knew she would miss him dreadfully when he moved on at Christmas. At first, she had resented having Hakim dumped on her, but it hadn't taken her long to become fond of him. It hadn't been easy for him, coming from a Muslim immigrant background. It was bad enough coping with the in-built prejudices of some of his colleagues without having to deal with the friction his chosen profession caused among many of his peers, who were jobless, angry and resentful at the way modern Sweden regarded and treated them. She also had a special bond with Hakim – he had saved her life, and she his.

Christmas would also see the retirement of Detective Henrik Nordlund. That would be a wrench, too, as Nordlund had been her unofficial mentor over the years. He had been the sane voice in many a mad moment. The one person in the Criminal Investigation Squad she could turn to when things got rough. He was always there to advise her, and he had been the only member of the force to visit her when she had been suspended following the shooting incident on top of Malmö's tallest building, the Turning Torso. She had become the unofficial scapegoat. Since then, she had rehabilitated both herself and her reputation by helping to clear up a number of murders connected to a right-wing group of businessmen in the Wollstad Case, as well as another homicide linked to a series of art thefts. But even after these successes, it didn't mean it was all plain sailing. She still had to deal with chauvinist colleagues who found it difficult to come to terms with women working on the same level as them. Near the top of the list was Chief Inspector Erik Moberg.

Moberg was a huge man. That was the politest way to

describe a seriously overweight officer whose answer to any crisis seemed to be to eat more. Throw in an explosive temperament and an appalling attitude to the opposite sex, whether they were colleagues or not, and you could understand why he'd had two failed marriages and his third was hanging by a thread. Unsurprisingly, he had no idea how to treat his female inspectors. At forty-four, Anita was still lively and attractive, and that seemed to obscure Moberg's view of her as a competent detective. But he was no fool – he had never tried to take advantage of his position in any sexual way. That role was taken up by the reptilian Karl Westermark, Anita's *bête noire*. Though a few years younger, Westermark – handsome in a stereotypically blond, square-jawed way – didn't know whether his feelings towards Anita were those of loathing or lust. In fact, he experienced both. He saw her as his main rival in the team, and had done everything he could to denigrate her in Moberg's eyes, yet still he couldn't help thinking with his balls. To Westermark, any woman under a certain age was fair game, and it rankled that Anita had failed to succumb to what he thought were his obvious charms. Westermark had even resorted to trying to blackmail her into having sex with him. After that strategy had failed, his hold over her loosened dramatically when suspicion fell on him for tipping off the wealthy industrialist, Dag Wollstad, who had managed to evade justice by a matter of hours. Nothing could be proved, but he knew that Anita had suspected him. And that was enough to keep him at bay; a seething resentment never far from the surface. Except when he had drunkenly put his hand up her skirt at last year's police Christmas party. He wouldn't do that again.

Anita sighed and shut down her computer. She picked up the paper coffee cup on her desk and dropped it into the bin. Time to go home and open a bottle of red wine. Would Lasse be there when she got in? Would he have something for her to eat, or would she have to cook again tonight? She glanced at her son's photo next to the computer. He had his father's smile.

But until last summer, he had been the antithesis of Björn. Lasse was only ten when Bjorn left. Anita's almost overwhelming love for him had intensified when, even at that young age, he had shouldered his responsibilities and tried to take on some of his father's role. The inevitable split had been caused by Anita's academic husband's extracurricular activities with a string of female students. Since the break-up, she and Lasse had created a mutual-support system. They had done everything together, from going to cheer on their beloved Malmö FF to holidays in Spain. Lasse himself had actually organised the last couple of foreign trips. He was meticulous to a fault, which reflected his naturally tidy habits and flair for organisation. Domestically, Anita was chaotic, and her handbag had always been a standing joke between them. He called it her "black hole" as she could never find anything once it had disappeared inside. But the most important aspect of their relationship, as far as Anita was concerned, was that they could always talk. They had no secrets. After a bad day at the office, she would come back to their apartment in Roskildevägen, and he would be a sympathetic ear.

When Lasse had left home for university two years ago, she had been distraught. It was like losing a limb. Then he had found his first serious girlfriend. The awful Rebecka, as Anita came to think of her, was a selfish little piece and seemed to enjoy driving a wedge between mother and son. And, heartbreakingly, Lasse was too smitten to see that they were drifting apart. Young love truly is blind. In her more rational moments, Anita knew perfectly well that it was pure jealousy on her part. Then, at the end of last summer, Lasse was dumped. Anita's initial jubilation was tempered by the obvious hurt her son was suffering. She knew only too well how difficult it is to cope with rejection. The unfortunate side-effect of this emotional angst was that Lasse refused to go back to university – Rebecka was there. Anita suggested he move somewhere else. He wasn't interested.

In fact, he wasn't interested in anything at all, and just moped around the apartment doing nothing and getting under Anita's feet. After a while, her maternalistic understanding began to melt away as his behaviour started to irritate her. He no longer helped with the chores and left everywhere a mess. This was a boy whose tidiness had often put his mother's to shame.

Anita stood up. She was tired. It was getting dark outside. Winter wasn't far away. She gazed out of her office window over the park across the road from the polishus. The large police headquarters building, with its functionalist design and myriad windows, looked out onto Malmö's central canal on one side and Rörsjöparken on the other. The park was a good place to sit and relax on a warm summer's day. Beyond the park she could see lights starting to glow in the buildings on the other side of the wide, tree-lined Kungsgatan. As she stood back, she suddenly glimpsed her reflection in the glass. She stopped and stared at a face she hardly recognised. She felt she had aged in the last two years. Wrinkles were starting to appear around her eyes, noticeable despite the black frame of her glasses. Her blonde hair was short and seemed to accentuate her features. Maybe she should start to grow it again, or was she now too old? Little bulges were now evident above the belt of her jeans. She wondered if the popular 5:2 diet Klara Wallen had recommended would help, but even dieting only two days a week would still probably be too much for her self-discipline. She was conscious that her thighs were a little thicker than they should be. Her arse would be the next to go. That had been like a magnet to Björn's hands when he had been in love with her. But no one had touched it for ages. Unhappily, she turned away from the window. The beauty she had taken for granted was now starting to desert her. And her self-esteem was eroding. She hadn't had sex for what seemed like years. It was partly her own fault. She was in love with a man that she couldn't have any kind of physical relationship with.

She had put him in prison. Bloody Ewan Strachan. He was the man she had saved at the top of the Turning Torso when she shot film director, Mick Roslyn. And, as she later discovered, Mick was innocent – it was Ewan who'd murdered Roslyn's wife. She still went cold whenever she thought back to that scene in the restaurant when Ewan had confessed. But by then she had fallen for him, and it was only her professional pride, stronger than she'd ever suspected, which resulted in Strachan being incarcerated in Malmö's Kirseberg prison. It was a ludicrous situation. The relationship had no future. It didn't really have a past. Nothing had happened between them. There hadn't been time. She had tried to cut the emotional ties, but she had found herself making the occasional prison visit. The pretexts had always been related to the investigation. It was these trips that Westermark had somehow found out about and had tried to blackmail her with in order to get her into his bed. Now that was no longer an issue. She realised she had to make the break and lift her life out of this emotional limbo. And soon. This had gone on for a year and a half. Why were things so complicated?

Anita clicked off the lamp on her desk. She put on her battered, brown leather jacket, swung her heavy, black handbag over her shoulder and made for the door. Then the phone made her jump. She stared at it and let it ring. She hadn't the energy to answer it. It was too late. Then weary instinct took over and she picked up the receiver.

'Anita Sundström.'

'Klara here.' It was Klara Wallen, the other woman detective on their team. Anita gave an internal sigh. Klara probably wanted to go out for a drink and discuss her domestic problems. Anita wasn't in the mood.

'I've got this woman on the line. She's calling from England,' Klara explained. 'I think it's better if you speak to her because my English isn't very good.'

Anita had spent two childhood years in northern England,

as well as a year on secondment to the Metropolitan Police in London, so anything that came up which involved speaking English, she was expected to handle. That's how she had ended up meeting Ewan Strachan. Now she reluctantly agreed to take the call. She waited for the woman to be put through.

'Hello, this is Inspector Anita Sundström speaking,' she said in her near-perfect accent. 'How can I help?'

There was panic in the voice at the other end of the line.

'My husband. He's gone missing!'

CHAPTER 4

Anita entered her apartment in Roskildevägen at twenty past nine. If it had been a couple of hours earlier, she might have considered a run in Pildammsparken opposite her home. But now she was far too weary. There was no sign of Lasse when she got in. So no food ready. At least he had gone out. Over the last few months, he had either hidden himself away in his bedroom chained to his computer, or been slouched in the living room watching rubbish on the telly.

The first thing she needed was a drink. There was a half-empty bottle of Chilean Shiraz next to the fridge. That would do for now. But what the hell? Tomorrow was Friday, and she had the weekend off. She would go down to the *Systembolag* and get herself a really nice bottle. Maybe two, as Lasse was sure to want some; not that he deserved any. She fished out a glass from the overhead cupboard and plonked it on the kitchen table. She poured out the wine. While it settled, she opened the fridge to see if there was anything to eat. She couldn't be bothered to cook. The shelves were sparsely stocked. That meant a big food shop, too. She couldn't rely on Lasse to do it. He was so weighed down with self-pity that he hadn't even the inclination to push a supermarket trolley. What was she going to do with him? What was she going to eat? There were four meat balls left from a previous meal. There was some beetroot. She could make a sandwich, and a salad to pad it out. But that could wait. She picked up her glass and wandered next door.

In the living room, Anita went over to the window and closed the blinds, which blotted out the tall trees that formed the dense perimeter of the park on the other side of the road. She switched on a lamp and curled up on her IKEA day bed. She didn't turn on the TV, as she was still mulling over the phone call she had had from England. It had taken a few minutes to calm the woman down. Eventually, Anita gathered that she was called Jennifer Todd and that she was ringing from Cumbria. It was an area that Anita had visited with her parents when they lived in Durham when her father was working at the nearby Electrolux factory. Anita had gradually coaxed some sort of coherent story out of her. Her husband, Graeme, had been on a trip to Sweden and had been due back that day. Jennifer had driven down to pick him up from Manchester Airport. He didn't emerge from the Easyjet flight from Copenhagen. And he wasn't answering his mobile phone. She hadn't spoken to him for three days.

Once Anita had got that information out of the way, she asked what Graeme Todd was doing in Malmö. It was a business trip. What was his business? He was a probate researcher. Jennifer had initially used the phrase "heir hunter". Anita hadn't come across that term before. Jennifer's explanation had been somewhat confusing, due to her agitated state, but it appeared that her husband was going to meet someone who would be the beneficiary of an old lady, a certain Doris Little, who had died without making a will.

Did Jennifer know who it was? No.

Did this person live in Malmö? She didn't know.

When was the last time she had spoken to him? She said he had phoned her when he had arrived at his hotel on Monday evening. He planned to have two days in Malmö and then fly back today, Thursday. Anita suggested that maybe he had missed his flight and was having trouble with his mobile.

Where was he staying? That was one of Jennifer's major

concerns. Graeme was meant to be staying at the Hotel Comfort. Anita knew it. It was behind the Central Station. It was also where Ewan had stayed on his ill-fated visit. But when Jennifer had rung the hotel, they said that they had never heard of Graeme Todd and he had certainly not stayed there. Even Anita conceded that that was odd.

All Anita had been able to do was to reassure the woman that she would hand over all the information to the Missing Persons Unit. She knew that they wouldn't actually do anything until Graeme Todd had officially been missing for three days, which meant nothing would happen until after the weekend. Not that she told Jennifer Todd that. It was the last thing the poor woman would want to hear.

Any further thoughts about the absconding Graeme Todd, whom Anita had assumed was probably playing away from home, as the British liked to refer to it, were banished when she heard the front door open and close. Lasse was back. He appeared at the door of the living room. He was tall and angular and, though he had Björn's looks, he had inherited Anita's high cheek bones and grey-green eyes. Fortunately, she hadn't passed on her poor eyesight gene, and he had no need for glasses.

'Anything to eat?'

'I was hoping that you'd have something ready for me.' She couldn't keep the annoyance out of her voice. Another argument was brewing. Until he had gone away to university, they had hardly exchanged a cross word. Now it was almost a daily occurrence.

'I'll help myself.'

'Where have you been?' she called after him.

She heard a muffled 'Out.'

This was driving her mad. She took a large gulp of wine.

It had been a good morning so far. Not much on, the weekend coming up, and she had a freshly brewed coffee on the desk, which was actually tidy for once. Then Chief Inspector Erik Moberg lumbered into the room. The light through the open doorway disappeared as he filled the space. 'Where's the kid?' he asked, nodding at Hakim's empty desk.

'He's doing something for me,' Anita lied. Hakim should be catching up on some much-needed sleep. Anita hoped that Moberg was here to thank Hakim and herself for their work on the arson case.

Moberg grunted. He held up a piece of paper in his meat plate of a hand. 'I hear you had a phone call from England last night.'

'Yeah. A woman thinks her husband might be missing in Malmö. I'm going to pass it on to Missing Persons, but he's only been unaccounted for since yesterday afternoon. Probably just missed his plane. He may even have turned up by now, or at least got in touch.'

Moberg pursed his chubby lips. 'I want you to check it out.'

'Fine.'

'If he still hasn't turned up, I want you and the Arab to look into it.'

Anita bridled at Moberg's turn of phrase, but she was also exasperated that she was going to be shoved onto some missing persons case.

'Why us?'

'Because the commissioner has got wind of it. Malmö has suffered enough bad publicity recently with shootings, race problems and an upturn in crime, without a foreign visitor disappearing as well. The city wants to encourage tourists and business people. This won't help.'

'But it's not what we do normally,' Anita protested.

'Well, you shouldn't speak English so bloody well, should you?'

'What about the attack on the pensioner in Segevång? I thought you'd want me to help Henrik, now that the arson business is sorted out.'

'Westermark can help Nordlund when he comes back from holiday on Monday.'

Anita was about to protest further when she saw that Moberg was becoming angry. The warning sign was the reddening of his cheeks.

'Just do it.'

He turned away like a Baltic ferry manoeuvring out of harbour, and left. Not a mention of the successful arrest of the arsonist. Fucking typical.

CHAPTER 5

'You're sure you haven't seen this man?'

The hotel receptionist screwed up her eyes to show that she really was concentrating. She shook her head again. Anita was showing her a photo that Jennifer Todd had emailed to her. Graeme Todd was a man of about sixty, with dark-brown hair, thinning at the front. It was obviously dyed – the colour was uniform. Why did men of a certain age dye their hair?, Anita wondered. It made their faces look older, their features more severe. Todd's eyebrows were thick and his chin had fashionably short stubble. He had a mole close to his right nostril. The eyes were brown and piercing. Not a flicker of a smile. The man staring out from the A4 sheet of paper was confident, and probably a little vain. That was Anita's interpretation anyway. She could be miles off the mark, though she had learned to make snap judgements about people over the years. Often she had been right.

'And no one named Todd has checked in over the last few days?'

Again there was an apologetic shake of the head.

Anita was following up the call she had made to the hotel last night. It always paid to double-check. Maybe Todd's wife had just got the wrong place.

'Were you full on Monday night?'

'No,' the receptionist answered emphatically. 'We only had half-occupancy on Monday. And Tuesday.'

Anita thanked her. She left the hotel and shoved the picture of Graeme Todd into her bag. Maybe he was running away from his wife. Sweden was an excuse to leave and he had gone elsewhere. Her instinct was that he would turn up soon. She had Hakim checking incoming flights to Kastrup Airport. At least that would show that he had made it as far as Copenhagen. Standing on the pavement outside the hotel, she remembered how she had gone to see Ewan Strachan the day after the body of Roslyn's wife was found. The journalist had been eating his breakfast. It was their second conversation. Now he dominated her thoughts in a way that a lover does. She took out her tin of snus, picked out a little sachet of tobacco and planted it under her top lip. If she couldn't smoke, this was the next best thing to calm her down. And a visit to Ewan always caused her some anxiety.

Anita was standing outside Malmö Kirseberg prison when her mobile phone burst into life.

'Anita Sundström.'

'Hakim here.'

'Any luck?'

'Yes. A Graeme Laurence Todd arrived at Kastrup on an Easyjet flight from Manchester last Monday, October the first. The plane landed at 13.45.'

'OK. That's fine. I'll think we'll forget about it until Monday. He'll probably have surfaced by then. Have a good weekend.'

'Aren't you coming back?'

'No. Something's come up that I need to attend to.'

'Need any help?' She wished she could sound so enthusiastic these days.

'It's all right, Hakim. This is something I need to do myself.'

Anita tramped along the same corridors each time she visited Ewan Strachan. They always met in the same room. She always used the same excuse. It was "police business". Ostensibly, she was still trying to find out if he had also killed his student lover after Mick Roslyn had stolen her from him and then cast her aside. She knew the answer. Ewan had admitted pushing the girl off the cathedral tower in Durham back in his days at the university. She hadn't mentioned it to the authorities, as he was going to be charged with the murder of Mick Roslyn anyway. That had plagued her conscience and she hadn't really known why she'd done it until, after a certain amount of drink-fuelled analysis, she had admitted to herself that she wanted him to stay in Sweden. She hadn't gone to the jail for several months. She knew it would be a futile exercise. She was in love with – and was loved by – a man who would spend the next twenty years of his life in prison. And he deserved to be there, which made her feelings even more contradictory, more confused and more tormented. She had tried to put an end to it by just not going any more. But then she went back. Not that Ewan was aware of this internal conflict between head and heart. She never articulated her feelings toward him. He was just grateful to see her and spend a few minutes in her company, for the visits were always short. Yet she could confide in him about her problems in a way that she had never been able to with Bjorn, and told him things she would never tell another living soul. Not even her few close friends. Ewan would listen, he would understand and he would often quietly advise. Then he would make her laugh. No one else could still make her smile, even when her world was at its most wretched. Yet the whole situation was preposterous – what a paradox! She was a cop. He was a murderer. A double one. And yet she still waited in the sparse, windowless room with its battered plastic table and three uncomfortable chairs, in a state of nervous anticipation for the man who was publicly *persona non grata* but who dominated her thoughts.

Ewan didn't look well. She hadn't seen him for nearly three months and the change was marked. He was even gaunter than he had been on her last visit. The shaved head didn't help. The plump cheeks, the red hair and the mischievous, twinkling eyes that had been part of the man that she had surprisingly fallen for were now all gone. Though he did manage a smile, Anita couldn't disguise her shock at his condition.

'Christ, do I look that bad?' This was accompanied by his customary smirk.

'No. It's just that you're so thin. Aren't you eating properly?' She had reverted to her maternal default setting.

He played with his hands in a distracted manner. She could sense that there was something wrong.

'What's up?'

Ewan glanced up at her. 'You haven't been for a while.' The tone was matter-of-fact and not admonishing. He was changing the subject.

'Been busy. And now Lasse's at home all the time, I have my hands full.'

'It must be good. I mean having Lasse around.'

She sighed and pulled her snus tin out of her bag. 'He's driving me mad at the moment. I don't know what to do with him.' She went on to explain why he was causing her so much angst. Ewan listened, as he always did.

'He'll come good,' he said when she had finished. 'Give him time. Space.'

They fell silent.

'You know, Anita. You're the only visitor I've had in a year and a half. Except for the suited half-wit who calls himself the British Consul. He came a couple months ago to make sure I was being treated properly – probably thinks he's upholding the Geneva Convention, or something. I don't think he can wait for me to drop dead or be transferred.'

'Do you want to go to a British prison? Maybe near your brother?'

Ewan raised a laugh. 'You're kidding. He's a respectable lawyer. He only deals with genteel crime. Fraudsters, insider traders... not with your common-or-garden murderers. He's washed his hands of me.' He paused. 'Besides, you're here.'

An awkward stillness pervaded the dismal room. Their eyes engaged. She wanted to say so much to him, but the words stuck in her throat. She was afraid.

'I love you.'

Anita was exhilarated and embarrassed at the same time. It wasn't the first time that he had said it to her. She had never told Ewan that she loved him, even though she yearned to. It was a psychological barrier she couldn't overcome. It seemed like an eternity before she said, 'I know.'

Now it was her turn to change the subject. 'I can see that something's troubling you. Tell me.'

Thoughtfully, he ran his hand over the top of his shaven head.

'Nothing really.' Then he sat up in his chair. Was he going to tell her? She didn't find out because her mobile suddenly started ringing. She pulled an apologetic face as she took out her phone and saw who it was. 'Lasse,' she mouthed.

'Hi. What's up?'

'Mamma. You'd better come home.'

'Is it important?'

'It's Dad. He's here!'

CHAPTER 6

As soon as she let herself into the apartment, the tall figure of Lasse was there to greet her.

'What is it?' she said with concern. As Lasse hadn't been forthcoming over the phone, she had dreamt up all sorts of awful scenarios on the drive back from the prison. 'What's he done now?' It was an instinctive reaction. What on earth had brought Bjorn down from Uppsala?

Lasse nodded his blond head in the direction of the kitchen.

'He's in there.' Then he raised a disapproving eyebrow. 'He's pissed.'

Anita was not at all happy to have been dragged away from Ewan just to have to cope with her wretched ex-husband. And a drunken ex-husband at that. Lasse's call had put her into a panic and she had left Ewan hurriedly. Not even a proper goodbye, just a hurried 'see you sometime'. Her last image of Ewan was of resigned disappointment on his face.

Björn Sundström was slumped on one of the two chairs in the small kitchen. He had obviously brought a bottle of red wine as a peace offering. It stood in front of him half-empty, a thimbleful left in the bottom of his glass. That didn't improve her mood. He looked up at her. He must have been drinking all day. His eyes were glassy, trying to focus on her. It was a strange sight. Despite the fact that Björn had always been a party animal – they had first met when she arrested him after a rowdy gathering – he had usually been able to hold his drink. He liked to be in control. He had put a bit of weight on since she had last seen him three years previously when she had gone to his mother's funeral in Örebro. She had always got on with her mother-in-law, even after the divorce, and had kept in touch for Lasse's sake. Björn's handsome face, that had so captivated her when young, had become jowly. The blond mane that used to be just long enough for him to casually flick over his ears for effect was now cut shorter. It didn't suit him, as it accentuated how thin his hair was becoming. There was a pin-cushion of fair stubble, like a newly harvested corn field, around his chin. Again, this wasn't like the old Björn, who had always been clean-shaven. He still wore his regulation black attire – trousers, T-shirt and jacket – though it seemed he hadn't changed them recently, judging by their crumpled state. An impish Irish acquaintance had once described Björn, with his mop of blond hair and all-black clothing, as looking like a pint of Guinness. It had amused Anita – Björn had taken offence. He hadn't taken himself so seriously when they were first married, but as he climbed academe's greasy pole he had become more vainglorious and egocentric. Björn had been able to make her laugh in the early years of their marriage. Later, he had been better at making her cry.

'I know I should have waited for you,' Björn said with a wave of his hand in the direction of the bottle.

She walked over to a cupboard, took out a glass and put it on the table. She poured herself some wine. She didn't offer to top up his.

'I don't usually have a drink at four in the afternoon,' she said, 'but this is Friday.'

He took the bottle and poured himself a glass before thumping it back down on the table. It was empty.

'Have you come to spend some quality time with your son?'

For a moment, Björn gazed at her blankly before he took in what she had said.

'Ah, sarcasm. I blame the years you spent in England for that. They love their fucking sarcasm and irony.'

'You should know. You've taught their literature for long enough.'

'So I have. And brilliantly, I may say.'

He took a slurp of wine before running his jacket cuff across his mouth.

'So, if you're not here to see your son, why have I the dubious pleasure of your company?'

Björn straightened up. He held out his hands in an expansive gesture.

'To see my beautiful ex-wife.'

'Very ex-wife.'

'But you are beautiful. Still,' he added as an unnecessary caveat.

'Crap. What do you want?'

Björn picked up his glass and clutched it in both hands, as if it may try to escape him. Then he spoke in English.

'All love at first, like generous wine,
Ferments and frets until 'tis fine;
But when 'tis settled on the lee,
And from th' impurer matter free,
Becomes the richer still the older,
And proves the pleasanter the colder.'

'I've no idea what you're on about,' Anita said in exasperation.

He cocked his head and looked at her with a squint. 'I think Samuel Butler got that wrong. When love goes cold, there's nothing more unpleasant. But he got one thing right... *The souls of women are so small, that some believe they've none at all.'*

Anita couldn't suppress the annoyed sigh. 'A bloody woman. It's always a bloody woman!'

'But she's special.'

'Aren't they always until you betray them? Remember, I've been there.'

He put his glass down on the table, spilling some wine in the process. 'She's disappeared.'

Anita suddenly burst out laughing.

'She's dumped you! At last, a sensible woman!'

'You don't understand. Greta's vanished.'

'So, what's that to do with me?'

He slid his right hand across the table and earnestly grabbed Anita's wrist.

'I want you to find her.' She pulled her hand free. 'Anita, I'm begging you.' And then he began to weep.

He had parked his car near the bridge at the bottom of the hill. The night was windy. It whipped the clouds across the sky, allowing the moon to appear only fleetingly. But it was enough to light his way. At least it wasn't raining. And it usually rained in Cumbria in his experience. He crossed the bridge and climbed up the steep incline that led into the village. He knew where the house was that he was going to break into. The instructions had been very specific. He had no choice in the matter. The threat had been specific, too. It would have been easier to park in the village, but he didn't want the risk of someone waking in the middle of night and spotting his car. The bank up from the bridge was almost vertical, and he was soon out of breath. Not getting any younger, he thought. It was madness to be here in the first place, but the consequences would be dire if he didn't go through with it.

As he passed the first houses, he was relieved that there was no sign of life in any of them. At three o'clock on a Saturday morning, he reckoned that late-night revellers would have gone to bed, and it would be too early for farmers to be out and about.

At the top of the bank, the village opened out, with a green running up the middle, on either side of which ancient cottages clutched each other as if trying to keep warm in the chill air. At the other end of the green, he could just make out a vast tree, imperious in its solitude. Even from this distance, he could hear the leaves rustling eerily in the wind. Some were being prematurely ripped off their branches by the gusts. In a month they would all be gone. To his right was the chapel, and on the left, the village pub. He had clocked the landmarks on his drive through yesterday afternoon. He had needed to get his bearings. The house he had been sent to was behind him. Like many of the buildings in the village, it was 18th-century. It was large and sturdy and may well have been a farmhouse in a previous life. An owl hooted; it was so close that it made him start. There was no sign of life at the front of the house. He knew the only occupant slept on this side. His goal was the office at the back, overlooking the garden. He quietly retraced his steps. Right on cue, the moon made another brief appearance. It was out long enough for him to make out the gleam of the wrought-iron garden gate. He had been given very precise information about where to get in. How he got in was up to him. Once inside, he knew where to go. Through the small hallway and the kitchen, along the corridor, and the office was at the end. He wouldn't have to waste precious time trying to find what he had been sent to get. He had been told exactly where it was located.

He carefully stepped along the stone path through the garden. Only when he reached the back door, did he dare turn on his torch. The door was half-glazed with six clear panes. He knew it would be. This was the risky bit – breaking the glass. It might disturb the occupant, or possibly some light sleeper in the house next door. He nudged the pane closest to the handle. To no effect. He was being too pussy-footed. This time he gave it a juddering blow with his elbow. It smashed, and the cacophony made his heart leap painfully. It seemed as if the shattered glass was hitting the stone-flagged floor inside the house in slow motion. Fortunately, he was just calm enough to realise that the wind would muffle the sound. He waited for a few moments to hear if he had disturbed anyone. Nothing. He took a deep breath and gingerly poked his hand through the broken pane and flicked the latch. He was in.

CHAPTER 7

Anita let Björn lie in. She had managed to steer him onto the opened-out day bed in the living room the night before. He had made a cursory effort to seduce her by cupping a breast in his hand. She had easily evaded any other attempt. With Björn it didn't actually mean anything – it was just a reflex action. There was one wistful moment when she saw him curled up on the sofa and remembered how wonderful their sex lives had been. Even when things had started to go wrong, the sex had been good right up to the end. Anita left him to go out for a run round Pildammsparken. It was her way of letting off steam or giving herself time to think.

She ran through the trees that lined the path, and into the park. At the end was the area called "The Plate", a large, circular, grassy space surrounded by tall beeches clipped to form an imposing boundary. It was one of the city's most popular destinations. At midsummer it was full of picnickers listening to live entertainment. Anita's normal routine was to run three circuits of "The Plate", but this time she veered off and headed to the lake on the other side of the park. She skipped up the bank and stopped at the top. She surveyed the calm water, which was glinting in the weak sun. A middle-aged woman was feeding the geese, who were noisily gobbling up the bread thrown in their direction. Anita suddenly felt tired and looked for an empty bench. She found one with a view of the old water tower, its conical roof looking like a wizard's hat, on the other side of the lake.

She hadn't slept much. Björn's reappearance in her life had been unsettling. Her ex-husband had been the only man she had fallen in love with – until Ewan. But she knew that with Ewan her relationship was totally abnormal. With Björn she had always thought that it was a meeting of kindred spirits, though, if she was being honest, she had also been rather in awe of him. He was eight years older than her and, after her father had died in the *Estonia* ferry tragedy, Björn had helped to fill the void. Of course, Björn was super-intelligent and was already starting to make an impact in academic circles. Maybe the real attraction – other than the lashings of lust which were imaginatively served up – was that he was so different from the people she knew and mixed with. He was exciting, and his cerebral world of ideas had been a good counterpoint to her own practical one of facts. Björn had enjoyed her being a policewoman. It shocked his friends that the great liberal was married to a figure representing the conservative establishment. Had their relationship simply been his way of being provocative? Certainly, she was often made to feel uncomfortable in the presence of the academic set. Despite all this, Björn had loved her and cared for her. He was thrilled with the arrival of Lasse, and for a few years she had never been happier.

Then it slowly began to dawn on her that if she wanted Björn, she was going to have to share him. He had always had a roving eye. She had had her suspicions, but the instincts she was developing in her career as a cop helped her to consolidate them. Then the lies became more frequent. His weakness for younger versions of herself became too obvious to ignore. Eventually, she asked him to leave. It wasn't a decision taken lightly, as Lasse had worshipped Björn. Till yesterday. Her son had disappeared first thing that morning, and she could understand why. He couldn't bear to see his father in such an emotional state. He had come into the kitchen just as Björn had broken down in tears. The look of horrified disdain on Lasse's face would remain with Anita the rest of her life. The fall of a hero. In many ways, her reaction had been the same. She had never seen Björn so out of control. So powerless. And all because of some stupid girl. But this was different. The great stud, who had simply moved on to the next conquest when he got bored, had made the mistake of falling in love. It had turned him into a pitiful old man. That was what Anita was finding so hard to come to terms with as she levered herself up from the bench and started to jog back in the direction of her apartment.

Anita took a thermos of strong coffee into the living room. She had showered and changed after her run and was now in a pair of black jeans and a white top. She put the thermos on the table next to two mugs.

'I think you need this,' she said, pouring the steaming black liquid into the mugs.

Björn sat, bleary-eyed, on the day bed. The duvet was crumpled at one end. He was in his black T-shirt from the night before, blue boxer shorts and white socks. She had removed his jacket, shoes and trousers, but that was as far as she'd gone.

'Thanks,' he muttered as he took the coffee.

She sat down. She watched him as he cupped his mug. It bore the cartoon of a goofy-looking man with a ball and chain round his ankle. The caption ran: *En lydig man är en lycklig man* – an obedient man is a happy man. Björn would have been appalled at the sentiment, if he'd been switched on enough to notice.

'Sorry.'

Anita smiled. It hadn't been a word she had often heard him say while they were married.

'I acted like an idiot last night.'

'Yes. Your son won't forgive you in a hurry.'

Björn looked startled. 'Is he...?'

'No. He's gone out.'

He sipped at his coffee and grimaced.

'Christ, you still make your coffee too strong!'

'It kept me awake all those nights I waited up for you to come back home.' She surprised herself at her own vehemence.

Björn gazed at her. The blue eyes were sad. He shook his head. 'I really fucked things up.'

'That's all in the past.' She had done enough dwelling on their marriage as she had lain in bed last night, and on her run this morning. She didn't want him to stay any longer than was necessary, so she had better find out about the woman who was causing him so much grief. 'Greta? Tell me about Greta.'

He took another sip of coffee before answering. 'Greta... Greta Jansson is the woman I love.'

'I gathered that from all the whimpering last night.' She found herself being short with him. The horrid truth was that she didn't like to hear him say that he loved another woman. Even after all the years apart, it was a difficult thing for her to come to terms with.

'I know it sounds pathetic. Greta's only twenty-three. And I'm...'

Though tempted, she didn't say anything. Anita knew that he had turned fifty a couple of years before. Maybe that's why he suddenly felt so vulnerable.

'Greta was one of my students.' Björn managed a wry grin when he saw Anita's eyebrows head skywards. 'Yes, I know. My record isn't good. But Greta was different. Bright, funny... and, unlike some of the others, she was mature for her age. Maybe with me becoming...' He broke off again, unable to admit that he was well past his half century. This led to another reflective slurp of coffee.

'Though we slept together, she wouldn't move in with me.'

She really was bright, thought Anita sardonically.

'Anyhow, she got a job teaching English down here in Malmö. In August. A high school in the centre of town. Kungsskolan.'

'A long-distance romance?'

'Not exactly. But I came down yesterday because I was worried that I hadn't heard from her for a while.'

'Maybe she doesn't want to see you.' As soon as she had spoken, she saw the hurt in his eyes.

'Greta's not at her apartment. And she hasn't been at the school this week.'

'She might have gone away for a break.'

He shook his head slowly. 'The school said she had suddenly left.'

'Well, there you are. Maybe the job just got too much for her. If it's Kungsskolan, there are some tough kids there.'

'Greta doesn't give up on things. She's a dedicated sort of person. Look, Anita, I just know that something's wrong. She's not answering her mobile. I need you to find her.'

'Sounds as though she's just gone off somewhere. Perfectly innocently.'

'She hasn't taken anything with her.'

'How do you know?'

'I've been in her apartment. I have a key,' he muttered as an afterthought.

'Should you have let yourself in?'

'She's my girlfriend, for Christ's sake,' he replied angrily. Anita wasn't so sure that was true. The more he talked, the more it sounded as though this wasn't a straightforward relationship. She knew Björn too well. She had learned the hard way when he wasn't telling her the whole truth. 'Please, can you just ask around? That's all I'm asking. I just want to know that she's all right.'

Another missing person. Had Greta Jansson and Graeme Todd got something in common? Were they just trying to escape from unwanted partners?

'OK. I'll make one or two discreet enquiries. But I'm not going to make a big fuss over this.'

Björn nodded his head like a grateful hound.

'But there's a condition. I want you to have a long talk with your son. He's driving me demented. I can't get him to do anything with his life. Like you, he's mooning over a floozy. He doesn't listen to me anymore. So act like a father for once, and talk some sense into him.'

'Does that mean I can stay the rest of the weekend?'

Anita inwardly groaned.

'You'd better be on the train back to Uppsala first thing Monday morning.'

CHAPTER 8

Five minutes after Anita had reached her office on Monday morning, she phoned Jennifer Todd. Though there was an hour's time difference, she reckoned that Graeme Todd's wife would be up. Worried women rarely slept well. Men seemed to cope better. Anita had given Jennifer Todd her mobile number so that she could contact her over the weekend if her husband turned up or got in touch. She hadn't rung. Anyway, Anita had had enough on her plate with a love-sick Björn and listless Lasse. On Saturday night she had sent them out to hit the bars of Malmö. She thought a bit of bonding might pave the way for the man-to-man talk she hoped the two of them were going to have. But it hadn't been a great success, as Björn had got drunk again and Lasse had had to chaperone him back to the apartment. According to Lasse, his father had spent most of the time saying how much in love he was with Greta Jansson, but also that he had been an idiot to leave Anita. Anita was furious with Björn for wasting the opportunity to deal with his son, and was happy to shove him out early that morning to catch the six o'clock train. Before he left, he'd extracted a promise from her that she would make some enquiries about Greta. This had been given reluctantly, as she didn't want to get involved in any aspect of Björn's messy domestic life. Eleven years had been enough.

Anita paused with her hand on the receiver. She was sure that Graeme Todd had done a bunk. Jennifer Todd knew he was working on the Doris Little case, but had no idea why it had taken him to Sweden. He must have kept her in the dark, which made his behaviour suspicious. Her money was on another woman. The call was answered almost immediately. Jennifer must have been hovering near the phone. She probably had been all weekend.

'Have you any news?' she blurted out even before Anita had time to say anything other than her name.

'No. I'm afraid nothing has come in.'

'You must do something. This isn't like Graeme. He always keeps in touch whenever he's away from home. Please, please find him.' It all came out in a garbled rush. 'I can get a flight across to Sweden. I'll be there tomorrow.'

'Wait a minute, Jennifer,' interrupted Anita. 'I can call you Jennifer?'

'Yes. Yes, of course.'

'I think you'd better let us look into this first.'

'I'm so worried.'

Anita tried to sound pleasantly professional so that the woman at the other end of the line would calm down. And she certainly didn't want her coming over to Malmö until she had a better idea of what might have happened. It wouldn't make the investigation any easier with a hysterical wife on her hands.

'Look, Jennifer, can you give me any more details about this search for a beneficiary? I need as much information as possible.'

She heard a sniffle at the other end. 'Sorry, I'm just all over the place.'

'Don't worry. I just need you to think. We know he flew into Copenhagen a week ago today. And you were right, he hadn't booked into the Hotel Comfort. But he phoned you that night, so he must have been staying somewhere. Did he mention that he'd changed hotels?'

'No.'

'This person he had come over to see. Any idea who it might have been?'

'It was to do with the estate of Doris Little, who died in Carlisle in 2009. That's our nearest town. Carlisle.' Her voice was more controlled now.

'I know where it is. I lived in the north of England when I was younger.'

'Oh,' Jennifer said in surprise. 'I thought your English was good.'

'This old lady,' Anita prompted, 'What was the Swedish connection?'

'I just don't know,' Jennifer said with a hint of frustration. 'I'm a nurse, but I sometimes help Graeme out when he's busy. But this case was different.'

Anita changed from going through the motions to being more alert. She sensed that this might be crucial. 'Why "different"?'

'He became secretive. Wouldn't tell me much. But he was excited. I could tell that. A couple of days before he left, he said that this was the "jackpot".'

'The "jackpot"? What did you think he meant by that?'

'Well, money. When someone dies intestate – that means they haven't made a will – and there are no obvious relatives, the money goes to the government. The Treasury. Heir hunters like Graeme try and find blood relations and sign them up so that he can put in a claim to the Treasury for the estate on their behalf. An heir hunter makes his money by taking a percentage of a successful claim.'

'So, this Doris Little must have had a big estate?'

Jennifer didn't say anything for a moment. 'Actually, that's the strange thing. When Graeme got onto it, the estate wasn't worth a huge amount. She only had a small house in Carlisle and only a little in a building society. I remember him telling me that. I know he's dealt with far bigger estates than hers over the years.'

'Where does the "jackpot" come in then?'

'I have no idea.'

After Anita had put down the phone, she sat at her desk wondering about Graeme Todd. Maybe, just maybe, there was something deeper about this mystery. He must have gone somewhere after he landed at Kastrup. He might be in Denmark for all she knew. And his "jackpot" reference sounded as though he was onto some financial bonanza. Running away from his wife didn't seem to fit in with that scenario. Why had the death of an old lady in Carlisle brought him to Scandinavia in the first place? She needed to try and establish whether Todd had actually crossed the Öresund Bridge and entered Sweden. That meant having a word with Chief Inspector Moberg – not one of her favourite pastimes.

Moberg was eating a bun. She had noticed that he was having his breakfasts in the office these days. Unless it was his second breakfast. Relations with the third fru Moberg must really be bad. While he munched away, Anita explained what little she had gleaned from Jennifer Todd. She ended up by asking whether this was officially regarded as important enough to get hold of CCTV footage from the Central Station, or if Todd had been missing long enough to put out his general description on the television and in the local press.

Moberg still had food in his mouth when he answered.

'Our beloved commissioner thinks this is vital. He's already been on the phone asking for an update at ten. God, haven't we got more important things to do?' he said moodily. As he spoke, some excess bits of bun flew out of his mouth. He flicked them off his desk with his stubby fingers. Anita tried not to look. 'OK, get the CCTV and check the usual places – the hospital and all the hotels. Hold off on the television. We'd look fucking stupid if we publicly put out details and he turns up.'

As she left the office, she saw Karl Westermark coming

along the corridor. Last week it had been a relief not to have had him around. He might no longer be the same threat to her as he had been before the Wollstad case, but he was still a disquieting presence around the polishus. She still dreaded having to work too closely with him. She just didn't trust him any longer. She had made the decision to adopt an attitude of polite detachment. She forced herself as she passed him to say, 'Good holiday?'

To her surprise, Westermark simply grunted something which she didn't catch. No cocky manner, no supercilious smirk, no barbed observation, and no lecherous leer. What was wrong with the man?

By the time she was back in her office, she had dismissed Westermark from her thoughts, and it was back to business. Hakim was now at his desk.

'Good weekend?' she asked as she swung into her chair.

'I've had better.' Hakim was usually cheerier.

'That doesn't sound good.'

'It's my sister.'

'Jazmin?'

Hakim groaned. 'She keeps winding my parents up. They don't know how to handle her. Keeps getting into trouble, and then they want me to try and sort her out. That only makes things worse.'

Anita laughed. 'I'm glad I'm not the only one suffering.'

'You're having problems?'

'Long story. Maybe your Jazmin should get together with my Lasse. Second thoughts, not a good idea. Anyhow, to work.'

'No sign of the Englishman?'

'No. But the commissioner's on the case, so we'd better start doing something. I'm going to the station to see if there's any useful CCTV footage. At least we can find out whether he made it to Malmö. I want you to get on the phone and call the hospital and then go through all the hotels, bed and breakfasts...

you know the sort of thing. As he was supposedly going to the Comfort, start at the cheapest and work your way up. British guests. You've got the days he was meant to be here.'

'Is it worth also checking flights out of Kastrup for that Thursday and the day after? British destinations.'

'Not a bad idea.'

Hakim stood up. 'I think I need a coffee to keep me going. Want one?'

'No thanks. I'm going out now.'

Hakim hesitated at the door.

'Do you think there's something sinister going on?'

'Well, according to his wife, he was very secretive about what he was doing over here. The only thing he said to her about his trip was that this was the "jackpot". He was obviously expecting to make a financial killing of some sort.'

Hakim left the room and Anita put her jacket back on. She glanced out of the window and saw a middle-aged man strolling across the park. He was carrying a briefcase. Yes, Mr Todd, what *was* your "jackpot" and how were you going to collect it?

She was still staring out of the window when her hand inside her jacket pocket touched something unfamiliar – the key to Greta Jansson's apartment. Over there, beyond the trees that lined Kungsgatan, was the school where Greta Jansson should be teaching this morning. But she wasn't. Why?

CHAPTER 9

It was nice to get out of the office, especially when the weather was as bright as it was today. Typically, the weekend had been the usual mixed bag of showers and brief sunny spells. Now that everybody was back at work, the sun had come out first thing. Sod's law.

Instead of following the canal round towards the station, she cut along Fredriksbergsgatan onto the busy Östra Förstadsgatan that ran up to Värnhem and the square which was an important interchange for city and regional buses. She knew the area well, not only because it was close to police headquarters, but because the Roslyn murder had taken place in an apartment at the corner of the square. Her destination was the less salubrious, grey concrete apartment block on the other side of Östra Förstadsgatan, above a jeweller's and the now-empty *Systembolag*. This is where Greta Jansson lived. Or had until a week ago.

Someone was coming out of the apartment block as Anita reached the main door, so she didn't have to buzz anyone to get in. Inside was a board with the list of residents. Next to *Number 15*, Greta Jansson's name was written neatly in biro. Not a professional print job – this was a temporary home. Anita took the lift up to the first floor. She came out onto a featureless corridor and walked the few paces to Number 15. She rang the doorbell first, just in case Greta had returned. When there was no reply, she took out Björn's key and opened the door. Inside, all was quiet. The traffic in the street outside was muffled by the triple glazing. Straight ahead of her was an open door to the one bedroom. To the left was the living room, to the right the bathroom, and round the corner, a very small kitchen.

Anita started in the living room. The furniture – dining table and chairs, cupboard, sofa and easy chair – was heavy and elaborate. It wasn't what you'd expect a young, twenty-three-year-old woman to surround herself with. But this was a sub-let – it wouldn't be hers. There were a few books on the middle shelf of a dark-oak bookcase. Anita glanced at them. English authors – Dickens, George Eliot, the Brontës and Björn's favourite, Thomas Hardy; some poetry books, both English and Swedish. And a couple of modern novels – judging by the titles, they were for light relief. There were also half a dozen English text books, which presumably were to do with her job. Except for a small pile of CDs – none of the artists' names meant anything to Anita, though Lasse might be familiar with them – there was very little of Greta in this room. Anita had to stop and remind herself that this wasn't an investigation. She was already mentally treating it like a crime scene, trying to get into the mind of the occupant. She even found that she had absent-mindedly slipped on the latex gloves which she always carried with her for such occasions. In reality, she was merely doing someone a favour, and the sooner it was sorted out, the sooner she could banish Björn from her life again.

The bedroom didn't yield much. There was a large suitcase in the bottom of the wardrobe, still with some clothes in it. Seems the girl wasn't anticipating a long lease. But everything was neat and tidy, and the bed was made. She pulled back the clean duvet and noted the fresh sheets underneath. It hadn't been slept in. The pillowcases had been changed, too. Among the things in the drawer of the bedside table was Greta's iPod so, wherever she had gone, that hadn't been important enough to take with her. Lasse never left home without his these days. But there was no sign of a handbag or mobile phone, and there was no computer either. Presumably she would have one. In the bathroom, there was a T-shirt and a pair of knickers hanging on a clothes line above the small bath. Again, there was nothing unusual in that. She noted that there was no toothbrush or toothpaste, which pointed to Greta going away.

The only place where Anita was surprised was the kitchen, which was crammed into the space next to the bathroom. There was just enough room for a table, big enough to seat two people at a push, and it had a window that opened onto Östra Förstadsgatan. There wasn't much in the way of foodstuff in the overhead cupboards, yet the fridge was well-stocked. Yogurts, milk, cream, three types of cheese, spreadable butter, a couple of pizzas, a packet of mince, a pack of salami, four eggs, a jar of mayonnaise, a couple of jams, some vegetables, the inevitable tube of caviar and a bottle of white wine. She sniffed at the milk – it was off. She looked at the sell-by dates on the products. The cream was old and the yogurts had run out yesterday. If Greta had gone, then it must have been on an impulse. She wouldn't have bought all this if she'd intended to go away. Anita poured the sour milk down the sink and put the carton into the bin, but not before seeing if there was a shop receipt among the rubbish. There wasn't. She could tell from the packaging that the items had been bought in the supermarket on the ground floor of the large *Entré* shopping centre, which had sprung up behind the square a couple of years before. She had used it herself, as it was handy for the polishus.

As she came back into the living room, she heard a baby crying through the wall. That meant that the neighbour was in. It was worth having a quick word. It took some time before the door was opened and a harassed young mother, clutching a weeping baby in her arms, peered out at her. Her dark hair was randomly scraped back and she still wore the T-shirt and pants she had probably slept in.

'Sorry to bother you, but I just want to ask you about your neighbour, Greta Jansson.'

'Who are you?' she demanded, with one eye on the baby.

Anita produced her warrant card. 'Anita Sundström.'

'I haven't seen her.' She made no attempt to ask Anita in.

'And you are?'

'Wilma.' She didn't volunteer a surname.

Anita smiled at the baby, whose crying was turning into grizzling. 'And the baby?'

'Nathalie.' Wilma stroked the baby's head.

Despite the obvious stress, Anita could see she was a proud mother. 'Can you remember when you last saw Greta?'

Nathalie went quiet. Wilma gently rocked the baby in her arms as she thought about an answer. 'A couple of weeks ago. Yes, she was coming back from the school and I was taking Nathalie out for a walk.' Then, as an afterthought, 'I did hear voices one night. Just over a week ago. It was late. I was up feeding Nathalie.'

'Did you often hear voices in there?'

'No. Funnily enough, that was the first time I can remember. Sounded like an argument.'

'An argument?'

'Yeah. Raised voices.'

'OK, that's all.'

'Is there something wrong?'

'Nothing particularly important.' Anita took her small writing pad out of her bag and scribbled down her name and number with a pencil. She handed it to Wilma. 'If you see her, can you give her this?'

Wilma took the piece of paper.

'Sorry to disturb you... and Nathalie.'

Anita turned away and was heading for the lift when Wilma called down the corridor. 'Greta's dad was here.'

Anita swivelled round. 'Her dad?'

'Yes. I gave him our key to the apartment.'

'Your key?' Anita said in surprise. She knew that Swedes didn't tend to trust their neighbours with spare keys; family yes, neighbours no.

Wilma read Anita's mind. 'It's only because we were renting Greta's apartment before. We moved in here because it's got two bedrooms, and with a kid on the way... Anyway, we've sublet it to her since August and we've always held on to a key.'

'So when did her father call?'

'It would be the Saturday... the one before last. He called to ask if I knew where Greta was. I said I didn't know, but gave him our key so he could let himself in and wait for her.'

That seemed to clear up the mystery, thought Anita. She's gone off home with her father.

'He forgot to give the key back, but I'm sure Greta will return it when she comes back.'

When Anita got back to her office an hour later, Hakim was on the phone. She had picked up the CCTV footage that covered the station concourse. There were three trains an hour from Kastrup. A visitor to Malmö would alight there first, before heading off into the town. As they knew Todd's plane had landed at 13.45, Hakim had worked out that the first train he would physically be able to catch, given that he got out of the airport quickly enough, was the 14.26, getting into Malmö Central twenty minutes later. That's if he really was heading for Malmö in the first place. They decided to look at the footage up until midnight. She would let Hakim do the trawling as he had better eyesight.

Hakim put the phone down with a resigned air. 'Nothing there.' He tapped a piece of paper on his desk. 'Nothing from the hospital. Drew a blank with health centres, too. I'm ploughing through the hotels. Done all the budget ones, and bed and breakfasts. No luck so far, and now I'm up to the pricier places.'

'Take a break. We'll have a coffee, then I'll take over the hotels and you can look through the CCTV.'

'Oh, yes... another thing. Graeme Todd didn't leave on any British-bound flights on the fourth, fifth or sixth from Kastrup. Unless he used another name.'

An hour later, Anita wasn't having any luck either. 'How are you getting on?'

Hakim was staring at his computer screen. 'I've been through it twice, and there's no sign of him. What about you?'

Anita glanced down at the list. 'No. I'm now down to the Radisson, Grand, Hilton, Mayfair, Rica, Duxiana and Renaissance. And they all cost well over a thousand kronor a night. The exchange rate isn't very good for the British at the moment, so that's over a hundred pounds. That doesn't sound like Graeme Todd's price range if he was supposedly booking into the Hotel Comfort.'

Hakim tore his gaze away from the screen. 'Of course, he could have got off the train at Triangeln, and not gone through to Central Station.'

'That's a point. Because he said he was going to the Comfort, we've assumed that he would get off in the centre of town. Well, it's a sunny day, so get yourself down to Triangeln and look at their CCTV. But you can have your lunch first.'

Anita sat on the grass in the park and enjoyed the rays of the sun. It even felt unseasonably warm. It might be the last time this year. Not bad for October 8th. She took out her crispbread and salami. This was her first step towards losing some weight. And alcohol only at weekends from now on. As she took a bite, she wondered whether she should ring Björn and tell him what she had found out. Yet she found herself prevaricating. Was it because she didn't want to speak to him? Or was it that she wasn't entirely satisfied with her scrutiny of Greta's apartment? The contents of the fridge still niggled. Then again, if Greta's father had appeared, it might be that there had been a family emergency that had suddenly called her away. An ill mother?

'What are you thinking about?'

Anita looked up, and standing in front of her was Henrik Nordlund. She broke into a smile. She always enjoyed seeing him. The sunken eyes always gave Nordlund a glum expression, exacerbated by the angular, pale face, and balding pate with a few wisps of grey hair clinging, limpet-like, to the back and sides. Though not a jolly man, he was amiable. He was an excellent detective who still believed in the job he was doing. Unlike most of his colleagues, he had never developed a cynical view of their work, or the world that they were asked to police. He was one of the few people at headquarters about whom no one had a bad word to say. Other than Westermark, of course, who didn't rate anybody except himself. Nordlund was too cautious and too methodical for the younger detective. Now Nordlund was on the cusp of retirement. Anita would miss him terribly, as he had not only helped guide her career, but had more than once acted as a rock in a stormy sea. She also worried about what he would do with himself. His wife, who had also worked on the force, had died of cancer a few years before, and they had had no children. Without his work, she feared he would be left facing years of loneliness.

'Oh, missing people.'

'May I join you?' Anita nodded, and he lowered himself onto the ground with some agility. He may have been twenty-odd years older, but he was still lithe. She offered him some of her lunch, which he politely declined. He pulled out a chocolate bar.

'Is this your English person?' Nordlund asked before taking the first bite. Anita looked on enviously. She had cut out chocolate, too. 'Yes. We don't even know if he reached Malmö. Still searching. Mind you, it's often difficult to find someone who doesn't want to be found.'

'That's what you think?'

'I don't know. He looks like the sort of vain male who's tired of his present wife and wants to start a new life.'

'You gained that insight from a photograph?' Nordlund said with some amusement.

'OK,' she smiled, 'but he was very secretive about why he was coming here, other than that he was going to make a lot of money. His wife doesn't know how. Keeping secrets in a marriage shows there's something wrong.' She knew from bitter experience.

'Maybe he's being secretive to protect her from something.'

'Maybe.' She didn't really agree, but didn't want to say so. They munched in silence and enjoyed the sun.

'Graeme Todd's not the only one.' She wasn't going to tell anybody about Greta Jansson, but it just came out.

Nordlund cocked his head quizzically.

'My ex-husband seems to have misplaced his latest girlfriend.' Anita went on to explain briefly what had happened; about Greta leaving her job suddenly and her own visit to the apartment in Östra Förstadsgatan. 'I don't know why I'm even doing it for him. The sod doesn't deserve it. All unofficial, of course. Moberg would burst a blood vessel if he knew I was using police time to find Björn's latest bit of stuff.'

'Well, it sounds as though it must be a family matter with her father turning up.'

'Yes. That's obviously it.'

Anita put away the remains of her lunch in her bag and got up. Nordlund followed suit. He saw her hesitate.

'Are you heading back?' he asked, his thumb pointing in the direction of the polishus.

She still hovered. Nordlund smiled.

'The school's just over there. But I wouldn't be too long.'

CHAPTER 10

The school was a large, red-brick building with uniform rows of windows over four floors, which managed to make it slightly less severe. In a street with many elegant blocks, the school didn't make much of an effort to fit in with its neighbours. Anita went up some steps and entered the foyer through one of the two double glass doors. She sought out someone who could direct her to the English department, and was taken along a seemingly endless corridor by one of the school secretaries. Anita hadn't made a fuss when she arrived as this was not an official enquiry.

She was ushered into a classroom. There were rows of empty desks.

'That's Alex Fraser over there.' The secretary pulled an apologetic face. 'He's British,' as though that was the only explanation for the tall, young man with the goatee beard and the long, curly black hair swept back in a pony-tail, who was bending over an iPad in the corner of the classroom. It gave Anita a jolt. She recognised him from her occasional visits to The Pickwick pub in the centre of town. It was the haunt of expats. She knew that Fraser was one of the two Britons whom Ewan had briefly befriended on his arrival in Malmö. He was the sort of person who stood out in a crowd.Fraser looked up enquiringly as Anita approached. His smile was friendly, but he obviously didn't know who she was.

'Sorry, are you a parent?' he said in Swedish. For a moment, a worried frown creased his face as though there might have been a meeting that he'd forgotten about.

'No, I'm here about Greta Jansson,' she replied in English.

'Ah.' He fiddled with his iPad distractedly for a moment. 'Just a second,' he said, reverting to English. She heard the unmistakable Scottish brogue in his voice. He completed his manoeuvre. 'That's it. Tough class this afternoon,' he added as explanation.

'I'm just here to ask a few questions about Greta.'

'In what capacity?' he asked suspiciously.

'Sorry. I'm police. Inspector Anita Sundström.'

He stared at her. Then his expression creased into recognition.

'Haven't I seen you in The Pickwick?' He clicked his fingers. 'And weren't you the policewoman who was involved in arresting Ewan Strachan?'

Anita didn't answer either question. 'I'm here unofficially. On behalf of a friend of Greta's.'

'She's OK, isn't she?'

'Hopefully. I only want to establish the circumstances around her leaving.'

Fraser ran a hand over his head. 'Bit abrupt.'

'So I understand.'

'She gave no indication that she was about to leave on the Friday afternoon. I thought she was enjoying the job. Well, maybe "enjoying" is too strong a word. Surviving, more like,' he grimaced. 'She only started this term. I know it's difficult here, but she seemed to be coping.'

'The Friday afternoon?' Anita prompted.

'Yes. She was quite upbeat. Going to meet a friend from Stockholm who was down on business. University connection.'

'Sex?'

'Pardon? Oh, I see. Female. Can't remember the name. Might have been Ulla.'

'So how did you know she wasn't coming back?'

'A call came in on the Monday morning. Said she wasn't returning. Some family thing, apparently. I suppose it wasn't a total surprise. This place takes its toll. There's always a big turnover of staff. This is my second year, and I'm the most senior English teacher in this section.'

Anita gazed around the classroom. The smell. Memories of her own school days in Simrishamn started seeping back. Not entirely happy recollections.

'Do you know who rang in?'

'No. But the secretary who took the call said it was a man. Of course, it left us in the shit and we had to get cover quickly. Extra bloody lessons for me, for starters. I thought Greta might have given us some warning.'

'Would she have a computer?'

'Yeah,' Fraser said, pointing to the one he had just been working on. 'We all get issued with an iPad. Actually, Greta should have handed it back if she was leaving.' He shrugged. 'Not that anyone round here will probably notice. Chaos most of the time.'

'Thank you, Alex.'

'Any help?'

Anita nodded. 'Seems to fit. Her father turned up that weekend.'

She made her way back to the doorway.

'Don't be a stranger!' he called after her. She turned. What did he mean? He grinned. 'The next time you're in The Pickwick, come and say hello.'

Hakim was beaming when she returned to the office.

'I sense someone's been a clever boy,' said Anita as she threw her bag over the back of her chair.

'You could say that. I've found him!' he announced triumphantly. He pointed to his screen. 'He got off the train at Triangeln.'

Anita squeezed round the desk and stared at Hakim's computer. It was frozen on an image that she now had firmly planted in her mind. Hakim clicked the mouse, and Graeme Todd began to move along the platform. On the screen, the time started spooling from 14.44. He was wheeling a small suitcase along the platform, and slung on his shoulder was a computer bag, presumably containing a laptop.

'He's heading out towards the shopping centre side,' Hakim confirmed.

Anita watched Todd as he got on the escalator.

'He couldn't be going to the Hilton, could he? That's the nearest hotel.'

Hakim's grin widened.

'Yes. He booked in that afternoon.'

'You have been busy.' Anita was learning to admire her young colleague's thoroughness.

'I've arranged to go down and see someone at the hotel. Want to come?'

The Hilton abutted the glass facade of the Triangeln shopping centre. Towering over the rest of the complex, it was one of the tallest buildings in the city. Anita and Hakim stood in the massive glass atrium. Outside, the street was packed with shoppers. Inside was hushed calm. An elegant staircase wound its way through the centre of building, while a glass lift with a blue illuminated undercarriage, glided up from the foyer, ferrying guests silently to the upper floors. To the left of the reception area was a bar and restaurant. Anita had often looked through the window from the street and wondered if she would ever meet someone who could afford to take her there for a meal. They sat down in the comfortable chairs on the other side of the reception. Anita felt she was in a goldfish bowl. Hakim looked around in awe. This was definitely how the other half lived. Anita was more interested in the fact that someone like

Graeme Todd had booked into a place that, according to his wife, would normally be beyond their means.

They stood up as they were approached by a small, dark-haired woman in a neat black skirt and jacket. The woman switched on a meet-and-greet smile. She was immaculately turned out, and Anita was conscious of her own, more casual, appearance as a manicured hand was held out for her to shake.

'Erica Tufvesson, deputy manager,' she introduced herself. 'The manager, herr Nørgaard, is back in Denmark for a two-day conference. Can I get you some coffee?'

'No, thanks.' Anita wanted to get straight down to business. 'I believe that you had a Graeme Todd staying here last week.'

Tufvesson produced a black, leather-bound notebook and flicked through some pages.

'Since your colleague rang, I've done some checking. Yes, a herr Todd did book in on Monday, October the first.'

'For how long?'

Tufvesson again consulted her notebook. 'Three nights. He was due to leave on Thursday, the fourth. But he never checked out.'

'When was he seen last?' asked Hakim.

'He had breakfast here on the Wednesday morning but he didn't come back that night. Certainly his bed wasn't slept in.'

'Did he leave anything behind?' Anita was quite happy for Hakim to take over the questioning. He had got them this far.

'Yes. A small suitcase. I have it in my office.'

'We'll take that with us if you don't mind,' Anita put in. 'Was there a laptop with his belongings?'

'No. After he failed to turn up, we cleared out his room and kept everything in case he returned. But we had to get the room ready for another guest arriving on the Thursday.'

'So the room was totally cleared?' This was Hakim again.

Tufvesson nodded. 'Sorry.'

'Were his bathroom things still there? Toothbrush,

toothpaste, that kind of stuff?'

'Yes. Everything's in the suitcase.'

'So, it seems he was expecting to return from wherever he went that morning,' Anita mused.

'It doesn't appear that he was just avoiding paying his bill,' Hakim added.

'Do you mind if we have a word with whoever was on reception or serving breakfast so we can get a description of what Todd was wearing last Wednesday?'

'Of course.' Tufvesson's smile was appropriately toned down.

After talking to the staff, they took the suitcase back to the polishus. It only confirmed that he had packed for a short break and not a long-term stay. There were no documents or files that could hint at what he was doing or whom he was going to meet. The only significant item was in one of the zipped compartments. It was a photocopy of his return Easyjet boarding pass, dated for Thursday, October 4th – destination Manchester. He had certainly planned to return home. So why hadn't he? And where had he disappeared to? As far as Anita was now concerned, Graeme Todd was officially missing in Malmö.

CHAPTER 11

Moberg wasn't too pleased when Anita reported back to him that Graeme Todd really was missing. 'The commissioner will get his knickers in a twist over this.' However, he did agree that they needed to get Todd's description out via the press and television. They had the photo of him, and they now knew what he was wearing when he left the hotel – beige slacks, buff-coloured jacket with a lime green jersey and a white shirt underneath. 'You'd better inform his wife,' Moberg added. Anita had already had that planned, though it wasn't a call she was looking forward to making. 'And see if you can get more information out of her about what Todd was doing over here.' Anita doubted that she would extract anything more revealing than she had already. Basically, Todd had kept his wife in the dark. Why he had done so was a mystery in itself.

Hakim had a coffee waiting for her when she returned to the office.

'Do you think something bad has happened?' he asked as he settled down to his drink.

Anita stared out of the window.

'I don't know. If we knew what he was doing in Malmö, we'd be in a position to speculate.'

'He could have had an accident. Should I widen my search of the hospitals? He might have been going somewhere else in Skåne.'

'Yes. Good idea. But I don't think he could have gone too far afield, as he was obviously coming back to the hotel.'

She sipped her coffee thoughtfully. She knew that what she was really doing was postponing the phone call she had to make. All she was going to do was confirm Jennifer Todd's worst fears.

It was with a glass of red wine in her hand that Anita sat down in front of the television to watch the local news. There was a brief mention of Graeme Todd at the end of the broadcast. The photo that Jennifer Todd had emailed to Anita was used, and it filled the screen for twenty seconds while the newsreader said that the police were appealing for any information concerning the whereabouts of this British national, last seen on Wednesday, October 3rd. Then the weather forecast came on. The warm weather they had just been enjoying was about to change – colder, cloudier and the chance of showers. Anita flicked off the TV with the remote.

'Is that yours? The missing English guy?'

Anita hadn't noticed Lasse standing in the doorway.

'Didn't know you were in.'

Lasse strolled over to the armchair and slumped down. His long legs stretched out across the floor.

'Yes. That's mine.'

'Didn't think you did missing persons.'

'Neither did I, but my lovely boss thought that as this particular missing person is British, I was perfect for the job.'

Anita's mind flashed back a couple of hours to the call she had made to Jennifer Todd to tell her that they now regarded her husband's disappearance as official. At first, Jennifer had been quite hysterical, and it had taken Anita a few minutes to settle her down. In between floods of tears, Jennifer kept repeating, 'I knew something was wrong.' Then she was ready to rush down to Manchester to catch a flight to Sweden. Again,

Anita managed to persuade her that there was little that she could do while they made their enquiries. Were there any relatives around that she could turn to? It transpired that she had a sister in Lancaster, who had come up to be with her for a few days. Jennifer explained that she was nervous staying by herself as she had had a break-in over the weekend; though the burglar must have been disturbed as nothing seemed to be missing. Anita promised that the moment she heard anything she would be straight on the phone.

As for getting any further with Graeme Todd's reason for visiting Sweden, Anita drew a blank. Other than that it was something to do with the old lady who had died in Carlisle a few years previously, there was no clue as to who Todd had been hoping to meet. Jennifer was just as baffled as they were.

'What about Dad?' said Lasse. 'Did you find anything out about his girlfriend?'

'Damn. I'd forgotten about that. I'd better phone him. It's something or nothing.'

Anita took a swift gulp of wine before taking the home phone out of its cradle. Despite everything that had gone on between them, she still had Björn's number on her phone. It was purely practical, as they had had to communicate from time to time about Lasse and his holiday visits to Uppsala when he was still at school.

Björn answered almost immediately. Anita decided to get straight to the point so she didn't have to talk for long.

'Greta Jansson has definitely left the school she was teaching at and, according to the neighbour, her father came to visit her. She gave him the key to Jansson's apartment. And the school said that she wasn't returning for family reasons. So it all fits. You've nothing to worry about.'

There was silence at the other end of the line.

'Did you hear what I said, Björn?'

At last he spoke. 'Greta's father died of cancer last year.'

CHAPTER 12

During the morning, two reported sightings of Graeme Todd came into the polishus. The first was from the city library and the second was from the Malmöhus museum. Both were for the day before he disappeared. But both needed to be followed up. Anita decided to send Hakim to the castle. It was a tourist attraction and therefore an obvious place for a first-time visitor to Malmö to go. Over the centuries, it had been a fort, a royal mint, a prison and now a rather eclectic museum, which featured everything from period furniture to a stuffed elk. She decided that she would take the library as it was a more intriguing place for Todd to visit.

Anita walked through the drizzle along the canal towards Slottsparken. The weather matched her mood. Her brief conversation with Björn had thrown up more questions than the simple answer she thought she had uncovered. Greta Jansson's whereabouts were no longer a straightforward matter, but she knew she had to shove that to the back of her mind. Graeme Todd was the priority. It was official. Reluctantly, Anita had again promised Björn that she would ask around, but only when she had time. It had been enough to get him off the phone. It was after overhearing the conversation that Lasse had poured out his confused feelings for his father. Lasse had been upset at seeing him in such a drunken and maudlin state. During his teenage visits to Uppsala, he had met a succession of increasingly youthful girlfriends. The fact that they were far nearer his own age than Björn's had been amusing at the time. What unnerved him was that he had never seen his father so besotted. All these years, he had harboured the dream of many children of divorced parents that there would be some sort of reconciliation. Of course, Lasse now knew that he had been deluding himself, and that his mother would never turn back the clock. He still hoped that his father would realise that he had made a mistake, change his philandering ways and try to mend their fractured family. But seeing Björn so upset by the disappearance of his latest girlfriend brought home the harsh reality that his father had moved on and would never come back. He would never change. He saw him now as an old man who was making a fool of himself over a girl only a couple of years older than his son. Björn made him feel sick.

Anita was torn. She was saddened that Lasse had such negative feelings for his father, who was behaving like a complete idiot. She hated to see her son so upset. It was a tough lesson having to reassess a parent. Yet she was pleased that they had been able to talk together again, as in the pre-Rebecka days. It was their first proper conversation since Lasse's return home. And when he had broken down in tears, she had taken him in her arms. She had missed that human contact, which had decreased as he'd grown up and he'd shunned her attempts to hug him. After she had gone to bed and left him watching his box set of *Curb your Enthusiasm*, she hadn't been able to sleep because she was so furious with Björn. His selfish actions were alienating a devoted son. What's more, he was intruding into her life again. She had fought so hard to banish him from her feelings that his reappearance was aggravating beyond measure – all the disappointments and resentments had come flooding back. Well, he could wallow in his self-pity. Fuck Björn and fuck Greta Jansson.

*

The city library was on the edge of Slottsparken. The older part of the building reminded Anita of a solid German schloss. She entered the foyer of the modern 1990s annex, which had a certain fascination despite its incongruity. The sheer glass walls captured each beam of light and threw it triumphantly over the central staircase. It was a bright and welcoming space, conducive to all activities, from both light browsing to intensive research. At the reception, she asked if she could speak to the librarian who had phoned the police about the missing person mentioned on the local news last night. The young man on the desk knew immediately who Anita was referring to. No doubt it had been a topic of conversation over the water cooler that morning.

'That'll be Paula. Paula Wennås. You'll find her up the stairs there,' he said, pointing up to the glass box. 'Red-brown hair, shaved on one side,' he added for identification.

Anita thanked him and made her way up the flight of stairs. At the top were rows of book shelves. Beyond was a structure which reminded her of man-sized pigeonholes on three levels. Each carrel must have housed a thousand books and had an individual work area. Because of the transparency of the wall beyond, it seemed as though those studying were suspended in mid-air. Anita spotted Wennås pushing a trolley past one of the bookcases on the main floor. The librarian stopped and put a couple of books back onto a shelf.

'Paula Wennås?'

The young woman turned. She had a pretty, round face and a lovely smile. 'Yes.'

'Anita Sundström. I'm here about the call you made to the police this morning.'

Wennås automatically picked up a book off the trolley and held it aloft, halfway to the shelf. 'The man you were looking for. I recognised him from the television. I remembered him because we don't get many British visitors.' She slotted the book into its place. 'It was a good excuse to speak some English.'

'When did Graeme Todd come in?'

Wennås trundled the trolley along to the next bookcase. Anita followed her.

'It was last Tuesday. Yes... a week ago today.'

'Time?'

Wennås smiled. 'A bit before half eleven. I remember because it was just before I went for a coffee break.'

'As you talked to him, I assume that he was after something specific.'

'Maps.'

'Maps?'

She fished another book off her trolley. 'Local maps.'

'Anywhere in particular?'

'Well, Skåne.'

'Do you know where in Skåne? It could be really important.' Anita was feeling that at last this could give her a clue as to where Todd had intended going.

Wennås adopted an apologetic expression. 'I'm sorry. I didn't find any maps for him. All I did was point him in the direction of the section where he could find them.'

Anita inwardly groaned.

'Nothing.'

'Snap,' said Anita in reply to Hakim.

'The man at the Malmöhus shop said he bought a couple of postcards. He thought it was about four o'clock, so we have no idea how long he was in there. I could look at the CCTV footage if you want.'

'Not at the moment. He was probably doing some sightseeing while he was here. Filling in time.'

'What about the library?' Hakim asked.

'He was after maps of Skåne. Trouble is, we don't know any locations as the librarian only sent him off to the relevant section.'

'At least it shows that he was probably leaving Malmö on the Wednesday.' Hakim fiddled with his computer keyboard thoughtfully. 'He must have been looking for detailed maps. Ordinary maps he could pick up at the tourist information or a bookshop. It sounds as though he might have been looking for a specific building or house.'

'Why not use Google Earth then?'

'Maybe he hadn't got a name to work with. I don't know. But he's out there somewhere.'

'But where?' Anita went to the window. The drizzle had now morphed into heavy rain. The leaves on the trees over on Kungsgatan were changing colour. Winter was on its way.

Then she turned decisively. 'Back to the train and bus stations.' Hakim gave a mock groan. 'We know he left the hotel after breakfast. So we'll start at Triangeln again. Then the bus station on Spårvägsgatan. That's the nearest to the Hilton. I'll see if Klara Wallen is available to help. Moberg should be OK with that, given that Todd has now been missing for six days.'

Anita sat down at her desk and picked up the phone.

'Do you think he could be dead?'

She glanced over to Hakim and shrugged her shoulders. She was starting to think that that might be a possibility.

CHAPTER 13

The good news was that Klara Wallen had been assigned to help. The bad news was that Chief Inspector Moberg was now going to oversee the case of the missing British heir hunter. With a flapping Commissioner Dahlbeck looking over Moberg's shoulder, it was going to be the foot soldiers who would end up in the firing line. The more pressure Moberg got from above, the more he would pass on to the team. At least Anita wouldn't have to work with Westermark, who was helping Nordlund with the investigation into the savage beating of an old man in Segevång.

Hakim was down at Triangeln station, while Wallen had gone to the bus station. The task that Moberg had given Anita was to once more ring up Jennifer Todd to see if she could provide any further information. She knew it was a pointless exercise, but she also knew that Moberg would check to make sure she had done it. This time Jennifer Todd's sister answered the phone. As a friendly warning, she explained how desperately worried Jennifer was at the moment. Anita said she understood, but insisted on speaking to her, even though she hadn't any fresh news of her husband's whereabouts.

Jennifer sounded calmer than during their previous conversations, and admitted that her feelings were ambivalent about the fact that there was no news. This took Anita aback. Though the possibility that Todd was dead had obviously crossed her own mind, she had expected the wife to assume that he was alive until told otherwise.

'I'm a nurse. I face death every day in the hospital. I have to be prepared.'

'I'm sure Graeme is fine.' She knew it didn't sound convincing.

'You don't have to soft-soap me, Inspector.'

'Call me Anita.'

'OK, Anita. What do you really think has happened? You've had a few days to think about it.'

Anita wasn't sure how to answer. 'If I'm honest, I have no idea. If we had any clues as to where he intended going, who he was trying to meet—'

'I think everything he had about the Doris Little case is on his laptop. I've checked his main computer, which is in his office downstairs here in the house, and there's nothing on that. I've also looked in his filing cabinet – nothing there either.'

'Did he usually have a physical file?'

'Oh, yes. He's a stickler about that. There's often lots of paperwork. Copies of birth and death certificates, census sheets downloaded from the internet; that sort of thing.'

'So you'd expect him to have a paper file on this woman?'

'Very much so. And I doubt he'd take it with him. When meeting a claimant, he usually puts all the relevant information on his laptop. Easier to go through than having lots of bits of paper floating around. Of course, official forms he'd need for signing up an heir, he'd take with him. That would give him permission to put in a claim on the beneficiary's behalf.'

Anita had a thought. 'You mentioned you had a break-in.'

'Saturday night. But nothing was taken.'

And then another thought: 'Could the burglar have been after the file?'

There was silence at the other end.

'Look, Jennifer, we've found out a couple of things about Graeme's movements. He was staying at the Hilton hotel.'

'What?' Jennifer sounded incredulous. 'Are you sure?'

'Yes.'

'But we can't afford that. What was he thinking? He's normally very careful with money.' She sounded cross.

'The other thing we discovered was that he paid a visit to the city library on the Tuesday. He wanted to find the map section.'

There was a little knowing snort at the other end of the line. 'That sounds more like Graeme. Loves his maps. Whenever we go on holiday, he spends hours poring over road atlases and ordnance survey maps to plan our routes and activities. Bit of an obsession. He's a bit obsessive. The Little case became an obsession.'

'So you wouldn't read anything significant into his wanting to look at some maps?'

'No,' she almost laughed. Anita took it that the map thing was a family joke. Another blank, she thought.

'But he does like to find out everything beforehand about a place we're going to visit. He usually Googles it, but he just loves proper maps. He's got quite a collection of them here.'

'All we know is that he was interested in maps of Skåne. Trouble is, that's about the size of your Yorkshire. Oh well, we'll carry on digging. As soon as we know anything, I'll be straight back on to you.'

There was a pause at the other end of the phone. 'Thank you for all your efforts, Anita.' Anita felt helpless as she had no idea what they were going to do next. Todd could have gone anywhere.

She was about to put the phone down when she had a thought. 'Apart from visiting Sweden for this case, was there anything about the country that interested him? I don't know... history, architecture, food, films.'

'Not really.' Then a moment later. 'Oh, there are the Wallander novels of course.' She pronounced the W as a W and not as a V. 'We saw some of the TV series. That actor. Brannigan? No, Branagh. Not really my thing, but Graeme had to read all the books. He took the last one with him to read on the flight.'

'Another obsession?'

'Once he's into something...' At least Jennifer Todd was being positive. She was still using the present tense.

Anita popped a sachet of snus under her top lip. She was glad the office was empty; she wanted time to think. Two potentially significant pieces of information had emerged from her conversation with Jennifer Todd. Firstly, the obsessive Graeme Todd might well have gone to Ystad, home of the fictional detective, Kurt Wallander. There was now quite a tourist trail built around the character that featured in Henning Mankell's books and various TV series. The easiest way for him to travel to Ystad would be by train, direct from Triangeln. It was only forty-five minutes away. He could do that in a morning and then be back in Malmö for his meeting, whoever that was with. Unless the meeting was out of town. The moment Hakim got back with the CCTV, she would get him onto that. As they had nothing else to go on, they might as well pursue that as a possible angle.

The second piece of information was more troubling. Had the break-in at the Todds' home been an opportunist one that had been disturbed, as Jennifer assumed? Or, was the burglar after the Doris Little file? Was it significant that it had taken place two days after Todd disappeared? If the burglar's sole intention was stealing the file, then someone was going to great lengths to ensure that no trace was left of the reason for Todd's visit to Sweden. And, if the two were interlinked, it also meant that someone in Sweden was powerful and influential enough to organise a break-in in another country. Was she being too fanciful? What she did know for certain was that Todd had uncharacteristically forked out to stay at the Hilton, he was secretive about his heir-hunting investigations, and now he had disappeared. Three things that added up to one – the death of an old lady in Carlisle in 2009 which had inadvertently triggered off a series of events that Anita had a nasty feeling wasn't going to end well.

CHAPTER 14

Linnea Kotiranta was seriously hacked off. She was more than a little drunk, too. Carlsten was being such a prick. As usual. This was meant to be such a pleasant evening out. They were making up. Carlsten had taken her to that nice sushi restaurant in Limhamn. The one on the main street. He had been at his most charming and accommodating. At first.

She stumbled forward, not quite sure where she was. She knew that she had been walking for about half an hour and had just passed a lot of fancy apartments. Ahead of her, she could hear the sea. Bright lights behind her, darkness in front. She wanted to sit down. The high-heeled shoes she was wearing were meant for looking good, not for tottering along endless concrete pavements. Now she could feel yielding grass beneath her feet.

She and Carlsten had split up twice already. The first time, she had moved out. The second, she had refused to budge and he had had to leave. After three weeks apart, she was more than ready to take him back. She missed the sex. She missed him, despite his slovenly ways. He never lifted a finger around the apartment. And when she managed to get him to take the dirty clothes down for their weekly washing slot in the apartment block's laundry, he moaned. And then there were his friends. Slobs. Except for Halvar; he was all right. He was the only one brave enough to admonish Carlsten when he was treating her badly in public.

Linnea felt her heels sink into the grass. It had rained most of the day. As she extricated her shoes from the enveloping turf, she realised where she must have staggered. It was Ön. "The island" attached to Limhamn. Down to the left, she could see the lights running along the length of the Öresund Bridge. She could make out a train as it flashed between the girders underneath the road. She lurched forward. Down in the other direction, she could see the myriad lights of the Turning Torso piercing the night sky. It made her feel dizzy.

The argument had started to brew even before they had left the restaurant. It was always the same one these days. His commitment, or lack of it, to be more precise. She was nearly thirty. They had been together for over five years. She wanted to cement their relationship and start a family. She was even prepared to forgo marriage if it would make Carlsten feel less trapped. He was always using that as an argument. He wanted to retain his "freedom". She suspected that that meant he could shag other women. She was open to compromises, but not that one. In her heart of hearts she knew that he'd never settle down. 'You'll never change him,' her mother had warned in the early days. But her love for him had made her think otherwise, and she had resented her mother's unflattering observations. When the simmering argument had blown up into a fully fledged row on the street outside the restaurant, the drink had given her the courage to say what she really felt. Their shouting had appalled the respectable citizens of Limhamn on their evening constitutionals. Her final, yelled 'Fuck off!' hadn't been the most original parting line, but had eloquently summed up the failure of their attempt to make up.

As her head swam, she veered away from the lights of the buildings behind her and stumbled off in the direction of the Torso. The developers hadn't reached this end of the small spit of land. The grass felt soft on her bare feet; she could no longer take the pain her expensive shoes were inflicting upon her. She could make out some boulders just ahead. She would sit there and try and gather her thoughts. The neatly cut grass made way for stony, rough ground, which scuffed and tore at her feet. She half fell into a bush before righting herself. With great difficulty, she put her shoes back on and tottered towards the lapping sea. Now she felt queasy. Maybe, if she got to the shoreline, she could dab her face in cold water. She made it to the edge and plonked herself down on a boulder. She took some deep breaths. They didn't stop her from feeling sick; she'd drunk far too much. She knew that Carlsten had been trying to get her pissed to ensure he got her into bed. Water. She needed cold water on her face. The sea was only a couple of paces away. Easing herself off the rock, she stepped forward. She groped down into the darkness and plunged her fingers into the freezing water. She whipped her hand out. That had been quite a shock. So, more carefully this time, she leant down on her haunches and gingerly lowered her hands towards the sea. But this wasn't what she expected. The water had more substance to it. Perhaps it was seaweed. No, it was something more familiar. What was it? Stretching out further, the full horror of what she was touching began to creep over her. A few seconds later, she started to scream.

CHAPTER 15

Anita was totally disorientated. She could hear the knocking on the door, but all was blackness. Her sleep had been deep.

'Mamma.'

It was Lasse calling. She rubbed her eyes. The digital clock clicked to 01.36. What on earth did he want? What was he still doing up at this time? Watching some unsuitable programme on the telly most probably.

'Come in.'

Lasse, still fully dressed, came in clutching her mobile phone.

'You left it in the living room. It was buzzing. It was Klara Wallen.'

'God, what does she want?'

'She says you should get down to Ön as soon as possible.'

'What?' Anita was still half asleep.

'They've found a body.'

'Honestly, it'll probably be some floater.' She began to stir herself. 'Or someone's jumped off the bridge, like that ferry company boss in the summer.'

Lasse handed her the phone. 'She thinks it might be your Englishman.'

It wasn't more than a ten-minute drive from Anita's apartment at that time of night. The streets were virtually deserted. She put her foot down. The rain from the previous day made the tarmac on the road glisten in the headlights. She fervently hoped that the body wasn't Graeme Todd's. They had made a breakthrough yesterday afternoon when Todd had shown up on the Triangeln station CCTV, getting on a purple Skånetrafiken train heading out of Malmö. It was the train to Ystad and Simrishamn. She had arranged to meet Hakim at Triangeln that day, take the Ystad train and see if they could retrace Todd's steps. But, if he was lying dead on Ön, then he must have returned to the city that Wednesday afternoon or evening.

It was just after two when she drew up next to a couple of police vehicles in the car park of one of the smart apartment blocks. She remembered being down on Ön a year and half or so ago to interview a Danish copywriter about the murder of his boss. She knew that the fantastic views of the Sound made the apartments round here very desirable. She ran into a uniformed officer who pointed her in the direction of where the body was discovered.

Anita crunched her way over the rough ground towards the shoreline, where two policemen were erecting a cordon with police tape. She could see that a couple of arc lights had been brought in to illuminate the area. A temporary privacy shield had been set up. A tent would probably follow later. There were a number of people in plastic overalls hovering around the crime scene. She was met by Wallen, who had obviously been roused from her bed, too. Her black hair had been quickly scraped back. She had an old anorak over the protective clothing. It made Anita realise how cold it was. Wallen was clutching a copy of the photo of Graeme Todd. Before Anita could say anything— 'I think it's him.'

'Accident?'

Wallen shook her head. 'You'd better have a word with Eva Thulin.'

As Wallen was speaking, Anita noticed Westermark hovering in the shadows. He was dressed in a tracksuit.

'What's he doing here?'

'Lives in the apartment block over there. Heard the police cars and got up to see what was happening. Don't know why he's still hanging around, though. He's a creep.' Wallen didn't like Westermark any more than Anita did. Anita sometimes wondered if Wallen's aversion to him was his obvious lack of sexual interest in her.

Anita put on overalls, latex gloves and plastic overshoes. She was greeted with a weary smile from Eva Thulin, the best forensic technician Anita had worked with in recent years. She was a bit younger than Anita, but they seemed to view life – and their colleagues – from a similar perspective. Anita wondered why they had never met up socially. In fact, even after working with Thulin on a number of cases over the last five years, she didn't actually know whether she was single, married, attached or divorced. Anita also liked Thulin's dark sense of humour, which presumably was a prerequisite for a forensic technician's gruesome trade. Thulin pulled the mask away from her mouth.

'My husband thinks I must have a lover as I keep slipping out of the house in the middle of the night.' That answered one question.

'Klara says it wasn't an accident.'

'No,' Thulin answered emphatically. 'Unless he decided to cut his own hand off.'

Anita felt a sudden wave of sickness. For a moment she thought she was going to vomit.

'Want to have a look?'

'Not really.' But she knew she had to.

'We had to pull him in a bit because his feet were still in the water,' Thulin explained as they stood over the crumpled body. It was the face that Anita noticed first – the mole close to the nostril. The features were bleached out and the seawater had played havoc with his dyed hair. But it was unmistakeably Graeme Todd. Thulin pointed to the victim's arm. Todd still wore a sleeveless shirt, now torn and dirty. As soon as Anita caught sight of the stump, she quickly turned away. It wasn't the sickening sight of dismemberment that caused her reaction, more the realisation that she was going to have to tell Jennifer Todd.

'Is that what killed him?'

'Not sure yet. His body has taken a savage beating. Might also have drowned, but I'll let you know.'

Anita noticed that Westermark was no longer there. That was a relief. 'Eva, I know you'll need to take the body back to Lund for a more thorough examination, but is there anything you can tell me now? Apart from the obvious,' she added, turning back to look at the man who had come to Sweden to pick up his "jackpot", and instead had met a horrible fate.

'This certainly isn't the crime scene. His body was washed up here.'

'Where from?'

'Well, you know how weird the currents are in the Sound. The Baltic meets oceanic saltwater here. So the surface stream tends to be northbound.'

'So he could have been dumped south of the bridge?'

'That's my guess.'

Anita stared down towards the Öresund Bridge. Even at that time of night, there was traffic criss-crossing between Sweden and Denmark.

'How long do you think he's been dead?'

'Can't be certain. I'm pretty sure he's been dead longer than he's been in the sea. As you can see, there's very little bloating and he hasn't been nibbled. Makes time of death a bit of a lottery. How long has he been missing?'

'Just under a week.'

'Might have a better idea when we get him back to the lab. After we've photographed everything, can we remove the body?'

'Yes. If it's not the murder scene, there's not much more we can do here. But your people had better give this area the once-over when it gets light. You never know.'

Thulin turned and started to issue instructions to one of her assistants.

'Oh, Eva, when can we expect to get some preliminary results? It's just that Moberg is heading up the investigation...' She didn't have to explain further. Thulin knew the chief inspector only too well.

'Just my luck! First I'm going to go home and do some explaining, then I'll have a look at your friend here. This evening?'

'Fine. And thanks, Eva.'

Anita left Thulin to organise the removal of the body. She went over to Wallen, who was talking to a uniformed officer.

'Klara, who found the body?'

'A Linnea Kotiranta. She's over in the car park in one of the squad cars.'

Anita sat in the squad car next to a very upset young woman. She was wrapped in a blanket but still seemed cold. There was nothing that Linnea Kotiranta could tell Anita, other than how she had stumbled across the body. After initially being freaked out, she had run back to the car park and told someone from the apartments who'd just driven in. He had phoned the police.

'Any reason why you were out here?' Anita asked.

Kotiranta looked away. 'I had an argument with my boyfriend,' she mumbled. Anita decided not to probe any further.

'Thank you, Linnea. I'll get an officer to run you home.'

Kotiranta nodded gratefully in response.

'It's been an awful experience for you. If you want to talk to someone about it... get professional counselling, just let us know.'

She shook her head. 'I'll be all right.'

Anita watched the squad car drive off. She cast her eye round the car park. Some expensive vehicles. One stood out. A black Porsche, three bays along from her new old Peugeot. The Porsche was a Cayman S. Must have cost a small fortune. She glanced up at the apartment block in front of her. There was a light in a window on the fourth floor. Someone was watching her. She realised it was Westermark. He quickly disappeared from sight, and the light went out. Anita knew the car was his; the whole of the Polishus knew it was his. It had caused quite a stir when he had bought it last year. He might be a bachelor, but his police salary didn't run to such extravagance. Was this the price for tipping off Dag Wollstad? No one knew where the multi-millionaire industrialist had fled to, though there were plenty of rumours. South America was his most likely hide out.

But she had far more on her mind at that moment. Graeme Todd was no longer a missing person. What was still missing was any clue as to what he had got himself involved in.

CHAPTER 16

Moberg hadn't been happy when Anita woke him up with a phone call at half past three in the morning, but, as she pointed out, he wanted to be kept up to speed on developments, and a dead body with a hand missing was as big a development as they come. He grunted that he would be in at six, and that he wanted to see her, Wallen and Mirza to get a full run down on the case so far. That meant there was no point in Anita going home to try and snatch a little rest. So she made her way to headquarters. That would give her time to phone Hakim and gather her thoughts. They were too jumbled to make any sense of at the moment.

By the time Hakim came in at about half past five, Anita's brain was no clearer. She had already gone through three coffees, and the bin was full of half-mangled snus.

'You should have called me,' Hakim said.

'There was no point in us both losing our beauty sleep. If it'd been the actual crime scene, that would have been different. But Graeme Todd was washed up on the shore. He was murdered somewhere else.'

'Have we anything to go on as to where he might have been killed?' he asked, stifling a yawn.

'What do you think?' Anita answered wearily and a little irritably. 'But that sums up this entire investigation.'

Anita, Wallen and Hakim had to watch Moberg plough his way through his McDonald's breakfast in the meeting room as they went through the sketchy evidence they had so far. But even he momentarily stopped eating when Anita described Todd's missing hand. Anita went through Eva Thulin's speculations – they would have to wait for her preliminary findings – and what they had discovered yesterday, which amounted to Todd's visits to Malmöhus and the city library, the maps, and his interest in Henning Mankell. The latter might explain why he had got on the train to Ystad that morning. The question was whether he met his fate while he was out of Malmö, or whether he had returned before being killed. What was certain was that he never went back to his hotel.

Moberg didn't speak until he had nothing left to eat.

'It'll be interesting to know how he died. Result of the beating or did he drown?'

No one could answer, so they remained silent.

'We'll need to get onto his local British police force and notify them. That's one for you, Anita. See if he had a criminal record. This smacks of a gangland killing.'

'What about going to Ystad?' asked Anita. That still had to be a starting point.

'Wallen and Mirza can do that. See if he left a trail. Of course, he might have got off at any of the stations along the line if he was meeting someone. But it's all we've got to go on. At least he was alive when he got on that train.'

Moberg slowly eased himself out of his chair.

'We'll meet again when you two get back from Ystad.' He lumbered his way towards the door. 'And Anita, as well as talking to the British cops, don't forget to inform the widow.'

She hadn't.

Normally, in the case of a dead national from another country, Anita would have contacted the deceased's local police first, who would then have broken the news to the next of kin. But, as she had been dealing directly with Jennifer Todd, it was only right that the news should be passed on by her, rather than a total stranger. This was never a pleasant task. It was always the worst part of the job.

Jennifer Todd had been initially stunned into silence before bursting out with, 'Why? Why? Why?' There weren't any tears, which somehow made it worse. It was as though Jennifer had already accepted the inevitable. Eventually, Anita had managed to explain that the body had been washed up on the shore, and that they were treating it as murder. 'How on earth can he have been murdered?' Jennifer had been incredulous. Anita didn't have the heart to tell her that her husband had had his hand cut off. That would come later when she identified him. Anita said that she would arrange for Jennifer to come to Sweden and at the end of the conversation, the distraught woman had thanked her for her help. What help? She hadn't taken Graeme's disappearance seriously until it was too late. As she put the phone down, she felt a stab of guilt. Could there have been more she could have done? Or was it too late anyway? Eva Thulin might be able to provide an answer.

The train had been updated, thought Wallen as she surveyed the carriage. Skånetrafiken must have invested in some new rolling stock since she last made this journey about a couple of years before. She had had a night out with Anita and her friends in Simrishamn. A boozy night. She reflected that that was virtually the last time they had been out together. At one time, they had seen quite a lot of each other socially. They'd once even had a holiday on Kos together. Anita was the nearest thing to a friend she had in the force. They were on amicable terms but they had drifted apart. Probably because Anita didn't like her partner, Rolf. He could be full of himself. And she suspected that Rolf quietly fancied Anita, so maybe it was she who was doing the distancing. She had had too much disappointment where men were concerned.

The train sped through the outskirts of Malmö.

'How are you getting on with Anita?'

Hakim smiled. 'Fine.'

'She's a good detective.' Annoyingly, Wallen knew that Anita Sundström had a better record than herself. Wallen felt some resentment – she was just as competent, yet she hadn't had the same opportunities to shine. But she knew deep down that Anita's relative success was down to an inner determination that she didn't possess. Anita could stand up to Moberg, which she had never been able to do.

'Yes, I've learned a lot from her.'

'You'll miss her when you move on.'

'Yeah. I heard last week that I'm going to Gothenburg after Christmas.'

'Nice city.'

The conversation died. She didn't know what to say to Hakim. Having no children of her own, she wasn't comfortable relating to the young any more. That was another thing she envied Anita.

The train slowed down. They had reached Oxie. Wallen picked up a discarded copy of the *Metro*, which she read until they reached Ystad.

'Detective Sergeant Kevin Ash here,' said a bright voice at the other end of the phone. Anita had been kept waiting a while after she had first rung the Cumbrian Constabulary headquarters at Penrith to explain the Graeme Todd situation.

'Inspector Anita Sundström from the Skåne County Police.'

'And where's that when it's at home?'

'Southern Sweden. Malmo.' She dropped the umlaut so that it came out as the English pronunciation of the city's name.

'Malmo. Now don't tell me.' There was a momentary silence at the other end of the line. '1979. The European Cup Final. Nottingham Forest beat Malmo with a Trevor Francis goal. Brian Clough's team. The Swedes had an English manager, though.' She could hear him purse his lips. 'No, it's gone.'

'Bob Houghton.'

'Heavens, you're right!' Anita recognised the Estuary English in the voice from her time at the Met. She hadn't expected to hear it in an officer somewhere as far north as Cumbria.

'Now you've established where I'm ringing from, can we talk about Graeme Todd?'

'Sorry.' She heard the rustle of paper. 'I've been given a note here. There was a call logged at 9.14 am, Friday, October the fifth. Jennifer Todd said she thought that her husband had gone missing and that she had already been in contact with the police in Sweden. So, I assume from your call that he's turned up.'

'Yes. Unfortunately, dead.'

'Oh dear! Accident?'

'No, murder.'

'Are you sure?' There was a hint of disbelief in his tone.

'Someone chopped his hand off.'

She heard a sharp intake of breath. 'Shit!'

Anita waited for him to take in the information. 'We dragged him out of the sea early this morning. We don't yet know where he died.'

'Does Mrs Todd know?'

'I've just spoken to her.'

'Do you have any idea who might have killed him?'

'None at all. He's what his wife calls an "heir hunter".'

'I know the sort of thing.'

'He came over to Malmo, or Skåne anyway – that's like your county – to meet someone. According to his wife, he thought he was going to make a lot of money out of the visit.'

'So there must have been a big inheritance.'

'No. That wasn't the case. That's the strange thing. It was to do with some elderly woman who died in Carlisle a few years ago. Mrs Todd thinks the estate wasn't worth much at all. But he was secretive about the details, so his wife doesn't know that much.'

There was a pause. 'Blimey, your English is good.'

'I've spent time in England,' Anita said with a hint of annoyance. 'The point is,' she continued more forcefully than she meant to, 'that until we know why he came over here to Sweden, we have virtually nothing to go on. At the moment, we're trying to trace his movements.'

'If he's an accredited probate researcher, presumably he'll have a file on the case here in Cumbria.'

'It's not there. Jennifer Todd had a break-in on Saturday night.'

'We've got no record of a break-in.'

'That's because she didn't think that anything had been taken. But there was no sign of the file, and she's sure he would have had one. He may have brought it with him, of course, but Mrs Todd reckons that's unlikely. But if he didn't...'

'Then whoever killed Todd has someone over here,' Ash said, completing the thought process.

'That's only speculation.'

'Will you be coming over?' Ash asked. There was a hint of enthusiasm in his voice.

'Probably. The murderer or murderers may be here, but I think we'll find the answers in England.'

'Anything we can do this end?'

'Yes.' Anita was at her most businesslike. 'You could check out the break-in. And we need to find out about the woman that's at the centre of the probate case. She was called Doris Little.' Anita proceeded to give Detective Sergeant Ash the sketchy details she had gathered from Jennifer Todd.

'OK, I'll get onto that, Inspector Sund... Sorry.'

'Sundström. I'll be in touch,' she said and put down the phone.

CHAPTER 17

'Amazingly, given what his body had been subjected to, Graeme Todd drowned. But he was dead by the time he ended up in the Sound.'

They were in the meeting room – Moberg, Wallen, Hakim, Anita and Eva Thulin. Thulin was running through her preliminary findings. Nordlund and Westermark would be joining the investigation in the next couple of days after tying up the final details of the Segevång attack case. It was after seven. Hakim had been sent out to bring in pizzas and coffees. It promised to be a long evening.

'The water in the lungs shows that he didn't die in the sea. Not saltwater. Freshwater, possibly rainwater. So wherever he was murdered, he was dumped later.'

'That could have been to deflect us from looking in the right place,' reflected Moberg as he wiped some stray tomato away from his mouth. 'So the murder could have taken place almost anywhere.' He shook his head wearily. 'Time of death?'

Thulin pursed her lips. 'That's not easy. I reckon he couldn't have been in the sea for more than twenty-four hours, given the preserved state of the body. Death probably occurred four days ago. Maybe five.'

'As he disappeared on the Wednesday, he might have been killed on the Friday or Saturday,' said Anita pointing to a whiteboard on which she had sketched out a rough calendar, from the day on which Todd had arrived, Monday, October 1st, to today, Wednesday, October 10th, the day he was found. Some days had details of his known movements written in. Most of the days were blank.

'What about the missing hand?' asked Moberg.

'That's pretty gruesome. It was sawn off.'

Hakim winced.

'My guess is that they used one of those pruning saws. From the serrated marks left on the body, we might be able to establish the make and manufacturer. But they're freely available, as there are an awful lot of trees in Sweden.'

'See what you can do. That would give us something.' Anita knew they would be grateful for any scrap of help.

'The condition of the body,' Thulin continued, 'strongly indicates that the victim had been tortured. Trauma everywhere. He was hit, kicked; you name it. Broken ribs. Then there's the hand. Though it didn't kill him, added to the punishment, it must have put him near the edge. Then someone must have held his head under water until...' She didn't have to finish.

They took in what Thulin had just told them as she carefully laid out graphic photographic evidence of the injuries and pointed out each area of forensic interest in sickening detail. Todd's captors had been brutal. Anita was glad she had eaten her pizza before the pictures appeared. 'I can't be certain, but I believe there might be more than one perpetrator.' With a flourish of her hand: 'I think it would be too much for one person to take the victim captive, carry out all the beatings and torture, then get him onto a boat and dump the body. This is not a Danish TV crime series.'

The remark produced a few smirks.

'The question is: what did Graeme Todd know that made his killer or killers go to such lengths?' Anita picked up a photo of Todd's handless arm. 'And another one is: did they get that information out of him before he died?'

'Surely they must have,' observed Moberg. 'Why kill him otherwise?'

'Maybe they pushed too hard, went too far. He obviously didn't give up his knowledge without serious encouragement.'

After Thulin left, it was the turn of Wallen and Hakim to report on what they had found out in Ystad. Between them, they had been able to establish that Todd had been in the town on Wednesday, October 3rd. They had three definite sightings. He was recognised getting off the Simrishamn-bound train by one of the station staff. He had been in the Hotel Continental, where he'd asked the receptionist to take a photograph of him with his camera in the foyer. And then he'd visited Fridolfs café. According to one of the staff, he left around half past one. 'After that, nothing,' Wallen finished. 'Fridolfs and the Hotel Continental both feature in the Mankell books, so it fits in with his love of Wallander.'

There was a muted snort from Moberg, whose reading was confined to police reports and divorce papers. 'So he could have gone anywhere after he left the café.'

'We don't think that he came back to Malmö,' ventured Hakim. 'Well, not by train. We haven't found anything on the Triangeln CCTV.'

'That doesn't mean he didn't,' Moberg added unnecessarily.

'What we do know,' said Anita quickly before Moberg took any more digs at Hakim, 'is that Todd must have had a camera, a mobile phone and a computer with him, which are all missing. All might contain incriminating evidence.'

'Presumably, they're at the bottom of the fucking Sound by now, or destroyed,' mused Moberg.

An hour later they had got no further forward. The only thing they had was the means of killing and a hint of a motive. Whoever Graeme Todd had met up with wanted something from him badly enough to torture him. Whatever information he had had was dangerous knowledge. They had to agree with Eva Thulin – there must have been more than one perpetrator. Of course, as Anita had pointed out, the killers might well have been trying to shut him up. If the break-in at the Todd home in Cumbria really had been to remove Doris Little's file, they were obviously covering their tracks. Obliterating their identity. More worrying was the fact that they had enough clout to influence events in Britain from here in Sweden. Were they straying into the realms of organised crime?

'Let's not get ahead of ourselves,' weighed in Moberg. He pushed away an empty pizza box. He had finished Wallen's leftovers. 'Do you hope to get anything of any use from the English police?' he asked Anita with a stifled yawn. She reflected ruefully that he couldn't possibly be as tired as her – she'd been up since half past one that morning.

'We can only hope so. I certainly think that the key to the mystery lies in England, even if the murderers are over here.'

Moberg thoughtfully drummed his thick fingers on the table top. 'Well, I suggest you bugger off over there and see what you can dig up.'

CHAPTER 18

It would be a couple of days before Anita could get clearance to go to England and start prying into Graeme Todd's life. It had to be sanctioned officially through Commissioner Dahlbeck in Malmö and the Chief Constable in Cumbria. No one wanted to be seen stepping on anybody's toes. Dahlbeck was already worried that they had a dead British citizen on their hands. The Mayor wanted a quick resolution. That wasn't going to happen. There was also Jennifer Todd to deal with, as she was flying over to officially identify the body. She was glad that Nordlund would be able to help soon, even if it meant the loathsome Westermark would be involved as well. With no leads, they needed the full team on this case.

She had decided to go to Ystad herself. That was where Todd had last been seen. Hakim was going through hours of CCTV footage from various vantage points in Malmö. They had gone for the obvious locations like Triangeln, all the major squares, the Central Station and the busiest shopping streets, plus the two places they knew he had visited before – the main library and Malmöhus. A couple of the polishus IT staff had been commandeered to help, despite the protests of the head of the IT department. After having marched into Moberg's office to complain, he had left, ashen-faced, five minutes later. Wallen was designated to meet Jennifer Todd at Kastrup Airport and take her directly to the morgue in Lund for her last meeting with her husband.

Anita wasn't quite sure what her own trip would achieve. She knew Ystad well, having being brought up in Simrishamn half an hour along the coast. When she was a teenager, Ystad had been the biggest place to go and hang out with her friends. She realised that she was unlikely to pick up any fresh clues. Hakim and Wallen would have done a thorough job. Maybe she could discover a bit more about what made Graeme Todd tick. Other than the conclusions she had drawn from his photograph, and the tit-bit about his obsessions, she wanted to hear from Jennifer Todd what he was really like. Build up a picture of the man. What motivated him? Was he headstrong? Or obdurate? Or a dreamer? Or a gambler by nature? Was he aware of the potential danger he was obviously facing, or had he naïvely walked into a situation that he had no idea could be perilous? Whatever his character, the overriding question remained – what was it about the estate of Doris Little that could have led to Todd's gory ending?

As Anita parked her green Peugeot opposite Ystad station, her mobile sprang into life. The moment she answered it, she wished she'd checked the caller first so she could have ignored it.

'Björn, what do you want?'

'Have you heard anything about Greta?'

Anita slammed the car door rather too firmly with her left hand.

'Nothing. I've got my hands full with a murder case. I haven't the time.'

'Shouldn't it be official by now? Greta's been missing for nearly a fortnight.'

'Look, Björn, I can't make it official as her family hasn't reported her missing. The school hasn't either. Do you want to, as her *boyfriend*?' She couldn't help the scorn.

All she could hear was breathing at the other end of the phone.

'I've spoken to Ulrika.'

'Who's Ulrika?' She didn't bother disguising her impatience. She hadn't time for this.

'Greta's best friend at university. Lives in Stockholm. She's in some sort of business now.' This rang a bell.

'And?'

'She was down in Malmö on September the twenty-eighth. The Friday that Greta was last at the school. Ulrika had arranged to hook up with Greta for a drink, but her meeting overran and she couldn't make it. But she phoned her while Greta was waiting in the bar. She might have been the last person to speak to her before she went missing.'

'Which bar?'

'Ulrika wasn't sure, but she was pretty sure it was in Lilla Torg. The point is, she hasn't heard from Greta since.'

Anita sighed. 'I'm afraid there's nothing much I can do at the moment. As I say, we've got this murder case on and I've got to go over to England in a couple of days. Don't know how long I'll be away.'

'I'm getting desperate.' He didn't have to say it. It came through in his voice. It was so pathetic. But she didn't feel any pity for him – she despised him for being so weak. She just wanted the call to end.

'All I can do is mention it to a colleague.' Nordlund was aware of the situation, and she was sure that he would keep an eye on things as a favour to her. 'If he hears anything, he can contact me.'

'Thanks, Anita.' She was about to end the call. 'Ask your colleague to try and answer the question that's been driving me crazy. Who was the man who rang the school to say she wasn't going back?'

By the time she entered Fridolfs café, the sun had elbowed its way through the bank of cloud cover that had blanketed the sky for the entire morning. It had made for a gloomy wander round the old town. All she had done was visit the sights that any Henning Mankell fan would have on their hit list of places associated with the Kurt Wallander books. She preferred British crime novels herself. The cops, like their real counterparts, weren't so hidebound by rules. Rules were the plague of Swedish policing – and Swedish life. During her year with the Metropolitan Police, she had become aware of how much Swedes were governed by accepted norms. She had been appalled, yet strangely envious, at the way Met officers blithely bent or ignored the rules to achieve results. Westermark was the nearest thing her department had to a British detective.

Standing in Mariagatan, the real street where the fictional Kurt Wallander lived, it was its ordinariness that brought back memories of her first home with Björn. A red-brick block stuffed with apartments full of anonymous people living their own lives and rarely acknowledging their neighbours. Yet she had been so happy because she was sharing her life with a charming, charismatic man who worshipped her.

She was annoyed with Björn for hassling her but, more irritatingly, she found herself thinking about Greta Jansson rather than concentrating on Graeme Todd. Despite trying to convince herself that there must be a perfectly logical explanation for her disappearance, too many questions kept surfacing. Greta's sudden departure from the school, the empty apartment with the well-stocked fridge, the appearance of her "father", and no contact with her supposed best friend. Another niggle was that for all his protestations and obvious worry, Björn wasn't telling her the whole truth.

Seated at her table by the window looking out over the square packed with parked cars, a fresh coffee and a large piece of moist carrot cake in front of her, Anita had firmly brought her thoughts back to the matter in hand. She had already asked a member of staff about Graeme Todd and showed them his picture. She had got the same information that Hakim and Wallen had gleaned – Todd had been in the café and had left at about one-thirty.

She tucked into her cake with some glee. She hadn't realised how hungry she was. A crumb landed on the picture of Graeme Todd that was laid in front of her. She brushed it away.

'I recognise him.'

CHAPTER 19

The man who hovered over Anita's shoulder was pointing to the photocopied photograph of Graeme Todd. He was a tall man wearing clean, blue overalls, and with a neat ginger beard.

'Saw him in here about a week ago.'

Anita's heart began to race. 'What day, exactly?'

The man stroked his beard thoughtfully. 'Wednesday. Last Wednesday. I sometimes come in here at lunchtime when I've got a job on in Ystad. I'm an electrician,' he added by way of explanation. 'I was doing a job over the road. Down on the docks.'

'And this would have been about half past one?'

'Yeah. I noticed him because he was talking in English to the girl at the counter.'

'Did you see him leave?'

'Yeah. He went over there.' The man pointed out of the window at the square.

'What direction did he go in?'

'No, he was just standing there. On the other side of the road.'

Anita stared out over the cobblestoned road to the cars parked beyond.

'Looked like he was waiting for someone. I remember he glanced at his watch.'

'Did someone pick him up?'

'Presumably. He was there for a few minutes, I think. But I was busy eating and reading my paper. When I glanced up, he was gone.'

'You didn't see a car leaving the square?'

'There are cars coming and going all the time. Sorry.'

Anita's initial excitement was swiftly dampened.

'Did he have anything with him? Like a computer?'

'He had one of those fancy bags slung over his shoulder. Could have had a laptop in it.'

Jennifer Todd was a plump woman. She had short, wiry, grey hair. That surprised Anita. It was usually the woman who hid the grey, not the man. It was the other way round with the Todds. She was sensibly dressed for the weather in black trousers, a thick, brown polo-neck jersey and stout leather shoes. This was a woman who was used to spending a lot of time on her feet. There was a complete absence of jewellery and very little evidence of make-up. She had none of her husband's vanity. Anita could imagine that the brown eyes behind the spectacles were quick to smile, given the right opportunity. This wasn't one of those times. Anita had met her at the polishus. Wallen had said that fru Todd had been very quiet while identifying her husband's body. Though noticeably shocked by the injuries, there had been no histrionics, no crying. They were reserved for Anita, who'd taken her home to give her something to eat. Sitting in the car outside her apartment in Roskildevägen, Jennifer Todd had suddenly let out all her pent-up emotion. Tears streamed down her cheeks like the rivulets of rain running down the windscreen.

A cup of tea helped, though she only picked at the salad that Anita had hurriedly concocted out of leftovers in the fridge. She was being kind out of pity, but also she was being pragmatic; she had reasoned that she would get more information out of Jennifer in a domestic setting rather than in the intimidating and impersonal atmosphere of police headquarters.

'How could they do such awful things to him?' As a nurse, she was only too aware of the damage that had been done. 'And his...' She couldn't say the word. She had seen many serious injuries over the years. Car accidents, limbs lost in machinery; even once, someone trampled by a herd of cows. But it was the sheer brutality of the missing hand that was beyond her comprehension.

'I know it's early, but would you like a glass of wine?'

Jennifer Todd gave Anita a grateful smile and nodded.

Anita got up and went into the kitchen. She came back with a bottle and a couple of glasses. 'I'm afraid I've only got red.'

'That's fine, thank you.' Anita filled the two glasses. 'You've been very kind, Anita. Right from the beginning.'

No, I haven't, Anita thought ruefully. I thought Graeme had deserted you. The only consolation was that it had probably been too late to help Todd by the time she took the call from his wife. She wouldn't have been able to prevent his death even if she'd acted straight away.

Anita sat opposite the shaken woman. 'I'm afraid we're no further forward in our investigation. Though I did learn today that it appears that Graeme was waiting for someone in Ystad. But who he met or where he was taken, we have no idea. We need your help.'

'I'll do anything. You know that.'

'Maybe now is not the right time.'

Jennifer Todd fixed Anita with a steely gaze. 'No. Nothing can be any worse than in that morgue today. Anita, you must catch whoever did those dreadful things to Graeme. Now *is* the right time.' She stifled a sob.

Anita cleared away the meal before they sat down together on the day bed in the living room.

'I want to get an idea of what Graeme was like. As we have so little to go on, maybe there's something about his character – or something from his past – that might shed light on what went on here. You said yourself that you can't explain how he ended up staying at the Hilton. That seems to have been out of character.'

Jennifer Todd stared at the half-empty wine glass on the wooden coffee table in front of her.

'It wasn't really out of character as such,' she said slowly. 'It was more down to economics. It's not what we could afford. My salary at the Cumberland Infirmary isn't bad. But since Graeme gave up teaching, he hasn't made that much as an heir hunter. We're comfortable. We *were* comfortable,' she said suddenly realising that she was talking as though her husband were still alive. Then, for a moment, a hint of a smile flickered across her face. 'Graeme's mum always said he should have been born a duke. He had expensive tastes, but we never had the money to indulge them.'

'So, the fact that he thought that this trip to Sweden was the "jackpot", in his words, would particularly appeal to him.'

'I suppose so. He gave up teaching history because he thought there was more to life than dealing with kids who had no interest in the past. History was a passion of his and that's why he first went into genealogy. Tracing family trees and that sort of thing. He loved it, but there wasn't much money in it. Then he moved on to probate research. It was a natural progression, as you use many of the same research techniques and sources to trace the families of those who've died intestate. The heir hunting produced a better financial return on his time, though it was a bit hit-and-miss. He was always delighted when he managed to make a successful claim to the Treasury on behalf of the relatives he'd found. But often he might put in weeks of work for nothing. Either he couldn't find anybody, or another company had beaten him to it. It can be a very competitive business. He was a one-man band up against quite large firms with massive research resources. Or sometimes the people he'd found decided to put in a claim on their own, cutting out the heir hunter and his percentage. That would really anger him, as often they hadn't even been aware of their connection to the dead person in the first place. Just greed on their part.'

'Was he a driven person?'

Jennifer Todd took a sip of wine before answering.

'Yes. He was very dedicated to his work. Once he got his teeth into a project, he wouldn't let go.'

'And as a husband?'

She didn't answer immediately. 'We rubbed along together. It wasn't the most romantic of marriages. We married quite late. We met when he was still teaching in Wigton. I was thirty-eight by then, Graeme forty. Not love's young dream.' She touched her wedding ring thoughtfully. 'Twenty-one years. I was going to retire next year so I could help him with the business.'

'Have you any family?'

'You mean kids?' She sighed. 'I would have liked to be a mum. But by the time I married, it was too late really. As a nurse, I've seen the problems some older mothers have had. And their newborns. Not that we ever discussed it. I don't think Graeme would have been interested anyway.'

For a moment, Anita wondered where the hell her own "kid" was. She hadn't seen him all day. He was still in bed when she left for Ystad that morning and he wasn't around when she had returned with Mrs Todd.

'And how would you describe Graeme to someone who didn't know him?'

'His character? I haven't really thought about that for a long time. You just get so used to each other that...' She started to fiddle with her wedding ring again. 'He was considerate. At times. Didn't have much of a sense of humour. You know at work we're always having a laugh. Nurses together tend to be silly. Laugh at suggestive things. Probably a coping mechanism. Graeme didn't like that sort of thing. Bit of a prude, actually. Stubborn, too. Once he got a bee in his bonnet. Never liked to admit he was wrong.'

'I know a few people like that.'

'A little conceited, perhaps. Pedantic. Oh, dear! I don't seem to be painting a very good picture. But Graeme was loyal... very loyal. And I know he loved me. Not in a demonstrative way. He wasn't tactile. But we were right for each other. That's all I can say.'

'Thank you, Jennifer. I know it's difficult, but everything you tell me is useful.' Anita glanced at her guest's nearly empty glass. 'Some more?'

'No, thank you. I'm not really a drinker. Graeme liked the odd pint at the Queen's Head. That's the village pub.'

'You say Graeme was stubborn. I know this isn't easy, but do you think he was the type of person to be strong, even if he was being threatened?'

Her head jerked up. 'You mean the horrible things they did to him?'

Anita nodded.

'He was certainly pig-headed. He wouldn't be bullied. And he wasn't afraid to upset people. Some of the decisions he made as chairman of the Parish Council didn't go down too well in the village. Whatever these people wanted, Graeme wouldn't... you know...'

'I understand.' Anita looked around for her snus tin. She must have left it in her bag. It would have to wait. 'You mentioned about probate companies in competition for business.'

'Could be quite cut-throat. Some estates could be very lucrative.'

'It may sound stupid, but could all this be to do with business rivalry?'

'No,' was the emphatic answer. 'That was the whole point about this case. It had been investigated by a big London outfit. But they drew a blank and dropped it. It was only then that Graeme took it up. Not because it was worth a lot. More due to the fact that it was so local. We're only half an hour from Carlisle. It was also a challenge.'

'A challenge?'

'Yes, because he wanted to succeed where a whole team of posh London researchers had failed. That was typical Graeme. Prove people wrong. But Yorkshiremen are like that.'

While Jennifer Todd went to the bathroom, Anita boiled up a pan to make them another cup of tea. By the time she came back into the living room, Jennifer had returned. Her face was flushed, and Anita suspected that she'd been crying again. She was trying to be sympathetic, but she knew she had to try and discover everything that this woman knew about the case that her husband had been working on. There might be some seemingly insignificant detail that she hadn't mentioned before because it had slipped her mind. Anita had to cajole her memory; shake free some forgotten snippet.

'Jennifer, can you take me through everything you can remember about the Doris Little investigation, however trivial it might seem?'

'That Penrith inspector asked me the same. Ash, I think his name was. Called in last night.'

That sounded encouraging. Detective Sergeant Ash had got straight onto the case. She would phone him later about the break-in.

'Doris Little?'

'Yes. It must have been about six months ago that Graeme first mentioned her name. She lived near Dixon's chimney in Carlisle.' Anita looked nonplussed. 'It's a well-known landmark in the city. At first, it appeared that she owned her own house. That's usually what heir hunters look for first. It means a financial asset, and that's what most estates are made up of. Not many people leave thousands in the bank. The house would have attracted the London firm in the first place, otherwise it wouldn't have been worth their while. I remember she was eighty because that was the age my own mother died at. Doris had lived in a small terraced house. It was worth about sixty to seventy thousand pounds. Not huge, but a percentage of that would be worth the effort. I know Graeme did his usual research – birth, marriage and death certificates, and censuses. She never actually married. That makes it more difficult. Sometimes you have to go back a hundred years to trace a modern relative.'

'Are these the sort of things he would have had in a hard file?'

'Yes, normally, that's where he would put them. He always had backup photocopies too. Very thorough. There's not much else to say. I wasn't involved after he'd made his initial enquiries. He didn't seem to be having any luck with finding blood relatives, and ran into the same barriers that the London firm must have come across. The weird thing is that I thought he'd dropped the case, because it turned out that Doris Little had sold her house to a building society in the 1990s a few years before her death. It was some equity release scheme.'

'What's that?'

'They advertise these schemes in Britain a lot. People who own their homes tend to be property rich, but often cash poor. So, what they do is sell their home to a bank or building society or property company while still living in the house. They end up with plenty of disposable income, and when they die the property reverts to the building society. It's particularly appealing to retired people because it means they've money to enjoy their final years. Doris Little was one such. I've no idea what happened to the money. I do remember that Graeme was pretty downhearted when he discovered this, because there wasn't much left in her building society account. As I say, I thought that was the end of it.'

'But you told me he was secretive about it.'

'He was. It must have been about a month later that he

was obviously getting quite energised about something. He wouldn't say what it was about, other than there had been a development in the Doris Little investigation.'

'Do you remember exactly when that was?'

'Late July, early August. That's right. He went away for a couple of days.'

'Where to?'

Jennifer Todd shook her head. 'I don't know. He wouldn't say. That was really the start of him keeping everything close to his chest.'

'And that was unusual?'

'Very. But I just let him get on with it. I was having problems at work with our department being restructured and everyone having to re-apply for their jobs. A horrible time. Dispiriting for all the staff. Morale was really low.'

'And no clues as to what he was up to?'

'Not really. There was this air of excitement about him, though. But he sometimes went through these enthusiastic phases. I just thought it was one of them. That's it.' She suddenly frowned. 'Wait though.... He did once say it was better I didn't know anything. It would be safer.'

'Safer?'

'Yes. Safer.'

CHAPTER 20

'That was the word he used to her.'

Anita was recounting her conversation with Jennifer Todd to the team in the meeting room the next day. This time, Nordlund and a very sullen Westermark were in attendance. Anita couldn't figure out Westermark at all. He wasn't his usual slimy, bombastic self. Quite the opposite. He hardly uttered a word. Maybe he was pissed off that Anita had such a central role in the investigation and he was only going to be a bit-part player. Anyway, she had enough on her plate without worrying about him.

'So, Graeme Todd must have been aware of some sort of danger.'

Moberg scratched his ample stomach. It was a recognisable sign of tension. 'It still doesn't really get us any further forward. In many ways we've gone backwards because this old lady doesn't seem to have had much money. Did she have any connections with Sweden?'

'We don't know. I spoke to Detective Sergeant Ash this morning after I put fru Todd on the train to Kastrup. He's been to Todd's house and has started to make initial enquiries into the Little woman's background, so something may emerge there. But he does think that there was a break-in at the Todds' house in Fellbeck. He says that the burglar had a good idea how to get in without disturbing the occupant. However, nothing was taken, unless it was Doris Little's file. And we're not a hundred percent sure that there was a file in the house. Conceivably, Todd could have had it with him, though his wife doubts that. Ash also checked Todd's office computer, and there was nothing about the old woman on that.'

'What about this mysterious trip of Todd's before he came over here?' Nordlund was a man of few words but he was good at getting to the point.

'His wife has no idea where he went. It certainly seems to have been the catalyst for what happened subsequently. However, we're pretty sure that it wasn't Sweden. Hakim's been checking flights from Britain from early August, when Todd went away.' She glanced at Hakim, who nodded. 'He couldn't find anything.' So, it's likely to have been somewhere in Britain. Todd's bank details may throw something up if he made a cash withdrawal or used his credit card for some purchase. That's another thing that Ash is looking into... and I will when I go over there tomorrow.'

'Mirza,' said Moberg. The young man looked at the chief inspector expectantly. Was he going to ask him about his part in the investigation? He wanted to prove how heavily involved he was. 'Go and get some more coffees.' Hakim's face fell.

The coffees didn't help get them any further forward. The consensus was that they were going to have to concentrate their Swedish search in the Ystad area. That meant having to liaise with the force in Ystad without letting them muscle in on the case. Anita would have to work closely with the local British police and try and discover why Todd had come over to Sweden – and, more importantly, who he was planning to meet.

'One last thing,' said Anita as the meeting was breaking up. 'Jennifer Todd wants to know when we can release the body so it can be flown home. The British consul in Malmö is coming in soon, as he wants to make arrangements.'

Moberg grunted. 'The forensics people want to hold onto it for a few more days. I'm afraid the widow will have to wait.'

While the team was filing out of the room, Anita managed to catch Nordlund's eye. He waited until everyone else had gone.

'Henrik, can I ask you a favour?'

'Of course.'

Anita started to gather up the plastic coffee cups that had been strewn around the table.

'Can you keep an eye on this Greta Jansson thing?'

'Your ex's girlfriend is still missing?'

'Yes. Still unofficial, as no one, including Björn, has actually reported her missing.'

'But you're worried about it?'

'I thought it was a simple case of her going off to see her family, or being fed up with a job she couldn't cope with. Then it occurred to me that she might just be escaping from Björn. He seems obsessed with her.' Now all the coffee cups were stacked up. Anita took them to a bin in the corner of the room and dropped them in. 'Her disappearance is too sudden. I mentioned the fully stocked fridge to you before. And it turns out she seemed to be enjoying the teaching, according to the colleague I spoke to. But as Björn points out, a man rang the school up and said she had to leave for family reasons. Both her parents are dead yet her "father" was supposedly looking for her at the time she disappeared. Even her best friend hasn't heard from her, according to Björn. It's starting to nag.'

'Have you got a photo of her?'

'I'll drop one in to your office. I don't want you to investigate; just keep an ear open in case she turns up. If she turns up.'

CHAPTER 21

'Oh, dear.'

Martin Tripp, the Malmö-based businessman who had been lumbered with the role of British consul, was shaking his head. A dapper, fussy man in his late thirties, he didn't like dealing with awkward situations. A dead British national, and a murder victim at that, was ghastly enough. But having to give up his Friday afternoon game of golf – the ritual start to his weekend – to try and sort out the removal of the body from Swedish soil was just too much.

'The widow... em...'

'Jennifer Todd,' Anita helpfully supplied the missing name.

'The poor woman must be desperate to get her husband back and buried as soon as possible.'

'We appreciate that, but we need to carry out further investigations before we can release the body.'

'Oh, dear,' he repeated. Anita knew exactly what was going on in Tripp's mind. Ewan had given her an amusing description of his meeting with the British consul when he had first been arrested and held in custody. As though by telepathy, he launched into his next grumble.

'It's bad enough having that awful journalist fellow in prison here. Now that was a bad business. Not good at all.'

Anita was tempted to say something nasty back but she bit her tongue. Despite what Ewan had done, she hated anyone saying disparaging things about him. As soon as she got back from England, she would go and see him. She was feeling guilty enough for leaving him so abruptly the last time. He'd be interested in her visit to the north, though she wouldn't be going near Newcastle or Durham on this occasion.

'Why Malmö?' Tripp whined. 'Couldn't they have done this sort of thing in Stockholm?' Then a thought struck him. 'It doesn't do the Swedish reputation any favours if you go round killing British visitors.'

'We don't tend to do it as a habit,' Anita snapped back. Tripp was just annoying her now. 'Look, Mr Tripp, I'll get someone in the department to give you a call and tell you when you can organise the body's transportation. Then you'll have done your duty.'

'Quite so.' He glanced at his watch. He might just have time to squeeze in nine holes before it got dark.

Before she left the office, Anita briefed Hakim. She stressed that he must get in touch with her immediately anything came up at the Malmö end. 'You'll be working with Klara so, hopefully, you won't have to put up with Westermark. But if you have any worries, speak to Henrik Nordlund.'

She realised that she was fussing like a mother hen and not a professional colleague.

'It's fine. I'll be OK.'

Anita smiled. She knew he would be. He was a bright young man who could handle himself. He'd proved that during their time together. But she was naturally protective of him.

'What are you doing this weekend?' she asked, changing the subject.

'Avoiding Jazmin.'

'What's your sister up to then?'

'She's just a pain at the moment. She's always giving my parents a hard time. And me. Says it doesn't do her credibility any good having a brother in the police. And we're all stuck in that apartment together. At least when I get posted to Gothenburg, I'll be able to move out.'

Selfishly, Anita had hoped they'd have found something for him in Malmö. It hadn't happened. She would miss him.

'I expect she's just going through a rebellious phase.'

'My parents want her to get a good job or settle down and get married. She doesn't want either. She's now working at the supermarket round the corner.' Anita remembered it well. The "Malmö Marksman" had picked off two of his ethnic victims there. 'No ambition,' said Hakim incredulously. He was very single-minded when it came to his career. 'Where she spends her money, I have no idea. But she usually comes in late. My father stays up until she returns, and demands to know where she's been. When she refuses to answer, they argue and wake me up. Of course, it doesn't help that my dad's always comparing her to me. The whole thing just drives me mad.'

Anita had a thought.

'I'm flying out tomorrow. Why don't you have a few days at my place? Or at least the weekend. Nothing's going to happen with the case in the next couple of days. Give you a break. I'll change the sheets and you can have my room.'

Hakim looked unsure.

'That's very kind... but what about Lasse?'

'It'll be company for him.' She avoided mentioning her ulterior motive. In Lasse's present state, she was worried about leaving him alone. She had no idea how long she would be away, and it would be perfect if Hakim could keep an eye on him. Lasse would object, but she knew he liked her young colleague. And as Hakim didn't drink, he might be a sobering influence on her son, at least while she was away. She had heard Lasse being violently sick in the bathroom at two o'clock that morning after he had staggered in from God knows where.

'If Lasse doesn't mind...'

'He'll be fine.' Lasse would forgive her eventually.

On her way home, Anita decided on a whim to pop into The Pickwick. With a bit of luck she might have the chance to sample a British pub when she was over in Cumbria – she was due to meet Detective Sergeant Ash at Penrith station late tomorrow afternoon. Her time in London had given her a taste for traditional hostelries, which The Pickwick pub mimicked in an over-the-top way in its layout and decor. British beers behind the bar, a dartboard on the wall, and a model of a spitfire suspended from the ceiling to remind visitors that two wars had been fought while Sweden had remained neutral. Not exactly diplomatic. The bar was full of the early-Friday-evening crowd. She ordered a pint of Bombardier from the Scots manager.

'Any luck?'

She turned round and saw a grinning Fraser, clutching a half-drunk pint to his chest.

'No.'

'Have a pew,' Fraser said, pointing to a couple of vacant seats under the hovering spitfire.

Anita put her pint on the table and settled down in a comfortable mock-leather chair. It was nice and warm after the distinctly chilly wind she'd battled through on the way from the polishus. A storm was brewing.

'Cheers!' said Fraser, raising his glass. 'I'm celebrating tonight.'

'What are you celebrating?'

Fraser pointed to the wall. She had noticed the line of small bronze plaques before. Each bore a name. She had no idea of their relevance.

'Got my name up there at last. It's taken a lot of years and a lot of pints. Shows you're a regular. Had my name on a couple of cups at school but this beats everything. I've made it!' he laughed.

'Skål!' she smiled back before taking a long sip.

'Nothing about Greta, then?'

'She's completely disappeared.' Anita put her glass back down on the beer mat. 'It's very strange. But maybe she has her reasons.'

'I didn't know her that well because she hadn't been at Kungsskolan that long, but she didn't seem to be the flaky type. Not the sort to suddenly up sticks at a moment's notice.' That's the impression Anita had gained from Greta's apartment.

'Was there anyone at the school who was close to her?'

'Not really.' Then he smirked. 'I tried to...'

'A date?'

'I did ask her out, but she said she wasn't ready for anything like that just yet. She told me she was getting over some fella. Actually, got the impression he was over-possessive and she was trying to distance herself from him.'

'Did she say who it was?'

'No. I assumed it was someone at uni in Uppsala.'

Anita found that very interesting. If Greta was attempting to get over someone, then it must have been Björn. It certainly didn't sound as though they were still an item, as Björn had claimed. It might explain why she was down in Malmö, but not why she left the city so abruptly. And it wasn't as though her escape had been triggered by Björn finding her hiding place, because he didn't turn up in Malmö until a week after she disappeared.

Anita changed the subject and, after she mentioned that she was flying over there the next day, they exchanged stories about Britain and British life.

As she left the pub three quarters of an hour later, the wind was whipping the rain into her face. Now she wished she had brought her car to work. She would get seriously buffeted on the walk home. But that was nothing to her mental turbulence on finding out about Jansson's real relationship with Björn. If she was in Malmö trying to get away from him – and they weren't a couple any more – how the hell had he got hold of a key to her apartment?

The breakers came rushing in from the Sound. It was not a night to be out at sea. The water crashed against the concrete wharfs that stretched like a giant's fingers out into the harbour. Even the biggest ships rocked to the rhythm of the storm, and the skinny quayside lampposts swayed back and forth, casting pinpricks of light on normally darkened corners of the dockside. Plastic crates, an old tyre, bottles, bits of rope and rotten wood; the usual flotsam and jetsam of every large port, ebbed and flowed around the old jetty at the edge of Nyhamnen. Now fenced off, it had not been used for some years – too close to the burgeoning buildings of the university around the Inner Harbour and the phalanx of new apartment blocks further along the Outer Harbour. Among the rubbish, something else was being unceremoniously tossed by the waves onto the ravaged concrete, and used as a battering ram against the fencing, constantly thrown at the unyielding mesh. A flickering beam from the nearest lurching lamppost picked it out – only for second – a crumpled, broken body with bedraggled hair, the blonde strands gleaming in the light.

CHAPTER 22

The train didn't zip through the countryside; it rumbled quickly. The rolling stock on the Manchester Airport to Edinburgh route wasn't of the intercity sleekness of the Virgin pendalinos that whizzed through the fringes of the Lake District. For that, Anita was grateful. She could take in the beauty of the mountains. It was such a contrast to the flatness of Skåne. Memories of childhood visits with her parents came rushing back. Her father had loved the hills and would have quite happily settled among them had their circumstances been different. She remembered one camping holiday outside Keswick. It had rained continuously, and her mother was not a happy camper. Her father was oblivious to the weather and had dragged her up the fells while her mother went shopping. Though she would rather have been inside, watching the television or playing with friends, she did it to please her father. The higher they climbed, the more relaxed he became. She had revelled in his contentment. It was just the two of them on top of the world. Inseparable. Sadly, it would be short lived. Within a year of their return to Sweden, her parents divorced. She had always wondered if there was something she could she have done to save the situation. Of course not, but it did plague her teenage years.

Anita also felt guilty about Ewan. As she was rushing out of the apartment that morning, her mobile had rung. Like every trip she made, she had left her packing until the last minute. She had also prized Lasse out of bed so he was awake when Hakim came round. Lasse had been less than enthusiastic that he was going to have a flat-mate for the weekend. She was dragging her case along the pavement on the way to Triangeln to catch the train to Kastrup, so she answered breathlessly.

'It's Ewan.'

She couldn't hide the surprise in her voice. Prisoners were allowed to make regular calls, but Ewan had never rung her before.

'Are you OK?' he asked when she didn't immediately respond.

'Yes.'

'Is this a bad time?'

'It is really. I'm off to the airport.'

'Oh.' Ewan sounded disappointed.

'To England. On a case.'

Anita hovered at the crossing on Carl Gustavs väg, waiting for the pedestrian lights to change.

'Will you be away long?'

'I don't know.'

The light went green and Anita hurried across the road.

'This is obviously a bad time.'

'Was there anything specific you want to talk to me about?'

There was a pause. 'Yes.' Anita nearly dropped the phone as the wheels of her case bounced off a raised paving stone, and she didn't quite catch what Ewan said.

'...but it doesn't matter.'

'Ewan, can I get back to you? I'll come and see you when I get back. I promise.'

There was no sound at the other end of the phone. All she could hear was her own heavy breathing.

'Send my love to Britain,' he said at last.

'I'll bring you something back.'

'Anita...' It sounded as though he was about to say something. But all that eventually came out was a clipped 'Goodbye.'

He was gone, and Anita had put her mobile away and managed to get to the station just as the Copenhagen-bound train was pulling in.

The sun glinted on the rugged, green Howgills with their patchwork of dry-stone walls clinging at precarious angles to the steep slopes. Sheep could be seen grazing, even in the upper reaches of the fells. The train snaked through Tebay and passed its colourfully painted railway houses. There was something about the way Ewan had said goodbye that stuck in her head. It was so final. But any further thoughts about him were pushed to the back of her mind as the train came out of the hills. In the cool, late-afternoon sunshine, she could see the buildings of Penrith sprinkled over the valley and up the slopes of the wooded Beacon Hill. The sandstone station, with its red-painted stanchions supporting the glass and wrought-iron canopy, matched Anita's idea of what a Victorian British station should look like. The huge, old-fashioned clock hanging above the platform added to her romantic notion. The other travellers alighting with her were mainly walkers, who would be heading off into the heart of the north Lakes.

The man who was obviously waiting for her didn't fit her pre-conceived image of Detective Sergeant Ash of the Cumbria Constabulary. He was smaller and thinner than she had expected. He wore a crumpled, grey suit and light blue tie, which was loosened at the neck. She had never understood why British plain-clothes policemen dressed so formally. His hair was severely cropped, though there wouldn't have been much of it even if it had been allowed to grow. He hadn't shaved that morning, so there was a stubbly frame around his lined face. What caught her attention most were the brown, humorous eyes that lit up when he spotted her. She put him in his early fifties. Later, she found out that he was only forty-eight. She was greeted by a wide smile followed by a firm handshake.

'Inspector Sundström, I presume. Welcome to Cumbria.'

Inspector Henrik Nordlund stood on the jetty in the mid-afternoon. The atrocious weather of the previous night had long abated and there were even hints of blue sky between the scudding clouds. The body of the young woman had been removed a few hours earlier by the forensics team. All that was left was the official tape cordoning off the scene. He didn't mind being there, as he hadn't planned to do anything special this weekend. He never had plans. No children to visit. No one to share his weekends with. He knew why he had come back to the scene of the body's discovery. Simply for something to do. Truth be told, he wasn't sure how he was going to fill his time when he retired at Christmas. All the plans he had made with Hannah had disappeared in that faceless hospital cancer ward. That last night he had stayed in the small bedroom until the dawn broke. He had squeezed onto the bed to hold her one last time. He had no idea whether she knew what was going on. She had breathed her last as the first light peeked through the drawn blinds, and he'd stayed on the bed, clinging to her, not believing that all their dreams were now dust. Sailing round the Baltic had been their great retirement plan. He hadn't gone near a boat since she died.

The water slapped at the edge of the jetty. He glanced around. To his left, two red pilot boats swayed gently in the swell. Just beyond was a large confection of concrete and glass – offices. Behind him was the unexceptional Bylgahuset, which housed Sweco and VASYD. Again, offices. The simple conclusion was that when the body was dumped, it had most probably been done at night when no one would be around. And dumped it had been, according to Eva Thulin's preliminary findings. It had been battered by the storm and had experienced a huge amount of trauma, but Thulin had said there was the strong possibility of strangulation being the cause of death. The likelihood was that hands had been used, so someone had been strong enough to throttle the life out of the victim. There wasn't much else she could tell him until she had had time to investigate further. She couldn't give him an idea of how long the body had been in the water because of its severely bloated state, through the inevitable loosening of the skin. She hazarded a guess that it was over a week. One thing in their favour was that, despite the mauling and the effects of the water, the head was still just recognisable, though one of the eyes had been eaten. She explained with relish that though on land the head degrades first, at sea it is often the reverse. However, if the victim had lingered in the water much longer, it would have been increasingly difficult to identify the remains. One important point of interest was that she was still wearing one small hooped earring in her pierced left ear. The other earring was missing, either coming off in the sea or during the attack. Thulin suggested it was a case of checking missing persons – a natural blonde female aged between twenty and thirty. Westermark was already on it. As there wasn't a great deal that they could do on the Todd murder until Anita unearthed some clues over in Britain, Moberg had put him, Nordlund, on the new case, with Westermark helping. It wasn't a situation that he was entirely happy with, as he knew Westermark would try and take over and bulldoze his way through the investigation. But Nordlund did trust the younger man's instincts. In fact, he had been surprised that when Westermark had been hauled in by Moberg, he hadn't complained about his weekend being ruined. He seemed up for the task. Nordlund reflected that this would be his own last case. He was determined to crack it before they handed him his leaving present on Friday, December 21st; a date seared on his brain. At least he had a good start; he was pretty sure he knew who the girl was. Greta Jansson.

CHAPTER 23

When Anita drew the curtains, she saw the rain had set in. The room in the Carrock Guest House was traditionally comfortable, without a hint of modern flamboyance. It was situated in a Victorian terrace in the centre of the town. Ash had explained that it would be more comfortable and have more character than the local Travelodge. For that she was grateful. Ash had taken her briefly to the county police headquarters at Carleton Hall, on the edge of Penrith, where he was based. In a cramped office, he had shown her the few bits of information he had managed to gather so far. He'd got hold of copies of Doris Little's birth and death certificates from the General Register Office in Carlisle. Nothing obvious had leapt out from the documents, but they would form the core of their research. He had also obtained building society details. On her death, Doris Little had had £5,633.76 in her account. That was the full value of her estate. Ash remarked that he could understand the London probate researchers giving up so easily after finding their reward would be so paltry. On the other hand, it certainly didn't explain why Graeme Todd had got so excited. Afterwards, Ash had dropped Anita off at the guest house.

Anita had gone out and had a pizza at an Italian restaurant close by. Before finding somewhere to eat, she had wandered round the centre of the small town to get her bearings. It was based around the market square with its distinctive Musgrave Monument clock tower. Behind the square, she had found

St. Andrew's Church. Originally 13th-century, all that remains of the medieval building is the tower. The elegant Georgian nave and chancel had a soothing ambiance, and Anita had spent a few contemplative minutes sitting in one of the pews. Ewan seeped into her thoughts. She couldn't get his phone call out of her head. She found herself about to offer up a silent prayer for him before mentally admonishing herself. Her father would have been most disappointed. When Anita was at her most impressionable, his fierce atheism had won out over her mother's limp Christianity. It had been an easy battle, and nothing in her life had given her cause to recant. After her meal, she had retired early to her room. It had been a long day. She was in bed by nine o'clock.

She was reading a book she had picked up at Kastrup airport when her mobile buzzed. As she took the phone from the bedside table, she assumed it was Lasse. He must have had an argument with Hakim. She was surprised to see Henrik Nordlund's name on the screen.

'Hi, Henrik. It's late over there.'

'Hope I'm not interrupting anything, but it's important.'

Of course; with Nordlund it would be. She waited for him to tell her just how important.

'A young woman's body has been found. Nyhamnen.' Anita's mind raced to Greta Jansson. 'Thrown up by the storm.'

'Blonde?'

'Yes.'

'Age?'

'Between twenty and thirty.'

'You think it's—'

'Greta Jansson? Yes. Westermark has been through recent missing persons of roughly the same description and nothing has come up. Of course, it might be someone who, like Greta, hasn't been reported missing yet.'

'But unlikely.' Anita was wondering how Björn would

receive the news if the body really was Greta's. He was a wreck already. This would finish him.

'Accident?' she asked without conviction.

'I'm afraid not. It's not easy working with a corpse that's been in the water for some time, but Thulin reckons she'd been strangled.'

'Oh, God!' Anita's heart sank. This was another missing victim that she hadn't taken seriously.

'There's another thing.' Anita wondered if it could get any worse. 'It appears that the young woman was probably raped first.'

'Shit!'

'Problem is, there's no semen because she's been in the water too long.'

'So no attacker's DNA.'

'The first thing we need to do is establish if it is Greta Jansson. Who do you think we should contact for identification purposes? The body's in a bad way.'

Björn was an obvious choice, but Anita didn't want to put him through the experience in his present emotional state. It was going to be difficult enough telling him. Anyway, he was up in Uppsala.

'For speed, I'd get one of Greta's colleagues in the English department at Kungsskolan. The one I spoke to was a Scottish guy called Alex Fraser. I haven't got a number for him, but you'll probably find him at The Pickwick pub on Malmborgsgatan.' Anita glanced at her watch. It would be half past ten in Sweden. 'He'll probably be there now. It's his regular haunt.'

'Thanks, Anita.'

'Henrik. If it is Greta, can you tell me as soon as it's confirmed? It's best that it's me who breaks the news to Björn.'

'I will.'

She couldn't believe that her mother had asked her to take it round to the policewoman's apartment. Her bloody brother.

He was so damned perfect. She never got a look in. Constantly criticised. And yet he was able to escape for the weekend to stay at his boss's fancy pad. He was only going to be gone two days, and yet her mother had badgered her to take round the plastic box filled with couscous. Just because it was his favourite! Ponce! It wasn't even Iraqi. But he thought eating North African food was more sophisticated than what they usually ate. She was happy with the McDonald's on the other side of the main road. Now she was having to trudge round to the edge of Pildammsparken. She had a good mind to throw the box away. It would serve him right. He was too big for his boots now he was a policeman. What an awful thing to be – they're all racist and fascist. Why couldn't he have stuck to painting? He was good at that. He was a serious embarrassment. Her friends were always taking the piss, especially the boys. Some wouldn't even speak to her because they knew what he was. They didn't trust her. In a moment of anger, she flipped off the box's lid. She could see the food by the light of the street lamp. She looked for somewhere to tip it out. Then she checked herself. She was bound to be found out when Hakim came back, and her father would go berserk.

She approached the apartment. It was on the ground floor. She could see there was a light on. It wasn't as smart as she had expected, but it was a hundred times better than their run-down block. She sauntered up to the door and rang the bell. She knew that the policewoman was away. At first she just wanted to hand over the box and get away, but now she was here, curiosity got the better of her. See how Swedes really lived. The only homes she had ever been in were those of other immigrants. She had no white friends. Maybe she would get Hakim to show her around.

When the door opened, she was taken aback not to see her brother. A tall, blond young man with grey-green eyes was standing in a pool of light. He smiled.

119

'You must be Jazmin.'

Suddenly she found herself tongue-tied. She had been preparing something rude to say to her brother. Now she was struck dumb. She could only nod stupidly.

'Do you want to see Hakim?'

'Not if I can help it.' It just came out in a rush.

Lasse laughed. 'It's OK. He's not in at the moment.'

Jazmin held out the box of couscous. She wished he would just take it and she could escape. For some reason all she could feel was embarrassment.

'Why don't you bring that in?'

Jazmin hesitated. For one daft moment she became very conscious of her hair, severely shaved at the sides and with an outcrop running across the top of her head. Like so many white kids, Lasse had blond, floppy locks.

He smiled again. 'You can bring that Red Cross food parcel in only if you promise not to mention the sodding police.'

Jazmin tried hard to suppress a grin as she stepped inside the apartment.

Though Anita had turned off her bedside light at about ten o'clock, the chance of an undisturbed night's sleep was now out of the question. Voices drifted up from the street outside, before tailing off. There was a pub at the end of the road, so there was probably more Saturday night noise to come. Not that it mattered. Her mind was racing anyway. She started to worry about Fraser. It wasn't really fair that he was going to have to identify a dead body when it should be Björn, but it would be quicker. He was on the spot. She would owe him a few pints if he stayed on speaking terms with her.

But it was Björn who really occupied her restless thoughts. Hearing about Greta Jansson's body turning up had been a shock. She had had a bad feeling about the business for a few days now. As she turned in her bed, her mind went back to Greta's apartment, and the little signs that hadn't meant a great deal at the time took on a new significance. The contents of the fridge. The made-up bed. Some things had gone, but others hadn't. Someone had cleared up afterwards. And the only person she knew who had been there was Björn. She was now sure that he hadn't told her the truth about his present relationship with Greta. She knew, from their last couple of fraught years together, about his propensity for lying when it came to young women. The key. She had given it to Nordlund, along with the photo of Greta. Again, that nagging thought – how had he got hold of it?

What was worse was the unthinkable – was the man she had lived with for over a decade, and the father of her child, capable of rape and murder?

CHAPTER 24

The next morning was cold and grey. The weather matched Anita's mood. She stood outside the guest house waiting for Ash to pick her up. They were going to drive out to Fellbeck to see Jennifer Todd. Ash had offered to show her round the area on that Sunday and then begin the job on Monday. She had declined the offer and said that she would like to begin the investigation as soon as possible. He hadn't looked very happy at having to give up his day off, but he had been given strict instructions that he had to do everything in his power to help the representative of the Skåne County Police. He must be seen to be as co-operative as possible.

Anita may not have had much sleep but at least she wasn't hungry. She had had an enormous full English breakfast – bacon, eggs, sausages, mushrooms, black pudding, fried bread and baked beans. In fact, she felt bloated. She did enjoy British food, and had developed a taste for pub food like steak and ale pie, and sticky toffee pudding during her time in London, but she could never understand the huge breakfasts. One colleague in the Met had a cooked breakfast every day. Yet he managed lunch and, presumably, an evening meal when he got home. British arteries must be under constant pressure. A couple of coffees and some yogurt should be enough for anyone first thing in the morning. That was another thing – she had forgotten how weak the coffee was over here. A further irritation was that she had forgotten her snus. She was always disorganised when it came to packing. The same with everything really, except her police work. In her mind's eye she could see the round tin on the kitchen table. Now, she was craving its soothing nicotine fix. She was awakened out of her reverie by a car horn. A silver Honda Civic drew up at the pavement. Inside, Ash gave her a cheery wave.

They drove out of Penrith northwards, before veering west and heading over the motorway and onto the road to Wigton. Initially, it was a straight, picturesque, tree-lined route, before the cover broke and the fells appeared on their left. The roadside fields were full of grazing sheep, oblivious to the rain. About fifteen minutes later, after a big dip in the road, Ash turned the car off sharply to the left. The signpost read *Fellbeck, 2 miles*. After mounting the first incline, a pleasant valley was revealed in the lee of two mountains, which were now starting to emerge from the wreaths of cloud that had enveloped their upper slopes. The winding road passed through a small hamlet with a humpback bridge, before making its way past a number of farms. When they reached the old Victorian school house, they were at the edge of Fellbeck village.

Throughout the brief journey, Ash had hardly stopped talking. Anita didn't know the man, yet she had got his life story. Why were the British so open? This would never have happened with a total stranger in Sweden. In similar circumstances, few words would have been exchanged, but here was someone who was coming out with intimate details of his life that would only emerge after a much deeper and longer acquaintance in her native country.

Ash was from Essex, and, as his words bubbled out, she had to listen carefully to catch everything he said as she attuned herself to his strong, elongated southern tones. What she gathered was that he had joined Northumbria Police after marrying a Geordie girl and had worked his way up the ranks until his divorce. Then he'd got a transfer to Cumbria to get away from the North East, yet be close enough to see his two daughters. He had been based in Penrith for five years and was at last getting used to the countryside and rural crime, though he did miss the city streets. 'A more interesting sort of crook over there. We get sheep rustlers over here.' Anita thought he was joking until Ash assured her that it was a real problem. One farmer near Fellbeck had lost over thirty animals last autumn. 'And there's a hell of a lot of sheep to steal round these parts, as you can see.' Anita could tell he was quite excited about the Todd case. 'We don't get many murders on our patch. Except when that lunatic Derrick Bird flipped and went on his shooting rampage back in 2010.' Anita remembered seeing the coverage on Swedish TV. Bird had travelled round the county picking off innocent people. She had been really taken aback, as Britain hadn't got a gun culture like America, or Sweden for that matter.

On their left, they passed some cows grazing on common ground, before they reached the main part of Fellbeck. Anita loved English villages, and this one was just right. No thatch, not too picturesque, but a traditional working village with colourful houses, an inviting pub, a busy shop and a pretty green. Nothing was out of place, and the whole vista, with the fells supplying the backdrop, was so pleasing to the eye it made her smile. Ash turned the car to the right and parked in front of a large, old, white-painted house.

'Here we are, Inspector. Hopefully, this is where we'll find out why Graeme Todd was killed.'

Nordlund watched the forensics team at work. Prints would show who had been in the apartment. Westermark had been sent off to try and find Fraser, who hadn't been at The Pickwick the night before. He'd been at a party in Trelleborg and wasn't expected back until later this morning. They had tracked down where he lived and Westermark was going to pick him up and take him to Lund to identify the body. Nordlund was glad that he had the field to himself. Westermark was unusually moody at the moment. Something was bothering him and he wasn't being very co-operative. He probably resents having to work under me, thought Nordlund. Well, he'd have to live with it.

Nordlund had already been next door to speak to the neighbour. The only visitors she had been aware of in the last fortnight were Jansson's "father" and a female police detective. All had been quiet since. The last physical sighting of Jansson was when she had left the school after work on the Friday. They would have to piece together her movements after that. Again, he knew from Anita that she was due to meet an old university friend somewhere in Lilla Torg. The information had come from Anita's husband. That needed checking out, too. But from what the neighbour had said, the "father" had been trying to find Jansson. Was she already dead by then? Hopefully, fingerprints would shed light on this mysterious figure. One thing they were sure of was that Jansson was alive late on the Friday night, as the neighbour had heard voices. She was fairly sure that one of the voices was male. Quite deep. Were they arguing? The neighbour thought they were. Once she had fed the baby and put her back in her cot, she had gone back to her bedroom, which wasn't next to Jansson's apartment wall, so she hadn't heard any other sounds.

Nordlund stood in the middle of the living room. Jansson and her male visitor must have been in here for the neighbour to hear them. Was the argument the preamble to the rape and murder, or the cause? Nordlund went into the bedroom. Did they come in here to finish off the evening and something went wrong? The sheets on the bed hadn't been slept in. Was she raped in the apartment or somewhere else?

In the kitchen Nordlund looked in the fridge. Anita had been right about the contents – it didn't appear that Jansson had been planning to go anywhere, though Anita had told him someone had taken her bag, mobile, iPad, toothbrush and toothpaste to make it look like she had gone away. That someone was smart enough to try and cover their tracks. Nordlund's mobile rang.

'Nordlund here.'

'Westermark. I'm with Fraser. That's him puking up in the background. He's just identified what's left of the body. He's as sure as he can be that it's Greta Jansson. There's a little telltale scar near her left temple which the fish hadn't had a go at.'

At least they weren't going to have to waste valuable time trying to discover who the victim was. That gave them a head start.

'Take him home. But on the way ask him what he knows about Greta Jansson. Who was she friendly with at the school? Did she socialise with her colleagues? Try and get as much background as you can. But Karl... be gentle with him.'

Jennifer Todd brought in a tray with a teapot, three mugs, and a plate of shortbread biscuits. They were in her living room. A fire was spluttering in the grate. The sofa and armchairs might have been chic twenty years ago, but now looked dated. Uncomfortable too, thought Anita as she moved her bottom once again to try and find a softer spot. The blue and red flowery curtains would probably have got away with their gaudiness in a retro Stockholm apartment, but here in the old, whitewashed farmhouse, they looked cheap and incongruous. The plain magnolia walls looked dingy and needed more than two dull watercolour paintings to liven them up. Jennifer Todd put the tray down on the glass-topped coffee table, leant over the log basket and put some more wood on the fire. It immediately hissed.

'We've had such a bad summer. Nothing but rain,' she said by way of explanation.

'You can certainly say that, Mrs Todd,' Ash said in doleful agreement.

No one spoke until Jennifer Todd had gone through the ritual of pouring out the tea. Ash helped himself to some milk and four spoonfuls of sugar. Anita had hers neat.

'Jennifer, we need your help in reconstructing Graeme's file on Doris Little.' Anita watched the woman opposite tightly clutching her mug. She knew it would be a painful process for her. Jennifer Todd nodded.

'Well, I'll get the ball rolling, ladies,' said Ash as he opened a thin file he'd brought with him from the car. Such a patronising endearment from a male Swedish cop wouldn't have gone down well. From Ash it sounded entirely natural. 'On Friday, I went to the Register Office of Births, Marriages and Deaths in Carlisle.' He fished out a couple of official pieces of paper and laid them down on the coffee table. He pointed to the first one. 'This is a copy of Doris Little's birth certificate. Doris Alma Little was born in Carlisle on March 5th, 1929. As you can see, her parents were James and Florence Little.' Ash shoved the first certificate to the side so that they could see the other document. 'Death certificate. Died: August 17th, 2009. So she was eighty. There was no marriage certificate, so we can assume there were no children.'

'Is this where Graeme would have started?' Anita asked Jennifer.

'Yes. His next step would be to look at Doris's parents. That would throw up uncles and aunts and potential cousins. And we'll have to discover if Doris had any brothers or sisters. Nephews and nieces would be entitled to the estate.'

'So, exactly who is entitled?' asked Ash, his mouth still half-full of a shortbread biscuit.

'Basically, it's the deceased's spouse or civil partner – there isn't one in this case – or children. Again, this doesn't seem to be relevant. That leaves blood relatives. That can be siblings and their offspring, or blood relatives descended from any grandparent of the deceased.'

'So people marrying into a family don't qualify,' remarked Ash who had now finished his biscuit. 'Sisters-in-law and that sort of thing? Or ex-wives?' he added with a wry grin.

'No. They have to be blood relatives.'

'I still don't really understand the process of heir hunting.'

'It's really a case of people like Graeme finding relatives of deceased people who didn't make wills. Over three hundred thousand people die intestate every year. The estate automatically goes to the Treasury unless genuine heirs can be found to claim their inheritance. Every Thursday, the Treasury releases a Bona Vacantia list of unclaimed estates. There are about twelve thousand of these cases a year, so it can be a profitable business. The Treasury used to give them a value, but now that's all changed. But each estate is worth at least five thousand pounds.'

'Hence Doris's,' put in Ash helpfully. 'Hers was worth just over five grand.'

'Probate research companies,' Jennifer continued, 'then go after the ones they think will be the most lucrative. It can get very competitive because they only make their money if they can find heirs to make a successful claim.'

'But without a property to sell, Doris Little's estate probably wasn't worth chasing?'

'That seems to be the case, Inspector. A London firm worked on it initially, but gave up. As you say, probably not worth their while financially. But, according to Graeme, they also drew a blank.'

'No blood relatives?'

Jennifer Todd shook her head.

'But he must have found something?'

'Yes. But I don't know what.'

'So, can you help us, Jennifer?' Anita asked with a certain amount of impatience. She didn't want to waste time. The longer they took, the harder it was going to be to find Todd's murderer or murderers.

'I'm on compassionate leave. And I need to keep busy, so I'm all yours.' Jennifer scrutinised the two certificates. 'The parents are the only people we have to go on, so we need to find out more about them. They should show up on the 1911 census. Or certainly James Little will. That should throw up any siblings. I doubt they were married before that date, so Florence will be under her maiden name, which we haven't got.' She looked across at Ash, who was about to bite into another biscuit. 'If you go into Carlisle tomorrow, you could find their marriage certificate. That's assuming they were married in the area. That would give us Florence's maiden name. Then we can start to piece together a family tree.'

'Sounds good to me,' Anita said decisively. This was a start.

CHAPTER 25

The day was clearing by the time Anita and Ash emerged from Jennifer Todd's house. A hint of blue sky could be seen to the west. Ash immediately took out a packet of cigarettes. He'd lit one automatically before realising that he should offer one to Anita.

'I don't smoke.'

'Good for you. Filthy habit.' The smoke was playing havoc with Anita's senses. There was no way she could buy any snus round here; she knew it was banned in Britain. She was sorely tempted to succumb to a cigarette, but fought the urge. Instead she pulled out her mobile phone. She still hadn't heard anything from Nordlund about the identification of Greta Jansson.

Ash smiled at her. 'You won't get a signal up here. Too wild and woolly. You'll have to wait until we head back to Penrith.'

Anita registered her frustration with a heavy sigh.

Ash let out a cloud of smoke. 'By the way, I'm visiting the Cumberland Building Society tomorrow. That's where Todd kept his business account. Try and find out where he disappeared to in August.'

'Weren't there any bank statements in the house?'

'Apparently, Todd would check them when they came in and then shred them. Was scared of identity theft. Didn't bank online.'

Ash took another deep drag of his cigarette. He flicked off

the precariously-balanced stack of ash he had created. 'When I've finished this, why don't we pop over there for a pint? It's a cracking pub.'

Across from where they were leaning against the wall of Jennifer Todd's front garden was The Queen's Head. 'Brew their own beer behind the pub.'

'All right.' It might ward off her tobacco cravings.

Nordlund put away his mobile phone.

'Still no answer.'

'She's probably run off with another British murderer,' Westermark said sarcastically. Nordlund ignored the remark.

'Where are we up to then?' asked Moberg as he barged through the door of the meeting room. He had quite happily called Nordlund and Westermark into headquarters on a Sunday afternoon. It avoided another excruciating day with his wife. They barely spoke these days. When they did, it was to argue about something petty. It was the same pattern as his last two marriages. The only reason he hadn't let this one wind down to the inevitable divorce was a purely financial one. His present wife wouldn't be as reasonable as the last two. She would want her pound of flesh and he wasn't inclined to give it to her. There was a kind of masochistic pleasure in denying her access to his hard-earned cash.

'The victim is Greta Jansson. That's been confirmed by one of her teaching colleagues this morning.' Nordlund glanced across the table at Westermark, who nodded in confirmation. 'She was twenty-three and had only been in Malmö since August, when she took up a teaching post at Kungsskolan across the park.' Nordlund gestured with his head in the direction of the window. 'No parents alive, so we don't know who the next of kin is. She was last seen Friday, September the twenty-eighth leaving the school. She was due to meet an old university friend in Lilla Torg for a drink. The friend, Ulrika Lindén, couldn't

131

make it, as her business meeting overran and she had to fly back to Stockholm that night. One thing she did confirm was that Jansson had left Uppsala in a hurry. The job at the school down here was a last-minute appointment. Lindén was under the impression that Jansson was going to tell her the reason she had left Uppsala so quickly.'

'Where were they going to meet?' asked Moberg.

'Lindén doesn't know. She was going to ring Greta to ask. Of course, that never came up when she did call, as they couldn't meet up anyway. I was with forensics this morning going over her apartment. I also talked to the neighbour, who said the only recent visitors were Jansson's father and Anita.'

'What the fuck was *she* doing there?' It didn't take much to make Moberg angry when Anita Sundström was mentioned.

'Greta Jansson was connected to Anita's ex-husband.'

'How?' Moberg snapped.

'Jansson was a student of his. They were also an item.'

'Jesus,' Westermark hissed. 'Old git dipping his wick. Disgusting.'

Nordlund knew his next remark would set Moberg off again, but it couldn't be avoided. 'Björn Sundström asked Anita to look for Jansson. He thought she had disappeared.'

'Was the silly bitch doing this on police time?'

'I doubt it.' Nordlund hoped it would qualify as a white lie.

'And when was this?' Moberg was still angry. If Sundström had been doing some private investigating, then she would get seriously bollocked. Just as well she was in England.

'About the time that she disappeared. He had a key to the apartment, which he gave to Anita. She went there and checked it over. Thought there were a few odd things about it.'

'What odd things?' asked Westermark.

'It appeared that Greta had gone away. Toothbrush and toothpaste missing. But the fridge had been recently stocked. The bed had been remade with fresh sheets and duvet cover. Of course, now it seems as if someone had gone to the trouble of making it look like she'd taken a trip. No bag, no cell phone, no iPad; but her iPod was still there.'

'And what about fingerprints?' Again this was Westermark, who was now paying rapt attention.

'Jansson's obviously. But not in the bathroom, where the toothbrush and things would have been kept. Nor the obvious ones you'd expect in the bedroom. No prints on the table in the living room, where we know she was with someone that Friday night. That was confirmed by the neighbour. Heard voices through the wall. Basically, someone seems to have wiped those areas clean.'

'So the person knew what he was doing?' Moberg asked rhetorically.

'We did find Professor Björn Sundström's fingerprints in the apartment.'

'You're kidding!' exclaimed Moberg in disbelief. 'Why would a professor be on our database?'

'He was arrested twenty-five years ago for a breach of the peace. Anita was the arresting officer.'

'What?' Westermark was incredulous.

'Didn't you know that's how they met?' Even Moberg had to laugh.

'Wait a minute,' said Westermark. 'You said that the neighbour saw Jansson's father, but before that you said that her parents were dead.'

'The man who said he was her father obviously wasn't.'

'Could it have been the professor?' asked Westermark.

'We can't say yet. We need to find out his movements. The "father" appeared the day after we think Jansson disappeared. Then again, we don't know for sure when she was killed because the sea has done too much damage. Forensics may turn something up, but we don't even know where the crime was committed.'

Moberg drummed his fingers heavily on the table top.

When he stopped, he spoke: 'Where's the professor now?'

'Uppsala, I assume. That's where he works.'

'We need to talk to him. And you need to talk to Anita and get everything out of her that she knows about her husband's involvement with Greta Jansson. He's our only potential suspect so far.'

'Well, maybe not.' The older men stared at Westermark. 'I think it might be worth looking into the school staff... I'll start with Fraser.'

Ash placed two pints on the small, round wooden table. Though the pub was full, they managed to secure a place near a freshly stoked fire that was roaring up the chimney. The atmosphere was cosily British. Pewter tankards alternated with dried hops hanging from the beams which criss-crossed the low ceiling. Old pictures of the village hung on the uneven walls. The clicking of pool balls came from the room beyond the bar, behind which the jovial, bearded landlord was cracking a joke with one of the regulars. This was the part of the culture that Anita most enjoyed.

'This is good,' smiled Ash after he taken a substantial part of his draught. '*Skiddaw* is a nice pint.' Anita took a tentative sip of her *Scafell Blonde*, a lighter beer. She thought it prudent to keep her wits about her.

'You see, they've named the beers after the fells... that's the local word for the mountains here in the Lake District. Hence, Fellbeck.'

'I know. Our word for mountain is *fjäll*. That's where you get the word from. The Vikings.'

'Well, you learn something new every day. We used to come across here for weekends when the kids were young. Camping outside Keswick. Usually bloody rained and we'd all huddle round the Primus stove. Why are you smirking?'

'Sorry. Sweden again. Primus is a Swedish company.' She

couldn't help grinning. 'And without Gideon Sundbäck, you wouldn't have had a zip on your tent.'

'Thanks! Now every time I go to the toilet, I'll think of Sweden.'

Though Anita kept mentioning Sweden, she was enjoying using her English again. She found it so easy to switch. Before the conversation had a chance to continue, Ash was out of his seat, empty glass in hand. 'Want another one?'

'I thought they had drink-drive laws over here,' she found herself saying automatically. She regretted it as soon as it came out. Damn rules again. Ash didn't seem remotely offended.

'It helps to be a copper.' With an exaggerated wink, he stood up and squeezed his way to the bar.

When he returned to the table, Anita got back to the business in hand. To ensure that Ash didn't try and sidetrack her again, she had pulled out her notebook.

Ash sat down and smacked his lips. 'Interesting session with Mrs Todd. At least the family tree is under way.'

Anita glanced over her notes. 'We've established that Doris's father had three siblings – John, David and Daisy. They were all still at home in the 1901 census. John, the eldest, was thirteen then. Doris's father, James, only seven. By the 1911 census, the boys were still there. They were all working on the railways like their father.'

'Only natural, really. Carlisle's always been a big railway town. One of the main employers. At one time, seven different railway companies shared the railway station.' Anita arched an eyebrow. 'I like trains,' he said bashfully.

'Daisy is missing. She would have been eighteen in 1911. According to Jennifer, she had either moved out and was probably in domestic service, or was dead. Are you going to check them out tomorrow at the Register Office?'

'Yeah. It'll show whether they had any offspring. They'd be Doris's first cousins. And it's their kids who would be the likely beneficiaries. That's if Doris didn't have any siblings.' Ash gazed at his pint reflectively. 'Unfortunately, I don't think it's going to be that simple. The original London heir hunting company gave up; and they had huge resources.'

'Is it worth getting onto them to see how far they got? Might save some time,' suggested Anita.

'Good idea. Are all Swedish policewomen so sharp?'

'Of course,' she said pulling a face.

He picked up his glass. 'Well, it looks like our friend Mr Todd managed to track someone down. Trouble is, someone might not have taken kindly to being found.'

CHAPTER 26

Anita bit into the last bit of her Karl Fazer chocolate bar. As far as she was concerned, it was the best thing to come out of Finland. The chopped hazelnut was her favourite. That would be another of her staple supports that she wouldn't be able to buy in Britain. For a moment, she felt a ridiculous pang of homesickness. She would ring Lasse and discover how he and Hakim were getting on. But first, she had to make one of the most difficult calls of her life. She had to tell Björn that Greta Jansson had been murdered. Raped. For a split second, the unthinkable thought surfaced again. Did he already know? She dismissed it almost as swiftly.

On the drive back to Penrith, Anita's mobile phone had started bleeping. Seven missed calls. They were all from Henrik Nordlund. When she had rung back, he had confirmed that the body in the harbour was that of Greta Jansson. He thought it best that she broke the news to Björn, and tell him he would have to travel down to Malmö as Moberg wanted him interviewed as quickly as possible. Nordlund also wanted Anita to give him any information she had on the Björn-Greta relationship. From Nordlund's tone, Anita realised that Björn must already be on the list of potential suspects, yet she was unwilling to tell her colleague everything she knew until she'd spoken to her ex-husband.

'Hello.' Even from the one word utterance, Björn's speech sounded thick. He must have been on the booze the night before.

'Anita here. I'm in England.'

Silence.

'Are you OK?'

'I've been better.' He coughed as though clearing his throat. 'Sorry. Life's not good.'

It wasn't going to get any better, thought Anita.

'Whereabout? Whereabout in England are you?'

'Cumbria.'

'Ah, the Lakeland poets. Wordsworth, Coleridge, Southey, De Quincey.' She could hear the enthusiasm awaken in his voice. 'Remember that Southey conference we went to in Keswick?'

'No.'

'The one where we went out with Caroline and em... Mike Evans. She was a Byron expert and he was into some obscure Welsh poet.' He paused. 'William Jones, that's it! They were from Swansea University.' He had started speaking English. It had been their language of choice for arguments. There were more expressive words and more expletives to play with when angry.

'You must have been with someone else.'

'Ah. Possibly.'

They both knew the call was about Greta Jansson, but were putting off the subject for as long as possible. It was Anita who took the plunge.

'It's Greta.' All she could hear was his breathing. It had quickened. 'I'm sorry, she's dead.'

She could make out Björn gulping for air, followed by a low moan.

'There's no other way to tell you, Björn. She was fished out of the harbour.' He began to sob quietly. Anita waited. Further details would just make things worse.

Eventually, he spoke, his tone uneven. 'I knew she was missing. I *knew*.'

'You were right.'

'Was it... was it an accident?'

This time it was hard for Anita to speak. 'I'm afraid not. She was murdered.'

'Oh, my God!'

Anita let the information sink in before adding, 'That's not all; you'd better know – she was raped before being killed.'

'This can't be true. It can't be...' The voice trailed away to a whisper.

'Björn, you're going to have to be strong. Now listen to me.' The practical Anita was taking over. 'My colleague, Henrik Nordlund, will be ringing you shortly. He'll want you to go down to Malmö.'

'Why?' The question was barely audible.

'They'll want to interview you. You're going to have to think clearly.' Nordlund was a probing interrogator. And if Westermark was involved, she knew, due to her own strained history with him, that he would give Björn a particularly hard time. 'They'll want to know all about your relationship with Greta. More importantly, they'll want to know your exact movements over the weekend she disappeared. You'd better be prepared.'

'They can't suspect me! Can they?' Anita was finding it difficult dealing with this new, crushed Björn.

'Just tell them the truth. You have told me everything, haven't you?'

'I loved Greta. I *really* loved her.'

'I know.'

As Fraser approached the front entrance of the school among a throng of morose students, most of whom were too sleepy at ten to eight in the morning to talk about their weekend activities, he noticed the blond policeman loitering by the main door. He was chewing a toothpick. Fraser had taken an instant dislike to him when Westermark had turned up at his apartment the day before and whisked him off to see the bloated, grotesque body of his former colleague. His face was arrogant, with its piercing blue eyes, wide mouth and square jaw. Add to that his cropped hair, and Fraser reckoned he wouldn't have looked out of place in an SS unit. This was the last thing he wanted right now. His mind was full of the lesson on English adjectives that he was going to try and drum into an unresponsive class.

'Morning,' Westermark said in Swedish. There was no warmth in the greeting. He didn't even bother to remove the toothpick.

'What do you want?' Fraser asked irritably.

'I need a word.'

'It's not very convenient. I've a class in ten minutes.'

'I'm sure they can wait.' Westermark was momentarily distracted as a couple of giggling girls in short skirts waltzed past. He watched them disappear through the swing doors. 'We can either talk here or over there at headquarters,' he said, jerking his thumb over his shoulder.

'OK, here. But make it quick.'

Westermark moved away from the door and headed for the tree-lined path that ran the length of Kungsgatan. He kicked at some recently fallen leaves.

'How well did you know Greta Jansson?'

Fraser adjusted his knapsack. It held a number of the old books he'd used when first teaching English as a Foreign Language. They were heavy. 'She was a colleague.'

'Let me ask you again. How *well* did you know her?'

'What the hell are you implying?' Fraser's tone was belligerent.

'Greta was an attractive girl. She came down from Uppsala. Didn't know anyone here. Lonely. Vulnerable. What the fuck do you think I mean?' Fraser was taken aback by the sudden switch to angry aggression.

'You've got it wrong. I didn't know her well at all.'

'But you fancied her?'

'Who told you that?'

'I saw you yesterday. You were nervous as shit.'

'Of course I bloody was,' he exploded. 'You were taking me to see a corpse. Unlike in your profession, it's not something teachers do every day.'

Westermark stared at Fraser before letting a supercilious smile play upon his lips. 'Did you ever ask her out? For a date?'

'For a drink,' replied Fraser, injecting as much defiance as he could muster that early in the morning. 'She wasn't looking for a relationship. Too busy getting over some guy from the university... up in Uppsala. Anyway, I told your colleague all this,' he snapped. 'Didn't she tell you?'

'She?'

'Anita Sundström.'

Westermark swore under his breath. 'When was this?' he snapped.

Fraser thought for a moment. 'A week ago. She came here. And I ran into her at The Pickwick on Friday.'

'Had a cosy pint together, did you?' Westermark sneered.

Fraser found all this hostility aggravating. Westermark was one of the few Swedes he'd come across who was confrontational. Most were totally the opposite.

'What are you hanging around here for? Haven't you got a class to teach?' A still-incensed Fraser stepped back a few paces before turning. 'We'll talk again soon,' Westermark called after the retreating school teacher.

Anita was due to meet Jennifer Todd at ten o'clock outside Morrisons in Penrith. After doing her shopping, Jennifer was taking Anita back with her to Fellbeck to continue their research. Ash was in Carlisle visiting the Register Office and the head office of the Cumberland Building Society. He was then returning to Fellbeck to report on his findings.

After a lighter continental breakfast – she couldn't take another full English – Anita had wandered out into the town. She walked down the main street past the Alhambra cinema, and, to kill time, called into Joseph Carr's antique shop. Porcelain seemed to be the main items on display. She was taken aback by some of the prices – even when she mentally converted them into kronor, with an advantageous exchange rate, they still appeared extortionate. All the time she was browsing, she knew she was putting off the inevitable. She beamed apologetically at the owner as she left, somehow feeling guilty for not buying anything. Joseph Carr, a bearded, bespectacled man in his late sixties, who had hardly raised his eyes from his book all the time she had been in, bade her farewell with a faint smile. She went straight into the newsagent's next door. She could no longer cope without her snus, and asked for twenty cigarettes. She handed over eight pounds. As she was leaving, the woman behind the counter called, 'You've forgotten your change.' Anita looked at her blankly. The woman proffered some coins in the palm of her hand. 'Eight pence.'

Anita took the money. 'I'm sorry. We don't get öre back in Sweden if the price is less than a krona.'

'Fancy that! So are all your prices rounded up?' The woman was enjoying engaging a visitor to the town in conversation. She had had a few Norwegians in before, but never a Swede.

'No, often they're not.'

'Heavens, if we kept all our change, we'd make a handy little profit.' The encounter ended in a mutual laugh and, as Anita left, the next customer was being told all about how weird the Swedish monetary system must be.

Her pack of cigarettes was still in her grasp when she got to the park opposite the station. Near one of the remaining walls of the ruined 14th-century castle, she slipped out a cigarette and felt the old, familiar thrill as she rolled it around in her fingers. She put it in her mouth. It had been a long time since she'd smoked. Snus had become her crutch. A wave of self-loathing flooded over her, but needs must. Shit! She had forgotten to buy matches. With a curse, she pushed the cigarette back into the packet. Ash would have a light, if she could wait that long.

Anita made her way across the road to the Morrisons store. As she was early, she decided to take a look inside the supermarket. It was more lavish than the average Swedish equivalent – a treasure trove of consumables. She found herself at the drinks section and marvelled at the selection. The only alcohol you could buy in a supermarket back home was under-strength beer. She picked up a bottle of Australian Shiraz and examined the label. It was similar to one that had been recommended by an old school friend who worked at the Nordic Sea Winery in her native Simrishamn. He was a useful contact.

'Shall we get that?'

Anita spun round and saw Jennifer Todd with a small trolley, which was nearly full.

'No, I'll buy it. Maybe we could have some later.'

'Just put it in the trolley. It's my treat. Besides, you look as though you might need a glass or two.'

'Do I look that bad? Must admit, I've had a sleepless night. But that's a long story.'

Jennifer took the bottle and placed it in the trolley.

'I know what will buck us both up. We'll pop over the road to Booths and have a cup of tea.' Anita smiled. The British answer to every crisis. It was coffee in Sweden.

They were soon ensconced in a window seat in the Booths restaurant, with a large pot of tea. It was on the first floor above the shop. Jennifer Todd had explained that, despite its modest size, Penrith had an inordinate number of supermarkets. Through the full-length window, Anita could see virtually the whole town, and the Pennines stretching away to the far distance. The view lifted her spirits.

'Graeme used to call this our Café Nervosa,' said Jennifer Todd as she poured tea into the two cups. For a moment, Anita thought Jennifer might start crying, but she brought any emotion under control.

The reference escaped Anita.

'Café Nervosa. It's in *Frasier*. The American comedy. It's where Frasier and Niles go.'

'OK. We get that in Sweden, too.'

Jennifer took a sip of tea and sighed. 'That's better.' She replaced the cup on the saucer. 'I expect you want to hear if I've made any progress.'

Anita nodded.

'Well, I've hit our first two dead ends. Doris's uncles – James Little's older brothers – were just the right age to be involved in the Great War, so I thought it was worth pursuing that route. Both John and David initially joined the Border Regiment and, according to the National Archives and military records sites, neither made it through. John died at Ypres in 1915 and David two years later at Paschendale. David's body was never found. Lost in the mud. Imagine losing two of your sons.' She shook her head in disbelief. 'Anyhow, neither were married, so no children there. We need to know about the sister, Daisy, and whether Doris had any siblings. If she had, are there any offspring? They would be in line to inherit, as opposed to any obscure relatives going back through Doris's grandparents.'

Anita glanced out of the window. 'I expect we're going to come across a lot of dead ends. If the London heir hunters couldn't find anything, then we're looking for a needle in a haystack, as you say over here.'

'But Graeme found someone.' There was a hint of pride in Jennifer Todd's voice.

Anita's gaze was fixed on a distant peak. 'He did, didn't he?'

*

'Bloody Sundström was investigating this case before the fucking body even turned up.' Westermark was furious. Nordlund sat passively while Moberg devoured a sandwich. 'It's bad enough that she went poking around Jansson's apartment, but she'd also interviewed Fraser. Twice!'

'We know that her ex-husband was worried about Jansson and thought she'd gone missing. He asked Anita for help,' Nordlund explained calmly.

'If he was so worried, why didn't he come to us? That's our job.'

'You can ask him yourself soon. I spoke to him this morning and he's coming down by train today.'

This didn't seem to placate Westermark. 'What else was Sundström up to? What did she find out?' Then a thought struck him. 'If the professor killed Jansson, maybe Sundström has been covering up for him. Wiped away the prints.'

'Don't be so fucking stupid!' Bits of sandwich came flying out of Moberg's mouth as an accompaniment to his howl of indignation. 'She might be a pain in the arse, but she's a straight cop.' He turned to Nordlund. 'Do you think she knows more than she's told you?'

'Not that I'm aware of. But I'll speak to her again.' This was to placate a simmering Westermark. He wanted co-operation, not confrontation if this investigation was going to succeed.

Moberg seemed happy. 'Right, Westermark, what about the teacher?'

'I'm pretty sure he had the hots for her. I can tell.'

'We bow to your experience,' Moberg said sardonically. 'Have you anything more than a bollock-based hunch?'

'Not really,' he admitted. 'But I would like to pull him in for a serious chat. Put a bit of pressure on him. There's something not right about him.'

Moberg sighed. 'Not yet. I think our priority is the professor. By the way, what's he professor of?'

'English literature,' Nordlund replied.

'No wonder he and Miss Aren't-I-Brilliant-At-English teamed up. As soon as he steps off the train, I want him in here.' Moberg grinned at Westermark. 'Try rattling his cage.'

Ash arrived before twelve. Jennifer Todd went off into the kitchen to make him a cup of tea while he took a seat in her husband's snug office. There was a battered, battleship-grey filing cabinet, a tall bookcase with books and directories, a couple of small chests with drawers full of microfilm, and a computer on the desk. Above the computer were two wall shelves devoted to Todd's large collection of maps.

'Did you have any luck?' Anita asked when Ash had made himself comfortable.

'Yes and no.'

Ash dropped some pieces of paper on the table in front of the computer. The top one was a marriage certificate. Anita's eye immediately went to James Little's spouse, Doris's mother. Florence May Oxley. Just then, Jennifer came in bearing a small tray with a mug of tea and a plate of digestive biscuits.

'My favourites!' said Ash as he grabbed a biscuit off the plate before Jennifer had a chance to put it down. 'Absolutely starving. Didn't have time for breakfast.'

Jennifer placed the tray next to Ash as she glanced at the marriage certificate. 'Oxley is a good name to work with; it's not that common. But I see she doesn't have any parents named on the certificate.'

'Well, I hate to put a dampener on things, but I've also been on to the London probate research company, Lampard & Horne. They grudgingly gave me some info after I said this was to do with a murder investigation. They're adamant that there were no leads from the maternal side. Florence Oxley had been born in a workhouse in 1899. Barrow-in-Furness; it's at the tip of southern Cumbria,' he said in reply to Anita's enquiring look. 'It was at 1, Rampside Road, if you're interested. I didn't think workhouses existed by then. Smacks of Charles Dickens.'

'What's a workhouse?' asked Anita.

'It was where the poor were shoved when they had nowhere else left to go,' Jennifer explained. 'They did unpaid work in return for food and accommodation. A lot of old people who couldn't survive outside ended up there, too. Grim places. They lasted until the nineteen twenties or thirties. You know the guest house on the corner near the pub? That was originally built as a workhouse.'

'You know, I'm learning so many new things on this case, you wouldn't believe,' said Ash with a wide grin. 'Anyway, Florence Oxley's origins are unknown. Father unknown. Mother probably staggered off to the workhouse to have her kid. It was definitely illegitimate. She died when Florence was still very young.'

He took a long swig of tea before dunking his second biscuit into the mug and chewing on the gooey result.

'We've drawn a blank on James' siblings. We know that the brothers died in the First World War. Jennifer's phone call saved me looking for them. The sister Daisy died in 1904. Pneumonia. Only three days past her seventh birthday.'

Anita was beginning to get despondent.

But Jennifer said: 'I know what would be useful! It's something Graeme did when he was hunting for information. He talked to the neighbours. You could try and speak to people in Doris's street. She hasn't been dead that long. People will remember her. Unless she was a total recluse, you'll get information. They tend to be pretty chatty in Carlisle.'

'I've just come from there!' Ash groaned. 'But you're right, Mrs Todd, that's the way to go.' He suddenly brightened. 'You want to come, Inspector?'

'You might as well, Anita. Not much you can do to help me here.'

'OK.' She turned to Ash. 'Didn't you say you had some good news?'

'I did, didn't I?' Ash said smugly. 'Better news, anyway. Well, I think it is, though I don't have a clue how it fits in. The Cumberland Building Society was very helpful. I've discovered where Graeme went on his mysterious trip in August. He must have paid for the train by cash, as he took out two hundred and fifty pounds from his business account at an ATM in Penrith on the morning of August the fourteenth. He must have also used cash for wherever he was staying. Certainly didn't use his debit or credit card. But he can't have had enough for an evening meal, because then he used his plastic. On that Tuesday evening, he dined at an Indian restaurant.'

'Typical,' sniffed Jennifer. 'I wouldn't let him have curries. Not good for him.'

'But where?' Anita said in exasperation.

'Oh, sorry. Worcester.'

'Worcester?'

'That's right. It's in the Midlands. Beyond Birmingham.'

'The mysterious way Graeme was acting, I always assumed that his trip was something to do with the Doris Little case.'

Ash picked up his third digestive. 'We've got to find out who he went to see... and why.'

CHAPTER 27

Björn Sundström paced around the interview room liked a caged animal. He hadn't seen anyone for an hour since that rude blond detective waiting for him to alight from the train had dragged him to the polishus. He hadn't even been offered a coffee. What had really hacked him off was the farce of him coming here of his own volition, though he knew he had no real choice. Anita had made that plain enough. The man Nordlund, who had phoned him, had sounded reasonable. So why this lack of action? And, on a practical level, where was he going to stay the night? He could bunk down at Anita's, as she was out of the country. But he wasn't sure what sort of reception he would receive from his son. He was conscious that he had made a fool of himself in front of Lasse. It pained him that he might have irreparably damaged their relationship. Maybe a hotel would be a better idea. He just wanted to get the interview over, and then he could go back to Uppsala and start putting his life back together. He now wished that he hadn't singled out the pretty, little, blonde student in his English Romantic Poets group two years ago. The special attention he had shown her had led him to this frustrating and worrying impasse. What's more, he didn't like cops. Anita was the only one he had had any time for. After seeing her again, he now knew what a fool he had been to let her go; to freeze her out of what had been a great relationship. Too many younger temptations. Anita was still a fine-looking woman. And level-headed. She hadn't been dazzled by his reputation, unlike so many of the others. He had had to make an effort with her. But she had been worth the chase. What a fucking idiot he was!

'Sorry to keep you waiting.' The tall, balding policeman spoke as he pushed the door open. When the blond one came in behind him, Björn's heart sank.

'I'm Inspector Henrik Nordlund and this is Inspector Karl Westermark.'

'Unfortunately, I've already had the pleasure.'

'Please sit down, Professor Sundström.' Nordlund smiled. Westermark scowled.

Björn took a seat at the table. He readjusted his light linen jacket. It was a stupid choice to make as he had rushed off to the station that morning. It was too thin for this time of year. And this room wasn't warm enough to stop him shivering. Westermark immediately took it as a sign that the professor was frightened. He didn't intend to let him relax.

Nordlund sat opposite Björn, while Westermark, arms folded, leant against the closed door. No escape.

'Thank you for coming down from Uppsala.'

Björn waved it away.

'How long did you know Greta Jansson?'

'She was in her second year when she came into my Romantic Poets group. That would be just over two years ago. She was a keen student.'

'I bet she was,' Westermark sneered.

'She loved the English romantic poets. Shelly, Byron, Keats, Coleridge, Blake.' Björn noticed Westermark pull a face. He beamed at the detective. 'If you're interested, I can recommend *The Longman Anthology of Gothic Verse*. It's a good place to start.'

'Don't be so fucking funny.'

'I prefer our own poets.' Nordlund spoke quietly. 'Gustaf Fröding.'

'Ah, Fröding. Interesting choice. He studied at Uppsala. A lot to be said for him.' Again Björn fixed Westermark with a mocking stare. 'Fröding wasn't very successful with women.'

'And you fucking are, I suppose.' Westermark was becoming belligerent. He was now standing next to the table, hovering over Björn.

'I wouldn't be here if I wasn't.'

Björn was amazed at the ease with which he had got under Westermark's skin. It would make him a less effective interviewer.

'Karl, that's enough,' ordered Nordlund. Westermark retreated to the door and took up his former position. He would make this Sundström pay.

'What was the basis of your relationship with Greta?' Nordlund continued.

'After a few months, we became lovers.'

'It became a steady relationship?'

'After time, yes.'

'Was that ethical? Impressionable young student and older tutor.'

Björn shrugged. 'It happens.'

'So, you were very much a couple?'

'Yes. We loved each other.'

Westermark shook his head. It was plain what he was thinking.

'And were you still a couple when she came to Malmö?'

'Of course.' For the first time, Björn was on the defensive.

'Only, one of Greta's colleagues had the impression that she was escaping from someone.' Westermark had regained control of himself and was back in the fray.

'That wasn't me.'

'Yet her departure from Uppsala was quite abrupt, according to her friend Ulrika Lindén. I assume you know her from her Uppsala days?'

'Yes. She was a good friend of Greta's from university. And the reason Greta's departure was so quick was because the teaching job in Malmö suddenly came up. Good opportunity for her. Foot on the ladder.'

'Did you visit her after she moved here?'

Björn hesitated. 'No.'

'Isn't that strange for a couple of lovers?'

Björn regained his composure. 'I was very busy with a new term and Greta wanted time to settle into her new surroundings.'

'Yet you've been to the apartment.'

'What makes you think that?'

'Your fucking fingerprints are all over it.' Westermark knew that wasn't entirely true, as certain areas of the apartment had been wiped clean of any prints. However, the comment had the right effect, and he was enjoying Björn's growing discomfort. He now took a seat alongside Nordlund. Björn found his close proximity across the table intimidating.

'Once. The weekend before last. I had a key. Let myself in. She wasn't around. That's why I approached Anita. Inspector Sundström. I thought something was up.'

'And how did you get the key?'

'Greta sent it to me.'

'And was she expecting you that weekend?'

'Well, no. It was a surprise visit.' Björn began to weave tiny patterns on the table top with his fingertips.

'So why did you think something was up?' Nordlund sounded almost sympathetic.

Björn appeared to be studying his finger movements. Then he gave a nervous little cough. 'The truth is that I hadn't heard from her for a few days. That's why I came down to Malmö.'

'Maybe she didn't want to hear from you.' Björn just wanted to hit Westermark.

'I didn't hear from her because she was dead.'

'When was it you last actually spoke to Greta?' The level,

precise tone of Nordlund's voice contrasted with Westermark's aggressively acerbic outbursts.

'I can't remember. About a week or so before she disappeared.'

Nordlund gave Björn a half-smile. 'We'll have to take a look at your mobile phone.'

'What the hell for?'

'It may give us some useful information.'

'I can't see how.'

'Just hand it over.' Westermark thrust his hand across the table. Björn looked at it before slowly reaching into his pocket. He wavered for a moment before placing his mobile in Westermark's outstretched palm. Westermark flashed an immaculate set of white teeth at Björn. The urge to belt him was almost insuppressible.

'There's one other thing we need to clear up, Professor,' Nordlund continued. 'Where were you on the weekend of September the twenty-eighth and twenty-ninth? It's the weekend we believe Greta disappeared.'

Björn raised his eyes to the ceiling. 'Uppsala.'

'You can prove that?'

'If I have to.'

'Well, you may have to, because a man describing himself as Greta's father turned up on the Saturday morning.' Westermark glanced up at Nordlund as he was flicking though Björn's mobile.

'Her father's dead,' said Björn, bringing his gaze back to his inquisitors.

'We know that. The neighbour met this man. In fact, she gave him a spare key.'

'I don't know who it was.'

'Karl. Have you a camera on your phone?' Westermark nodded. 'Good. Can you take a picture of Professor Sundström and then go over to Greta's apartment block and ask the neighbour if she recognises him.'

Westermark's mouth creased into a sizeable grin. 'Of course. Professor, would you be kind enough to pose for me? I want a really good likeness.'

Björn held up a restraining hand. 'Don't bother.'

The drive into Carlisle took about twenty-five minutes. The ancient city had seen its fair share of violent history over the centuries as warring Scots and English families had clashed. The whole Border area between the two fractious countries had been like the American Wild West, and Carlisle was the Dodge City of the Middle Ages. The two symbols of certainty and safety in those troubled times remained – the red sandstone cathedral with its maternal air; and the proud, inviolable medieval castle, now rudely and ungratefully severed from the rest of the town by a dual carriageway. The other significant landmark that towered over the city was the tall and slender Dixon's chimney, a relic of the industrial age when Carlisle's textile mills did a roaring trade and the sophisticated railway network sped their products to all parts of the country and the empire beyond. At the crossroads in front of the chimney, close to the offices of Cumbrian Newspapers, Ash turned left into a street of back-to-back brick houses, a legacy of the days when the city grew dramatically in the second half of the 19th century. Ash managed to find a parking space in the tightly packed road.

'That's where Doris Little lived,' he said, pointing to a neat front door across the street. 'We knock on a few doors and see what we come up with.'

It was the fifth door Ash knocked on that was opened by the friendly, talkative neighbour they desperately needed. Every street has one fount of all knowledge, and Ethel Braithwaite was it. A woman in her seventies, she was neatly dressed with fiercely permed hair, as though she was constantly ready to receive visitors at short notice. Her gestures were expansive and her chatter non-stop. Despite Anita's protests, she had insisted on serving up a pot of tea. Ash had cheekily suggested that some cake would be nice too. At least when she was in the kitchen, they had a break. The living room was immaculate and littered with souvenirs from various seaside resorts. A rotating pendulum clock with a transparent case adorned the mantelpiece, antimacassars were draped on the sofa and chairs, frilly net curtains keeping out prying eyes covered the windows, and the obligatory photos of family and friends cluttered the sixties sideboard. In the corner, on an antique gate-leg table, was a bottle of port with two glasses. She must have had regular company.

'Doris was a lovely neighbour. Friend really. I've been in this street for nigh on twenty years. Came here after Bob died.' She paused so they could take a reflective glance at her husband's photograph, which took pride of place on the wall above the small bookcase. 'And she spent most of her life here. Funny you should come asking about her. That man who traces family trees came to see me, too; the one they had that article about in the *Cumberland News* last week that died in Iceland or somewhere.' Her words came out in a joined-up gabble and Anita was having difficulty understanding everything she said, as her Cumberland accent was quite thick. While Mrs Braithwaite had been in the kitchen, Ash promised he would act as interpreter. 'As I say, couldn't have been nicer, though in the last few years she kept herself to herself. I used to go round and do little jobs for her. Keep her company. Couldn't believe it when she died. Just went in her sleep – best way to go, I suppose.'

It was only when she stopped to take a sip of tea that Ash was able to jump in with a question. 'Do you know if she had any brothers or sisters?'

'Just a sister. Now she was very pleasant too. Always wore nice coats. Hoopers' best. I like people who make an effort to look nice.' This was accompanied by a reproving frown in Anita's direction. The customary blue jeans, old, red jersey and brown leather jacket obviously didn't come up to scratch, particularly for a woman in a position of authority. But she was foreign. She was pleased to see the polite British policeman was wearing a suit and tie.

'Name?' Ash prompted.

'Isabelle. Of course, we all knew her as Belle. She would come and visit her sister once a week, regular as clockwork. Always had a pleasant word for me if I was there. Naturally, I would leave them to chat. Didn't want to overstay my welcome. Of course, that stopped when Belle died. Now when was that? Certainly after 2000. Did you see the Millennium Bridge they put over Castle Way? Don't think much of it myself. It corroded in no time—'

'Sorry to interrupt, Mrs Braithwaite, but what was Belle's surname?'

'Didn't I say? Ridley, of course.'

'Why "of course"?'

'Sorry, you don't come from round here, do you? You sound a bit southern to me. Ridley's, the butchers. Up on Scotland Road. Stanwix. Belle was married to Richard Ridley. That's how she could afford to shop regularly at Hoopers.'

Ash scribbled the names down on the incomplete family tree that Jennifer Todd had drafted before they set off for Carlisle.

'Is Richard Ridley still alive?'

'Oh, no. Long dead. I have an idea that Belle played the merry widow after he went, if you know what I mean.'

Ash raised his eyes in recognition of what she was implying.

'Any kids?'

'Yes. Two, I think. Bit wild they were. Had a reputation for it.'

'Can you remember their names, Mrs Braithwaite?'

156

'Call me Ethel, for goodness' sake.'

'Well, Ethel?'

'Michael was the boy. He'd started in his dad's shop. But he was into motorbikes. Killed in an accident on Hartside.'

'Hmm, I'm afraid, despite our warnings, the bikers still wipe themselves out up there,' Ash shook his head sagely. 'Dangerous bends. Do you know when he died?'

'Sorry, dear, it was so long ago. He wasn't that old. Well before his dad.'

'Was he married?'

'Too young. Such a shame.'

'That means he had no kids.' He flashed a disappointed glance at Anita. 'I assume, from what you said, the other was a girl. That would be Doris's niece?'

'Yes. What was she called? Tearaway. Carol, I think.'

'Is she still about?'

'Not that I've heard. Carlisle was too small for her. Left when she was young. I don't know what she did, but Belle and Doris never mentioned her. Funny that, actually. As though she didn't exist.'

CHAPTER 28

'He's in trouble.'

These were not the words Anita wanted to hear when Nordlund rang on her return to the guest house after the visit to Carlisle.

'He's admitted that he was in Malmö the weekend that Jansson disappeared.'

'The "father"?'

'Yes.'

Deep down, she had already reached that unwelcome conclusion.

'What did he say he was doing?'

'He said that he'd come down to see Greta Jansson because she wasn't returning his calls. Said he was getting desperate.'

'The idiot!'

'It fits in with what her colleague had said about her trying to get away from someone. It *was* Professor Sundström. He'd gone to her apartment. She wasn't there. He saw the neighbour and, on the spur of the moment, pretended to be Greta's father and borrowed the key. That's why we found his fingerprints.'

'What did he do after that?'

'Got drunk. Then went back to Uppsala the next day. He came down the next weekend to see you and get you to try and find her.'

'What about the phone call to the school?'

'He denies that.'

Anita took off her glasses and rubbed the bridge of her nose with her left hand. It always seemed to be sore when she was stressed.

'Have you got him in custody?'

'No. But I've told him to stay in Malmö. Westermark wasn't very pleased, but he's been very touchy lately.'

'What? More than usual?'

Nordlund gave a little laugh. 'I've put him in charge of going through all the CCTV from the Lilla Torg bars. A trawl through the footage of that Friday night might show where she went. And also who she left with, if that's where she met her murderer. We have to start somewhere.'

'Her university friend thought she was already in a bar when she rang to cancel their drink together.'

'I've dragged in Hakim to help. He's got a good eye.'

Anita sighed. 'Poor sod.'

'He's strong enough to cope with Westermark.'

'I hope you're right.' Anita was being overprotective again.

'Oh, one bit of potentially bad news.'

'You mean there's more?' she said warily.

'Your ex-husband is staying at your apartment.'

'Brilliant!' Anita put her glasses back on. 'That'll cause ructions which I won't be there to sort out.' She suddenly thought about Hakim holing up there. That would put an end to his little domestic escape. 'Thanks for keeping me in the loop, Henrik.'

'You'd better call Moberg. He wants to know what on earth – not that he used that phrase – you were up to investigating Greta Jansson on your own. I'm afraid Westermark jumped on that.'

'I'll call him in the morning,' she groaned. 'Maybe I can distract him with the Todd case. We've made some progress. We've been told about a living relative, but we've no idea where she is or how any of it is connected to Sweden. Not that that will please our beloved chief inspector.'

'Good luck.'

She was about to finish the call. 'Henrik. Do you think Björn killed Greta Jansson?'

'I don't know. But it's not looking good for him.'

Westermark sat alone in his office. He was lost in thought. He was still brooding over Nordlund letting Björn Sundström go. The old fucker didn't know what he was doing. Putting that bitch Anita's ex-husband away would be a great way to get back at her. Despite everything that had happened in the past, she had re-emerged ahead of him in the team's pecking order. He could understand it if she had flashed her tits to get there, but she was above that. Too principled for a tough job like ours, he thought bitterly. He was more than happy to cut corners to get quick convictions. Moberg didn't care as long as nothing rebounded on him. Westermark flicked through Björn's mobile for the umpteenth time. He had made a lot of calls to Greta Jansson's phone. Many after she was dead. His mind went back to Anita. Even he had to admit that her results were impressive, but she was a lucky cop. She got those breaks that others didn't get. However, he knew that what was really gnawing away at him was that he wanted to get into her knickers, and she had evaded every attempt. He wasn't used to women turning him down. He didn't like it. The more Anita spurned him, the more he wanted her. He couldn't count the number of times he had imagined ravishing her over his desk. He had looked on in dismay when he could see that she had fallen for Ewan Strachan. His satisfaction at Strachan's conviction and subsequent imprisonment had been tempered by Anita's visits to the jail. He had failed to use that to his advantage, and instead of getting her into bed as he had planned, she had managed to turn the tables. It was time she paid.

Westermark threw the mobile back onto the desk. He would head for home, take the CCTV footage from Moosehead and Mello Yellow with him, and flick through them over a whisky or two. He had left the other bars in and around Lilla Torg to the Arab. That would keep the little wanker out of the way.

Though the handsome professor was definitely in the frame, he wasn't going to overlook Fraser. Another fucking Anita connection. Someone was going to go down for Greta Jansson's murder. He would see to that. And if it hurt Anita in the process, all the better. But the first thing he was going to do was apply a little pressure on her ex. He picked up the phone.

'I'm at home.' Anita had thought it best to check on how Hakim was. 'You know your husband has come to stay? But thanks for letting me use the apartment, anyway.'

'Sorry about that.'

'It's not a problem. I appreciated the break from home.'

'How is Björn?'

'A bit shaken up, actually. It can't have been easy for him being stuck in an interview room with Westermark.'

Anita refrained from asking him whether he thought Björn was guilty. She might not get the answer she wanted. 'Is Lasse OK about his dad staying?'

'I don't know. He was out. He was hardly there over the weekend.'

That didn't sound good. She thought it better to get back to business. 'I hear you've been put with Westermark checking out CCTV.'

'Yes. But we've split up the bars, so I don't have to work with him. I've found no sign of Greta Jansson yet. Maybe Westermark will turn something up.'

'Any luck on the Graeme Todd front?'

'Wallen went back to Ystad, but hasn't unearthed anything new. She's been liaising with the Ystad police. What about over there in England?'

Anita gave him a brief account of their latest findings. Not that there was much she could tell him. By the time she hung up, she felt quite deflated. Her case was at that infuriating stage where nothing seemed to be happening. One step forward, two steps back. And the Greta Jansson murder was even more unsettling. She thought about ringing home to see if Lasse and Björn were all right, but she resisted the urge. She couldn't cope with Lasse giving her grief about his father and she didn't want to compromise herself by talking to Björn. After all, she couldn't escape the fact that he might well be a killer.

Billy Hump drained his glass and thumped it down on the bar. 'Another,' he slurred unsmilingly at the barmaid. She took a fresh glass and started to pull a pint. She did little to disguise her contempt for the regular she had learned to loathe over recent months. Why he had come back to the area, she had no idea. His family had disowned him and they wouldn't be seen dead drinking in the same pub as him. When she looked up, he was no longer at the bar. He was over by the door.

'Just gannin' for a fag. I'll pay when I gets back.'

If he came back. Once the drink was in Billy Hump, there was no knowing what he might do. He'd already had six pints and wasn't very steady on his feet. They'd had to call the police on a couple of occasions when he had got aggressive. The landlord said he was on a last warning. If she had had her way he would have been barred months ago, but she suspected the landlord was a bit afraid of him.

Billy Hump wandered outside. The two other smokers immediately threw their stubs onto the pavement and vanished back inside the pub. He was alone on the street. Painstakingly, he took out his crumpled packet of cigarettes. He fumbled with the pack until he managed to squeeze out the last one and slide it into the side of his mouth. He flicked his plastic lighter and managed to unite the cigarette with the flame. He didn't notice the car further up the street rev into life. Billy Hump stared up into the starry sky. He watched the smoke funnel out of his mouth into the night air. It was only when he heard an engine gunning that he half turned round, just in time to see a car mounting the kerb and heading straight towards him. With a booming thud that alerted the regulars of the Cross Keys, Billy Hump was thrown up into the air. He landed in a broken heap on the dry, cold pavement. His cigarette rolled to the pub doorway. It was still burning.

CHAPTER 29

'Where do we go from here?'

Ash looked enquiringly across at Jennifer Todd. Along with Anita, they were sitting in the Todds' dining room. On the long, mock-Georgian dining table was a new, rudimentary family tree. Doris Alma Little's name was in the middle, highlighted in yellow. Jennifer had double-checked that Doris's sister, Belle, had been her only sibling, and she'd filled in all the names and dates of known blood relatives.

'Summing up,' said Jennifer, looking down at the left of the diagram, 'Florence's mother died when she was only two. Father unknown. So no relatives there that we're ever likely to find.'

'So who is this lot?' Ash said, pointing to the names on the right-hand side of the tree.

'I thought I'd look into the Ridley side of the family.'

'Can any of them inherit?' Anita asked.

'Not Richard Ridley, our Stanwix butcher. He married into the family, so he's not a blood relative and neither are relatives on his side.'

'So what's the point?'

Jennifer folded her arms emphatically. 'Well, we're faced with two alternatives. One, we know Carol Emily Ridley, born April 10th, 1959, is the main heir, but we can't find her. Two, we can go back a couple of generations to James Little's parents and find someone there.'

'Shouldn't we do that then?' Ash's suggestion seemed to make sense to Anita.

Jennifer pursed her lips. 'I think the London heir hunters would have tried that route before they decided the financial returns weren't worth the effort. That suggests they found nothing there. And they probably didn't bother with the Ridley side of the family. They won't have messed around. With their staff and resources, they would've taken about a day to sort all this out and make the decision to go no further. And you can bet that if they'd got as far as Carol Emily Ridley – and they must have done – they would have checked out everyone that's in this country. But they obviously cut their losses. That's why they didn't bother sending someone to interview Doris's neighbour. Their nearest agent is probably based in Manchester or further south, so the cost of getting someone to dig around on the ground wasn't worth it. Again, that decision would've been made within hours.'

'Do they work *that* quickly?' There was a hint of admiration in Ash's voice.

'Oh, yes. Remember, they're often competing with other large probate research outfits, so if they don't find heirs within the first day or so, their rivals will. That's why I believe Graeme found Carol. Or found out something about her.'

'OK. So, how far have we got?'

'Well, as you can see, Richard Ridley had two brothers, William and Douglas. William died in the Korean War. He wasn't married.'

'This lot have been unlucky in war,' observed Ash.

'Douglas, the youngest, had a son called John, who was born in 1960. I phoned the Register Office and they have a record of a John Douglas Calthwaite Ridley marrying in Carlisle in 1984. The Church of Scotland on Chapel Street. His bride was a Vanessa Janette Johnson. The thing is, John's Carol's first cousin and there's only a year between them in age. I thought, if we can find him, maybe we can find her.'

'That's where we can take over. I'll get onto headquarters.' Ash was about to whip out his phone when Jennifer Todd held up her hand with a broad grin on her face.

'No need. John's names helped. He was obviously named Douglas after his dead uncle, but it was Calthwaite that was unusual. Probably a family name going way back. Anyway, I put John Douglas Calthwaite Ridley in a couple of search engines and came up with a match. An obituary.'

'That's no fuc...bloody use,' cursed Ash, quickly correcting his oath.

Jennifer was still smiling. 'The obituary was from two years ago. It was in the Worcester Evening News.'

Anita clapped her hands. 'Well done, Jennifer!'

'So why did Graeme go down to Worcester if John was dead?'

'Isn't it obvious? He went to see the widow. Vanessa Ridley.'

The sun was shining when Fraser emerged from the main entrance of the school. He was glad to be out. The listening lesson hadn't gone well. The students hadn't listened. He wandered over to the centre of Kungsgatan; the long, tree-lined pedestrian avenue that swept up to St. Pauli Kyrka and beyond. Curling, brown leaves were fluttering down and another autumn was imperceptibly taking hold of the urban landscape. The weak sun still had some warmth in it, and Fraser plonked himself down on a bench next to a green lamppost, and closed his eyes. He was grateful that he hadn't ended up further north. Swedish winters could be unrelentingly severe on both body and soul but were easier to cope with in Skåne. Often the season was no worse in Malmö than he'd experienced growing up in Glasgow. It just seemed to go on longer and sometimes seemed to skip spring altogether before jumping straight into summer.

'Can I join you?'

Fraser glanced up. He didn't bother suppressing a heavy sigh. 'What do you want?'

'Another chat.' Westermark sat uncomfortably close. Fraser shifted along the bench. Westermark was pleased with himself. *Sydsvenskan* had run a short but prominent piece on the Greta Jansson murder and had alluded to a romantic connection to an unnamed professor from Uppsala. The other papers would soon be on the trail, and he knew that they would be camped outside Anita Sundström's apartment. Of course, Moberg had gone berserk when he saw the article, claiming that he would castrate the person responsible. The chief inspector might well suspect him of the leak but he wouldn't be able to prove it. For Westermark it was a win-win situation. The spotlight was on Anita's ex-husband – that would put pressure on the professor and embarrass Anita. And his tip-off to the attractive reporter at *Sydsvenskan* would be worth a quid pro quo shag.

'Last time we spoke, you said you fancied Greta Jansson.'

'No. *You* said that.' Fraser couldn't control his temper. He wondered if Anita Sundström had said something to this sleazy cop. It had been indiscreet to mention that he had asked Greta out on a date.

'Touchy, aren't you? Anyway, the day she left the school for the last time was Friday, September the twenty-eighth. Do you remember what you were doing that night?'

Fraser tried to calm himself. 'Not specifically.'

'It was only just over a fortnight ago.' Westermark managed to inject a dollop of disbelief into his voice.

'Most Friday nights I have a drink with colleagues after work. Then I usually end up at my local, The Pickwick.'

'You English are obsessed with pubs.'

'I'm Scottish.' This guy was really winding him up.

Now Westermark knew why he didn't like this man. Another bloody Ewan Strachan.

'Did you go anywhere near Lilla Torg that night?'

'I don't think so.'

'Are you sure?' barked Westermark.

Fraser looked startled. 'Well... I think—'

'You were in Mello Yello early that evening.'

'I can't rem—'

'We've got you on CCTV. Six twenty-two.'

With a flicker of panic in his eyes, Fraser backtracked. 'Yes, of course. I was going to meet some pals there. But they didn't turn up, so I went off to The Pickwick.'

'What time?'

'I actually went home to get something to eat first. Then on to the pub.'

'How long were you in The Pickwick?'

'I don't know. Until about ten.'

'I'll double-check.'

Fraser shifted on the bench. The wooden struts were biting into his backside. 'What's the big deal about Lilla Torg?'

'That's where Greta went to meet a friend. We think she may have met her killer there. You weren't following her, were you?'

'Of course not. Look, I don't know what crazy thoughts you're conjuring up, but I didn't kill her. I don't know why you're harassing me – there were plenty of people who fancied her.'

Westermark's eyes glinted. 'Like who, for instance?'

Fraser tapped his feet nervously on the ground, scuffing away some fallen leaves as he did so. He was already regretting his impetuosity.

'Just spit it out.'

'Andreas. Andreas Holm; my head of department... *he* liked Greta.'

By the time they reached the Thelwall Viaduct south of Manchester, the M6 traffic had grown heavier, and Ash was forced to reduce his speed. For this, Anita was thankful. Britain had too many huge trucks, too many fast cars and too many bad drivers. It was a combination that had her wistfully thinking how calm Swedish roads were. There, she felt safe. Here, it was like the dodgems. And Ash's erratic driving wasn't helping.

The decision to head off to Worcester had been taken quickly. A call to directory enquiries had produced a number for Vanessa Ridley, and Ash had managed to catch her before she left for the shops. She gave him her address. Fort Royal Hill. Ash had estimated that he could do the trip in four hours. They would be at Ridley's house by half past two. They had high hopes that this was the lead they were after, especially as Ridley confirmed that she had been visited by Graeme Todd in the summer. Before they left, Anita had pressed Jennifer Todd to see if she could remember any other trips that her husband had made after his visit to Worcester. Nothing had come to mind until they were getting into the car. She had come rushing out of the house. There had been one. In late August. Graeme had gone across to the North East for the day, but she didn't know exactly where.

Ash was muttering as the car was reduced to a crawl. 'They're always having accidents along this stretch. It'll be just our luck.'

Anita's mobile started to vibrate in her pocket. She took it out with some dread. After leaving Fellbeck, her phone had come to life as soon as they neared Penrith and the motorway. There had been five missed calls from Björn. She just didn't want the hassle. It was still ringing in her hand.

'Aren't you going to answer that?'

It was Björn again. Reluctantly, she answered. It seemed to be the only way to get rid of him. 'What do you want, Björn?' she said wearily.

'The fucking press!' he shouted at the other end. 'There are masses of reporters outside your door.'

'What?'

'Reporters. I tried to go out and they started bombarding me with questions. I rushed back in. When Lasse went out, they did the same to him. But he managed to run off.'

'I don't understand.'

'Some shit has tipped them off. It was in *Sydsvenskan* this morning. Didn't name me as such, but hinted. Someone has told them where I'm staying. Must be one of your lot. Only they knew where I was going to be.'

'No. Can't be.' Then she fell silent. Of course it could. She knew exactly who would play that sort of trick.

'And the police think I did it.'

'Did they say so?'

'They didn't have to. What am I going to do?'

Anita was fed up. Why should she have to sort out Björn's mess? He had used her and lied to her. She was tempted just to let him wallow in his own muck, but it would affect Lasse – and probably her if Westermark was behind this.

'Does Inspector Nordlund want to see you again?'

'Yes, I'm due at the polishus at three.'

'Right. There's a back door to the apartment block. You can make your way onto Kronborgsvägen. After your interview, book into some quiet hotel and keep your head down.'

'That's what I'm trying to fucking do!' he said angrily.

Anita snapped her mobile shut, cutting Björn off. She, too, was furious. Ungrateful bastard. A few moments later, the mobile rang again. Anita switched it off.

'Trouble?'

'Long story.'

The traffic was now bumper to bumper. Ash waved at the serried ranks of vehicles ahead. 'We've got plenty of time.'

'Tell me about Andreas Holm.'

Fraser had regretted it the moment he had mentioned his

colleague's name. He had panicked. This bloody detective had put him on the back foot. He was pushing and needling him, and he needed to divert his attention. But it *was* true. Andreas Holm did pay too much attention to Greta. Now that he had blurted out his name, he was unsure about how much he should reveal to Westermark.

'Holm appointed Greta.'

'And?'

'And he tends to appoint young, attractive women if he can. I slipped through the net.'

His joke didn't wash with Westermark. 'But presumably there's more to it?'

Fraser was paying more attention to his shoes than to his questioner. He found Westermark's unrelenting stare difficult to match. 'He's a bit creepy around some of the female staff. I could tell Greta was uncomfortable.'

'How old is he? Married?'

'Late thirties. Yes, he's married, but I've never met his wife.'

'Other than being a creep, what makes you think he might have gone that bit further with Greta?'

Fraser fidgeted with his hair. 'There were rumours.'

'What rumours?'

'Before he came to Malmö, he worked up north. Not sure where. But I heard that something happened at the school he was working at. Don't know the details. Don't even know if it's true. But apparently he left under a cloud.'

'Fiddling with kids?'

'No, nothing to do with the students. He's not like that. It was a female member of staff.'

'So, you can see he's in a bit of a fix.' Anita summed up her edited explanation of how Björn had come to be a suspect in the Greta Jansson murder.

'Bit awkward for you, Inspector.' Ash sympathised.

The traffic had cleared and Ash had cranked up the speed. They weren't far north of Birmingham now. He reckoned they would be in Worcester in an hour. Anita gazed out of the window. The landscape had flattened out. She marvelled at how green everything was. Autumn wasn't as far advanced here as in Cumbria.

'So how long ago did you split from Björn?'

'I left him in 2000. It was my Millennium present to myself.'

Ash laughed. 'And I take it from what you've told me, it was his interest in young female students that was the problem.'

'Not for him. I know you British think that Sweden is obsessed with sex and is the home of the open marriage and all that, but that isn't my style. Björn's, yes. Mine, no.'

'Funnily enough, not mine either.'

Anita gave him a sceptical glance. Ash grinned again. She had come across too many randy cops in her time; Karl Westermark being top of the list. She had seen too many police marriages hit the rocks. Long hours away from home. Colleagues thrown together. These things happened.

'Like your Björn, my Leanne had a penchant... that's the word, isn't it? She had a penchant for policemen of a higher rank than her husband. And there were a lot of them. She didn't think I was ambitious enough. She wanted to mix with a better sort of cop. Go to those fancy dos where the bigwigs hang out. I think you'd call her an "aspirer". Bloody Thatcher produced a nation of those, and we're living with the consequences now. Self-interest everywhere.'

Ash paused, as if to collect his thoughts.

'Good looking, Leanne. So she had plenty of takers. I loved her enough to turn a blind eye for a while. Persuaded myself that it wasn't really happening. Except, as a policeman, your instincts never stop working. I knew what was going on, but wouldn't accept the truth. Until one of them started to boast about it. You know what cop shops are like for gossip. Whispers behind your back. Sniggers when you walk into a room. It made the job untenable.' He started to drive even faster, and Anita watched the twitching speedometer with alarm.

'So, I applied for a transfer. Leanne wouldn't come with me, so we divorced.'

'Did she end up with this man?'

'Roller? No, he was married. Dumped her when he thought it might cause him a problem. Probably was told to stop the affair because it might harm his chances of getting to the top.'

'"Roller" is a strange name.'

'Ah, that's his nickname. He's called Royce Weatherley. Rolls Royce. We call the car a "Roller". It's probably a British thing. We're big on nicknames.'

The car slowed down to a manageable 80mph.

'Is he still on the force?'

'Oh, yes. He's the bloody Deputy Chief Constable of Northumbria Police.' The car speeded up again.

Anita thought she had better change the subject quickly.

'You're not from the North, so what brought you up?'

'Leanne. She's from Wallsend.' The new tack hadn't seemed to work, but he did slow down a touch. 'Met her on holiday in Majorca. Free and single. I'm an Essex boy. Born and bred in Braintree. Great little town. My kid sister, Sarah, still lives there. Her husband Calum's a Jock, but he seems to love it there, too. I was on the Essex force. Our holiday romance turned into marriage, but she never settled down south, so when Abigail was one, I got a transfer to Northumbria Police. Of course, they think that anybody who comes from south of Middlesbrough is a Cockney. So that became my nickname. They've no idea of geography. Mind you, they're friendly enough people, but I never really fitted in. The accent didn't help. Always an outsider.' Anita could sympathise. She wasn't a true Scanian like most of her colleagues. Her accent was different too. 'Then Roller came along.'

Again, the speedometer began to climb.

'Interesting that Jennifer said that Graeme went to the North East. I wonder why?'

This had the desired effect. Ash manoeuvred back into the middle lane.

'I was wondering that. First Worcester, then across the Pennines. He was certainly following a trail. I only hope Vanessa Ridley can supply an answer, otherwise our trail is going to go cold.'

CHAPTER 30

Moberg wanted an update on both the Graeme Todd and Greta Jansson cases. More importantly, he didn't want to go home. His wife was now refusing to cook him meals. In one way, it was a godsend, as her culinary skills weren't the reason he'd married her. However, it was inconvenient, as he had to buy a meal for himself on the way home. And, once through the front door, her silence was more maddening than her constant nagging had been. If he could have afforded it, the divorce would already have been under way. He dismissed from his mind the decision whether to call in at the China Box or pick up a pizza, and concentrated on the two matters in hand.

Round the table in the middle of the meeting room – now turned into the nerve centre of the two investigations – were gathered Nordlund, Westermark, Wallen, Hakim, and forensic technician, Eva Thulin. Another young detective, called Mjallby, had been brought in to help. On both of the walls running between the door and the window were whiteboards, on which there was a plethora of names and photographs. The images of the two victims featured prominently – two bodies; the only obvious connection between them was the sea into which they had been unceremoniously dumped.

'Let's begin with Graeme Todd. Wallen, in Sundström's absence, you can fill us in.'

A nervous Wallen cleared her throat. Moberg was so intimidating that she had hidden in the ladies' toilet until the last minute. She always felt better when Anita was by her side. She could stand up to the chief inspector if the going got tough.

'I spoke to Anita an hour ago. She was on her way to some town that's impossible to pronounce.' She wrote WORCESTER on the whiteboard.

Moberg glanced enquiringly around the table. No one else knew where it was either.

'She and the English detective have discovered who, in theory, would be the beneficiary of the will. The only problem is that no one seems to know where the woman is.'

'So why is she going to this place?'

'She hopes to talk to someone who is connected to the family.' She stared down at the notes she had taken from her brief conversation with Anita. 'Anita was going to see a cousin's wife. The woman is called Ridley. Apparently, Todd did the same.'

'Does she think it's promising?'

Wallen gave a little cough. 'She hopes so. If not, then she's not sure what they'll do next.'

'She'd better find something to justify the fucking flight and expenses. The commissioner was giving us earache about budgets only yesterday. How are we meant to do our job?' Moberg was beginning to redden. It was a danger signal they all recognised. 'Right, anything at this end?'

Wallen shook her head. 'Not really. I've talked to the Ystad police and they're asking around. I've revisited the places we know Todd went to on the day he disappeared, but nothing new has emerged. There's no CCTV covering the place in the square where we think Todd was picked up. Or at least was seen waiting to be picked up.'

Moberg waved a gorilla-like hand in Nordlund's direction. 'Henrik, please have some better news.'

Nordlund stood up and went to the Greta Jansson wall. 'We've now three potential suspects, thanks to Karl's digging.'

Wallen noted that Westermark's smugness had returned. 'First, we have Professor Björn Sundström. I'd like to leave him until last. The other two,' he said pointing to two photographs, 'were colleagues of Greta's at Kungsskolan. The man with the long hair is Alex Fraser, who is from Glasgow in Scotland. He's lived in Malmö for five years. He met a Swedish girl while on the hippy trail in India and followed her back here. They split up. At present, he's single.'

'Fraser denies that he was interested in the girl, but I don't believe him,' chipped in Westermark. 'He's lying about something. More to the point, he turned up on CCTV in Lilla Torg on the evening that we think she disappeared. He was in Mello Yello at the time Greta was meant to be meeting her university friend.'

'Has she turned up in any footage?' asked Moberg.

'Mirza and I have been through it all from every bar and restaurant in Lilla Torg, as well as visiting each one with a photo, but there's no sign of her. We'll have to widen our search to Stortorget and Skomakaregatan.'

'We're sure she was down in that area somewhere,' put in Nordlund. 'When I spoke to Ulrika Lindén, she was positive that Greta was sitting in a bar when she phoned. She could hear the background noise. And Greta had mentioned Lilla Torg when they were setting up the meeting.'

'Of course,' continued Westermark, 'we can't be sure that she met her killer in a bar. He might have turned up later; the voice the neighbour heard in the apartment. Basically, we don't know her movements between the phone call with her friend and being heard by the neighbour – that's approximately five hours.'

'What about that guy there?' said Moberg, pointing at a chubby, bespectacled face whose cheeks seemed to have pushed the eyes back into the head. The hair was reddish and unruly, the puffy lips thick and unappealing.

'Karl?' Nordlund made way for Westermark.

'Like Fraser, we downloaded the photo of this gorgeous creature from the school's website. He's called Andreas Holm. I was given his name by Fraser. He's head of the English department that Greta worked in. He appointed her. Fraser said that Holm fancied Greta, and he had a habit of appointing attractive young women to the department. What makes him interesting is that he has a history. Fraser said there were rumours but didn't know any details. I've done some checking. Before coming to Malmö three years ago, he worked at a high school in Sundsvall. I've spoken to one of the head teachers. Holm left under a cloud. There was an official complaint made by one of his young colleagues, that he was stalking her. Out of school, he would suddenly turn up when she was in a bar or a shop, or would appear near her home, though he lived with his family in a totally different area. He also made inappropriate remarks to her. At first, she let it go because he was a senior colleague. But she acted when he grabbed her in an empty classroom. The school was going through a bad patch at the time; poor inspection report, a lot of problem kids, low morale among the staff. They didn't want any more bad publicity, so they persuaded the teacher to drop the complaint and told Holm to get a job elsewhere. To make sure that happened, they didn't give him a negative reference. So, basically, it was swept under the carpet and lucky Malmö got him instead.'

'Any record of physical violence?' Moberg asked.

'No. But the first incident never got to that stage. It might well have done with Greta.'

'Have you spoken to him?'

Westermark smirked. 'He's next on my list.'

They reached Worcester half an hour later than Ash had estimated. They pulled off the M5 motorway and found themselves heading down London Road towards the heart of the city. The trees here were only just starting to turn. Ahead was the tower of the cathedral. Ash, a cricket fan, recognised it at once. New Road, in his view, was one of the most picturesque grounds in the country. Rain was on the way. The sat nav directed them up a sharp turn to the right and along a street of red-brick terraced houses. To the left was a grassy park, beyond which the cathedral was revealed in all its graceful glory. In the distance, the Malvern Hills rose serenely from the Severn plain. Not as high as the Lakeland fells, they had a beauty of their own. Gentler, softer, more homely, they were sculptured onto the landscape like an artwork. Anita knew from Björn that his favourite English composer, Edward Elgar, had roamed their slopes to seek inspiration. She had liked the music as background, but Björn's real legacy to her had been Santana.

Ash brought the car to a standstill in front of Number 4. Vanessa Ridley's house stood in a small row at the top of the hill. Ash hesitated. He stretched his arms and yawned. 'I'm gasping for a fag.'

'That'll have to wait,' Anita said sternly. 'Vanessa Ridley comes first.'

Ash rang the doorbell.

'Sorry we're late. Traffic,' he added to his apology.

The woman standing in the doorway was fifty-two. Anita knew her exact age from Doris Little's family tree. Her shoulder-length, jet-black hair came courtesy of a bottle. The thick, red lipstick and black eye make-up fought their way through the perma tan. The brown slacks were tight and the cleavage of the cream blouse low, both showing off a well-preserved body. The smile of welcome wasn't faked, though. Neither was the half-smoked cigarette delicately protruding from the immaculate black-varnished fingernails of her left hand. Ash immediately noticed the rising smoke and gave Anita a smirk.

'I'm Detective Sergeant Kevin Ash from the Cumbria Constabulary and this is Inspector Anita Sundström from the Swedish police.'

Ridley gave Anita the once-over. 'If you want any make-up tips, you've come to the right place, pet.' The northern endearment was dripping in condescension.

'Can we come in?' Anita asked, ignoring the put-down.

'Of course. You've come about that bloke who does family trees, haven't you?' She stood aside to let them in. 'Is he in trouble?'

'You could say that,' answered Ash, who was already fishing in his pocket for his cigarettes.

'Right,' said Nordlund, 'let's get to Professor Sundström. I had him in again this afternoon. He was very unhappy because, somehow, the press have got wind of him being a suspect, despite nothing official coming from here. And the press also turned up on Anita's doorstep this morning. No one knew he was staying there except us.'

'Not quite true.' Moberg drummed his fingers on the table in irritation. 'I reported that information to Dahlbeck last night after you'd interviewed Sundström. Our revered commissioner was desperate for suspects so he had something to give the public to show we're on top of things. I said it was too early for that, but the moron must have leaked it to the newspapers.'

Hakim watched Westermark intently while the chief inspector was speaking. He hadn't batted an eyelid, but Hakim was sure as hell that it hadn't been Commissioner Dahlbeck who had tipped off the media.

'That apart, Sundström appears to be our main suspect. He'd had a relationship with the deceased in Uppsala, where she was a student. I don't know what went wrong, but she came down to Malmö to get away from him. This is borne out by what Fraser gathered from her comments. The professor was obviously still in love with her and tracked her down to Malmö. Except, according to his version of events, he couldn't find her and turned to Anita for help. He certainly has a potential motive. Jealousy. Can't take rejection. I get the impression he's a man who's used to getting his own way. Likes being in control.'

Nordlund reached over to the table and picked up a clear polythene bag containing a mobile phone. 'Karl's looked into mobile phone calls made by Björn Sundström and Jansson. Sundström phoned Greta Jansson fifty-seven times in the three weeks leading up to her disappearance. Seventeen afterwards. Maybe this was a ruse to make us think that he was still trying to get hold of her.'

'I've managed to track Greta Jansson's call log,' added Westermark. 'Though we haven't found her mobile, which is probably in the sea somewhere as we can't get any signal from it, I've discovered that she had an account with Telenor. She didn't actually make any calls on Friday, September the twenty-eighth but she received some.' He glanced at his notebook. 'Four from Sundström, which weren't answered. The last from Ulrika Lindén, which was made at the time we think Greta was in the unknown bar.'

'Anyhow,' Nordlund carried on, 'he's admitted he was in Malmö the weekend Greta disappeared – though, initially, he lied about that both to us and Anita – and his fingerprints were found in Greta's apartment. That gives him opportunity.' Nordlund put down the phone, picked up a plastic cup of water and took a careful sip. 'The trouble is, if Sundström is our prime suspect, why did he approach Anita to find Greta? All it did was draw attention to himself.'

'I would have thought that was obvious,' weighed in Westermark. 'He gets Anita to look for someone he's already killed. It makes him look like the worried boyfriend. He's the last person you'd expect to be guilty when the body was found. And it was bound to turn up eventually. Where his plan has backfired is that we know the relationship was over.'

'Wait a minute,' interrupted Moberg. 'Let's get back to the apartment.'

'Yes.' This was Thulin's first contribution. 'There's a strange pattern, or rather lack of the sort of pattern you'd expect. It's not what we found, it's what we didn't find. For example, the bed had been remade with fresh sheets. No semen stains, hairs, et cetera. So, either Greta had changed the sheets after getting up that morning or the murderer had changed them after the rape. Either way, any evidence there might have been has been obliterated. There was no sign of the old sheets, and she wasn't on the block's laundry rota for that day or the day before, which points to the second scenario. Then there's the fingerprints, or again, lack of. The bedside table had no prints at all. You'd expect it to be covered with both Greta's prints and possibly the previous owner's, as she had taken the apartment already furnished. There were no prints at all in the bath and on the bathroom basin. The only ones we found were on the toilet seat, which was raised by the way, and they belonged to Professor Sundström. The coffee table was wiped clean too. So was the kitchen sink. Greta's prints should have been evident in all these places.'

'That makes sense,' suggested Westermark. 'We know Sundström entered the apartment on the Saturday posing as Greta's father. He went back to clean up and cover his tracks.'

Thulin nodded. 'That could be true. But his prints did turn up on the fridge door and on the front door. In the living room, some of the books had his prints on them, as well as hers. It just seems odd that he was so careful in one respect, and yet left telltale signs in another.'

'Presumably, he was concentrating on the areas where he remembered he'd been with Greta the night before.'

'Westermark's got a point,' agreed Moberg.

Thulin shrugged.

'It does beg the question about why he borrowed the key from the neighbour,' offered Nordlund. 'If Sundström raped and killed Greta, then he would have got hold of her key. Her bag was missing, so the killer must have had access to it.'

'Maybe he just got rid of it at the same time he dumped the body,' Westermark interjected, 'and then realised later that he had to go back and sort out the apartment. After all, if you've just killed someone, you don't always act rationally.'

'Eva,' Moberg turned his attention back to Thulin, 'where do you think the rape and murder took place?'

'Though the evidence has been cleared away, I think the rape probably took place in the apartment, even though there's nothing in the forensics to support that theory. I think the lack of prints in the bedroom points to that being the location of the rape. But I'm not sure about the murder, though it could have happened there. There are no signs of a struggle. And there's the practical problem of getting a dead body out of the apartment and down to a car to take to the harbour.'

'So, to summarise,' Moberg said, 'Greta either met her killer in a bar, or she had a visitor when she returned. Then she could have been raped in the apartment and taken away and strangled somewhere else before being thrown into the harbour.'

'Couldn't he have raped her elsewhere, too?' ventured Hakim. Everybody looked at him in surprise, not because of what he had said, but because he had had the courage to voice an opinion in front of Moberg. 'If he raped her in the apartment, wouldn't it have been difficult to get her out of there if she was still alive? There would have to be some level of co-operation on her part.'

'Maybe he just coaxed her out,' ventured Wallen. 'She would be traumatised by the experience.' She had come across enough rape cases to know this could be possible.

'The perpetrator could have slipped in some Rohypnol,' Thulin said looking up from her notes. 'It's the rapist's drug of choice. Of course, if he had, there'd be no trace after all this time. But we know she'd been in a bar, so she may have been drunk. In such a state, she could have been led out of the apartment. Unfortunately, the blood and tissue samples don't show up any alcohol, but that doesn't mean she hadn't had a few drinks. Again, the sea has covered those tracks.'

'If, hypothetically, Rohypnol was used, where was it most likely to have been slipped into her drink?' Nordlund asked.

'Could have been the bar, but the physical effects can kick in within half an hour. That would have been risky. Much more likely back at the apartment.'

'OK. Anything else on the forensics side?' asked Moberg.

'Only this.' Thulin produced a small evidence bag. They could see it contained a small, gold hooped earring. 'Greta had pierced ears and this was still in one of them when she came out of the water. The other's missing. It either came off in the struggle or it's at the bottom of the sea.'

Moberg didn't seem to be listening. Something else was on his mind. 'Did Sundström have a car down here that weekend?' It was a pertinent question that no one had previously asked.

'I don't know,' said Nordlund shaking his head.

'And that goes for our other two suspects. I suggest you bloody well find out!'

CHAPTER 31

'Well, I never! Murdered!' Vanessa Ridley shook involuntarily. 'And he was sitting here in my lounge just a few months ago. Doesn't bear thinking about!'

Despite her protestations, Vanessa didn't let her cigarette spill any ash on the garish, swirly-patterned carpet. Instead, she delicately flicked it into a large glass ashtray on the occasional table next to her armchair. The whole room was caught in an eighties time warp, from the cream woodchip wallpaper, to the stone cladding around the fireplace. To Anita, the decor seemed totally inappropriate for a 19th-century terraced house. The sharp-eyed Ridley read her mind. 'Fort Royal Hill wasn't my idea, love. John liked old houses. I would have preferred one of those nice semis in St. John's across the river. But he gave me a free hand with the interior. And I've become fond of the place. It's also easy to walk into town. I work in Boots; on the cosmetics counter.' She stubbed out her cigarette.

'Meet all sorts of people in that job, I should imagine,' chimed in Ash, who had lit up the moment he took his seat next to Anita on the lime-green Dralon sofa. Being surrounded by tobacco smoke made her fidgety. She just wanted to get on and find out what they could. This was not the time for small talk, but she could see that Vanessa liked the detective sergeant and was relaxing. She would have to let Ash lead the questioning.

'Oh, yes. Fascinating. But not as interesting as some of the people you've come across, I'm sure,' she giggled knowingly.

'They certainly don't smell as nice as your customers, and their idea of a facial is usually rearranging your nose. But that's when I was working in Newcastle. They're easier to handle in Cumbria.' Vanessa gave an unladylike honking laugh.

'I love the Geordies, don't you? I was no stranger to Newcastle in the late seventies. Used to get the train across and go to Scamps. On Waterloo Street. Goodness, there were some wild nights. Sorry,' she said smiling sweetly at Ash, 'can I get you something to drink? A cup of tea or maybe something stronger? I know it's a bit early, but it's my day off.'

'I could murder a cuppa, please, Mrs Ridley.'

'It's Vanessa.' Turning to Anita. 'And you?'

'The same would be fine.'

Anita was impressed at how easily Ash ingratiated himself with these women and had them eating out of his hand. She couldn't see any of her male colleagues doing the same. Ash was able to turn on the empathy, so she was sure that if Vanessa knew anything, she would tell him.

Five minutes later, Vanessa returned with a tray with three bone china tea cups and saucers, and a plate with neatly arranged assorted biscuits.

'I'm amazed you can do police work with them glasses,' Vanessa remarked as she looked over the top of her tilted tea cup after taking her first sip. Ash couldn't hide his smile. 'Don't they get in the way? You see, I have contact lenses. No one notices.' As if to prove the point, she stared widely at Anita.

'I don't have a problem. It helps me see whether I'm dealing with good people, bad people, or just stupid people.'

'Let's get down to business, Vanessa,' Ash put in quickly before international co-operation vanished.

Anita's retort had totally passed over Vanessa's head. She turned her attention to Ash. Her flirty beam was a signal for him to proceed.

'Graeme Todd visited you in the summer. What was the purpose of his visit?'

'Carol. He was trying to find Carol. It was something to do with an old aunt of Carol's who had died and left some money. I didn't quite understand the ins and outs. I think he mentioned the Treasury.'

'This is Carol Ridley? She was your late husband's cousin?'

'Yes.'

'And you knew Carol through your husband?'

'No. I knew Carol before I ever met John. I was at school with Carol. Best friends. Truth be told,' she leant towards Ash confidentially, 'I had the hots for Michael. Carol's brother. Then the poor sod killed himself on his bike.' She took a contemplative sip of her tea. 'That's probably why I ended up with John. He had a look of Michael, but without the sense of fun. I don't think John ever approved of Michael. And he certainly didn't approve of Carol. She was a bit of a goer.' She gave Anita a sideways glance. 'She probably doesn't know what that means.'

'It means she liked to fuck.'

Despite her bronzed complexion, Vanessa blanched, and she was temporarily lost for words.

Again Ash intervened quickly. 'You used to knock around with Carol. Did she go on your trips to Newcastle?'

Vanessa still sounded stunned when she mouthed, 'Yes.'

'And did Carol marry?' Ash prompted.

She regained her composure. 'That caused a rumpus, that did. That's where she met Nicky. Newcastle. Scamps.'

'Why the rumpus?'

'Well, Mr Ridley, the butcher, didn't like Nicky. To be honest, he didn't like his kids having a good time. Methodist family. Went a bit funny after Michael's death. Seemed to blame Carol, though it had nothing to do with her. He got more disapproving and she got wilder. Nicky was the last straw. I don't think they ever spoke after her engagement. Carol moved over to Newcastle and moved in with Nicky. I was the only one from Carlisle at the wedding. There were only four of us at the registry office. Carol, Nicky, a friend of his and me. Went to the Gosforth Park Hotel afterwards. Real champagne. I'd never had it before.' She pulled a face. 'And precious little since. My John wasn't a boozer.'

'Why was Nicky the last straw?'

Vanessa pursed her lips and a smile of reminiscence crossed her tanned face. 'Nicky was beautiful. Mad as a hatter, of course. But so charming. He could charm the birds off the trees. He liked the good things in life. But he was only an art student and couldn't afford them. That's when he started to go bad. Thieving. Selling drugs. Didn't touch them himself, but with all those students around Newcastle, there was a big market for that type of thing. He was doing so well, he dropped out of university. I didn't see much of them after their marriage, though I kept in touch with Carol for a while. She was over there and I was in Carlisle. She got into different things. Like Nicky's plinky-plonky jazz stuff. Music with no tune. What's that all about? Nicky was nuts on that rubbish. Obsessed. I was more into Elton John. ABBA, of course.' She flashed her perfume-counter smile at Anita. 'Your lot. I've seen *Mamma Mia* three times at the theatre and seven times at the cinema. I've got the DVD too. They give you tunes.'

'And then?' encouraged Ash, who could see that Vanessa was only too happy to go off at tangents. Goodness knows what her customers had to put up with.

'Anyway, my social life changed and I started going out with John. We got married and eventually we moved down here.'

'What was Carol's married name?'

'Pew. She became Carol Pew.'

Anita noticed Ash tense.

'Pugh? P U G H?'

188

'No, P E W.'

Ash went quiet. Then he nodded his head at Anita. He obviously wanted her to carry on.

'Do you know what happened to Carol and Nicky?' Anita asked.

'Nothing good. I don't know what he was up to, but I heard they split up. He left the country for some reason. Escaping the law, no doubt. I think Carol got a divorce. Then she disappeared.'

'But you heard from her again?'

'That's right. I got a postcard out of the blue. It was weird. From Sweden of all places.'

'Do you still have it?'

Vanessa shook her head gravely. 'Sorry. Gave it to Graeme Todd.'

Anita felt deflated. She glanced at Ash, who seemed to be consumed by his own thoughts. Anita couldn't help being annoyed. He should be more involved.

'What did Carol say on the postcard?'

'That she was fine. Starting a new life there. Not to worry about her. That was it. No address or anything, so I couldn't get back to her. Maybe that's the way she wanted it. Maybe she was just embarrassed by the whole Nicky thing. Fresh start. I don't mean to be rude, but why the hell would you want to live in Sweden?'

'We've got ABBA.'

'Fair point, but I wouldn't want to sit in a snowdrift for nine months of the year.'

Anita couldn't be bothered to contradict her.

'Can you remember what the card was of? The picture.'

'I can, actually. A whole lot of old stones. I thought it was a strange thing to send.'

'Old stones?'

'Yeah. Just sticking out of the ground.'

'In a circle?' Anita's mind was quickly indexing all the ancient stone circles which were well-known enough to be on a postcard.

'No, it wasn't in a circle.' Vanessa pondered for a moment. 'I know. It was like a boat.'

Anita felt that little tingle of excitement in the pit of her stomach that she got when she stumbled across something really significant in a case.

'I know exactly where that is.'

CHAPTER 32

Anita and Ash were sitting on a bench in the park on Fort Royal Hill overlooking Worcester Cathedral. The dark clouds were thickening and the Malvern Hills had disappeared in a bank of rain that seemed to be heading across the plain towards the city. They were on part of the site of the Battle of Worcester of 1651, in which Oliver Cromwell's Parliamentarians defeated a young Charles II and his Scottish allies during the English Civil War. Anita was also in a fighting mood by the time they had left Vanessa Ridley's home. Why had Ash gone AWOL half way through their interview?

'At least we know the area that Carol Ridley, sorry Pew, lives in. It all fits with Graeme Todd going to Skåne. The stone ship is a place called Ales Stenar.'

Ash didn't answer.

'I suppose it's our equivalent of Stonehenge, but not as old and a lot smaller. There must be about sixty upright stones that are arranged like a Viking ship, on a flat-topped hill overlooking the Baltic. It was some place of worship and sacrifice.' Still no reaction. 'The point is,' she said tetchily, 'it's near a place called Ystad. And that's where Graeme Todd was last seen alive.'

Ash pulled out his packet of cigarettes. He silently offered it to Anita. She huffily refused. He slowly took one out himself and popped it in his mouth, but didn't attempt to get out his lighter.

191

'At least we got that out of her.' Anita couldn't keep the increasing irritation out of her voice.

At last Ash took out his lighter, flicked it on and drew on his cigarette. His gaze was fixed on the cathedral tower as his exhalation of smoke whorled in its direction. 'We got a lot more than that, Inspector.'

Anita stared at him in surprise. They'd established the name of the husband and Vanessa's youthful friendship with Carol, but what else was there?

'It's not Carol that struck a chord, but her husband.'

'Pew. As in the church pew.'

'Nicky Pew.'

'You know of him?'

'Oh, yes. He was involved in a famous case back in the North East.'

'Were you on it?'

'No. Just before my time. A year before I joined Northumbria Police. But people were still full of the tale.'

'I think I will have a cigarette. Then you'd better tell me.'

They were both smoking when Ash started.

'Nicky Pew was a flash local villain. Very charming and very dangerous, just as Vanessa said back there. Lived the high life in Darras Hall. That's a posh ghetto outside Newcastle, near the airport. He did all sorts of things, but well-planned robberies were his *forte*. He had a gang who carried out the raids. The clever bit was that he never did a job on his home turf. So the local cops never had a reason to pick him up. Police all over the country were chasing shadows. He did a job in Essex when I was down there. A fancy jeweller's in Chelmsford. But no one could ever prove it or find evidence. His house was searched a number of times; and those of his associates. Never found anything. He was too smart. Behind the bonhomie, he was ruthless. Apparently, one of his gang fell foul of him and disappeared. They reckon the bloke is somewhere out in the North Sea.'

Ash took out a second cigarette before continuing. The sky was now almost black above the cathedral.

'Then he broke his criminal pattern and pulled off a local job. A consortium of jewellers was buying a large consignment of diamonds from Amsterdam dealers. They were to be brought in by ship to North Shields and handed over to a representative of the consortium. It took place at night so as not to attract attention. Anyhow, Nicky Pew somehow got wind of it and must have thought it was too good an opportunity to miss. But something went wrong on the night and a security guard got shot.'

'So he was now a murderer.'

Ash gave a grim smile. 'Well, at least a murder that could be proved. Of course, he had to get out. Fled the country.'

Big, fat raindrops began to plop. Ash looked up. 'Better get back.'

They stood up and made their way as quickly as possible to his Honda. By the time they reached the car, they were both soaked. As they sat inside, the rain streamed down the windscreen, and the view in front of them was obscured. Anita took her glasses off and began to wipe them dry.

'You should take them off more often,' Ash commented.

She ignored him and put them back on firmly. 'So, you think that Graeme Todd tracked down Nicky Pew through Carol?'

'Not that simple.'

'Why?'

'Nicky Pew died in 1994.'

Ash brought over a pint for himself and an orange juice for Anita. They were in a pub on London Road. Ash had said that he was buggered if he was going to drive all the way back in the torrential rain. Anita knew it was just an excuse to have a drink. She was quite happy to comply, as they had a lot to absorb after their chat with Vanessa Ridley.

'Thank you,' Anita said as he put her drink down on the

stained beer mat.

'My pleasure, Inspector.'

'It's Anita. You can call me Anita.'

He gave an exaggerated sigh of relief. 'That's better. I didn't want to upset a female colleague, especially a visitor to our shores. And it's Kevin.'

They virtually had the bar to themselves, as the rain was keeping customers away. Just one regular, who had obviously been in position long before the heavens opened.

'Why did you go quiet in there?'

'Well, because Nicky Pew's name came up. I knew it rang a bell.'

'That wasn't all, though.'

Ash screwed up his eyes as he faced Anita across the table. 'You're not just a pretty face. A very pretty face, if that's not an unacceptable thing to say to a female officer.'

'It is. Back home you'd be halfway to a gender appropriateness course by now.' She grimaced. 'But, as you've just bought me a drink and I've taken one of your cigarettes, I'll let it pass.'

Ash pushed his seat back from the table and stretched wearily. He settled back before he spoke. His voice was quiet. 'The other thing. There was a detective who made his name on the Pew case. It's not someone I want anything to do with, but we've no choice.'

Anita looked at Ash enquiringly. 'Roller?'

''Fraid so.'

'Well, you've got to be totally professional about it. Put your feelings aside.'

Ash toyed with his pint glass. 'If I'd found someone else since... you know, Leanne, it might be different. But no one has come along.' Then he snorted. 'Pathetic, isn't it?'

'Not at all.' Anita could see the vulnerability behind the affable exterior. She felt some sympathy.

'And you? Have you been close to anyone since

whatshisname? Sorry, can't remember...'

'Björn.'

'Since Björn?'

'Yes. There's someone.' The stab of guilt she felt had more to do with the fact that she hadn't even thought about Ewan for a couple of days. Had she deliberately shoved him to the back of her mind? Maybe it was because he had been trying to tell her something and she hadn't had the time to let him. Yet it also felt strange that she was acknowledging to a virtual stranger that Ewan was part of her life.

'Is he in the force?'

'No. It's complicated.' Ash took the hint and didn't press any further. 'Anyhow, let's get back to Nicky and Carol Pew.'

'There's not much to tell. After the robbery, a couple of the gang were picked up locally. Roller Weatherley did the collaring. Pew and the fourth member of the gang disappeared. But then a few months later, they surfaced in Australia. I know Weatherley went out there and came back with Dobson.'

'And what of Pew?'

'He died in a chase, apparently. I don't know the circumstances but Weatherley was there when it happened.'

'Did they ever retrieve the diamonds?'

He gave a hollow laugh. 'No.'

'Could Carol have them?'

'Now that's a thought. It might explain why Graeme Todd believed he was onto a winner.'

Oxie was an unremarkable satellite town of Malmö. It was an unimaginative urban sprawl of neat, featureless houses, typical of today's Sweden, thought Nordlund. The twenty-minute drive from the polishus had taken them past the large Jägersro course, the home of the Swedish Derby, and one of the few tracks that accommodated both horseracing and trotting. His wife had enjoyed the odd visit there. He hadn't been back since her death.

Westermark parked the car in front of the swimming pool. They had already been to Andreas Holm's house. His anxious wife had been alarmed at two detectives turning up at her door. Nordlund had explained it was to do with the death of one of her husband's colleagues and reassured her that they were just making routine enquiries. She told them that each Tuesday – he worked a four-day week – Andreas took their youngest daughter, Helena, to a baby swimming class at the local pool.

They were greeted by the smell of damp and chlorine as they went through the glass doors of the main entrance. There was a small reception and an area where mothers could feed their young. Three baby chairs were stacked up in the corner. Through a glass wall they could see a small pool. Beyond was the main pool. In the former, an enthusiastic woman was in the centre of a circle of parents who were clutching their offspring. They were singing, and manoeuvring the babies in the water in time with the rhythm of the song. Nordlund watched with a twinge of envy. Hannah had had two miscarriages. He would have loved to have had children. And grandchildren to keep him occupied in his old age.

'There he is,' said Westermark pointing at a rotund man with flattened red hair. He wasn't wearing his glasses. He appeared to be enjoying the session and was joining in the singing enthusiastically. 'Shall we go in?'

Nordlund went over to the reception desk and asked how long the session was due to last. He was told five more minutes. 'We'll wait.'

'Don't you think we should just go in? It'll put the pressure on. He looks the sort of fat shit who molests women.'

'No, we wait,' Nordlund replied firmly.

Fifteen minutes later, a bespectacled Holm emerged from the changing rooms with young Helena in his arms and a backpack slung over his shoulder. Already, a couple of mothers had set up the highchairs for their babies and were busily feeding them. One yowled as it refused the proffered yoghurt.

'Andreas Holm?'

Holm stopped and looked at Nordlund. And then at a scowling Westermark.

'Yes,' he replied warily.

'I'm Inspector Henrik Nordlund and this is Inspector Karl Westermark. We'd like a word. About your colleague, Greta Jansson.'

Nordlund could see that Holm was embarrassed to be confronted in such a public area.

'I really should get Helena home. It's time for her feed.'

'We could take you to headquarters in Malmö if you prefer,' Westermark said nastily, conscious that the mothers were paying more attention to what was going on than to their children.

'We can do it here,' Holm said quickly. 'But outside.'

Nordlund opened the door. It was chilly outside and Holm hugged Helena to his chest as the baby began to whimper unhappily.

'Let's go to your car,' suggested Nordlund.

It took a few minutes before Holm managed to secure Helena in the baby seat in the back of the vehicle. He sat in the back alongside his daughter, who had a dummy in her mouth and was fiddling with a woollen doll. Nordlund and Westermark sat in the front.

'I can understand your reticence about talking to the police,' Nordlund began. 'Especially after what happened in Sundsvall.'

'How do you know about that?'

'We're bloody policemen,' said Westermark. 'That's what we do. Check up on creeps like you.'

'It was blown out of all proportion. The woman was delusional. Nearly ruined my life and my family's.'

'But do your present employers know about your past?' Westermark's smile couldn't have been more unfriendly.

Holm lowered his head so he didn't have to look at the piercing blue eyes of the blond detective who had swivelled round from the driving seat of the car.

'We're not here about Sundsvall. It's Greta Jansson we're interested in.' Nordlund's measured tones managed to take the edge off the hostile atmosphere. 'Is it true that you appointed her?'

Holm found it easier addressing the older detective. 'Yes. She was a late appointment. The person who'd been lined up for the job found another school. Probably a better one. But that wouldn't be hard. Greta was available at short notice.'

'Did you get close to her? As a colleague, I mean.'

'Not really. She wasn't with us long enough.'

'Was she particularly friendly with any of the other staff?'

'Not really... I suppose Alex Fraser. Yes, they seemed to get on well.' Nordlund and Westermark exchanged glances.

'Do you know if she was dating anyone?'

'Oh, no.'

'That sounds very definite.' Westermark immediately latched on to Holm's quick reply.

Holm became flustered. 'Well... that's what I heard anyway.'

'Did you know where she lived?'

'No. Yes. I remember her telling me. It was close to the school.'

'Did you stalk her?'

Holm was forced to look at Westermark's craning head. 'No!' He spoke so vehemently that he set Helena off crying. It took a couple of minutes to settle her down.

'Where were you on the night of September the twenty-eighth?' Nordlund asked. 'It was a Friday.'

Holm made a great play of thinking back. 'Greta didn't turn up on the Monday, so it was the Friday before. I worked late that night.'

'Late on a Friday?' Westermark asked incredulously.

'I had lots of marking.'

'Then what did you do?'

'Went home. And that's it.'

'Can your wife vouch for you?'

Holm blinked nervously. 'Not exactly.'

'What do you mean by that? Either she can or she can't.'

'We've a weekend place. Nybrostrand. Outside Ystad. Next to the beach.'

'I know it,' confirmed Nordlund.

'Lamija took the girls there on Friday afternoon.'

'Lamija?' Westermark queried.

'She was born in Bosnia.'

Westermark didn't hide his contempt. 'So you were by yourself on Friday night?'

'I went across first thing Saturday morning for the rest of the weekend. Our last trip of the summer.'

'And your wife drove over?' asked Nordlund.

'Erm... no, she didn't. Took the train. I had the car at work.'

'So, you have no alibi,' Westermark said, pointing out the obvious.

Holm looked unhappy.

'This car?' Nordlund asked.

Holm nodded.

'We'll drive you home. Then Inspector Westermark will drive it back to headquarters.'

'Why?' Holm protested.

'Because we'll need to strip it down to see if Greta Jansson was in it the night she died.'

CHAPTER 33

Anita woke up late. The sun was peeking through the curtains and cast a beam of light through the glass of water by her bedside. She had spent the night at Jennifer Todd's. Anita had insisted, despite the late hour, that they call into Jennifer's to give her an update. Ash, tired after two long drives in the day, just wanted to go home. After a cup of tea, he had gone and Jennifer was adamant that Anita stay the night. Anita realised that Jennifer wanted some company. She could see that Jennifer needed to keep connected to reality, and helping to find out who was responsible for her husband's murder was her way of doing that. Until Graeme's body was finally released and returned to Britain, there would be no chance of closure and moving on. However, the news from Worcester was encouraging, even if it did do little to stem the emotional pain that haunted her every waking moment.

There was a light knock on the door. Anita managed a sleepy 'Yes?'

Jennifer came in with a mug of tea. 'Thought you'd probably need this. I'll have breakfast for you when you're ready.'

As Anita sipped her tea, she started to marshal her thoughts. The visit to Worcester had given the investigation a kick start. There was now a plausible reason for Graeme Todd to find Carol Pew other than the paltry inheritance she might get if the claim on Doris Little's estate was accepted. But Anita had to admit that that was based purely on the assumption that Carol had got hold of the stolen diamonds. What they now needed to know was what happened to Carol after her husband's diamond robbery ended in murder. Ash was going to make some calls this morning, probably followed by a trip across to the North East. It was a journey that Todd himself had made after his visit to Vanessa Ridley. But who had he gone to see? They would need detailed background on the whole Nicky Pew case, and one person knew it more intimately than anyone. If that meant Ash having to see Deputy Chief Constable Royce Weatherley, so be it. He would have to put his personal animosity aside for the sake of the investigation. She had sympathy for his predicament, but she wouldn't let it get in the way of discovering the truth and catching the killer. And from where she was standing, that person might be Carol Pew – or someone acting on her behalf. She didn't even know what she looked like. Vanessa Ridley didn't possess a photo of her. Ash was going to see what Northumbria Police had on file. As Pew's wife, she must have come under the spotlight at some stage.

As Anita showered, her mind was still whirring. She must ring Lasse to see how he was coping with Björn. She still couldn't bring herself to think that her ex-husband was a killer. It was bad enough for her to contemplate – it would be shattering for Lasse. With Björn in mind, she should also phone Nordlund and find out what the latest was on the Greta Jansson investigation. And she needed to report to Moberg. At least she had something to tell him now. Then there was Ewan. He'd just have to wait until she got back. But then her priority was to discover what he had wanted to tell her. Instead of feeling refreshed after her shower, she just felt stressed. Why was life so damned complicated?

Björn Sundström hadn't slept well. He stared into the mirror above the basin as he brushed his teeth. Neat stubble was turning into a beard. He couldn't be bothered to do anything about it.

He had too much on his mind. The grotty bed and breakfast he had moved into wasn't the kind of accommodation he was used to on his many conference and colloquium jaunts around the world. But it was in an area of the city where he could keep a low profile. He had returned to Anita's apartment to find that the press were still camped on the doorstep. Who the hell had tipped them off he didn't know, other than it must have come from inside the police. He had a left-winger's natural distrust of authority, and the police in particular. Anita had been an aberration. He had never taken to any of her colleagues and had gradually made a point of avoiding them. Basically, he didn't trust them, and the last few days had only heightened that feeling. Anita had been different. She was almost too honest for her own good, and had a refreshingly liberal attitude to everything from politics to immigration. She didn't have that fear of a changing society that troubled so many Swedes.

He stopped brushing and dropped the toothbrush into the horrid plastic mug next to the mirror. Maybe it was the mess he was now in that made him view his former marriage in a brighter light. They had been so happy at one time. The sex had been terrific. He may have been her teacher, but she had been a willing and inventive pupil. Strangely, he had no inkling of her subsequent love life. Lasse had never been very forthcoming. On the other hand, his own had been an open book. Lasse's visits to Uppsala had usually coincided with a new woman. Had any of the details got back to Anita? Suddenly it mattered what she thought of him.

He rinsed out his mouth. More importantly, he knew he was in a bad position. The police wanted to take in his car. He had handed over his spare set of keys. That obnoxious younger detective was going to Uppsala to pick the car up today. Why had he driven down that weekend when he could have got the train or flown? He hadn't thought it through. He had just wanted to find Greta. And now the university had got wind of his involvement with the murder. He had been told that when he had called a colleague from a pay phone to cancel his lectures and tutorials. They weren't happy, and he was sure to have received a lot of irate calls on his mobile, which was still at the polishus. He tore himself away from the mirror. He hadn't liked what he had seen.

'You shouldn't have.' She meant it. Anita surveyed with some dismay the huge English cooked breakfast that Jennifer Todd had laid out before her. This was definitely one of the 5 indulgent days. She took a sip of coffee and tried not to pull a face. Through the window she could see the main part of the village and the market cross. An elderly couple were standing next to the bus stop waiting to go to Keswick, the only service available from Fellbeck. And Wednesday was the only day the bus ran.

'What time will Kevin Ash be here?' Jennifer Todd had joined Anita at the breakfast table. She, too, had a coffee in her hand. Her breakfast had been eaten very early. She found sleep difficult since Graeme had first disappeared.

'Not sure. He had a few calls to make. We're also after a photo of Carol. We don't actually know what she looks like.'

Jennifer put her cup down thoughtfully while Anita tentatively cut herself a small slice of Cumberland sausage.

'I've just remembered something.' Anita watched Jennifer intently as she ate her sausage, which was far spicier than she had expected; it was rather tasty. 'Graeme was always closeted in his office, and when I went in one night, he was trawling through a foreign website. He told me it was Swedish. Anyway, he became very animated. "I've found her!" That's what he said.'

'Found who?'

'I kind of ignored it at the time. He was always finding people – that was his job. So I just forgot about it. But now we know there's a Swedish connection with Carol Pew, I think it must have been her.'

'On a particular internet site?'

'I didn't really see it properly, but I think it was probably a newspaper.'

'Was it an article or a picture?'

'I think it was a photo. But I can't remember what it was of.'

Anita put down her fork. 'Jennifer, please think very, very carefully. Try and imagine that you're back in the office with Graeme. There's the computer screen. On it is a photograph. Try and think.'

Todd shook her head slowly. 'No.'

Disappointed, Anita returned to her breakfast.

'I do remember Graeme saying something about jazz.'

Anita's head jerked up. 'Well, Nicky Pew was a jazz fanatic. Could it have been a jazz group? A concert? Some event?'

'Could have been a concert. I've got a feeling there may have been a number of people in the photo. Yes, now I think about it, there were. I suppose the woman Graeme was getting so excited about must have been in there somewhere.'

Moberg was eating a large bun. Nordlund didn't want to hazard a guess at what it contained. He assumed that it was the chief inspector's second breakfast.

'I've just had a call from Anita Sundström. She's starting to get somewhere. I'll fill you in later. But I'm more concerned about Greta Jansson at the moment. Where are we with the various cars?'

'We've got Holm's and Fraser's cars in. Eva Thulin's forensic team will be giving them the once over. Westermark flew up to Stockholm first thing this morning and he'll bring Professor Sundström's car down from Uppsala. We should know Thulin's findings in the next couple of days.'

'Well, that should turn up something.'

'That's if the killer got her to the harbour by car. It's

walkable from the apartment.'

Moberg huffed impatiently, 'Don't throw in any negatives, Henrik. We've only got these three suspects. So, the sooner we get evidence on one of them, the better. My money's on the professor. What do you think?'

Nordlund had had plenty of time to ponder the question. 'On the face of it, Professor Sundström certainly seems to have the best motive if Greta rejected him. It's a hard thing for a man to take. Rapes her, then realises what he's done. And he has the most to lose if the rape comes out. He's the one with the high-profile career.'

'Exactly my thoughts.'

'Westermark thinks both of Greta's colleagues had a thing for her. I've sent Hakim off to the school to talk to other members of staff to see if we can actually establish that. If Fraser's and Holm's interest was unhealthy, and she spurned any advances then...' Nordlund shrugged. 'Whoever did rape her was let into her apartment. So we can assume that she knew her attacker.'

Moberg happily finished the last of his bun. 'I don't think this will take long to clear up.' Then he looked at Nordlund and his faced dropped. 'OK, Henrik, I sense a "but".'

'You may be right. But the killer was smart enough and, I suppose, brave enough to go back to the apartment and try and get rid of any traces of his being there. Rape might have been the result of an emotional, overheated reaction to a situation. But cleaning up the apartment was done with cool deliberateness. Do any of our suspects fit that dual personality?'

'Oh, yes. Professor Sundström smacks of being just such a guy.'

CHAPTER 34

Though they didn't leave Penrith until the afternoon, the day stayed fine throughout their drive to Newcastle. They took the motorway up to Carlisle before turning onto the A69 and heading east. At Greenhead, Ash decided to take the scenic route along the old Military Road to avoid the convoy of lorries they were stuck behind. To her left, Anita could see the outline of some of the remains of Hadrian's Wall. Now a World Heritage Site, it had been built by Emperor Hadrian as a way of defining the edge of his empire. Everything south of the wall, stretching as far as Africa, was civilised Roman territory; beyond was nothing but barbarians. Ash had some colleagues who still thought the same.

As the road crested a ridge outside Once Brewed, Ash pointed out a lone sycamore tree in a deep dip in a crag along which the Wall was straddled. It was an image discordant with a bleak landscape dominated by rough grass, bracken and bogs. 'That's where they filmed Robin Hood. The one with Kevin Costner. A fugitive kid climbs that tree and Robin Hood saves him from the Sheriff of Nottingham's nasty henchmen.'

Anita nodded in recognition. Though she was no film lover, Lasse had made her watch it.

'And is Weatherley your Sheriff of Nottingham?'

Ash snorted. 'Not exactly. Just as slimy, but there's no denying he must be a good policeman. His record speaks for itself.'

'And where are we meeting him?'

'He's going to some official dinner, so that's why we're going directly to his home and not to police headquarters in Ponteland. He lives in Gosforth. That's posh to you and me. Success has its rewards.'

Earlier, they'd picked up her things from the Carrock Guest House. It was unlikely that the investigation would take Anita back to Cumbria. She and Ash would seek answers in Newcastle, and then she would return to Sweden and start the search for Carol Pew. She had told Ash about the jazz photograph that Graeme Todd had found. One of their priorities would be to find a likeness of Carol, though it was likely to be nearly twenty years out of date. Once they had something to go on, she would get Hakim to trawl the internet and through the local Skåne newspapers and find a jazz event. If they could match the two, then they were going in the right direction.

They headed down a steep road and found themselves stopped at the traffic lights at an old single-file bridge over the North Tyne at Chollerford, next to the George Hotel. Ash gave a sidelong look. He smacked his lips. 'Could do with a quick pint.'

'No,' said Anita firmly. She could sense that he was nervous. She could see this meeting with Weatherley was going to be difficult for him. 'Why don't we stop for a smoke?'

Ash managed to coax his car up the bank on the other side of the bridge. He was reduced to second gear to reach the first bit of level ground. He pulled into a lay-by. Beyond was a small church perched on the hill top.

'Why don't we go over there?' Anita suggested.

They wandered over a field full of grazing sheep, and entered the churchyard. Round the back of the church the view was unbroken. The late-afternoon sunlight cast a rich yellow glow on the rough-hewn terrain that rose and fell all the way to the horizon. Leaning against the dry-stone church wall, Ash lit two cigarettes and passed one to Anita.

'I love this countryside. Essex is beautiful, but it's too ordered. Too flat. This is untamed,' he said, with a flourish of his hand. 'The main drawback is that it's too bloody cold.'

'If you think this is cold, try a winter in northern Sweden.'

Ash laughed. 'Fair enough. Shouldn't complain. My girls think I'm a sissy because I'm always complaining about the weather. They were brought up here, so don't know any different. But the young don't seem to feel the cold. You should see them in Newcastle on a Friday night wearing next to nothing.'

'You're joking!'

'No. Even in the middle of winter.' He shook his head in disbelief.

'Why?' Anita couldn't conceive of going out in the cold without wrapping up, even on a night out with friends.

'Don't ask me. My sister says it's getting like that in Essex, too. Some of the sights are not for the faint-hearted either. It's worse when you've got daughters that age and you wonder what the hell they're getting up to. Safer for me to live in ignorance in Cumbria, I think.'

'My son is the same. He met this awful girl who then dumped him, and he changed completely. He was very level-headed, but now I don't know what to do with him.' She'd managed to track Lasse down earlier and he'd reported, with what sounded like relief, that his father had left the apartment and was staying somewhere else in town. The press had disappeared too. He had been his now-usual monosyllabic self and couldn't speak for long, as he was going out to meet somebody. Anita hadn't managed to worm out of him who it was before he'd ended the conversation with, 'Sorry, Mamma, I've got to go.'

'Bloody kids!' she agreed with Ash.

To take her mind off Lasse and the sense of loss she was feeling as a mother, she changed the subject back to the case in hand.

'What's the itinerary?'

'Roller first. Whatever he has to tell us will probably dictate our next move. But afterwards, I thought we might visit the scene of the crime.'

'Pardon?'

'Pew's diamond heist. See where this all began. It's near where I've booked us in. A Premier Inn in North Shields. Then tomorrow, I'll go to the North Shields nick and get all they have on Pew and the robbery. Then it should be easy enough for your lot to find Carol Pew in Sweden.'

'Don't sell the skin before you've shot the bear.'

It was Ash's turn to say, 'Pardon?'

Anita smiled. 'Swedish expression. It's the same as don't count your chickens before they're hatched.'

'I like shooting the bear better. Must remember that one.'

'I've already been onto Malmö about tracing Carol Pew – or Ridley; she may have reverted to her maiden name.' That morning, Anita had managed to get hold of Hakim, who had been at Kungsskolan doing interviews when she called. He said he would look into it as soon as he got back to the office. Other than moaning about Westermark, he'd seemed chirpy. 'I suspect that it's not going to be that simple, though. She might have a completely different name. Married again, or just wants to disappear.'

Ash tossed his finished cigarette over the wall.

'I still don't really understand why she would want to kill Todd. That's if she's responsible at all. Even if she did have the money from the diamonds, surely there's nothing that Todd could have done to put her in jeopardy. Torturing and killing someone is a bit of an overreaction.'

'Perhaps he was blackmailing her.'

'But with what? How could he prove anything?'

Anita had to admit that Ash was right.

Ash watched her finish her cigarette.

'I have to say, Anita, to use another British expression, we might be barking up the wrong tree.'

They came off the central motorway and up onto the road that crossed Newcastle's Town Moor. Which was exactly what it was – a large expanse of green, right in the middle of the city. Cows could be seen grazing in the distance. It was a surreal urban sight. As they headed down the bank towards Gosforth, Anita could see a line of large, smart houses with gardens backing onto the open space. At the end, there was a big apartment block that commanded fantastic views across the moor, the city, and Gateshead beyond. 'Expensive,' Ash commented.

The traffic lights at the bottom of the hill filtered them past a Kwik Fit garage and Ash took an immediate turn to the left. They were in Montagu Avenue, and now Anita could see the fronts of the grand residences, stylistically all at odds with each other. Ash drew the car up outside one, which was pretending to be late Georgian. It was a huge, cream-stuccoed edifice; covered in Virginia creeper, russet and gold in its autumn glory. The portal, flanked by Ionic pillars, had obviously been an afterthought and seemed out of perspective with the rest of the house. What had once been the front garden was now paved over, and a large four-by-four and a slick Mercedes were parked in front of a garage the size of a normal semi. A fierce laurel hedge lined the boundary wall and screened the ground floor from curious eyes. Ash turned off the engine and slid out his key. He just sat there looking straight ahead.

Anita put a hand on his. 'Kevin, don't let the situation get to you.' The last thing she wanted was this vital discussion dissolving into an unseemly personal vendetta.

He glanced down at her hand, which she quickly withdrew.

'Don't worry. I'll wait until he tells us what we need to know... then I'll kick the shit out of him.'

*

Mrs Weatherley ushered Anita and Ash into the spacious sitting room, explaining that her husband would be down soon. She was quite short with them and her body language made it obvious that she didn't approve of Royce bringing work home in the form of junior detectives cluttering up her home. A large flat-screen TV dominated the room in its position above the mock-Adam mantelpiece, which displayed a row of what looked like Royal Staffordshire figurines. A coal-effect fire created the illusion of a warm hearth. The room was big enough for three sizeable, heavy, black-leather sofas, which sank into a thick, white pile. Why were the British so obsessed with carpets? Anita idly wondered. Scandinavia was colder but, except for the odd scattering of rugs, Swedish floors were bare. All this compacted fibre everywhere can't be that hygienic; there'd even been carpet in the bathroom in the guest house she had just stayed in. Unlike the figurines, the art on the walls was not genuine. Even Royce Weatherley couldn't afford a real Constable or Van Gogh. A huge gilt mirror adorned the wall opposite the fireplace. Next to a silver drinks tray on a highly polished mahogany table, a large, silver-framed photograph showed the uniformed Deputy Chief Constable and his wife at an official function. In the growing gloom, Anita spied through the French windows one of the neatest gardens she had ever seen. It was laid out mainly to lawn, in the middle of which was a fountain presided over by a trio of cherubs delicately balanced on a central pedestal. Flowerbeds and rockeries bordered the lawn, and in the far reaches of the garden were crammed conifers and rhododendrons.

When Weatherley appeared, he certainly didn't look the Don Juan that she had expected. He wasn't much taller than Ash. Anita thought him presentable rather than handsome. His fair hair was swept back at the front. The darting eyes were sharp and observant as he took in his visitors. Maybe it was this air of confidence that had attracted Mrs Ash. He was wearing a dinner jacket and black tie.

'Sorry about the monkey suit. Rotary Club.' The accent was a strange kind of suppressed Geordie. Somewhere along the line he had tried to lose his local twang and hadn't quite managed it. To compensate, he overemphasised the wrong syllables, making his style of speech somewhat ridiculous.

'Well, if it isn't Cockney Ash.' He didn't offer to shake Ash's hand. 'How's life among the Cumbrian sheep shaggers?'

'Fine.' Anita could see how restrained Ash was being.

'And the missus?'

This time Ash flinched. 'I wouldn't know.'

'And this must be our guest from Sweden.' His face lit up momentarily.

'Inspector Anita Sundström of the Skåne County Police,' said Anita introducing herself.

Weatherley held out his hand. 'Delighted.' Anita shook it. 'Take a seat, Inspector.' As an afterthought. 'And you, Ash.'

As Anita and Ash took their places on the same sofa, Weatherley wandered over to the drinks tray and poured himself a large Scotch from a crystal decanter.

'I would offer you one, but you're both on duty. Rules is rules,' he smirked, before taking a long sip of his whisky. He moved over to the fireplace and stood watching them. 'Now, what's this all about?'

Ash briefly explained about the circumstances of the death of Graeme Todd in Malmö and how they had discovered that the connection was probably Carol Pew.

'What we need from you, sir, is a background to Nicky Pew and what you know of Carol's movements since he died.'

'So, you think Carol may have ended up in Sweden? Interesting.' Weatherley walked over to the drinks tray again and refreshed his glass. This time when he came back, he sat down on a sofa opposite his visitors.

'Well, you've come to the world authority on the Pews. Never met him properly until his end, but Nicky was quite a character. Charismatic, some said. A villain, of course, but up until that night in North Shields, he hadn't pulled any jobs on our patch. Presumably you know about the diamond shipment that was being collected that night on Commission Quay?'

Ash nodded. 'I've told the Inspector.'

'How he found out about it in the first place we've never discovered. Security was tight. It could have been anyone: one of the jewellery consortium, a Dutch source, someone at Imerson's Security or, dare I say it, one of us. I was based in North Shields at the time and there was a rumour that someone was in Nicky's pocket. But nothing was ever proved or fingers pointed. Of course, all hell broke loose when the security officer was killed. They made their escape with the diamonds across the river. That was a clever touch because they could disappear easily in South Shields on the other side. We found the dinghy abandoned.'

'But you caught two of the gang pretty quickly, as I understand it.'

Weatherley's eyes brightened. 'Yes, there were four of them. Nicky Pew, the brains; George Dobson, his right-hand man; young Billy Hump was the driver, or in this case, the man in the dinghy. And then the enforcer, Gary Chapman. He was a real hard bastard. Sorry, Inspector, forgive the language.'

'I'm fine with it.'

'Two days later, I picked up Hump and Chapman in a flat in Walker.'

'How did you find them?'

'Anonymous tip-off. To this day, I don't know who. Maybe a neighbour had seen something suspicious. Mind you, in these close-knit communities they don't easily give up their own. But it was a good start.'

'Are they still in prison?'

'Chapman died inside. Cancer. Billy Hump was released from Durham in 2007. His sentence was less because he hadn't been on the quayside when the shooting took place.'

Ash looked hopefully at Anita. 'Maybe we should have a word with him.'

'I'm afraid you're a bit late for that. He died in a hit-and-run.'

'When?'

'Two nights ago. Report came in from the Hexham station. Acomb.'

'Do they know who did it?' Ash couldn't hide his disappointment at the news.

'Not that I've heard. It'll be some drunken hick out there, no doubt. Hump was a charva and won't be missed.'

'What about the others?' asked Anita.

'Pew and George Dobson got out of the country. Dobson was spotted in Sydney some months later. I went over to help with the investigation. The local police found Dobson and he was brought back here, eventually. He's been in Her Majesty's Prison Doncaster since 1996.'

Ash turned to Anita, 'So, Todd didn't visit Dobson, but someone up here.'

'Hump?' Anita suggested.

'Possibly. Sorry, sir, carry on.'

'Well, to cut a long story short, we tracked Pew down to an area on the New South Wales coast around Wollongong. We hadn't got much out of Dobson, but he had let that morsel slip. I was down under for about a fortnight. One evening, I was accompanying a local patrol in Austinmer, near the beach there. We were doing house-to-house. At one particular house the door was answered by a woman. Attractive. About forty. When I showed her a photo of Pew, she started. She tried to cover up and said she hadn't seen anyone like that. But I knew she was lying. I asked myself in. There was an empty whisky bottle on the table. Then the back door opened. I'd never met the guy who walked in with a bag of booze, but I sure as hell recognised him. Nicky Pew. When he saw me, he was out like a shot and into a car. Frantically, I looked around for the two patrolmen, but they were nowhere to be seen. I couldn't wait, so I jumped in the patrol car and gave chase.'

Weatherley hadn't told the story for some time and was enjoying retelling it to a new audience. He was becoming so animated that he hadn't touched his second glass of whisky.

'I hurtled after him down the Lawrence Hargrave Drive. It's a scenic route that runs along the coast up to Helensburgh. Pew was driving pretty erratically, which I put down to the amount of booze he must have had. Though it was going dark, it was a clear evening, so I never lost sight of him. The fact that there wasn't much traffic made it easier. I've been back since; they now call the route the Grand Pacific Drive. It's a swish new motorway, but in the nineties it was a cliff-hugging road prone to rock falls. Whether his car hit a bit of debris, or because he was drunk, I don't know, but Pew crashed. I stopped my car. By that stage, I'd managed to call for backup but I had no idea when they'd arrive.

'I saw Pew stagger out of his car. He had a gun in his hand. He took a shot at me and it smashed my windscreen. Luckily for me, there was a police gun in the patrol car. He moved away to the edge of the road, which was high above the sea. I got out and shouted for him to stop or I'd shoot. He turned and shot again, hitting my left arm. I had no choice but to fire.'

He paused for effect. His story was well-rehearsed.

'As I say, it was a clear evening. I can see it all in my mind's eye, as if it were yesterday; Nicky Pew dropping his gun, grabbing his chest and keeling over the edge. The backup arrived moments later and I was carted off to hospital to be patched up. Yet I was annoyed. As I'd been on the case since the beginning, I so wanted to bring Nicky Pew to justice. He was the one who'd shot dead the security guard. Dobson was little consolation.'

'I can understand that,' said Anita. 'Did you ever recover the diamonds?'

'No. That was another disappointment. I assumed he'd fenced them by the time he reached Australia.'

'But what about Carol all this time? Could she have got hold of the diamond money?'

Weatherley paused for a swig of his whisky. He smacked his lips.

'No, the poor cow missed out there. We brought her in after Nicky did a bunk. Of course, she denied knowing anything about his nefarious practices. And we hadn't enough evidence to prove otherwise. She was genuinely shocked to hear that Nicky had killed someone. I believe the love died there and then. She stayed in Newcastle for a couple of years after Nicky's death. Had to give up the smart home in Darras Hall, as the bank accounts were all frozen. The last I heard was that she'd gone to New Zealand to start a new life. I'm surprised to hear she might be in Sweden.'

'Well, this heir hunter was keen to track her down,' said Ash. 'She was the only one in line for the inheritance, but that wasn't much. But if she'd had some of the money from the robbery, then it might have been worth his while. Blackmail.'

Weatherley's smile was patronising. 'I think you're on the wrong track there, Cockney. Firstly, I think there's no chance that Carol got hold of Nicky's ill-gotten gains. I heard that when she was in Auckland, she was living like a church mouse. Worked in some menial secretarial job. Hardly the high life. And Nicky was living with another woman before he died, so he was unlikely to let Carol near his cash. But even if she had managed to get hold of his money, how could this Todd character prove it enough in order to blackmail her? So, whoever was behind the murder of your heir hunter, I'd lay heavy odds against it being anything to do with Carol Pew.'

CHAPTER 35

'Where the hell does that leave us?' Ash may have asked the question out loud, but it was one that Anita had been asking herself. Ash had already lit up as they got back into his car. They had just watched Deputy Chief Constable Weatherley get into a taxi.

'I don't know,' Anita sighed. 'It was quite a story.'

'That case made his name,' Ash said bitterly. 'Word is, he was a very ordinary cop until the Commission Quay robbery. It's like those film stars talking about their lucky break. That was his.'

'You were very good in there,' Anita said reassuringly. 'You didn't hit him once.'

Ash laughed. 'I didn't, did I? Maybe a beer will help us think this through. First, we'd better check into the Premier Inn and then I'll take you to Commission Quay. That might provide some inspiration.'

Moberg was on the point of dragging himself home when his office phone rang. It was almost a relief to delay the inevitable.

'Moberg,' he barked into the receiver.

'Westermark here. Just to let you know I've delivered Sundström's car to forensics. It's up to them now.'

'Good. Do you know if they've had any luck with the other two vehicles?'

'No. They're short staffed at the moment. One sick and another on paternity leave.'

'Paternity leave!' Moberg shouted in frustration. 'This fucking, useless country.' Not having any children of his own, the thought of giving fathers six months' paternity leave was anathema to him. 'No wonder nothing ever gets done round here.'

'They do have three cars to totally strip.'

'I don't fucking care. If they have to drag the sod away from his breastfeeding or nappy changing, or whatever the idle tosser's doing, then make Thulin do something about it.'

Moberg slammed down the phone. His job was stressful enough without this gumming up the works. He needed food.

It was hard to imagine what Commission Quay had looked like nearly twenty years before. Now, as they sat in the long car park which stretched over two thirds of the quay's length, there were no sizeable vessels in sight. The most prominent boat was the Earl of Zetland, a floating restaurant. Behind them was a marina with masts bobbing uncoordinatedly, trying to keep time with the tide. Fringing the marina were modern blocks of flats and town houses, none of which would have been built when Nicky Pew had planned his audacious robbery. The whole area had been redeveloped since then. Across the shimmering water were the lights of South Shields. That's where the gang had made their escape, leaving a dead security guard in their wake.

'Of course, it's all changed now. The QEII came in here on her last voyage a few years back, but not many big ships these days. The ferries go from along there,' said Ash, pointing further up the river. 'They used to go to Scandinavia, you know, but don't any more. Leanne and I went on one of those romantic weekend trips to Bergen from here. Won it as a prize in a police raffle. She spent most of the time heaving her guts out over the North Sea. And that was the romantic bit.'

Anita wasn't listening. She was trying to recreate the events of 1993. Everything had gone according to plan, until a security guard had bravely, or foolishly, tried to intervene. Had Pew taken the shooting in his stride? Or had it plagued him?

'I'm still sure that what happened to Graeme Todd was as a result of what happened here.'

'I hate to admit it, but maybe that prick Weatherley is right. Maybe we're wrong about the Carol Pew connection. What if Todd innocently went over to Sweden to find her as the heir to Doris Little's money, but ran into someone else? Maybe it was a mugging that went horribly wrong. Whoever did it believed that he had more money than he really had.'

'No. There has to be more to it. Todd stayed at the Hilton when he didn't really have the money to do so. He told Jennifer that this was the "jackpot". Whatever the reason for his visit, he thought he was onto something lucrative.'

'Well, Weatherley's right about one thing: even if Carol had somehow got hold of the diamond money, Todd wouldn't have been able to prove it. She could have sent him off with a flea in his ear, and he wouldn't be able to do anything about it.'

Anita rummaged in her bag and eventually found a handkerchief, which she then proceeded to clean her glasses with. She held them up in front of her and squinted until she was satisfied that they were clear. She popped them back on.

'And we know something's wrong over here. Someone breaks into Jennifer's home, and, we think, removes any information connected to the Little enquiry. Todd makes a mysterious trip to the North East – the chances are that it was to see Billy Hump to get some background on the robbery.'

'I can check that out.'

'Then Hump's suddenly killed in a hit-and-run. Is someone in Sweden manipulating events in England?'

*

The Magnesia Bank, or Maggie Bank, as it was known locally, was half-full on a Wednesday evening. Anita found a table on a raised dais round the corner from the front door. She sat next to the window, through which she could see a couple of smart apartment blocks silhouetted against the night sky. There was a gap between the blocks, and she gave a sudden start as she saw, at close range, an enormous container ship glide past. From her elevated position, she could look down on the wooden-floored bar where Ash was getting in the drinks. Suddenly, she remembered where she'd heard the name of the pub before. Ewan had mentioned it. This had been his local. Some of these people would know him. Certainly the bar staff. Her conscience stabbed her. She was going to have to do something about Ewan very soon. She wasn't being fair to him. She had to admit it was easier to be in love with him because there was no commitment involved. No day-to-day contact. No getting pissed off with your partner trying to run your life, as Björn had done. Maybe she was keeping the love going because it stopped anyone else getting close. She could shut them out. She could use Ewan as an emotional barricade. After she had got over Björn, she had been attracted to the idea of another life partner as a way of moving on. Someone to share the responsibilities; someone on the spot to offer Lasse the fatherly advice she couldn't. But Mr Right had never turned up and now that Lasse had grown up, it was dawning on her that she didn't want to go through the process of adapting to someone else's habits, foibles and human attachments. She had become too independent. Though the whole Ewan thing messed with her head, she had become used to the status quo. His love was unconditional. It would always be there. Maybe a lovers' limbo land was a safer, less demanding place to be.

'You seem miles away,'

Suddenly, she was aware of Ash standing above her with two pints in his hand.

'Sorry. Thinking about my next red day,' she lied.

'What's a red day?'

'Oh, like your bank holidays. I've used up all my leave this year.'

He placed the foaming glasses on the table. 'Workie Ticket. From a little local brewery. I think you'll enjoy it. Part of your education. Oh, by the way, they do grub here, too, so we might as well grab a bite. There's a menu on the board.'

They sat in silence as they both tried the beer. It was a different taste to anything that Anita had tried before, but it was very pleasant. She remembered colleagues at the Met being surprised that the "Swedish bird" liked beer. It had made her more acceptable to some – others took it as a sign that she was "easy". They had found out pretty quickly that she wasn't. Her lovers during that year had not been policemen.

'After what we talked about before, I think it'll be best if we divide up our work tomorrow morning. I'll go to Acomb and find out if Todd went to see Billy Hump; see if there's anything I can dig up. By the way, I've put in a call to Doncaster. The prison. See if George Dobson also had a visit from Todd. Just to cover all the bases.'

'And me?'

'You can go to the police station here in Shields. It's just along the road from here. I've confirmed that they've got a photo of Carol. You can get them to send it across to your people. They'll also show you the file on the Commission Quay case. Not sure you'll get much out of that, but it's worth a try. The bloke you need to ask for is a DS Tony Phillipson. Tony's one of the good guys.'

'OK.'

'Well, we might as well have a nice evening. There's nothing

221

else we can do until tomorrow.'

That was the problem, Anita thought. They were stuck. She had a horrid feeling that tomorrow wasn't going to bring them any good news.

CHAPTER 36

Anita found the police station opposite a park in an area dominated by regulation council houses. Its front elevation was long and squat, and occupied most of one side of the street. A row of police cars were lined up outside. As the dark clouds scurried across the sky, the brightness of yesterday was already a memory. Anita's head wasn't at its clearest, either. They had stayed in the Maggie Bank too long and she had been persuaded by Ash to have too many drinks. However, he had been the complete gentleman and hadn't taken advantage of the situation to try anything on. She knew a few who would have done so in the same situation. That had been a relief.

She attracted a mixture of strange looks and admiring glances from the staff inside the building. The tight black T-shirt under her leather jacket was a mistake, but it was the only clean top she had left from her hasty packing. After a ten-minute wait, a stocky officer in a smart grey suit and tie appeared. Detective Sergeant Phillipson had a chubby, rosy face, black hair receding from his temples and an eager-to-please smile. A chunky hand was proffered in greeting as he introduced himself. He showed Anita into a sparsely furnished interview room. There were two thick files and a thin folder on the table.

'Can I get you a coffee?' Phillipson asked pleasantly.

'Water would be fine.'

He came back a couple of minutes later with a plastic cup of cold water.

'How's Cockney these days?'

'Spending his time catching sheep rustlers.' Phillipson laughed politely.

'It was a pity about... well, it was pity he had to leave. A good detective.' He could see that Anita wasn't in the mood for small talk. 'I'll leave you to it. If you need me, I'm the second door on the left down the corridor outside. The ladies' toilet is just beyond,' he added helpfully.

It took her an hour to flick through the files. They covered the ground that she and Ash had already been over. Nothing new emerged, though she could see how lucky Weatherley had been. The anonymous tip-off leading to the arrests of Hump and Chapman was a break from which he'd never looked back. Ash had said that the word was that he was favourite to become Chief Constable of Lincolnshire Police. That would be the next stepping stone to one of the really top jobs.

It was only the thin folder that contained anything useful. It had a photograph of Carol Pew. As it wasn't a mugshot, Anita could read more into the face. She was a striking woman. It was the eyes that caught Anita's attention. They were dark and piercing. This was a woman who knew her own mind. The hair was black and in the fashion of the early 1990s; it was straight and cascaded down over her shoulders, giving her a Jennifer Aniston look. The lips were full and the nose was probably stronger than Carol would have liked. Her make-up was subtly applied and suited her dark complexion. There was also a cutting from a local magazine of the same period with a photo of her and Nicky at some social event. She looked stunning with an exquisite coiffure and a designer dress. He was only seen in profile, as he was talking to somebody behind his wife. He was tall and lean with short, dark-brown hair. This must have been the same photo of Carol that Todd had found, enabling him to identify her on the Swedish newspaper website. But the photos were pretty much it. Carol was obviously clever enough to keep herself detached from her husband's "business" dealings. The size of the file indicated how little they knew about her.

Anita took out her mobile and picked a number from her contacts.

'Hi, Hakim. How are you doing?'

'Busy.'

'Well, I'm about to make you busier.'

'Haven't had any luck with finding a Carol Pew. Been through all the usual channels, including the *Skatteverket* website. Whatever she's doing, she's not paying tax under that name. Not under Ridley, either. And, as a long shot, I translated Pew directly into the Swedish "Kyrkbänk". Still zilch.'

'That's commendably thorough, but not to worry. I've managed to find a photo of her. I'll get the police here to send it over. It was taken about twenty years ago. I want you to get the techies to age the woman to what they think she might look like now – different colour hair... that sort of thing. Then I want you to go through the archive sections of all the local newspapers looking for photos of jazz events – concerts, jam sessions; whatever jazz people do. Your job is to find Carol Pew in one of them.'

'You're joking.'

'I'm afraid not. If Graeme Todd could find her, then a bright spark like you should have no trouble.'

'At least it'll get me away from Westermark. I don't think Nordlund's enjoying working with him. If you ask me, Westermark seems to be trying to take over the Jansson investigation.' Anita hoped not, as that would be a pity, because this would be Nordlund's last case before retirement. But it was a typical Westermark manoeuvre.

Anita left North Shields police station with a copy of the Carol Pew photograph. It still niggled her that Weatherley could well be right, and that Carol Pew really did have nothing to do with the Todd murder; but she was the only lead they had. The least they had to do was track her down and eliminate her from their enquiries. And if they did do that, then they really would have nowhere left to go. But what else would have taken Todd to Sweden?

She wasn't sure what to do next, as Ash hadn't called in. The dark clouds were still rolling across the river from the direction of the sea, though the rain was holding off for the moment. It was chillier than when she'd entered the police station and she wished she'd put on a jersey. She wandered towards the centre of North Shields, passing a Netto store. It made her think of home. She remembered that Ewan had made a joke about Netto being regarded as quite downmarket in Britain. It had surprised her, as she had always regarded the popular Danish supermarket chain as quite good. Ewan. He had lived in North Shields right up to his imprisonment. Now what had been his address? If she could find a street map, she might remember the name. There was a map in Bedford Street, the main shopping thoroughfare. After scrutinising it for a few minutes, her eye alighted on Etal Court. That was it. It looked close by. She turned into Nile Street, opposite the Metro station entrance. The centre of the town was busy, but it had a feeling of neglect, in contrast to the redevelopment on its fringes and along the river. She crossed Albion Road and walked past a row of Victorian terraced houses. Ahead of her was an unassuming spread of three-storey blocks of flats, probably built in the 1970s. Ewan had described them as full of pensioners; people who had downsized. He had said that he fitted in well, as his neighbours were quiet and no one bothered him.

Anita followed the pavement round the blocks. She couldn't remember the number of his flat, not that she would have been able to tell which was which. It was just as she was nearly at the end of the cul-de-sac at the back of the buildings that her mobile began to vibrate, a setting she had put it on when she had entered the police station earlier. As she took it out of her pocket, her heart sank. It was Karl Westermark. What the hell did he want? He had nothing to do with her case.

'Hi, Anita.' Westermark's voice was almost cheery.

'What do you want, Karl?'

'It's OK. Nothing to do with the case, though I'm sure you're having lots of fun in your beloved England.'

'Just get it on with it,' she responded with annoyance.

'Some news. I thought you should be the first to know.'

'What news?'

'About your boyfriend.'

Anita was nonplussed. 'Who?' Then it suddenly dawned on her who he meant.

'Strachan. Your murdering journalist.'

'What about him?' Anita asked warily.

'Topped himself last night.' There was glee in his voice. 'Managed to get pills from somewhere. Easy thing to do in our crap prisons. So, one less piece of shit bunging up the system.'

Anita didn't hear any more. She was barely conscious of holding the phone to her ear. She just stared at the flats in front of her. She was too numb to react. She had no idea afterwards what she did in the next few moments.

'Are you all right, pet?' Anita slowly swivelled round and saw a small, white-haired woman in a blue, woollen winter coat bending down and picking her phone up off the ground. 'You dropped this.' The woman now held it out to Anita. 'You look as though you've seen a ghost.'

Anita took the phone. 'Thank you,' was all she could manage.

'Do you want to come in for a cup of tea? You look as though you could do with one.'

'No. No, I... I'll be OK.'

Only after further assurances, did the woman let Anita go. She wandered aimlessly back through the centre of North

Shields and found herself on the road above the fish quay. She watched the waves battering the Victorian harbour walls. They were rising and coiling above the stone parapets like some spitting sea serpent. The fermenting water wasn't the result of any storm, but what an aged fisherman in Simrishamn had once described to her as an "old sea".

How could Ewan have taken his own life? Why? It was the "why?" that kept returning and tormenting. And then the guilt. The searing guilt that festers in the mind and gnaws at the soul. She had left their last meeting abruptly because of her bloody ex-husband. Then Ewan's last call had been brushed aside because she had been rushing off to the airport. She'd had no time for him. He had been trying to tell her something. Was it a call for help? Could she have prevented him taking his life? A feeling of overwhelming sadness made her physically shudder. And the one regret that would live with her forever was that not once had she told him how she felt. His love for her was total. She had never said to Ewan that she loved him.

Her phone buzzed again. She reluctantly pulled it out of her pocket. She didn't recognise the number.

'Kevin here,' came the cheery voice. 'Are you there?' Anita hadn't realised that she hadn't even bothered to say anything.

'Yes.'

There was a pause at the other end. 'Any luck at North Shields nick?'

Her professionalism took over. 'Photograph of Carol. I've sent it through to Sweden.'

'Well, my trip to Acomb hasn't been wasted either. I'm on my way back. Meet you at the Maggie Bank in half an hour.'

'OK,' she said blankly.

'Do you mind if I walk with you?'

Hakim glanced to his left and saw Henrik Nordlund striding up to him along the pavement by the canal.

'Of course not,' said Hakim. It was a cloudy day that didn't promise rain, but the first blasts of a winter wind coming off the Sound between Sweden and Denmark had made Hakim turn up the collar of his jacket on leaving the office for his lunch break.

'Grabbing a sandwich?' Nordlund asked.

'Actually, I was going to pop into Moderna Museet.'

Nordlund knew of Hakim's love of art. It was a passion that had saved Anita's life eighteen months before.

'I've never been there. Is it good?'

Hakim smiled. 'It depends on your view of modern art. There's a Didi Dandano exhibition I wanted to see. It's about to finish, so this is my last chance.'

They turned to the right and headed across Paul's bridge, which spanned the canal.

'If you don't mind, I'll come with you.'

Hakim couldn't help a little chuckle. 'I hope you've got an open mind.'

Nordlund liked Hakim. Anita spoke highly of him, and he could see how their professional relationship had blossomed. In some ways he envied the young Muslim, as he was just at the beginning of his police career. He hoped that in today's force, his creed and colour wouldn't be the obstacle others had had to contend with in the past. Things were changing for sure, but maybe not fast enough. The old prejudices were still there, and suspicions of those with immigrant backgrounds still too evident. No excuse, he knew, but the police were just a more exaggerated reflection of the country's natural conservatism and the difficulties many native Swedes still had accepting incomers.

But Hakim was the representative of a new generation of police officers. And he was very good at his job. Nordlund had been impressed with the perceptive conclusions the young man had reached from the interviews he had carried out with the colleagues of Fraser and Holm. His approachable style had encouraged the staff to confide in him. He had learned that Holm was regarded as a bit of a lecher. Female colleagues were uncomfortable in his presence. Fraser was liked, though a couple of members of his department thought that he had a "crush" on Greta Jansson. This information made the CCTV evidence of Fraser being in the Lilla Torg area at the time that Jansson was meant to be meeting her Stockholm friend seem more suspicious. Apparently, Fraser could be vocal in departmental meetings and had strong opinions, which could spill over into anger if he felt that his views weren't being listened too. Could his temper have got the better of him if Greta Jansson hadn't responded to his overtures? His movements that night were hazy after he had left The Pickwick; and Holm had no alibi whatsoever.

From Stora Nygatan they quickly turned into Gasverksgatan, and the modern art gallery was in front of them. The main part was an attractive brick building with heavily shuttered windows over two floors. It had been an electricity plant in the early 1900s and was now cleverly renovated. At one end, an enormous, orange, perforated-steel annex had been added in 2009. This was to give the building's interior "an entirely new spatial order", as Nordlund read in the pamphlet he was given in return for his hefty seventy-kronor entrance fee. His growing doubts about the wisdom of accompanying Hakim were increased the moment he entered the main gallery area, which had been the turbine hall. After he had seen the first two paintings, Nordlund consulted his exhibition leaflet to try and understand the theme of the oddly grotesque, half-abstract, half-cartoon-style pictures on display. Apparently they formed "a surrealistically spinning narrative that sucks you into the brutal and contradictory world of the male of the species". Nordlund pondered that the artist must have come across some seriously appalling men in her time to issue such a blazingly harsh indictment of his sex. The images were disturbing. Many of the paintings were difficult to decipher, but some were blindingly obvious. One depicted a rape scene. This gave Nordlund a jolt. Had Greta Jansson's attacker worn the callous expression of the man in the painting? Was it someone who loved women or hated them? Nordlund found the exhibition hard to take, and excused himself to Hakim, who was engrossed in the work. Nordlund escaped upstairs in the hope of finding something lighter. He was disappointed. Despite the size of the gallery, there were few exhibits; mostly comprised of random explosions of paint and textile. One had so many spots of colour that he felt a headache coming on.

He was glad to be back in the open air. He would go and find a sandwich. Though his visit may not have increased his appreciation of modern art, it had enabled him to see the murder of Greta Jansson in a different light. He hadn't really thought about the mental make-up of the man behind the crime. The professor's love and rejection, Fraser's temper, Holm's weakness, none of them strong enough motives for such an abhorrent act. The rape of the painting was the deed of a monster. Underneath the superficiality of their characters, one of the suspects must have a much darker side to his nature. None struck Nordlund as being psychotic, but one of them was sick enough to rape an innocent girl, cold-blooded enough to murder her, and then cool enough to return to the scene of the crime to cover up his tracks. But which one?

CHAPTER 37

Anita had a pint waiting on the table for Ash's arrival. She had plumped for a fruit tea – had to be better than the coffee.

A couple of minutes later, Ash came breezing through the door.

'That's my kind of lunch!' As soon as he sat down he launched into his beer as though he hadn't had a drink for days. On replacing his glass on the table, he smacked his lips with satisfaction. 'Thank you. Needed that. Want any food?'

'No.'

'Are you all right? You sounded a bit off on the phone. Anything happened?'

'No,' she lied.

He could tell that something was preying on her mind, but was wise enough not to probe. He went to the bar and ordered a sandwich and a pork pie. On his return, Anita fished out the photo of Carol Pew. Ash studied it in silence. Eventually, he said, 'She was a bit of a looker.' Anita didn't pass comment. 'At least it'll give your lot over in Sweden something to go on.'

The young man behind the bar came across with Ash's food.

'Sure you won't have anything, Anita?'

She shook her head.

Ash shrugged and took a large bite out of his prawn mayonnaise sandwich.

He said, his mouth still half-full, 'There doesn't seem to be any sense of loss in Acomb for Billy Hump. Had a word with the police in Hexham and they're no further forward with the hit-and-run. They don't know whether it was deliberate or an accident. Apparently, he was good at making enemies.'

He took another sizeable chunk out of his second sandwich. Anita waited for him to continue, though she was finding it difficult to rustle up any enthusiasm.

'I did talk to a few of Billy Hump's neighbours, and I tracked down a cousin in the village. Since coming out of prison, he hadn't worked and had spent most of his time getting drunk and being objectionable. What I did gather was that when he was in his cups, he'd talk about Nicky Pew. He'd tell people, if they could be bothered to listen, that Pew had sold him down the river. Chapman too.'

'What do you mean?'

'Hump reckoned that it was Pew who'd set him up; tipped off the police. No one had known where they were hiding. It was Pew who'd told him and Chapman where to lie low until everything blew over.'

Anita managed to drag her mind back to the matter in hand. 'Why would he tell the police?'

'Hump maintained that it was so Pew didn't have to split the money four ways.'

'That makes sense.'

'If it's true. I think there's more to it than that. Pew was on the run because of the shooting. It would be easier for the two stars of the show to get away if the excess baggage was jettisoned. Throw the police a couple of titbits and it draws attention away from Pew and Dobson. And then, of course, Pew probably did the same thing again.'

'You mean in Australia?'

'Exactly! The heat was on, so he betrayed Dobson. Except it didn't do him any good in the long run. What a ruthless bastard! And he was also quite happy to dump his wife as well.

Maybe that wanker Weatherley did the right thing for once.' He took a rueful sip of his pint.

'And what about the diamonds? Or the money from them?'

'Pew must have salted that away somewhere. But with his death, that knowledge has gone. Probably sitting in some off-shore bank account to this day. If there's one thing to come out of this, it's knowing that none of them benefitted from the security guard's death. Three are now dead and the other... oh, by the way, I've been on to Doncaster. Graeme Todd didn't visit Dobson, but he did go to Acomb. That cousin of Hump's I mentioned was round at his house when Todd called. But she left before they discussed anything.'

'That's a pity.'

'There was one curious thing the cousin said, though. After the visit, Hump said he was going to come into some money. She just put it down to the drink talking. "His usual bullshit" was how she described it.'

'I wonder what Hump could have told Todd?'

'As they're both dead, we'll never know.'

'Unless...' Anita paused as though thinking something through.

'Unless what?' said Ash, who was now enthusiastically attacking his pork pie.

'Unless he took the picture from the Swedish newspaper to see if Billy Hump could confirm that Carol was in it.'

Ash nodded, a lump of pie restricting any speech.

'It still doesn't get us anywhere,' Anita sighed.

'I'm afraid you're right.'

'There's nothing more I can do here. I've got to go back to Sweden.'

Ash stared at her. 'That's a shame.'

'All I can do is to try and find Carol Pew. She may not be directly behind Todd's death, but we've nothing else to go on.'

*

The rain had passed, and the quayside was deserted. Standing in the car park, Anita watched the light of a fishing boat heading out to sea.

She had spent that afternoon in an almost-comatose state. She had gone through the motions of arranging an SAS flight out of Newcastle to Copenhagen for the next morning, but her mind was fixed on Kirseberg Prison. Ash, who seemed in no hurry to return to Cumbria, had gone off to see one of his daughters. He had returned in time for a dull meal at the restaurant next door to the hotel. She hadn't been much in the way of company, and it had been left to Ash to fill in the long gaps in the conversation. Afterwards, she had gone out for a walk.

She couldn't get her head round the fact that Ewan wouldn't be there in Malmö when she returned. Ironically, he would leave a huge hole in her life. How she had allowed herself to get this attached to such a man was a conundrum. But however much she chided herself for being so stupid, it didn't change a thing.

And what else would be awaiting her? A recalcitrant Lasse. An ex-husband who could be a murderer. An angry boss who would be quick to point out that her trip to England had been a waste of the department's time and money. A hopelessness enveloped her entire being. It was as though she could physically feel her confidence and any sense of self-worth draining from her.

'I was worried about you.'

She turned to see Ash's face illuminated by one of the streetlamps, like Humphrey Bogart in a black and white movie.

'Thought you might have got lost.'

Anita folded her arms against the cold. She didn't say anything.

'Returning to the scene of the crime?' The levity in his voice didn't lift her mood.

'Look, I'll piss off. I don't know if it's something I've done or said. Whatever, I'm sorry.'

'It's not you, Kevin.'

'I'm glad to hear that.'

'It's...' From nowhere came a surge of grief. It caught her totally unawares. It was like a tidal wave that she had no defences against. She grabbed her mouth with her hand, but it was too late. The huge sob just couldn't be controlled and the torrent of tears followed. Ash watched helplessly as Anita's body shook uncontrollably. He was embarrassed and had no idea what he should do. He tentatively held out a hand. Her convulsions began to recede and she took off her glasses and began to wipe them distractedly with her fingers. With pleading eyes, she looked at Ash.

She whispered, 'Hold me. Please.'

Hardly a word was spoken in the half hour it took Ash to drive from North Shields to Newcastle International Airport. He was confused, while Anita was ashamed. Ashamed that she had displayed such hysterical emotions in front of a new colleague. Ashamed that she'd allowed a sympathetic Ash into her bedroom. She hadn't particularly wanted him; she just needed someone. It wasn't the sex that was important; it was the physical contact. She just felt she needed the touch and caresses of another human being. In truth, the sex hadn't been that good. She wasn't the only one who was out of practice. Like an errant schoolboy, Ash had apologised for his poor performance. After he'd left, she had slept soundly. Over a continental breakfast, it had been business as usual. She could see that Ash was waiting for her to say something about what had happened between them, but that was in the past. She was grateful to him, but now it meant nothing to her. He would have to live with that.

As they hit the dual carriageway to the airport, the rain started again. A dismal end to a frustrating visit. They had agreed that while Anita would search for Carol Pew in earnest on her return to Sweden, Ash would see if there were any more connections he could dig up on the Doris Little front – and have another look at the events surrounding the Commission Quay robbery. They both had a feeling that there were still unanswered questions in England. Who broke into Jennifer Todd's? Was the sudden death of Billy Hump an accident or premeditated? Ash said that he might go and visit Dobson, the last remaining member of the gang, in Doncaster prison. Something might come to light. They both knew they were missing something, but what?

The only positive news Anita had received was a call from Lund that morning before she left the hotel. Graeme Todd's body was being released, and shipment back to the UK was being organised. Jennifer would have closure at last.

They reached a parking barrier and Ash leant out into the rain to take a ticket. A few moments later, he parked opposite the main entrance. An Easyjet plane, easily distinguishable by its orange tail, was just taking to the bleak skies. It would be nice to head somewhere sunny – to get away from it all. She wasn't looking forward to going back to Malmö. Ash took her small case from the boot of the car.

Ash wasn't sure what he had expected, but it was certainly more than a cursory 'I'll be in touch.' He watched her stride through the rain to the revolving door of the Departures section. He liked Anita. He had enjoyed working with her. More than that, he fancied her. And then last night. Had he taken advantage of her vulnerability? Or had she taken advantage of his? He had never been good at understanding women. If this was what Swedish women were like, he was both intrigued and bemused by them. All he could conclude was that Swedish men had their hands full.

Moberg could see the look of triumph on Westermark's face as he burst through the open door of his office.

'We've got him!'

'Where's Henrik?'

'I have no idea,' retorted Westermark, who didn't want anything to stop him giving Moberg the news he had brought.

'Get him, then you tell us both who you've got.'

Moberg could see that Westermark was trying to usurp Nordlund in the handling of the case. While *he* was in charge, that wasn't going to happen. He'd always had time for Henrik Nordlund. He could trust him. He was going to be sorely missed when he retired.

Westermark, still looking triumphant, returned three minutes later with Nordlund in tow.

'All right, what have you got?'

'The cars belonging to Alex Fraser, Andreas Holm and Björn Sundström have been totally stripped. And the technicians have come up with evidence that Greta Jansson was in one of those three vehicles.' He paused for effect. 'We've got him!'

CHAPTER 38

Anita's plane arrived fifteen minutes late. It took another half hour to get through passport control and reach the train station in the bowels of Kastrup airport. Having only taken hand luggage, she had avoided wasting time at the baggage reclaim area. However, travelling light also meant that she was desperate to get out of the things she was wearing, as she had survived six days with little in the way of a change of clothes.

When she boarded the train, she saw the latest edition of *Sydsvenskan* lying on the seat next to her. Her eye couldn't escape the headline: PROFESSOR ARRESTED FOR EX-STUDENT'S MURDER. Anita felt winded. She had tried hard to dismiss such a possibility. She stared out of the window and saw the waters of the Sound flicker by as the train flew past the girders of the Öresund Bridge. With Nordlund in charge, she knew that an arrest would have to be based on solid evidence. Prosecutor Blom wouldn't want any foul-ups either, as it would reflect badly on her if they had got the wrong person. This couldn't be a worse homecoming.

Lasse wasn't in when she reached the apartment on Roskildevägen. There was a pile of mail on the kitchen table, which she didn't feel she had time to open. She took a quick shower and changed into a clean pair of black jeans and a dark-blue top. The wind off the Sound was colder than she had had to put up with on

Tyneside, so she added a thick, blue polo-necked jersey to her downbeat ensemble. In search of food, she found the fridge nearly empty. She couldn't suppress her annoyance at Lasse's lack of action on the domestic front. He had nothing else to do all day, so the least he could do was some basic shopping. She toasted some rather stale bread and smothered it in lingonberry jam while the coffee was percolating. She went through to the living room and turned on the TV. As she munched her toast, she sipped her deliciously strong coffee and watched the last ten minutes of some English property show. That was another British obsession she had become aware of during her time in London. Now Swedish television was full of these programmes – she knew more about housing in Sussex than she did in Småland. She was tempted to have a second coffee, but resisted the urge as she felt she'd better report to Moberg and get the ordeal over with. What she was going to have for supper that night, she had no idea.

'Right, let's go back to the night of Friday, September the twenty-eighth,' suggested Nordlund. 'We know you were in Malmö that weekend. You'd come down to find Greta. By your own admission, you got into her apartment on the Saturday posing as her father. But did you see her the previous night?'

Björn didn't answer. He gave an exasperated sideways glance at his lawyer, but he didn't seem to be getting much help from that quarter.

'We believe she was raped in the apartment that night and then driven to the harbour, where she was strangled and dumped in the sea. Everything points to you, Professor Sundström, unless you can supply us with an alibi.'

When Björn did speak his tone was measured, his voice clear. 'I can't supply an alibi. I slept that night in my car, somewhere down near Limhamn.'

'If that's the best you can do, we might as well send you back

240

to your cell and get the prosecutor to sort out the paperwork,' scoffed Westermark.

Björn took a deep breath and said slowly and deliberately, 'I did see Greta that night.'

Westermark was about to jump in when Nordlund held up a restraining hand. 'Where?'

'I found out where she lived through a student who was still in contact with her. I waited in the square opposite her apartment. She came back about ten. I followed her in.'

'Are you sure you want to say any more?' put in the lawyer.

Björn gave him a scathing look. 'I waited until she had gone inside before I knocked on the door. To say that she wasn't pleased to see me is an understatement. I persuaded her to let me in. I could tell she'd been drinking. She was never very good at holding her alcohol. I tried to plead with her to come back to Uppsala so we could start again.'

'So much for you two being in love.' Björn ignored Westermark's sarcasm and didn't rise to the bait.

'We'd had a falling out. Things hadn't been going well for a while. I admit I'd been getting too possessive. She just upped sticks and was gone. I had no idea where. I was frantic for weeks. She wouldn't return my calls. I tried her friends but they wouldn't tell me where she was. I think some of them genuinely didn't know. Then I discovered she was in Malmö, which is why I came here.'

'What happened in the apartment?' Nordlund asked quietly.

'Not much. She was drunk enough to have the courage to say all the things she hadn't had the nerve to tell me in Uppsala. I was socially suffocating her, my behaviour was unreasonable. I can get angry at times, but I've never been violent.'

'Until now,' said Westermark, leaning across the table.

'I've never been violent,' Björn repeated, 'but I'm willing to make an exception for you.'

'I hope you're not threatening a police officer,' Westermark smiled back.

'The apartment?' Nordlund urged. Westermark's interventions weren't helping.

'After Greta told me exactly what she thought of me, I left. I could see that it was useless trying to have a conversation with her when she was in that state. Her parting shot was that she'd found someone else. I was too hurt to ask who this person was. I assume that's who she'd been out drinking with that night.'

'What time did you leave?'

'I'm not sure. Probably about eleven. I went back to my car and drove to the sea. I spent the night in the car feeling sorry for myself.'

'What about the next day?'

'I went back to try and discuss the situation sensibly. I convinced myself it was the drink talking the night before, not the real Greta. No one answered the door. Just then, I saw the neighbour with a pushchair. She looked at me suspiciously. On an impulse, I pretended to be Greta's father. It was the neighbour who suggested I borrow her key and let myself in and wait for her. I waited for about an hour. Then I drove back to Uppsala. When I heard nothing from her all week, I came back. This time by train. I still had the key. She still wasn't there. I was worried that I'd chased her away again. That's why I approached Anita. If anybody could find her, I was sure she could. I gave her the neighbour's key. You know the rest.'

'I'm afraid I don't believe a word of your story.' Westermark was going in for the kill. 'Except the bit about Greta telling you what she thought of you and you having a temper. Admit it, Sundström, you're a control freak. And you've just given us a motive – jealousy, possessiveness or whatever. The way I see it is this. You find out where Greta lives. You confront her. She's drunk, so you rape her. Probably horrified by what you've done, you take her down to the harbour in your car. After all, you've a lot to lose as a highfalutin Uppsala professor. You strangle her and chuck her in the sea. You go back the next morning because you realise that you might have left evidence in the apartment. You clean where you think you've been and you remove certain items to make it look as though she'd gone away. Then, the clever touch. A week later, you get Inspector Sundström to find your "missing" lover.'

Björn let him finish. 'Two things, Inspector. Why did I need the neighbour's key to get into the apartment? And, once in, why did you still find my fingerprints?'

'That's simple enough. You probably got rid of all Greta's stuff when you dealt with the body. Bag, mobile phone, key, et cetera. Then it dawns on you that you've left a trail. You go back, get the neighbour's key, and then try and erase any evidence of your presence. Except that you're an amateur. You don't do it thoroughly enough. Whatever lies you're trying to spin, there's no escaping the fact that you raped and murdered Greta Jansson. You're our man.'

With a look of exhilaration, Westermark pushed two small, transparent plastic bags across the table. Each contained a single gold hooped earring. He pointed at one. 'This was found on Greta's body. And this,' he said, pointing to the other, 'was found in your car.'

CHAPTER 39

'How did it go with the chief inspector?'

Anita had returned to the sanctuary of her cramped office with its two desks. Hakim had looked goggle-eyed when she had popped her head in on the way to reporting to Moberg. He was still trawling the internet. Above his screen, stuck to the wall, he had three pictures of Carol Pew. The first was the one that Anita had sent over from North Shields. The other two were mock-ups of what she might look like now. Given that she was fifty-three, the techies had been generous with the ageing process. In the first version she still had her natural black hair, but they had allowed for a touch of grey creeping in. In the other picture she was blonde, which softened the features.

'Could have been worse. He moaned a bit. Fortunately his mind is more on the Greta Jansson case.'

'Westermark was cock-a-hoop when they brought in your husband... sorry, ex-husband. He's being interviewed by Inspector Nordlund and Westermark right now, I think.'

She had to get hold of Lasse. What would he be thinking? It was an awful situation for him to cope with.

Anita forced herself to bring her thoughts back to the Todd case. She went on to explain all that had happened in England, including Weatherley's doubts about Carol Pew's involvement.

'We may be back to square one on this. We have to find her. Or you do!'

Hakim raised his eyebrows wearily.

'What you need is a coffee. So do I.'

Anita went to the kitchen to make up a pot. At moments like this the coffee machine wouldn't suffice. It had to be really strong.

Nordlund walked past the kitchen door.

'Hi, Anita. Welcome back.'

'Hello, Henrik. I hear you've been busy.'

He shrugged his shoulders apologetically. 'It's not looking good for Björn. Do you want to see him? He's downstairs.'

Anita shook her head. She couldn't face it. Not at the moment.

'I've got to go to a meeting in Prosecutor Blom's office, along with the chief inspector and Karl. Look, are you doing anything this evening?'

'No.'

'Come for something to eat at my place. We can chat things over. We can catch up on each other's investigations.'

Anita was taken by surprise. Despite Nordlund being friendly for a number of years, she had never been invited round to his apartment. He had shunned most work-related social events. He wasn't a mixer.

'Yes. That would be good.'

'Eight, then.'

Anita returned to the office with two steaming coffees on a tray.

'Anita!' Hakim cried the moment she entered. She nearly dropped the tray. 'I think I've found her.'

She quickly put the tray down on her desk, which was clear for a change due to her being away. She squeezed next to Hakim and looked at the screen. He had enlarged a photograph accompanying a short article in *Ystads Allehanda*. It was an outdoor setting; there was a cobbled courtyard. The caption mentioned Hos Morten Café. Anita had been there on a couple of occasions. There was a jazz group playing – the Göran Brante Trio. It was someone in the audience sitting at one of the surrounding tables that Hakim was pointing to – a blonde woman smiling broadly. Hakim increased the size again, which made the face blur slightly. Anita looked intently at the faces stuck up on the wall and then back down to the image on the screen. The style of hair was different – the woman listening to the jazz had a short crop – but there was no mistaking the face. It was Carol Pew.

CHAPTER 40

Anita went by foot, clutching a bottle of Shiraz. At that time of the evening, the market in Möllevångstorget had packed up for the day. The square was dark, even though lights were blazing from many of the surrounding buildings. The oriental shops and restaurants were still doing brisk business along Simrishamnsgatan. She turned sharp left and up to the small roundabout in the middle of Kristianstadsgatan. It was at a cross roads, with blocks of apartments on three corners. On the fourth was the edge of Folkets Park. Underneath a canopy of trees, the popular park's perimeter fence was used as a canvas for official graffiti artists. The early-1900s apartment buildings each had curved frontages, which mirrored the contours of the roundabout. In one – a tasteful combination of cream walls and rich red-tiled roof – opposite the park, Nordlund lived. Anita pressed the buzzer next to his name and the front door opened at her push. His apartment was on the second floor.

The apartment was as old-fashioned at she imagined it would be. Neat and tidy, it lacked frills. Hannah Nordlund had been a practical woman, not taken with fripperies. She had been a country girl, from what Anita remembered. And Henrik himself had been brought up on a Scanian farm. It was almost like a rural homestead in the middle of the city. Nordlund took Anita into the living room. There was an enormous beech sideboard against one wall, above which were a couple of ancestral portraits. A fire screen on the hearth displayed a faded tapestry of a wooded landscape, and there was an old, but good-quality, rug in the middle of the central area. The mantelpiece sported several framed photographs, mostly of Hannah, and one of a typical Scanian farm building with cobbled walls and an intricately thatched roof. It must have been taken in the 1920s. An old couple stood proudly outside the front door. They could have been 19th-century peasants.

'My grandparents. That's where I was brought up. Still in the family. My nephew now runs the farm, though my older brother keeps his hand in. It's just a few kilometres north of Sjöbo.' Nordlund had come in with a couple of glasses of white wine. 'I haven't exactly travelled far in my life.'

Anita accepted the wine and took a seat on the hard-backed sofa. Hannah hadn't been one for comfort either.

'But you've had a productive life. You don't have to travel the world for that.'

Nordlund took a seat opposite in a high-backed, wooden chair. It was well-worn and its arms were shiny from constant human contact. He stretched his long legs out.

'*Skål!*' He said, raising his glass.

'*Skål!*'

'I think I've done a decent job as a policeman. But soon that will be in the past.' He glanced across at one of the photos of Hannah. Though she was a plain woman, there was a smile playing on her lips that hinted at someone who hadn't taken life totally seriously. She probably wouldn't have let Henrik get too solemn, which he could at times. 'I've no one to share the final years with now. We had so many plans.'

This was what had been worrying Anita ever since he had announced his retirement. What would he do?

'There must be masses of things you can do. Maybe the travel you haven't had time for up till now?'

'Hannah and I had always planned to buy a boat.

We were going to spend the whole of one summer sailing round the Stockholm archipelago and call in on some of the islands. I learned to sail when I was serving as a young policeman in Karlskrona. I started to teach Hannah down at Limhamn. I used to hire a boat. But then she became ill. We said we'd take it up again when she recovered...'

'Why don't you take me out for a sail some time?'

A hint of a smile crossed Nordlund's face. 'Do you mean that?'

'Of course I do. I was brought up in Simrishamn, don't forget. Sailing's in the blood.'

It wasn't exactly true. She'd been an awful sailor. She had gone out a few times only because she'd had a boyfriend who was a member of the sailing club and, as he wanted to spend most of his spare time on the water, it was the only way to see him regularly. She'd nearly always been sick. Needless to say, the boyfriend had lost patience and found someone with a sterner stomach.

'Next summer I'll take you out on the Sound.' The thought cheered him up. Anita took a slurp of wine. The things one does for one's friends, she thought.

It wasn't until after Nordlund had cleared away the plates that the conversation touched upon professional matters. It turned out that he was a good cook. Cauliflower soup with watercress and cream was followed by a brisket of beef with root vegetables and Scanian mustard. Local, plain fare, but good and heart-warming. Anita was amazed that he had managed to whip up such a meal at short notice. But Nordlund had always been incredibly well-organised. She wished she was a better cook, but she could rarely work up any enthusiasm for it.

They returned to the uncomfortable seats in the living room. Rain beat on the window panes. Though it was dark over the park, there were lights from the apartments down the streets. Hardly a blind was drawn. She smiled to herself as she thought about Penrith after dark – curtains drawn everywhere by this time of night. Nordlund came in with a couple of cups of coffee.

'So how did you get on in England?'

'I'm not sure.' Anita told him about working with Ash and how they had followed various trails, culminating in the photographs of Carol Pew. But what Weatherley had said still niggled. He was sure that they were on the wrong track, and he should know, as he was the officer most involved in the original Commission Quay robbery case and its successful aftermath. He was sure that Carol couldn't have gained from the robbery. So why was Todd trying to trace her when her inheritance just wasn't worth the trip?

'There's something we're not seeing,' she concluded. 'Maybe it's something that Carol isn't even aware of. Anyway, I'm taking Hakim across to Ystad tomorrow to ask around.'

'Dragging the poor young fellow out on a Saturday.'

'It's his fault. He found a photo of Carol Pew at a jazz event that appeared in *Ystads Allehanda* last year. We should find her now.' She took a satisfying gulp of coffee. 'What about you?'

Nordlund patted his bald pate thoughtfully before answering.

'It's not looking good for Björn, I'm afraid.'

'I thought as much.'

'Did you know that he'd been in Greta's apartment the night she disappeared?'

Anita couldn't hide her shock. 'No, he never mentioned it.'

'According to him, he tracked down where Greta lived and confronted her when she came back from her night out. He says she was drunk. She said some painful things to him, so he left. He claims she was alive when he went. He slept the night in his car down in Limhamn, so no alibi. Then he went back to see her so he could talk her round. But she wasn't there.

That's when he met the neighbour and pretended to be her father so he could wait around for her.'

'And she was still missing the following weekend when Björn came to see me.'

'Westermark reckons that was just deflecting attention from what he'd already done. He's got a point. Nothing looks more innocent than asking a cop to find someone whom you've actually already killed.'

'Why didn't he tell me the truth right away?'

'If Westermark's right, he couldn't afford to. Björn didn't help himself, either. He admitted that Greta had run away from him because he was being too possessive. What makes it worse is that he also admitted he had a temper. That doesn't sound good when it's relayed in a courtroom in a case that involves rape and strangulation. I don't like to ask, Anita, but was he ever violent with you? You may end up being asked this by the prosecutor anyway if they try to establish a history of violence.'

Anita was still stunned by all she was hearing. Slowly, she shook her head. 'No. No, never. Björn did have a temper. He didn't like being proved wrong. That used to set him off. But physical abuse? Never.'

'That's something. Of course, the most damning evidence is the missing earring. Greta was wearing it the day she disappeared. It couldn't have got in his car without her being in there that Friday night, which, of course, he denies.'

Anita felt wretched. She no longer loved Björn, yet he would always be part of her life because of Lasse. That was an unbreakable bond. The fact that he had lied to her from the moment he had got her involved really hurt. It was betrayal all over again. What was even harder to digest was the reality that her ex-husband was a killer. It was just too ironic – could the only two men she had ever fallen in love with both be murderers?

'So, it's done and dusted?'

'Officially, yes. Blom and Moberg are happy that they've

got a watertight case.'

Anita noticed the hesitation in his voice. 'Is there a "but"?'

'There are one or two things I'm not entirely happy with. Björn did mention that Greta said that she'd met another man. Westermark is convinced it was just a ruse. However, if it's true, then it might bring Fraser and Holm back into the picture. One of them – or someone else – might have visited the apartment after Björn left.'

'The person she'd been drinking with?'

'Possibly. We know that Fraser was in the Lilla Torg area earlier in the evening. Then he went to The Pickwick. He could have gone round to her apartment later. So could Holm. He's got no alibi for that night, either.'

'At least you've got an open mind.' Anita was thankful for that. She wasn't thinking of herself. It was Lasse who was her greatest concern.

'There are things I want to double-check. I need to have another word with Eva Thulin.' He stopped and sat in silence. Anita could sense that there was something that was bothering him.

'Is anything up?'

Nordlund seemed hesitant. 'I just need to listen to the interview tape again. It's probably nothing.'

Anita didn't get any more out of him. After helping him to do the dishes – he had never seen the need for a dish washer – she prepared to leave.

'Thank you for a lovely evening, Henrik. Beautiful meal.' Nordlund's face creased into a pleased grin. 'If you need any help, just ask.'

'Anita, I think you've got enough on your plate.'

As they reached the door: 'I heard from Westermark that Ewan Strachan had committed suicide.'

'He told me.'

'I'm sorry.'

Anita was taken by surprise. Had Nordlund known all along about her feelings for Ewan? She left without another word.

Anita made her way back into Möllevångstorget. The rain had relented and the scudding clouds were visible above the sodium lights of the city. The cafés and bars were busy with Friday night trade. She hurried on, as it wasn't the safest place to be after dark. Suddenly, a familiar voice halted her.

'On a night out?'

It gave her an uncomfortable start when she realised that it was Westermark.

'This isn't a part of town I'd expect to see you in,' she responded. 'Bit beneath you.' What was Westermark up to?

'Out celebrating.'

'And what's there to celebrate?'

'Nailing your ex-husband for one. Pity Strachan's dead or they could have become prison buddies.'

Anita turned on her heel and prepared to negotiate the main road that bordered the square. An approaching bus stalled a quick exit.

'And where have you been?' Westermark was by her side as she waited.

'With Henrik.'

'Discussing work?'

'You'll have to ask him.'

The bus passed and she stepped out into the road.

'It's pay-back time, Anita,' Westermark called after her. His laughter was lost in the noise of another bus coming in the opposite direction.

Anita let herself into the apartment. The light was on, so Lasse must be back. That was good, as they needed to sit down to a serious chat about his father. Despite her tiredness, she felt she had to tackle the subject now. She dumped her bag on the hall table and strolled into the kitchen. There, sitting at the table, a bottle of water in hand, was Jazmin Mirza.

'Oh, hello,' Anita said in surprise.

Jazmin stood up. She seemed embarrassed. 'Hello, fru Sundström.'

Anita couldn't fathom what on earth she was doing here. 'Is Hakim with you?'

'No.'

That moment Lasse appeared at the door.

'Hi, Mamma.'

'I see we have a visitor.' Anita raised her eyebrows as a sign that she wanted an explanation.

'Jazmin needs to stay the night.'

Jazmin shuffled nervously on the other side of the table.

'Why?'

'Because her parents have thrown her out.'

'So why has she come here?' Anita was talking to Lasse as though Jazmin wasn't in the room.

'Because I'm the reason she's been chucked out.'

'What?'

'I think you need a drink, Mamma.'

Anita's tiredness kicked in with a burst of anger. 'No I bloody don't! Just tell me what the hell's going on.'

'I should go. I'll find somewhere else,' said Jazmin.

'No,' said Lasse firmly. 'You're staying.'

'Lasse. I'm waiting for an explanation.'

'We're going out together. An item.'

Anita looked askance. She couldn't think of two more unlikely people joining up. And how had they met? Hakim hadn't said anything.

'When Hakim was staying here Jazmin came round with some food for him. He wasn't in. We talked. That was it.'

'Why didn't Hakim say anything?'

'He doesn't know,' put in Jazmin. 'None of his business.'

'So how come Uday and Amira have asked you to leave?'

Jazmin shrugged. 'We had yet another argument. A shouting match, I suppose. It was about me coming in late. They said I was to stay at home until I learned to behave. I let slip that I'd been out with my boyfriend. That was bad enough, but when I said he was Swedish – white Swedish – my father went mad. Said he would never let me see Lasse again. When I told him I didn't care what he thought and that I'd see Lasse whenever I wanted, he told me to leave.'

Anita was astonished. Uday had seemed far more liberal than that. He was once a respected art dealer in Baghdad, used to western ways, before escaping Saddam Hussein's regime.

'Does Uday know that it's Lasse that you're talking about?'

'No.'

'Mamma, you've got to let her stay.'

Anita sighed. 'Just for tonight.' Turning to Jazmin, 'You can have Lasse's bed.' Lasse gave Jazmin a big grin. 'And you can sleep on the day bed in the living room.' She gave him a knowing look. 'I don't want to upset Jazmin's parents any further.'

'OK,' he agreed reluctantly.

'Now, I'd better ring Hakim and tell him and your parents that you're safe.'

'Jazmin's here.'

'Allah be praised!' Anita could hear the relief in Hakim's voice. 'I didn't know what had happened until I got home. Dad and I have been searching for her all over.'

'According to your sister, Uday chucked her out.'

Hakim sighed. 'Sort of. They had one of their arguments. He said she taunted him with the fact she had a white boyfriend. It's not the colour; it's the non-Muslim thing. He just lost his temper. They're as bad as each other. Mother soon impressed on him that he'd been hasty, and now he's worried sick.' He paused. 'So why has Jazmin come to you?'

'The white boyfriend. It's Lasse.'

The whistle from the other end of the phone spoke volumes. 'When did this happen?'

'When she came round here to deliver some food for you. Look, tell your parents she's safe with me. It's up to you whether you mention Lasse. We'll try and sort it out in the morning when I pick you up. Now, I just want this day to end.'

She switched off her mobile. She didn't want to speak to anyone again that night, however urgent it might be. Lasse and Jazmin were still in the kitchen, talking in whispers. She picked up her bag off the hall table and spotted a pile of unopened mail. It would have to wait. Then she noticed that the top letter was handwritten. That was unusual in this age of computer printers, emails and texts. She didn't recognise the writing. It was addressed to Ms A Sundström and had a Malmö postmark. It had been posted three days ago. The "Ms" alerted her immediately. She closed her bedroom door and switched on the bedside lamp before turning off the main light. She felt nervous about opening the letter. She just knew it was from Ewan. She sat down on the bed and looked at the envelope. Then she took a deep breath and ripped it open. Her throat went dry as she read:

Dear Anita,

I'm sorry to do this to you, but you are the only person in the world that I want to communicate with before I go.

Hopefully, by the time you get this, I'll have had the courage to duck out of this life. It's not an attempt to escape the horrors of Swedish coffee – though that's reason enough – but because I've been suffering from cancer. Spotted too late, and it's bitten deep. Your reaction on seeing me last time was confirmation enough of how much I'd changed. They were threatening to send me back to Britain to die. But I can't leave here. I can't leave you. That's what I wanted to tell you when I rang.

I know you never loved me, but I've always hoped you had some feelings for me. You made the effort to see me, even after all the awful things I've done. You know that I love you. I just wish I could have told you one more time. This will have to suffice.

Thanks for the visits. And the cigarettes and the snus. I've never regretted coming to Malmö, not for a minute. Meeting you was the best thing that ever happened to me. If I've complicated your life, I apologise.

Time to go. Goodbye, Anita.

Puss och kram, Ewan x

PS Don't worry about Lasse. He'll come good.

Anita let the letter slip from her grasp. It fluttered to the floor. Just at this moment, life was shit.

CHAPTER 41

Anita honked the horn of her car as she sat outside Hakim's parents' apartment in Sevedsgatan. Hakim appeared at the first-floor balcony to the immediate left of the front door and waved. Two minutes later, he climbed into the passenger seat.

'Are your parents OK?'

'Yes. They're grateful that you took Jazmin in.'

'And you told them about Lasse?'

Hakim hesitated. 'Not exactly.'

'I had half a mind to bring her over this morning, but she was still asleep when I left.'

'She wasn't in Lasse's room?' Hakim sounded aghast.

'Yes, but Lasse was in the living room.'

Hakim's sigh of relief was eloquent.

'First, we'll go and find Carol Pew, then we – and I mean *we* – will sort out the Lasse-Jazmin problem.'

Westermark drove his Porsche into the police car park. On a Saturday morning there weren't many other vehicles around. He had no intention of going into work. He was going to treat himself to a shopping spree. The main shops were an easy walk along the canal. Life was looking good again. The case was tied up, with the delicious irony that he had been able to put Anita's nose out of joint by establishing that her ex-husband was a murderer. And Strachan killing himself was just the cherry on the cake. To add to Anita's discomfort, the word around the water cooler was that she was struggling with her heir hunter investigation. That's what Wallen had reported anyway.

He tossed his car keys up in the air and caught them with an exaggerated flourish. Just as he was reaching the gateway, he noticed Nordlund's car. What was he doing in the building? The last thing he wanted was the old fucker buggering up his carefully constructed case. The sooner he retired, the better, then he could take his long face and ancient ideas on policing with him to some obscure backwater in rural Skåne. As far as Westermark was concerned, Nordlund should have been pensioned off years ago. Just beyond the gateway, he stopped. Curiosity got the better of him; the shopping would have to wait.

Westermark didn't even acknowledge Wallen in the corridor. He found Nordlund in the meeting room which was being used as the command centre for the team's two ongoing investigations. The walls were still covered in faces and gory photographs, maps and whiteboard scribblings. Nordlund was bent over the table going through a file.

'What on earth are you doing?' Westermark asked with obvious irritation. 'Shouldn't you be enjoying a weekend off? There's nothing we can do until Blom attends court on Monday.'

The older policeman eyed Westermark up and down.

'There are just a couple of things I want to get my head around. A loose end or two.'

Westermark exploded. 'There are no fucking loose ends! It's an open-and-shut case. What the hell are you looking for? Is this bloody Sundström stirring things up, trying to save her precious professor? I know she was round at your place last night.'

Nordlund appeared unmoved by the younger man's unprovoked outburst.

'Karl, you've nothing to worry about. It's nothing to do with Anita. And I'm not trying to take any of the glory away from you. You've done a very good job.'

This seemed to placate Westermark. 'I'm sorry, Henrik. It's just an important case for me. It'll help make my mark with the powers that be.'

'I won't be long. You go off and enjoy your Saturday.'

Westermark nodded and retreated. Once he was outside, he wasn't in the mood for shopping any more. He got into his car and drove back to Limhamn.

The day was verging on bright. The dark clouds that had greeted Anita when she emerged from a troubled sleep had been swept away, and a watery sun was doing its best to pretend it was still summer, even though they were now in the second half of October. Christmas was only two months away. That meant a visit to her mother and aunt in Kristianstad. She never spent Christmas itself with her mother if she could help it, but usually a weekend in the middle of December, when they swapped inappropriate presents, got on each other's nerves and spent the next few months thankful that they wouldn't have to see each other again until the summer. Her mother would criticise her clothes, her appearance, the way she was bringing up Lasse, and anything else she could think of which her daughter had disappointed her in over the years. Anita thought she would take Lasse with her this time. If they were still together, she could drag Jazmin along as well. That would upset Mamma and give her racist aunt apoplexy. No, she couldn't do it. It would be unfair on the youngsters.

They reached Ystad at quarter past ten. After they had parked the car, they made their way to the café, which was up a pedestrianised side street off the main Stora Östergatan. Hos Morten was housed in an old brick-and-timbered building dating back to the late 1700s. The cosy interior was enhanced by hundreds of books lining the walls. The door to the outside courtyard was closed at this time of year. Only a few tables were occupied, with people having an early Saturday coffee.

A young woman came across and asked if she could serve them.

'Hi, I'm Anita Sundström and this is Hakim Mirza from the Skåne County Police.' When Anita saw the worry flicker across the woman's plump face, she quickly added, 'It's OK, we're just trying to find someone. Hakim?'

Hakim passed over a copy of the photo from the *Ystads Allehanda* to the relieved waitress. He pointed to Carol Pew. She squinted at the picture and then she nodded.

'I know her. She comes in from time to time. English lady. Johansson. I think her first name is Carol. She likes it here because she says the garden outside reminds her of England. She's a good tipper.'

'Do you know where she lives?'

'I think it's somewhere out near Löderup. But I couldn't say exactly where.'

'You've been very helpful.'

The waitress beamed back. 'Would you like something while you're here?'

'Why not? Hakim, I'll let you order. I'll have some cake. I'm just going to ring in. Wallen's on this weekend.'

Five minutes later, Anita came in, clutching her mobile phone. Hakim was sat at a table with two coffees and two slices of carrot cake, one of Anita's favourite indulgences.

'Klara's getting onto the *Skatteverket* website. Now we've got a name, we should be able to get the address, though I believe Johansson is Sweden's most common name; but Carol's more unusual, of course.'

'That's if she's paid any tax,' Hakim noted wryly.

'Interesting that she hasn't changed her first name. And she's done nothing to hide her Englishness either.'

'Maybe she's got nothing to hide.'

'With any luck, we'll be able to ask her soon.'

*

Anita turned off the Simrishamn road and headed down Östra Kustvägen, which hugged the coast. The road bisected the flat patchwork of fields in this arable area which was dotted with houses in a variety of styles. Most had been farmsteads, now converted into domestic dwellings. They passed the turning to Kåseberga, the coastal village next to the prehistoric site of Ales Stenar, which had been featured on the postcard that Carol had sent to Vanessa Ridley. They hit a long, straight stretch.

'It must be around here,' said Hakim, studying the local map they had picked up in Ystad. Anita once again swore to herself that she would buy a sat nav.

'I think this is it.'

Anita slowed the car and manoeuvred it onto an unmetalled track. The tyres crunched over the surface of gravel and mud. The house in front of them was a low, modest building, with a detached barn set back in a clump of trees. However, on closer scrutiny it was clear to see that anybody was unlikely to be at home, as the windows were shuttered. Anita was glad to send Hakim into the biting wind coming off the sea.

'You'd better go and knock on the door, just in case someone's about. It would be typical if they're away.' Not only had Wallen found Carol Johansson on the tax register, she had also found she had acquired another husband called Peter Johansson.

Hakim got out and knocked on the front door, which was at the top of three steps. He glanced over to Anita and shook his head before heading off round the other side of the building. He soon emerged and got back into the car.

'No one there.'

Anita could see the track continued on round the rear of the property and on to further houses in the distance. 'We'll try the next one.'

On the next bend the road split. There was a house straight

in front of them; and another way up to the left, partly obscured by the usual clump of pine and birch. They tried the nearest house but, like the other, it was boarded up for the winter. 'Another holiday home,' was Hakim's verdict as he shuffled back into the passenger seat.

Taking the left-hand fork, they could see that the third house was bigger than the other two. In the nearest field, two bay horses were grazing contentedly. This was a more traditional farmhouse, with single-storey buildings forming three sides of a square, in the middle of which was a central courtyard. The property was in good condition; recently whitewashed, the window frames neatly painted. Where the sun poked through the protective cover of the trees, the walls dazzled. There was no car parked in the courtyard and Anita's hopes sank. They would probably have to come back on Monday.

This time she got out and left Hakim in the car. There was no reply when she rang the doorbell, nor when she knocked on the thick wooden door. Nothing stirred inside. As they'd driven in, she'd seen a large barn behind the right-hand wing of the house. Returning to the car, she noticed the barn door was open, an electric light blazing inside. Anita headed towards it, then suddenly stopped, her heart pounding. A large German Shepherd dog was bounding towards her. Never comfortable with dogs at the best of times, she immediately shied away as the animal began to bark loudly.

'Jingo!' commanded a strident voice from somewhere just out of sight. The dog instantly ceased barking, but hovered menacingly just a foot in front of Anita.

'Who are you?' demanded a voice in Swedish. Anita tore her eyes from the drooling jaw of the German Shepherd and saw Carol Pew standing there. She was dressed in working clothes – a scruffy pair of jeans, a thick fleece jacket and wellington boots. Even with dirty hands and dishevelled hair, she still managed to look elegant. She didn't seem to have aged; her face was unlined and her features still well defined. She was wearing a little too much eye make-up, but there was no disguising the sharpness in her gaze. 'What are you doing here?' The language was still Swedish, but the accent was unmistakably English.

'I'm Inspector Anita Sundström from Malmö. I need to speak to you.'

'What about?' she asked suspiciously, the voice gravelly.

'It's about a murder investigation.' Anita realised that she had lapsed into English. 'An Englishman called Graeme Todd. Does the name mean anything to you?'

Carol Pew didn't show a flicker of surprise. 'Yes.'

CHAPTER 42

They sat outside on a wooden picnic bench away from the house in a sheltered corner of the garden on the edge of the trees. The vista before them was of a flat terrain, only broken by the odd copse. A couple of tractors were working in a field in the distance. The wind had dropped a little, the sun was still shining, and Hakim was trying so soak up its pathetic rays while Carol went indoors to make them a drink. She came back with a tray on which was a teapot and three cups. There was a plate of biscuits too. British habits die hard, thought Anita.

'I'll be mum,' Carol said in English with a smile. There was no hint of Cumbrian left in the deep tones of her smoky voice. Using a tea-strainer, she poured out the tea. Only she took milk.

'Sorry Peter's not here. Kåseberga. Out on his boat. Mad fisherman. But I suppose it's me that you want to see.'

She sat down on the bench opposite Anita and Hakim. She offered them the plate of biscuits. Anita declined, while Hakim tucked in.

They had established that the conversation would be in English. Carol apologised that her Swedish wasn't brilliant – 'You all speak English so well over here that I don't have to use it much.' Anita and Hakim were quite happy with the arrangement. Once they'd all settled down, Anita began.

'As I said, we're investigating the murder of Graeme Todd, who was a probate researcher.'

'I can't really believe it. Where was he killed?'

'He was washed up in Limhamn. I'm surprised you didn't hear about it.'

'We don't tend to watch much Swedish television.' She pointed back to the house and the satellite dish on the roof. I tune into the good old BBC and Peter likes Sky. He's fanatical about the All Blacks, and Sky shows the rugby.'

'You said you knew the name... Graeme Todd's. Did he contact you?'

'Yes. He wrote to me about a month ago. Maybe a bit longer, actually.'

'Did he say what it was about?'

'Something about inheriting some money. He didn't go into details. Then he got on to me about three weeks ago and suddenly announced that he was coming over to Sweden and that we should meet up.'

'Did you know who you were inheriting from?'

'Well, at first I thought it was a bit strange as he said it was an aunt of mine. When I left England, I had three. Doris and Belle on Mother's side and an auntie by marriage called Louise on my dad's – she's my cousin John's mum. He married a friend of mine, Vanessa White.'

'I know; I met her. In Worcester.'

'Did you really?' Carol asked in surprised delight. 'How is the old bat? Is she still putting up with boring old John?'

'He's dead.'

'Oh. I doubt if she's over-fussed. She was bit of a girl, our Vanessa.'

'She said the same about you.'

'The saucy cow!' she exclaimed with a rasping cackle.

'Anyway, Graeme Todd?'

'Right. As it turned out, it was Auntie Doris. Sweet old thing; she'd already given me some money. When my ex-husband disappeared out of my life, leaving me destitute, it was

Doris who gave me the money to start again in New Zealand.'

'So that's where her house money went.'

Carol glanced at Anita quizzically. 'What do you mean?'

'Equity release. She sold her house to raise the money.'

'Oh no! God, that makes me feel awful. She never mentioned it at the time. I was just grateful for the help.'

'Back to Graeme Todd,' Anita prompted.

'To be honest, I thought it might be a scam. But then he phoned again saying he was in Malmö and could we meet up? He hadn't any transport, so I arranged to meet him in Ystad. I was to pick him up and bring him here. He wanted me to sign something so he could put in a claim on my behalf to the Treasury.' She picked up her cup of tea and sipped it thoughtfully.

'Did you meet up?' Hakim asked impatiently.

'No. He didn't turn up. I waited an hour and then headed back home. I put him down as a time-waster.'

'Did you tell anybody else about Todd's visit?'

'No. No one. Except Peter, of course. And he thought it was quite funny that, despite all my efforts to remain anonymous, someone had tracked me down.' She squinted up at the sun. 'It still amazes me that he discovered where I lived.'

'It was the postcard you sent to Vanessa that started him off. Ales Stenar.'

'Ah.'

'So how did you end up in Sweden?' Anita asked. She knew a lot of the story already. Now she wanted the gaps filled in.

'That's a long story, dear. An awfully long story.'

'We've got plenty of time.'

Wallen opened the door to the meeting room. She was bored seeing out her Saturday shift. At least Anita's call about finding Carol Johansson's address had given her something to do. She had a girls' night out planned for later. They were going to try out a new club that had just opened and was meant to be good.

She was surprised to see that Nordlund was still in there. He was surrounded by pieces of paper. He never looked in the best of health, but his face was drawn. Retirement would do him good, she thought. Get some colour back into his cheeks. She was envious. If she had the financial means, she would give up the police tomorrow. Modern policing had lost its appeal: too much red tape, too much accountability and too much interference. And life without the likes of Moberg and Westermark would be so much nicer. Nordlund would be a loss. He was a decent man.

'I can't believe you're still in, Henrik.'

'Just double-checking. Can't overlook anything when it's a murder case.'

'Can I get you anything?'

'No. I'm fine, Klara. I won't be long.'

Wallen shut the door and left him to it. Now, what was she going to wear tonight?

'This is a new life. One I want to protect.' Carol took out a packet of cigarettes. She offered them across the table. There were no takers. She lit up and exhaled a plume of smoke.

'If you found me, then I haven't done much of a job keeping a low profile.'

'It wasn't easy,' remarked Anita.

'I don't know how much you know about my background, but I was married to a guy called Nicky Pew. Handsome sod. Fell for him in a big way. This was in Newcastle, by the way. Not Carlisle. The only problem was that he was a crook. An educated, clever, charming crook. He was fun to live with. Oh, I can't pretend I don't miss the high life. Nicky had three weaknesses – money, jazz and women. He got me hooked on the first two and pissed me off with the third. He was a very successful jewel thief, but it all went wrong one night. He ended up killing a security guard in North Shields. I don't know how it happened. I only ever saw him once after that. He came home, stuffed a case full of money he had stashed in the house, and left in a hurry. Not a bloody word of explanation. The next thing I hear is that the bugger has surfaced in Australia. He left me right in the shit.'

Carol took out another cigarette and lit it from the dying butt of the first one.

'The grand house in Darras Hall went. The authorities froze our accounts. And I had a copper sniffing around. Weatherley. He was rounding up Nicky's gang. And he was doing his best to implicate me. Hadn't any proof, though. Then the randy sod tried it on.' Kevin Ash would recognise the scenario, thought Anita. 'I'll never forgive the bastard for that. He wouldn't have dared if Nicky had been around. Nicky would have killed him. Ironic that it was Weatherley who killed Nicky.

'Anyway, I was starting divorce proceedings before Nicky was shot. Saved me some lawyers' fees.' Another chuckle. 'So, I suppose Weatherley did me a favour. Even before that last robbery, I was tiring of Nicky's philandering. It was no surprise when I heard he'd been shacked up with some Aussie trollop before he died.'

Reflectively, she watched the breeze carry her cigarette smoke across the garden. Her nails were manicured, but there was a yellowish tinge of nicotine on her fingers. She was a serious smoker. Maybe Nicky Pew had driven her to it, reflected Anita.

'I stuck around in Britain for a bit. But the police harassment was getting too much. They hadn't recovered the jewels. Or the money Nicky had probably made from them, so they automatically thought I must have access to it.'

'It didn't come your way?'

Another guttural laugh, 'If only, my dear, if only.' She flicked a growing column of ash onto the grass. 'I headed to

New Zealand for a fresh start. They speak English of a kind. They swap their 'i's and 'e's so six sounds like sex and sex like six. Can make some conversations confusing, if you know what I mean. It's a pretty country though, but pretty dull too. And it's closer to Britain than you think. They're not so backward that they don't have the internet. The press got wind of where I was. The story of Nicky's death had been big in Australia, and that sort of thing floats across the Tasman Sea. By that time, I'd met Peter. He was born in Auckland, but his parents had emigrated from Dalarna. So he's a dual citizen. Met him in a jazz club in Auckland. I love jazz – that was Nicky's fault; he was passionate about it. Peter loves it too. He plays in a trio.'

'Ah, the Hons Morten Café,' said Hakim. 'The photo of the Göran Brante Trio in *Ystads Allehanda*. Peter Johansson was captioned. Drums.'

'That's right. They do a lot of Esbjörn Svensson material. Are you into that sort of stuff?'

'No. It seems like a lot of funny noises to me,' admitted Hakim.

'Maybe it's a cultural thing with you.'

Anita thought Hakim was going to react to her insensitive comment. A warning glance ensured he kept quiet. Anita wanted to take advantage of Carol's talkativeness, even though it didn't seem to be leading them anywhere at the moment.

Carol carried on, completely oblivious to any aspersions she may have cast. 'Peter's a kind and thoughtful man. The complete opposite of Nicky. We married. I realised that I couldn't have that new start I wanted over in New Zealand and, obviously, I wasn't going to go back to Britain. Peter wasn't averse to coming back to his mother country, so Sweden was an ideal solution. Swedes keep themselves to themselves. After all, you did spawn Garbo. Peter still had relatives in Dalarna, but I didn't want to live up there in the middle of nowhere, so this was a good compromise. Even though I haven't been back to

England for years, it's reassuring to know it's not far away. And this is quiet and peaceful, yet I've got Copenhagen and Malmö on the doorstep.' She waved a hand in the direction of the nearest houses. 'They belong to Stockholmers and Germans, so they're empty at this time of year.' She pointed to the distant tractor. 'That's our nearest full-time neighbour.' She paused. 'I must admit I thought I'd never be found. My past is a painful chapter in my life. All I want is to be left alone and live life in the present.'

'I'm sorry if we've raked up bad memories, but you were our only lead.' Anita felt a palpable wave of disappointment – they had reached a dead end. The one question that needed answering now was who intercepted Graeme Todd before he could meet up with Carol Johansson?

CHAPTER 43

'What did you make of all that?'

They were beyond Ystad and heading back on the E65 to Malmö.

'She sounded plausible,' replied Hakim. 'She wasn't exactly trying to hide anything.'

'Brutally honest.'

They drove on in silence while they wrestled with their thoughts. Hakim was the first to speak.

'It couldn't be the husband who got to Todd first?'

'Why?'

'I don't know. Didn't want to have Carol's new life disrupted. Trying to protect her.'

'It's rather extreme to torture him, cut his hand off and then drown him. He could just have easily warned him off.'

'It was only a thought.'

'No, Hakim, I think there's something more sinister here. But what the hell it is, I've no idea.'

Anita parked the car in front of the apartments at Sevedsgatan. She turned off the engine and looked across at Hakim.

'Come on, let's get this over and done with.'

Hakim produced his key and opened the front door. They went up the flight of stairs to the first floor and Hakim unlocked the door of the apartment. He called out his name and something in Arabic as he took off his shoes. Anita followed suit with her own footwear. That was one habit Swedes and Arabs shared. They entered the living room and were taken by surprise. There, sitting opposite Uday and Amira, were Jazmin and Lasse.

Uday immediately got to his feet when he saw Anita. 'How nice to see you again, Inspector. Please take a seat. Amira, get our guest something to drink and eat.'

'No, don't worry about that, Amira.'

'Are you sure?' Amira asked with some concern. She didn't like to think that they weren't being hospitable.

Realising her mistake, Anita said she would be pleased to have something. Amira appeared relieved. She scurried off to the kitchen while Anita took a seat.

'Your son has explained to us that there has been no inappropriate behaviour on his part.' Anita had doubts about that, but she admired his courage in coming to see Jazmin's parents. She wondered whose idea it had been. 'Naturally, we would have preferred that Jazmin step out with a Muslim boy.' Jazmin gave an audible groan, which her father ignored. 'However, we all have great respect for you, Inspector, particularly Hakim.' Hakim looked suitably embarrassed. 'And we have to accept that we have made our home in a Western country. Sweden has been good to us. And, as Jazmin keeps reminding us, she is Swedish. However, as you'd expect of a good father, I think that we should lay down some rules.' Before these could be outlined, Amira came bustling back in from the kitchen with a tray of cakes.

When Hakim eventually saw Anita and Lasse out of the apartment block's front door, he seemed thankful that he hadn't had to deal with a huge family trauma.

'It's only because you're Lasse's mother that he isn't making a big fuss,' Hakim confided. 'He wouldn't have entertained anyone else.'

'Well, you can have the rest of the weekend off without worrying. And as for the case, we'll start again on Monday.'

As they reached the car, Hakim called: 'Lasse, I think you're mad taking on my sister.'

Lasse couldn't help grinning. 'Someone has to do it.'

Anita spent the rest of the weekend trying to sort out her head. She mentally put aside the Todd case, as she had more immediate things occupying her mind. She had taken Lasse off to The Pickwick for a pint and a chat about Björn. Lasse had never been in the pub before and said how much he liked it. Sitting on one of the leather sofas, they had as good a talk together as they had ever done since the time before Rebecka had come on the scene. Naturally, Lasse was upset at the thought that his dad could have killed someone.

'Do you think he did it?'

'I wouldn't have thought it was in his nature, but I've heard the evidence against him. At least Henrik Nordlund still has doubts. I'm not sure what they are, though.'

Lasse surprised Anita with his mature and sensible approach to the whole nightmare. He knew it was something he'd have to get through. And he'd told Jazmin all about it, and she'd been really sympathetic.

'I really like her, Mamma. She's different from other girls I've met.'

She couldn't disagree.

'Who had the idea to face up to Uday?'

'I did. Jazmin thought I was nuts for suggesting it. She said they wouldn't let me in. But I just knew we had to do something. Didn't want to let it fester and spoil our relationship, or put you in a difficult position with Hakim, seeing him every day as you do.'

'I'm proud of you.'

'Proud enough to buy me another pint?'

274

Before they left, Alex Fraser had come in and looked uncomfortable to see her there. He didn't make any effort to acknowledge her and studiously avoided any eye contact. Anita could understand why. After dealing with Westermark, he was bound to be wary of the police. And she knew, though Fraser was now officially in the clear, that Nordlund wasn't satisfied and that he might well come back into the reckoning.

That night, Anita curled up in bed with Ewan's final letter and wept. In the morning, she burnt it.

The rest of Sunday she lazed about the apartment. There was cleaning to do. She couldn't be bothered. When there was a break in the rain, she went for a run round Pildammsparken. On her return, Lasse announced that he was going out to meet Jazmin. At least the girl had given him the sense of purpose that had been missing for some time. He had even gone out shopping that morning and made the lunch.

Anita was sitting watching something mindless on the TV when her mobile started ringing. She pressed the mute button on the remote control and picked up her phone. She didn't recognise the number.

'Anita? It's me, Kevin Ash.'

Anita's conscience was immediately pricked. She knew she should have called him to report back on the meeting with Carol Johansson.

'I was meaning to ring you.' Not quite true. 'But I didn't want to disturb your weekend.' That was more convincing.

'Are you OK?' he asked. 'It's just you weren't in the best of spirits when you left.'

If he wanted to talk about their night together, then he would have to think again. That had been confined to the category of another of her bedroom mistakes. She had had too many of those since leaving Björn.

'I'm fine. What I was going to tell you is that we've tracked down Carol Pew. Now called Carol Johansson. She seemed a straightforward lady who is rebuilding her life in obscurity in southern Sweden. Her story tallies with what Weatherley told us. The only interesting thing to come out of our conversation was that she claims that she never met up with Graeme Todd. She freely admits that he got in touch with her about the Doris Little inheritance, and even rang her from Malmö. She arranged to pick him up in Ystad, but he never showed up.'

'Wow! So someone got to him first. Any idea who?'

'Not really. She's got a new husband called Peter. He's from New Zealand, but of Swedish extraction. My partner suggested him as a possible suspect, but only because we've nothing else to go on. It's highly unlikely he's got anything to do with it. He's got no reason. After all, Todd was supposedly there to try and get money for Carol out of the British government. That doesn't exactly give the husband a motive.'

'Did you meet him?'

'No. He was away fishing somewhere. By the way, did Hakim send you the picture of Carol out of the newspaper?'

'Yes.'

'The husband is in the jazz trio. He's the one playing the drums. So, have you anything to report from sunny Cumbria?'

'Sun's nowhere to be seen. I just wanted to let you know that I'm going to Doncaster on Tuesday to see George Dobson. Now I'm having second thoughts after what you've just told me. Sounds like the Commission Quay robbery's been a red herring.'

'We've nothing to lose. If nothing else, it'll give you a day out.'

'Have you ever been to Doncaster?' he spluttered in amusement.

'No, but I'm sure you'll find a pub.'

This was followed by an awkward silence.

'Right, I'll let you know how I get on. And if there's

anything you want me to do, just get in touch. I've got your work email. Have you a personal one? Just in case I need to send you something when you're at home,' he added hurriedly in a voice that sounded increasingly dry.

Anita's first instinct was not to give him an excuse for even more contact. Then she relented.

'Right, got it!' There was a pause at the other end of the line. 'Thanks. Take care, Anita.'

'Goodbye,' she said more brusquely than she had intended.

As she was putting her phone down, she noticed that she had missed a call. It was from Henrik Nordlund. She listened to the message with increasing concern.

'Anita, Henrik here.' There was an urgency in his voice that she had never heard before. 'I need to speak to you. Tonight. It's about Greta Jansson. Don't come to the apartment, as I think I'm being watched. Come to the park opposite. Nine o'clock. Come through the Amiralsgatan entrance and I'll meet you at the back of Moriskan.' The message ended. Anita sat back and watched the silent characters moving on the TV screen. This was so unlike Nordlund. He was the last person in the world who would be described as melodramatic, yet that was exactly the tone of his message. She texted Nordlund back saying she would be there at nine. Now she had yet another thing to worry about.

Sunday night in Malmö was quiet. The traffic on the normally busy Amiralsgatan was down to a trickle. At the entrance of Folkets Park she walked past a semicircle of flags, whose cords flapped unharmoniously against their poles. The Cuba Café at the corner of the park was shrouded in darkness. The trees beyond were being tousled by the wind, and the minarets of the Moorish Pavilion, known locally as Moriskan, flitted in and out of view as the clouds raced across the moon. In daylight, this extraordinary Arabian Nights building, which had become the centre of this People's Park in 1902, was a wonderfully gaudy sight. In the dark, it was mysterious and forbidding. The nature of Anita's tryst only helped to make its shadows more unsettling. She steadied her nerves by reminding herself that this was a happy spot, where families came to play and picnic and ride on the amusements. In far off days, it had been a meeting place for workers expressing their political views, and in later years it had become an entertainment venue where many world-famous artists had performed; her mother remembered Frank Sinatra singing here in 1953.

Anita rounded the pavilion and made her way along the path towards the centre of the park. Ahead of her, there was an avenue of trees stretching to the right leading up to the original entrance with its pagoda-style portico. Between the rows of trees was a large, rectangular water feature with paths on each side. On the paths, benches were positioned at regular intervals. Though the light was dim, she could see a figure sitting on one of them. The straight back could only belong to Nordlund. A couple, hand in hand, were leaving the park through the portico. No one else seemed to be around. They would not be disturbed, which was presumably what Nordlund wanted, as he obviously had something vitally important to tell her.

Anita approached the figure. 'Hello, Henrik,' she called lightly. Nordlund didn't move. He was staring straight in front of him at the water.

She sat on the bench next to him. She leaned over and touched him on the arm. 'Henrik.'

Silently, he flopped forward and fell to the ground in front of the bench onto a carpet of fallen leaves.

'Henrik!'

She bent down. He wasn't moving. She put her ear next to his mouth to listen to his breathing. There was no sound. She felt in the dark for his wrist. There was no pulse either.

Then she realised her knee was becoming wet. It wasn't from the earlier rain – it was blood. She could hardly breathe herself when it finally dawned on her that Henrik Nordlund was dead.

CHAPTER 44

Below the tops of the trees, the arc lights illuminated the centre of the park. Together with the flashing lights of the police cars on the road outside, the roped-off entrance and the tent erected over the dead body, it made an eerie spectacle for the curious onlookers who had emerged from the nearby apartment blocks. There was activity all around Anita. Completely dazed at first, the enormity of what had happened was now slowly sinking in. Her first action had been to phone the polishus. Then, as the mental fog had begun to clear, the practical policewoman had taken over. She had called Moberg at home. Then Hakim, who had made his way quickly on foot. Eva Thulin and her team had appeared and quickly went about their gruesome business. No black humour from Thulin this time. This was serious. This was one of their own. Westermark had arrived shortly after Thulin, after Moberg had raised him on his mobile. Everything was carried out in efficient silence. No one felt like talking.

Moberg appeared from the tent and came across to Anita, who was standing on the grass above the water.

'Thulin has confirmed it was a stabbing. In the back. From your description of his position, she reckons Henrik didn't see it coming. Neat job.'

Anita was grateful that it must have been a very quick death.

'Anita, what I need to know is what he was doing here. And, more to the point, what were you doing here?'

Anita tried to clear her mind. It was important to act swiftly. If they wasted the first twenty-four hours, the harder the investigation would become. The time that had elapsed before Graeme Todd and Greta Jansson were found had caused the headaches that followed. This murder had just taken place; probably minutes before she had turned up. The attacker could still have been in the park when she arrived. Grieving had to be put on hold.

'He left me a message today saying he wanted to meet me here at nine.'

'Why here?'

'Because he thought he was being watched.'

'Watched? By whom?'

'I don't know. He wanted to speak to me about the Greta Jansson case. Something was bothering him about it.'

'But we've got your ex. As far as Blom is concerned, it's nailed down.'

'Henrik wasn't sure. Or he wasn't certain when I spoke to him the other night. Something must have changed over the last couple of days.'

'Could this have been a random attack? Some nutter? A robbery? Thulin thinks that his pockets have been rifled. His wallet is missing.'

'It could be an impulse robbery or drug addict after money. But it's quite a coincidence that Henrik wanted to meet me here because he thought someone was watching him, and he ends up dead. Maybe the attacker just wanted it to look like a random killing. Maybe the killer took something that he was going to show me.'

'So you're pretty sure it was something to do with Greta Jansson?' This wasn't the barking Chief Inspector Moberg speaking. It was a softer version. He was hurting as much as Anita. Henrik Nordlund was one of the few detectives he had had time for. He didn't have friends in the force; Nordlund had been the closest thing.

'Have you any clues as to what he was thinking?'

'Not really.' For some reason she found herself withholding the fact that Nordlund had wanted to listen again to the recording of Björn's interview, and to speak to Eva Thulin. She would do that herself first.

'You should go home.' Moberg put a huge consoling arm round her. She felt gratitude, not revulsion. 'I know he was close to you.'

'It's OK. I'll be fine. This has to be solved. Someone has got to pay for this.'

Moberg withdrew his arm.

'Take your time.' He then strode off back towards the tent. Westermark, Wallen, Hakim and a couple of other detectives were standing talking quietly, all still in a state of shock. 'Right, let's get fucking moving.' Moberg was back to his most bullish. 'I don't care who does what, but I want Fraser and Holm brought in now!'

No one could remember seeing so many lights on in the polishus at midnight before. As soon as the word had got out that Nordlund was dead, people had come in to see what they could do. Even Commissioner Dahlbeck, from his country retreat, was closeted with Moberg and Chief Inspector Larsson. Westermark had overseen the picking up of Fraser and Holm, who had been put into separate interview rooms. Everyone else was hanging around waiting for instructions. One notable absentee was Anita. After issuing instructions at the park, Moberg had decided that she must concentrate on her existing case, as she hadn't been involved in the Greta Jansson investigation anyway. Privately, he thought that her close relationship with Nordlund would affect her judgement. Even if Sundström and Mirza weren't exactly making progress on the Todd case, they couldn't afford to step back from it.

But Anita had no intention of detaching herself from

Nordlund's murder. As she left the forensic team to their work, she had been outlining in her mind a plan of action, which she knew Moberg wouldn't allow her to carry out. She had questions to ask, facts to check. After speaking to Moberg, she was worried that he and the team would end up concluding that it was a random killing. But she was convinced it was tied up with Greta Jansson. She knew it would be quickly established whether Fraser and Holm had alibis or not. If it was one of them, then the case would be swiftly solved. But one thing was certain; it wasn't Björn, who was safely in custody in Kirseberg prison.

Anita told Hakim to go home. Naturally, he was upset at Nordlund's death. He was fond of the old detective. She said they would review the Todd case in the morning. In truth, she had no idea how to proceed on that. Now, however, she was more interested in talking to Eva Thulin.

The forensic technician emerged from the tent looking pensive and drained. White-suited members of her team were searching the area under the arc lights for evidence. The entire park would have to be combed in the morning, when they could work in daylight. But there might be something that might turn up now. She spotted Anita and gave her a weary wave.

'This is the worst part of the job, when you have to examine someone you know.'

'Any initial thoughts?'

'It was quick and clean. It was either someone who knew what they were doing, or they were dead lucky; excuse the pun.'

'Eva, did Henrik come and see you or speak to you on the phone yesterday?'

Thulin pushed back the plastic hood on her body suit. 'He did, actually.'

'What was it about?'

'The fingerprints in Greta Jansson's apartment. He just wanted to clarify my findings. He wanted to know exactly which parts of the apartment had been wiped clean and which hadn't. He was interested in the discrepancy in the findings. Basically, where Björn Sundström's prints were or were not.'

'And?'

'Well, his prints were on the front door, in the kitchen, on the bedroom door, around parts of the living room. On books and things.'

'And where would you expect to see them where they weren't?'

'As we think the rape took place there, the bedroom would be the most likely. That was wiped clean of all prints, including Greta's. The bedding was fresh. The bathroom, too, was clean. Cleaner than mine at home. Oh, except for the toilet seat. Sundström must have had a pee. Some of the floors had been cleaned too. Apart from the ones left of Jansson's, the only fresh prints were yours and your ex-husband's.'

'Did Henrik make any comments on what you told him?'

'No. Just thanked me in his usual polite way.'

'Thanks, Eva. Sorry to keep you from your work. You're going to be under the cosh with this one. I'll let you get away.'

Thulin knew Anita of old. She recognised the glint in her eye. 'Do you know who did this?'

'Not yet. But I'll find out.'

CHAPTER 45

The next morning, Anita and Hakim held an impromptu meeting overlooking the canal outside the polishus. She hadn't slept much and had woken to heavy rain. That wouldn't help forensics' work in Folkets Park. Now, there was a rainbow arcing over the Turning Torso. Headquarters was still in a state of agitated alert. The sense of disbelief was palpable, as was a deep feeling of helplessness. Fraser and Holm had been allowed to go after providing alibis. Fraser had been in The Pickwick at the time of the murder; Holm with his family and his visiting mother-in-law. As Anita suspected, they were now talking about a random or opportunistic killing. The police were rounding up every criminal in Malmö with a history of violence, every drug addict and every undesirable they could think of.

It was a new, resilient Anita who leant against the canal-side railings with a paper cup of coffee in her hand and snus firmly embedded under her upper lip. The emotional traumas involving Björn, Ewan and now Henrik Nordlund had left her dazed and confused. But she realised that the only way to cope with all life's present slings and arrows was to be strong, put emotion aside and do everything in her power to find Nordlund's killer, even if it meant taking her eye off the Todd case. And to do that she would have to follow the methods and thinking that her mentor had passed on to her over the years. He had left her a couple of clues, and Hakim had a good idea as to what had gone on in the Jansson investigation when he had helped Westermark in the early stages. She needed to clear her mind, gather evidence methodically and combine it with her cop's instincts. Nordlund had often said she had a cop's nose for a case. She didn't always believe it herself, but now she needed to put faith in her own judgement and find his killer.

'Where do we go from here?' Hakim asked.

A very good question. 'We can look more into Carol Johansson. I doubt it'll throw up much but I think we have to go through the motions. Kevin Ash is visiting the last member of Pew's gang in prison tomorrow. I can't see that shedding much light. He's been in there since being found in Australia back in the 1990s. Must be due for release soon, I would have thought. If he'd been in Sweden, he'd have been out ages ago.'

'I've got an angle that I think is worth pursuing,' said Hakim before draining his coffee.

'OK, you've got a free hand. But first, I want you to go through everything that you were involved in while working with Nordlund on Greta Jansson.'

Hakim gave her a quizzical look. 'Isn't all that being handled by Moberg and Larsson?'

'I want to make sure that they haven't missed anything. Even if it turns out his murder was a random attack, Henrik was still onto something. I have to find out what.'

Anita spent the rest of the morning going through the information that Hakim had supplied her with. He had explained how he and Westermark had divided up the CCTV footage of the various bars in and around Lilla Torg – they had also double-checked, by physically going to each one with a photo of Greta Jansson. Nothing had turned up, despite the fact that Greta's friend Ulrika Lindén was sure she was already in a bar in that area when she called to cancel their get-together. Westermark had gone into Greta's call log and Hakim had been sent to interview

Fraser's and Holm's colleagues.

Anita had also slipped into Nordlund's office and managed to get hold of the recording of his interview with Björn. That had been a sad moment as she reflected on the number of times she had been there and asked for guidance, or just for some sanctuary when things were getting on top of her. There was a photo of his wife, Hannah, on his desk. Everything neat and tidy, just as he had been. In time, they would have to clear out all his possessions and pass them on to his nephew, who was acting for the family. Anita would take it on herself to sort out the office, but not just yet. She looked through his drawers. There was nothing that seemed particularly relevant to the case. Maybe there was something at home, so she would have to visit his apartment. She then went to the operations room. Westermark was already in there. He was taking the photos of Greta Jansson off the wall.

'Is the case closed then?' she asked in surprise.

He smirked. 'Oh, yes. Blom has already been in court and we've got your husband for the next two weeks. Moberg and she are now convinced that Nordlund's murder had nothing to do with the Greta Jansson case. Silly old bugger shouldn't have been out in the park. You get all sorts of weirdos hanging around these places at night. We'll nail it on one of the usual suspects soon enough.'

'You think that's what happened?'

'Why not?' He couldn't resist a condescending grin. 'Your conspiracy theory about Nordlund having some doubts about the Jansson case seems to be just that – a theory. Your professor murdered Greta Jansson, no question.'

Anita left before she let him really wind her up, but not before she had squirrelled a mug shot of Greta Jansson into her bag.

She looked in on Hakim, who seemed absorbed in his internet research, to tell him that she was going to work from home for the rest of the day. It would be easier to think clearly away from the bedlam of headquarters. If Hakim did find anything interesting, he was to get in touch – and if Moberg wondered where she was, he was to say that she was following up a lead. She suggested he keep it vague.

Listening to the recording didn't do anything to help get into Nordlund's head. It was a typical Nordlund-Westermark interview. Nordlund quietly trying to get to the nub of the matter, while Westermark blustered, threatened and sneered in equal measure. Björn had held his own, but the more information he revealed, the more it seemed to confirm his guilt. The fact remained that he had lied to her right from the beginning, both about his relationship with Greta and his movements around the time that she disappeared.

After another coffee and an over-ripe banana she found hiding at the bottom of the fruit bowl, she played the tape through again. And again she gleaned nothing, other than Björn appearing even more culpable. The only question that wasn't answered satisfactorily was the anomaly of the fingerprints. However, she had seen Prosecutor Blom in action in court, and she would put up a convincing argument as to why there seemed to be a discrepancy. The rest of the evidence seemed so overwhelming that the fingerprints might not even become an issue. They proved Björn had been in the apartment, which he had reluctantly admitted to. Whatever had worried Nordlund was more subtle, more imperceptible than Anita could discern in the clear-cut conversation of the recording. Maybe it was something that Nordlund had seen during the interview that had raised his doubts. She wouldn't even bother to attempt to get anything out of Westermark, who wouldn't make any effort to co-operate. And why should he? He had stolen the case – and the subsequent glory – from under Nordlund's nose. And she didn't want to approach Björn's lawyer, as that would immediately get back to Moberg and ructions would inevitably follow. This was not *her* case. The only person she could talk to who was in that room was Björn.

The irony wasn't lost on her. The last time she had been in this miserable room, deep inside Kirseberg prison, was to see Ewan. It had been their final meeting. Now it was the other man in her life that was brought into the room and plonked down in the chair opposite her. The shock this time was Björn's attire. The white T-shirt and faded, blue jeans was a dramatic sartorial change from his regulation black. He was pale and drawn, and confusion and fear were etched equally on his face. Anita didn't know whether to feel pity or anger.

'Hello, Björn,' she said after the guard had left the room.

'Is this another interrogation? It's a dangerous business talking to me. The last one who did is now dead, I understand.'

'This is no time for any of your flippant remarks, Björn,' Anita snapped angrily. 'Whether you're a murderer or not, this case is responsible for the death of Henrik Nordlund. He was a good man who didn't deserve to die. So I'm not taking any shit from you. You either answer my questions or I'll leave you here to rot.'

'I'm sorry,' he said contritely. 'How's Lasse?'

'Bearing up. He's got a new girlfriend to take his mind off things.'

Björn beamed. 'Chip off the old block.'

'I bloody hope not. Now, I need to know one or two things. Like why did you lie to me about your movements? You didn't tell me you went into Greta Jansson's apartment on three separate occasions.'

'I didn't think you'd look for her if I told you the full truth. I was desperate.'

Anita took out her tin of snus. She didn't offer it to Björn. 'The trouble is that it makes you look guilty. You were with her the night she died.'

'We argued. She threw me out. Then, when she wasn't around the next day, I started to worry.'

'The neighbour's key. That was another thing you failed to mention.'

'When she still wasn't around a week later, I really panicked. You were the only person I could turn to. The only person I could trust.'

I was convenient is what you mean, Anita thought ruefully. 'All right. I want you to think very carefully about each visit you made and where exactly you went when you were inside the apartment. Your exact movements in each room.'

She knew this shouldn't be a difficult task for Björn, who had always been a clear thinker.

'The first time,' he said contemplatively, 'I just went into the living room. That's where we had our confrontation.'

'Not the bedroom?'

'That's where I was hoping to end up. Greta had other ideas,' he said with a regretful grimace. 'So, no to the bedroom. Obviously, I was in the hallway when I came in and went out.'

'OK. You went back the next day when you pretended to be her dad.'

'Yes. Shows I can think on my feet.' He's had a lot of practice at that, Anita reflected bitterly. 'That time, I went into nearly every room. Living room, kitchen, bathroom... and I glanced into the bedroom.'

'Can you remember what you touched?'

'Nothing much. Opened the fridge. Went into the bathroom and had a pee. Noticed her toothpaste was gone. That made me think I might have frightened her away. Maybe touched some of the books in the living room. Two were mine, anyway!'

'What about the bedroom?'

'Why the obsession with the bedroom?'

'Just answer,' she snapped.

'Nothing, really. I didn't lie on the bed and pine if that's

290

what you're after. I just looked through the door.'

'Was the bed made?'

Björn looked pensive. 'It was, actually. Fresh sheets. She mustn't have had a chance to sleep in them.' The last words caught in his throat and she could see his eyes starting to well up. She knew he would fight any display of emotion. It was the Swedish way.

'And your last visit?'

He was back in control of himself. 'I was only in there a few minutes. I could see that nothing had changed and that Greta hadn't been back. I realised she had disappeared, so I came to you.'

Anita took out a notebook and scribbled a few lines.

'Did you make a call to the school to say that Greta wouldn't be going back?'

'Of course not. Why should I?'

'My colleagues think you did. Unluckily for you, it tied in with your stupid tale about being Greta's father.'

Björn sighed despondently.

'One last thing. You mentioned that Greta talked about a new man in her life. Any ideas who it was?'

'To be honest, at the time, I assumed she was just making it up to get me out of the apartment. But the more I've thought about it, the more I'm convinced there was someone. If there was, he must have been pretty new on the scene; she hadn't been down here that long.'

'Her colleagues talked about her getting away from someone, presumably you, but no mention of a new man. She may have kept it quiet, though.'

'She may only just have met him. And another thing, she wasn't a great drinker, which was why I was surprised that she seemed pissed when I saw her at the apartment. I think she'd been with someone earlier that evening. Perhaps he came back after I'd left.'

'There's nothing on her mobile call log to suggest she rang anyone after you'd gone.'

'Maybe the bastard just turned up.'

Anita wasn't listening. She'd just had an uncomfortable thought.

CHAPTER 46

Anita had another bad night, yet she was in a determined mood when she entered through the main door of the polishus at seven o'clock the next morning. Her mind had been racing as she had tossed and turned. A herbal tea at half past two hadn't helped. It was while she was in the shower that something Björn had said came back to her. She had listened to the interview yet again. Now she knew what Nordlund had heard. Now she had a clear idea of what action she was going to take.

Headquarters was already busy. A suspect had been hauled in during the early hours of the morning. Sejad Medunjanin was well known to the Skåne County Police as a serial thief and drug dealer with a history of GBH. A knife was his weapon of choice; it didn't make a noise. He had spent more time behind bars than on the streets. He wasn't the only suspect to be brought in for questioning, and it was taking a lot of manpower to check out the growing list of alibis. Commissioner Dahlbeck was no longer that worried about a dead British visitor when it looked far worse that one of his own officers should be murdered in a place used for family outings and relaxation. This suited Anita, as she was mystified as to what to do next in the Todd case. She was more concerned about finding out what her old friend and colleague had discovered; she was now convinced that Nordlund had been on the verge of solving the Greta Jansson murder.

By the time Hakim came in just after eight, Anita was engrossed in some notes she had found in Nordlund's file. She had also compiled some of her own. Hakim immediately knew it was nothing to do with their own case. But she was his superior, so it wasn't his place to question her, and he knew her well enough to trust that she knew what she was doing. However, he felt that they mustn't give up so easily on the Todd investigation. Here was a chance for him to shine. Help to solve the case, and he would leave Malmö on a high. It would make it easier for him to be accepted in Gothenburg when he started there after Christmas.

'Anita, can I borrow your car today?'

She gave him a quizzical glance. 'Yeah. Where are you going?'

'I thought I'd go back out and nosy round the Johanssons'. Just ask around. I assume they're still officially on the radar?'

'Yes. But why the interest?'

'I did some digging, and discovered that Peter Johansson is quite a rich guy.'

'Well, admittedly, it looked a nice house, but nothing out of the ordinary.'

'Did you know that he owns all the houses around theirs as well?'

'I thought she said— '

'I know – "Stockholmers and Germans". She lied. They also have a fancy apartment in Gamla Stan in Stockholm.'

'Do you know what he made his money in?'

'Property in New Zealand.'

'It just sounds as though he's doing the same over here.'

'Well, we've nothing to lose. And I'm expecting a call or email soon from New Zealand about something else.'

'What time is it over there?'

'Ten hours ahead, but the person I've been talking to is doing me a favour. She sounded nice.' He smiled at the recollection.

'Whatever. I'm going out and won't be around for a few hours.' Anita shoved some papers into her bag. 'Keep a low profile. We don't want a police harassment charge on top of everything else.' She gazed at him fondly for a moment then said brusquely: 'Just don't do anything stupid.'

'Are you sure? Are you *really* sure? You're not pulling my plonker?'

'Oh, yes. I'm sure.'

Kevin Ash was sitting in a large, deserted hall, lined with tables and chairs. It was where the inmates of HM Prison Doncaster received visitors, if they had any. The only two other occupants were a large, unsmiling prison warder hovering near the entrance, and the shaven-headed George Dobson sitting opposite Ash. The purpose-built prison on the site of the old power station in Marshgate was the most modern one Ash had visited.

He hadn't arrived with any real expectations. Dobson was a wiry man with darting, intelligent eyes. Now in his mid-fifties, he had kept himself in good condition. And he was more forthcoming than most prison inmates Ash had had dealings with. Maybe it was the light at the end of the tunnel – the prospect of his imminent release – that made him more accommodating. Ash had opened the encounter with the offer of a packet of cigarettes, which Dobson had surprisingly turned down. They had kicked off the conversation by talking about his time in prison – or "Doncatraz", as it was known by the incarcerated residents.

With his years in the North East, Ash had learned to interpret thick Geordie accents, which was just as well in Dobson's case.

'I'm into cookin' these days. Might try to get some chef work, like, when I get oot. If anybody gives us a chance.'

Ash was amused. 'And what brought that on?'

'Gordon Ramsey did one of his programmes in 'ere a few years back. By, that lad's got a filthy mooth on 'im. But he was all reet. So impressed wi' one of the boys, he offered him a job when he escaped from 'ere!' He had a guttural laugh.

Then they got round to Nicky Pew.

'What went wrong that night on Commission Quay?' Ash asked.

'The silly tosser of a security guard tried to be a hero. Must admit I was surprised it was Nicky who pulled the trigger, like. Gary was the one into shooters. Liked to think he was bloody Reggie Kray.'

'Who tipped you off about the diamond delivery?'

'Nicky always played his cards close to his chest. No one was ever sure what he was thinkin'. It was a bit weird, like, 'cos we never normally did jobs in our backyard. Suppose this was a biggun an' he couldn't resist it. Twat.'

'You know Billy Hump's dead?'

Dobson appeared genuinely surprised. 'I heard about Gary. When did Billy gan?'

'Beginning of last week. Hit-and-run. Outside his local boozer.'

'He was thick as pig shit. Mind, he was all reet. Just mixed with bad company from an early age. Like the rest of us, except for Nicky of course. Who ran him ower?'

'They don't know.'

'Typical police. If it were someone from somewhere snotty, they'd be like blue-arsed flies. A felon like Billy, an' they don't give a rats.'

'Chapman and Hump reckoned that Pew stitched them up.'

'Too bloody reet. I'm sure he did the same thing to me in Oz. He'd cocked up in the first place, so it was easier to cover himself by gettin' us oot the way. I'm glad the bastard's dead. If he wasn't, I'd track him doon after I got oot.'

Ash fished out the photograph of the jazz event in Ystad.

'Carol Pew's been tracked down in Sweden. Calls herself Johansson now.'

'Stuck up cow. Nicky was obsessed wi' her. Sharp as a knife, she was. Not a woman to be crossed. Vindictive. Always thought she might have been behind a lot of wor jobs. Nicky was all front. She was the brains, I reckon.'

'Well, if she was, it was never proved. Sounds doubtful to me; she didn't even get his money from the diamond heist. You know Nicky was with another woman at the time he was killed?'

'I heard that. Big surprise.'

Ash pushed the photo across the table. He pointed to Carol Pew sitting in the audience. 'That's her now.'

'Blonde now, then. Still a looker. Can't deny that.' Then Dobson went quiet. He started to shake his head very slowly. His eyes bulged, and Ash could see the vein on his forehead pulsing.

Minutes later, Ash was rushing down a corridor with a warder. He showed Ash into an empty office and pointed to a phone.

'Do you know what time it'll be in Australia?'

'Haven't a clue,' the warder replied. 'But I tell you something, I'd rather be there than here right now.'

'So would I,' said Ash as he hurriedly picked up the receiver.

CHAPTER 47

Hakim was enjoying the sense of freedom Anita's sudden lack of interest in the Todd case had allowed him. He drove round the outskirts of Ystad and headed out on the Simrishamn road. As soon as he moved to Gothenburg, he would buy himself a car – he'd be able to afford it then. And he would keep it in better nick than Anita's. The Peugeot was a mess.

He was looking forward to Gothenburg. He was dying to get away from the stifling environment of the cramped family apartment and, particularly, his annoying sister. He grudgingly admitted that recently she'd been less trouble, now that she was hooked up with Lasse, but his father still wasn't totally happy with the relationship, and there was still something of an atmosphere between them. What was weird was having your sister going out with your boss's son. He smiled. He wouldn't have to live with that problem after Christmas. He would miss Anita, of course. They had a good rapport, and he had learned a great deal under her guidance. That was why this was such an exciting possibility. If he could help solve this case, she would be impressed. It would be his leaving present to her.

He eased the car onto the coast road. Now Peter Johansson was occupying his thoughts. It may be just a hunch, but something wasn't quite right. Johansson was wealthy. He owned property. Four houses in the same place. Hakim had found no evidence that they were rented out in the summer. Of course, they might just be investments that he would sell on when the market was right, though Sweden wasn't suffering the same property slump that much of the rest of Europe was subject to. Yet it was odd that such an astute businessman wouldn't try to make some money on them instead of leaving them idle. Hakim decided to have a closer look at the properties. However, his first destination was going to be Kåseberga. Peter Johansson had his boat registered there. And it was the sort of place where he could pick up a bit of gossip.

Hakim turned the car off the road and made his way through the village. He reached the tiny harbour just below the cliff where the famous stone ship, Ales Stenar, was situated. Even at this time of year, there were a few sightseers trekking up the hill to the ancient site, which overlooked the grim, grey Baltic. He pulled up in the cobbled car park next to a German motorhome, which dwarfed Anita's old Peugeot. He gazed out seawards. The harbour walls enclosed a small haven where half a dozen craft rocked gently in the swell. Behind the car park, the little local museum and a collection of timber-built tourist shops were strung along the bottom of the cliff. Hakim got out and locked the car. He scrutinised the boats in front of him. One took his attention more than the rest. This vessel wasn't just for pottering along the Scanian coast. *Diamanten* was a gleaming-white, sleek-hulled craft with highly polished, light-brown decking and shining chromework. This was Peter Johansson's boat. Hakim first decided to visit the shops and herring stalls to see if anyone knew anything about the New Zealander. Then, if the coast was clear, it might be interesting to have a look round the boat.

The unremitting, grey cloud that blanketed the city gave it a drab winter feel, though it wasn't especially cold for late October. Anita's feet were uncomfortable. In her haste this morning, she had put on a pair of ankle boots; a rare fashion extravagance. She had paid handsomely for them, only to regret the purchase during their first outing. They were too tight, and the thick heels made her clomp around inelegantly. Now she was wobbling over the cobbles of Lilla Torg with a photograph of Greta Jansson in her grasp. The pretty face stared up at her. What a waste of a human life! The passing pedestrians heading for the shops, and the office workers returning after lunch could have no idea of the turmoil in the mind of the blonde woman with the glasses, tottering past the old telephone box in the centre of the square. She was almost trembling with excitement and anticipation. She might not be any closer to finding Nordlund's killer, but Greta Jansson's was another matter. She now knew that her mentor really had been onto something.

She was startled out of her reverie by her mobile phone ringing. She looked at the caller's name. It was Kevin Ash. She hoped he had some real news, and that it wasn't just some pretext to ring her.

'Anita here.'

'Hi. Can you speak?'

'Yes.'

'You might have to sit down, given what I have to tell you.' She could hear the animation in his voice.

'Just tell me.'

'Nicky Pew is alive.' At first, the words didn't register. She found herself staring at the half-timbered façade of the Lilla Torg Steakhouse. 'Did you hear me?'

'That can't be.' Anita was absolutely stunned. Her mind had been so full of finding Greta Jansson's murderer that she had filed away the Todd case in the "visit later" folder.

'George Dobson recognised him in the photo you sent over. He's one of the jazz trio. The drummer.'

Anita's head was reeling. She couldn't see how that was possible. Unless? 'Deputy Chief Constable Weatherley?'

'Oh, yes. He didn't kill him at all.'

'But he was so sure.'

'I've been on to Australia. The body was never actually recovered from the sea. The local police had no reason to doubt Weatherley's story, especially as he had been shot. He wasn't wounded seriously, of course, but enough to make it all look and sound believable.'

Anita was frantically processing this astonishing information.

'It makes total sense of everything.' In his growing excitement, Ash's words were running away with themselves. 'Pew and Weatherley faked the death, Pew re-emerges as Peter Johansson a few years later, with the same wife, and hides away in Sweden. It would've stayed that way if it hadn't been for the death of Doris Little and a tenacious heir hunter. Once Todd had found Carol and made the Nicky Pew connection, he must have checked the jazz photo out with Billy Hump, just as I did with Dobson this morning. Then he realised he'd hit his "jackpot". With Nicky still alive, it didn't take a genius to work out that he still had the diamond money – all the proceeds split one way, as he'd shopped his three accomplices to Weatherley, who emerges a hero. I suspect that Graeme Todd thought he could blackmail Nicky. Books into a posh hotel in Malmö because he thinks he's about to make himself rich. Big mistake.'

'So, he meets up with Nicky or Carol in Ystad,' said Anita as she pieced together the story from the Swedish end. 'They aren't going to give him anything, let alone leave him alive to give them away. But they have to discover exactly what he knows, hence the torture. God, the severed hand. It's probably no coincidence that Carol's a butcher's daughter.'

'I bet they've got a boat.'

'Well, yes. Carol said Peter had a boat moored in the harbour nearby. That'll be how they got the body out to sea. In the meantime, they feed back the information they've extracted from Todd to Weatherley, and he tries to tie things up at the British end.' Anita's mind was still racing. 'Kevin, you've done a fantastic job.'

'Thanks.' He sounded genuinely pleased at her congratulations.

Then she had a sudden thought.

'Hakim!'

'What?'

'Look, I'll ring you back soon. I've got to call a colleague before he does something stupid.' The moment Ash rang off, she punched in Hakim's mobile number.

Hakim glanced around him. No one was watching. He leapt over the small gap between the harbour wall and the stern of *Diamanten*. He had some difficulty regaining his balance as the boat rode on the lapping water. He was out of his comfort zone – dry land was his natural habitat. He ducked through the cabin door and found himself in the saloon area. It was not as luxurious as he had expected. Blue padded benches tightly abutted the legs of the vinyl-topped table. The galley was compact and functional. Beyond it was a high seat in front of the wheel and controls. Four paces took him to a step down, and into the bow area with a bedroom, and small shower room complete with basin and toilet. Somewhere on this boat Peter and Carol Johansson must have hidden Graeme Todd's body. He was now convinced.

The local storekeepers hadn't been much help. The New Zealander kept himself to himself, though he was always pleasant. But then, while he was having a coffee sitting on the harbour wall, Hakim had picked up an email on his mobile phone. It was from his police contact in New Zealand, and it brought him some startling news. Peter Johansson had been born in Auckland in 1955. And then he had died there in 1961. The Peter Johansson now living in Skåne was roughly the right age, and had obviously taken over the dead boy's identity. Hakim had no inkling who he really was, but now he was sure that he was behind Todd's death. Or certainly a party to it. He just couldn't fathom a reason. All he knew was that Todd had been taken by boat to near the Öresund Bridge and thrown overboard. He could have been tortured anywhere – the Johanssons owned four houses, after all; they'd bought themselves real privacy, with no prying neighbours to worry about. But the boat was a fact, and Hakim just knew it was *this* boat.

By this time, he was sitting on the double bed in the bow end. He heard a car draw up. He peered through the thin, horizontal cabin window. Out of a green Saab stepped a figure he recognised from the photo in *Ystads Allehanda*. The blond quiff of the jazz drummer was unmistakable. He had no time to slip off the boat, as Johansson was a few metres from the stern. He quickly nipped into the shower room and sat on the toilet seat as quietly as he could. The boat lurched as Johansson stepped on board. He was whistling. Hakim held his breath as he heard footsteps approach his hiding place. The whistling continued just outside the door. Hakim thought he was going to be sick. Through the thin wall, he heard Johansson opening a cupboard in the bedroom. Retrieving something from the cupboard was hopefully the reason for his visit to the boat, and he would now leave. Hakim could hear him jump up the step and go back into the saloon. Further creaks confirmed that he was heading back off the boat. Hakim was about to breathe a sigh of relief when his mobile phone went off.

Anita only got Hakim's answer phone. He would call back when he got the message. She started to worry. Where was he? She should never have let him go on his own. She should never have taken her eye off the Todd case. What a fool she was – and an unprofessional fool at that! By this time, she was moving through the crowds on Skomakaregatan and was soon in the wide thoroughfare of Södergatan. As she entered Gustav Adolfs Torg, she paused briefly to redial. Soon she was running, as fast as her boots would allow, along the canal back to the polishus. Her mind was whizzing ahead. She would have to get hold of a car, as Hakim had taken hers.

Minutes later, she was running into the car park, where she spotted Westermark's car. Her feet were in agony as she pushed her way through the glass entrance doors. She caught Westermark just as he was coming out of his office.

'I need you to take me to Löderup... or near there.'

'I've got stuff to do.'

'Fuck that, Karl! Hakim could be in serious trouble.'

'The silly shit—'

She hadn't time for this. 'Just bring your pistol. I'll fetch mine.' Westermark hesitated.

'Now!' she yelled at him.

CHAPTER 48

It was a relief to turn off the road onto the dirt track to the Johanssons' home. The first part of the journey had been undertaken in hostile silence, with Anita resisting the urge to slip off her ankle boots and massage her feet – she could already feel the blisters forming. Eventually, she thought it prudent to fill Westermark in on what she had just discovered from Ash. He had made little comment and had remained quiet. As they passed the first two houses, there was no sign of Anita's Peugeot. Maybe Hakim was fine. If she had dragged Westermark out here for nothing, then she would never hear the end of it.

'What do we do now?'

'I'll try Hakim again.' Again the answer message kicked in. Now she was in a dilemma. Hakim might well be safe, but she had no idea where he was. But, now they were on the spot, maybe she should have another word with Carol Johansson. She couldn't arrest her or her husband on suspicion of murder, as she hadn't consulted with Moberg or Prosecutor Blom. They would want more solid evidence before committing themselves. The least they'd require was an official statement from Ash about his conversation with Dobson. Anita sighed – perhaps rushing out here had been a mistake. What made it worse was that she would look a fool in front of Westermark, who would make a point of capitalising on her impulsiveness.

'Drive up to the house,' she instructed.

They were greeted by the barking dog.

'I hate fucking dogs,' Westermark mouthed.

Carol Johansson appeared from the front of the house. Her surprise at seeing an unknown car disappeared when she saw Anita get out.

'Jingo, heel.' The dog immediately obeyed and sat upright, though still alert. 'What brings you back?' she said in English.

'This is Inspector Karl Westermark.' Westermark nodded while not taking his eye off the dog. 'I wanted to have a word with your husband.'

Carol Johansson seemed completely relaxed. No sign of nerves. Anita had to admire the woman's coolness and confidence.

'He's away on business. Why do you want to see him?'

'Just routine stuff,' Anita said off-handedly, not wanting to alert her to the possibility that they were suspicious.

'We know he's Nicky Pew.'

Westermark's blunt statement was like a bolt from the blue. Anita wasn't sure whether she or Carol Johansson was the most startled.

Carol recovered first. 'Jingo!' she shouted, and the animal bounded towards Westermark, leapt up at him and clamped its jaws round his left arm, which he had thrown up to defend himself. He yelled in anguish as he grappled with the dog, while he desperately tried to manoeuvre his pistol out of its holster with his right hand. Carol ran to the open barn door. Anita went after her, leaving Westermark to fend for himself.

It was dark inside. Anita advanced carefully into the barn, her eyes slowly becoming accustomed to the gloom. There was a strong smell of horses and hay. She couldn't hear anything. Slowly, she pulled out her weapon. Then a shot rang out and all she could hear was the dog whimpering, accompanied by Westermark cursing. Another shot followed and the whimpering stopped.

In front of her, Anita could just make out the bottom rungs of a ladder, which disappeared upwards. She assumed it must lead to a hay loft.

'Carol, come on out.' Nothing. 'It's too late. We know that you and Nicky killed Graeme Todd.' She still couldn't detect any movement. 'Hand yourself in. It's the only sensible thing to do.'

But she knew that Carol wasn't going to give up that easily – she and Nicky had gone to great lengths to create this new life. They had even murdered to protect it. Suddenly, there was a sound behind her. She swung round.

Westermark was silhouetted in the doorway. 'Thanks for your fucking help, Anita.'

She ignored him. She was now in the centre of the barn.

'Karl, go round the back and see if there's another way out.'

As Westermark turned, Carol appeared out of the darkness. She was brandishing a pitchfork, which was aimed at his back. 'You bastard!' she shrieked hysterically. Westermark didn't have time to react as she lunged forward. A split second later, Anita's pistol fired. Carol spun away as the pitchfork harmlessly pronged a pile of loose hay. She was clutching her hand, and blood was dribbling thorough her fingers. 'You killed my beautiful dog, you bastard,' she howled at an ashen-faced Westermark. Anita was shaking with relief. Had she been a better shot, Carol Pew would be dead, and a lot of difficult questions would have to be answered.

'Carol Pew, you are under arrest for attacking a police officer.'

Carol glared at her. 'Shouldn't you read me my rights?'

'This isn't Britain,' Anita said dismissively.

Carol suddenly spat in Anita's face. Anita resisted the urge to slap her. She calmly wiped the dribbling saliva from her cheek.

'Is your arm OK?' she asked Westermark.

'I'll live. Ruined a great jacket, though.'

'Sod your jacket! We've got to find Hakim. There's no sign of my car round here.'

'Well, what about the other houses – or Johansson's boat?' said Westermark.

A look of alarm crossed Carol's face. Anita saw it and realised in an instant that the boat was where they would find Pew.

Hakim had never felt such pain before. His left eye was already so swollen that he couldn't see out of it. Blood was trickling down his chin from a cut lip. His ribs ached from the kicks and punches that Johansson had rained on him.

After his phone had gone off, he knew he would be discovered. He swallowed hard, opened the shower room door and found himself on the wrong end of a small handgun. Johansson, or whoever he really was, had frisked him and found his warrant card. Then Hakim's heart had stopped as Johansson had taken his phone and started to flick through it.

'I won't ask again.' The man spoke in Swedish with a pronounced foreign accent. He shoved his face menacingly right up to Hakim's. 'Who else knows about me?'

Hakim looked at him defiantly; he was playing for time. It resulted in another sideswipe, making him lurch back across the bed. With his hands tightly tied behind his back, he had no way of defending himself. The man grabbed his shirt collar and jerked him back into a sitting position.

'Well, if you're not going to talk, you're of no use to me. I think we'll go for a little boat ride.'

Anita was furious. 'You've forced our hand, you imbecile!'

Westermark had just shoved Carol Pew into the back seat of his Porsche. 'If she bleeds on my leather interior, she won't make it back alive,' he'd muttered darkly. They had bandaged her hand and slapped handcuffs on her wrists. She was still full of wrath and bile, primarily directed at Westermark.

Despite his obviously painful arm, he looked smug. 'Well, we've got the bitch. All we have to do now is arrest the husband. Case closed.'

'Christ, Karl! It's not that simple.' Anita was still seething at her gung-ho colleague. She knew there would be hell to pay. If they messed up Nicky Pew's arrest, they'd spend the rest of their careers in traffic. And where the hell was Hakim?

Despite wanting to wait for the backup from Ystad, she realised that they would have to move quickly. The only thing they had on their side was the element of surprise. She just hoped Pew hadn't gone out to sea.

Anita drove the Porsche. They raced along the country roads and down through the village of Kåseberga to the harbour. Anita spotted her own car straight away. Then she saw a new Saab was parked in front of a smart cabin cruiser. Anita noticed the name immediately – *Diamanten*. *The Diamond* must be an in-joke. This had to be Nicky Pew's boat. She was thankful that it was still moored. She parked the Porsche on the opposite side of the car park.

'He's probably on board,' said Westermark as he took out his pistol.

Anita glanced down at the weapon. 'We want him alive. We've got to go easy.'

Westermark stepped out of the car. Anita could see his blood was up, the adrenaline flowing. He would be difficult to control. She had to take charge before he got out of hand.

'I'll check the boat out. You stay with Carol.'

Westermark grunted. 'OK; I'll cover you.'

Anita looked around. She was grateful to see that there weren't many visitors about at what was now the fag end of the season. The afternoon murkiness would soon merge with the evening shadows. As casually as she could, she sauntered over to the boat and peered through the front cabin window. No one to be seen. Maybe Pew was below. She had no option but to go on board. She took out her own pistol. Her throat was dry. This was a man who knew how to use guns. Ruthless. She glanced back at Westermark, who was leaning against his car. He nodded as though giving her his permission to step aboard. With a gulp, she took the stride that got her onto the rear sundeck. The boat swayed under her feet as she readjusted her footing. She grasped her pistol in both hands and held it out in front of her in the firing position. She stepped through the door of the saloon. Her footstep made a loud, thudding noise. Her wretched boots! She immediately stood still. All she could hear was the lapping of the water from outside. But now there was another sound. Her body was taut. Her finger nervously fretted over the trigger of her pistol. This wasn't the instinctive reaction of the barn. This was the interminable waiting for the right moment. In front of her was a closed door. It must be the bedroom. For a moment, she thought of calling out Pew's name. Then she changed her mind. If he was armed inside the bedroom, he might fire through the flimsy wall. Now she was sure she could hear low breathing. Was Nicky Pew on the other side, waiting with gun in hand? She felt herself sweating in the cramped conditions of the saloon. Then there was a muffled moan. That didn't sound like someone waiting to pounce. Anita stood back, tensed herself, and with a sudden lunge, kicked the door open and dived into the room, pistol at the ready. Nothing happened. No shot, no attack. Pew wasn't there. But Hakim was. His hands and feet were bound, and he had gaffer tape over his mouth. Anita was shocked at the state he was in and she swiftly set about freeing him. She had to find a carving knife in the galley to cut the knots of the rope, which had been tied with the expertise of a sailor.

Hakim tried to speak, but found it impossible to get the words out through his swollen lips. Anita found herself cradling him like a child. Pew would pay for this. He must be somewhere near. His car was here and he wouldn't want to leave Hakim for long. She phoned for an ambulance and then instructed Hakim to lie on the bed and wait.

She stepped off the boat and saw Westermark wandering over towards her.

'What have you done with Carol Pew?'

'It's OK; she's safely locked in the car.'

'Hakim's in there,' Anita said, indicating the boat with her thumb. 'Badly beaten up.'

'No sign of Pew?'

'No. But he must be around here somewhere.'

Just then they heard a scream. It came from the Porsche. They could see Carol Pew's face pressed against the window. She was shouting. Though muffled by the glass, they could hear, 'Nicky! Run! Run, Nicky!'

Glancing over towards the shops, they saw the tall figure of a man with blond hair standing uncertainly at the edge of the car park, a large jerry can in each hand. His gaze quickly travelled from the car to Anita and Westermark. In a flash, he had dropped the cans and whipped out a gun. There was a single shot in their direction, the bullet loudly splintering off the concrete harbour wall behind them. Nicky Pew turned on his heels and made for the gap between the shops. He pushed past an elderly woman who momentarily blocked Westermark's line of fire. For a man in his mid-fifties, Pew was surprisingly fit and agile. He was mounting the steps that led to Ales Stenar, two at a time. Westermark made after him. Just then the squad car from Ystad came down the road. Anita rushed over to it and quickly gave instructions to the two patrolmen to keep an eye on both Carol and the injured Hakim on the boat.

She was soon running up the steps. Her feet were seriously throbbing. As she neared the top of the hill, she heard a couple of shots. On reaching the brow, she found a middle-aged couple cowering in the grass. She shouted 'Police!' at them and, without saying a word, they pointed along the path. Anita rushed on. There was no sign of either Westermark or Pew. A frightened young man was hiding behind the large site-information board.

'Stay there and get down!' she shouted at him.

Two more shots were exchanged as she reached a cattle-grid. She gingerly stepped over it, balancing on the metal rungs. The gunfire had come from straight ahead. In the dim light she could just discern the ancient stones of the ship, still impressive after centuries of wind and weather. The prow and stern were large, upright boulders, twice the size of the other stones forming the body of the vessel. She had often visited this megalithic monument of worship and burial and felt anger at its imminent desecration.

She scoped the site for any sign of Pew and Westermark. They must be hidden behind the stones. Out on the Baltic, the light of a tanker glinted in the dusk. A shot rang out, betraying the location of one of the men. It came from the side of the ship on Anita's right. Crouching, she ran across the wide expanse of grass separating her from the prow. On reaching the high end-stone, she threw herself to the ground. A bullet zinged off the side of one of the smaller stones, only metres away. This was immediately followed by a volley of shots.

And then nothing. All Anita could hear was her heart thumping and her uneven breathing.

She eased herself up to a squatting position, her back pressed against the cold rock. Very slowly, she manoeuvred her way round the side of the stone. Still no sound. She wanted to call out Westermark's name, but that would draw attention to her location. But she couldn't stay here forever. If the light went, Pew would be able to make a dash for the fields beyond. She had to do something now. She steeled herself, counted to three, and swung out of her hiding place, pistol in firing position. Half way down the ship she could see the silhouette of a man standing, weapon in hand, over a lifeless shape on the ground.

'Freeze!' she shouted.

CHAPTER 49

'I believe this initiative will help make our communities safer, and will be an example to other forces around the country.' Deputy Chief Constable Weatherley looked very pleased with himself as he beamed at the cameras of the television crews from the local BBC and ITV stations. Standing on the steps of Newcastle's Civic Centre, he was immaculately dressed in his police uniform, the peak of his cap gleaming almost as brightly as his confident smile. This was a man that the public could trust.

'One more question. And then we've got to get this show on the road,' he joked.

An attractive reporter with brown, shoulder-length hair poked her microphone towards Weatherley and asked with a knowing smile: 'Is it true that you're about to be appointed as Chief Constable of Lincolnshire?'

Weatherley looked suitably humble. 'I cannot deny it. So, let's just say that this initiative is my leaving present to the people of Northumbria, whom I have been honoured to serve for so many years. Thank you.'

Weatherley gave a little bow to show that the interview was formerly terminated. As he turned away, he saw Kevin Ash hanging around close by, with a cigarette dangling out of the corner of his mouth.

'Hello, Cockney. Can't keep away?'

'Must be your magnetism.'

Weatherley glanced back at the film crews, who were

starting to pack up their gear.

'I'll be on TV a lot more once I take up my new job. Has television reached Cumbria yet?'

'Very funny. Can I have a quick word?'

'Supersonic. That quick enough for you?'

'You are on good form, Roller.'

Weatherley wasn't pleased. 'It's "sir" to you.'

'Not for long,' Ash smiled. There was a hint of alarm in Weatherley's eyes. 'I've come to tell you that you've been rumbled at last. After all these years.'

'And what the fuck do you mean by that?'

'That's not the sort of language they'll expect to hear from their Chief Constable in Lincolnshire. But, of course, you should never sell the skin before you've shot the bear.'

'What on earth are you babbling on about?'

'Basically, it means you'll never take up the job. It's a Swedish saying; I'm surprised you've not heard it. Know a bit about Sweden these days, don't you?'

Weatherley was furious. 'I'm not putting up with this shite from you. You're messing with the big boys now.'

Weatherley was about to turn away.

'I just wanted you to know that Nicky Pew's dead.'

Weatherley stood stock still. 'Of course he's dead,' he said slowly. 'I killed him.'

'No, I mean he really *is* dead this time. Not pretend dead.'

'Say any more and you'll be in serious trouble, Ash.'

'Shall I call the TV people back? I've got quite a story for them. And I think it'll go beyond the local telly. Might even make Cumbria.'

Weatherley went quiet. Ash flicked away his cigarette butt.

'I know you fabricated Pew's death. After all, you were in his pocket.'

Weatherley was about to argue the point before deciding against it.

315

'You've been his man since the 1990s. It was you who tipped off Pew about the diamond shipment when you were serving in North Shields. Watch it, did you? Must have crapped yourself when it went wrong and Nicky shot that guard. But then it all suddenly worked out a treat. Nicky gives you Chapman and Hump. Suddenly your standing goes up. Then he disappears to Oz with Dobson. You follow, because Nicky's got an even cleverer plan up his sleeve – give you Dobson and then the big one. You kill Nicky trying to escape. Nice touch, him winging your arm for credibility. You return a glittering hero while Pew vanishes and reappears as Peter Johansson in New Zealand. Then he starts a new life with his wife in Sweden. And he still has all the loot. I wonder how much of it he gave to you? Anyway, it's all hunky-dory with everybody coming out a winner.'

Ash pulled out another cigarette. Instead of lighting it, he used it to point at Weatherley.

'Then a few weeks ago, Pew's new life, your reputation, the money – they're all put in jeopardy when some nondescript probate researcher follows up the death of an old biddy in Carlisle. And the path leads, indirectly, to Carol. But who'd have thought that Graeme Todd would be clever enough to link Carol with Nicky? Not only that, but he finds out about the Commission Quay robbery. He goes to drunken old Billy Hump with a photograph from a Swedish newspaper. He confirms Carol's identity, then, low and behold, there's Nicky, risen from the dead. And that means money. Trouble is, Todd is greedy. He doesn't realise how vicious the people are he's trying to blackmail. They can't afford to let their secret out. After all, there's only one other person who knows it – and that's you, Roller.'

'You're talking through your southern arse,' Weatherley interjected.

'I haven't come to the best bit yet. Nicky and Carol torture the poor old heir hunter. Carol even uses the skills she picked up from her old man in his butcher's shop in Carlisle. What they needed was to find out how much Todd really knew. Turns out he still has stuff on them back in his office at home. So Nicky calls you. Out of the blue, I imagine. That must have given you a nasty jolt. Not someone you wanted to hear from now your career's on the up. Did he threaten you? He was good at that. So, you're sent off to Fellbeck in the middle of the night for a little bit of breaking and entering. But that's not all. They've also discovered that Billy Hump is in on the secret. That has to be dealt with, too. You run the poor bugger over. And you're in a position to make sure that's one hit-and-run that's never solved. It was still a helluva risk, though.' Ash shook his head in mock admiration. 'But you carried it off, Roller; I'll give you that.'

Weatherley had regained his composure.

'Facinating story. Might make a crime novel one day. Trouble is, Ash, you haven't a shred of evidence linking me to any of this.'

Ash lit his cigarette and sent a cloud of smoke in the direction of the council offices above.

'George Dobson described Carol Pew as vindictive. Very apt, as it turns out. You should have heard some of the things she's been telling our Swedish colleagues over the last couple of days. When she realised that you would probably get off scot-free – no doubt you'd come out with some tale about not actually seeing Nicky die when he fell over that cliff – it all tumbled out. Do you know what your big mistake was, Roller? You think with your dick. And I should know. You fucked up my life. But trying it on with Nicky Pew's woman was a step too far. When he was safely out of the way in Australia, you tried to move in on his territory. But Carol was the love of his life, and he hers. She wasn't in a position to resist your advances; she didn't even tell Nicky because they still needed you to help start their new life. But she never forgot, nor forgave.'

A suited PR man approached them. 'Excuse me, sir, *The Journal* wants an interview now.'

Weatherley stood open-mouthed. His upper lip was sweating.

'What?'

'*The Journal*. They're waiting.'

'Yes,' he said distractedly. 'Em... no... mustn't keep them waiting.' He walked away from Ash like a man who had been dazed by an unexpected punch. Ash decided it was time for a celebratory drink.

CHAPTER 50

Anita left the hospital on foot at about five in the evening. She was back in sensible shoes. The rush hour traffic was heavy, with vehicles bumper-to-bumper stretching along John Ericsson's väg and into Ystadvägen. It was easier to walk home than drive, even at the risk of being mown down by Malmö's army of cyclists. The clocks going back at the weekend and the cold breeze off the Sound were portents of winter. Hakim had seemed cheerful enough and was due to go home tomorrow. The last three days had been stressful. Interviewing Carol Pew had been an unpleasant experience. She blamed everything on Nicky. And thanks to Westermark's sharp-shooting, he wasn't alive to contradict her. The tactic had worked in England; it wouldn't work in Sweden. They had found the pruning saw. The grooves matched those on Graeme Todd's wrist. It was her prints that were on it, not Nicky's. Eventually, the whole sordid tale came spilling out; the details of which Anita had relayed to Ash.

Then there was Greta Jansson. She had been busy on that front, too, though Björn was still wallowing in a cell, with another court appearance due in a week. As for Nordlund, Sejad Medunjanin was still firmly in the frame, and a huge number of officers were being employed to try and prove it. His funeral was scheduled for the following Tuesday, and Anita had been asked to say a few words on behalf of the department. She wasn't sure she was emotionally up to it.

As she reached the edge of Pildammsparken, her mobile rang.

'Hi Anita, it's Kevin. Kevin Ash.'

'I know. Your name came up.' She found herself grinning.

'Just thought I'd let you know that Roller Weatherley has been arrested by Northumbria Police for the murder of Billy Hump. They've got a bucket load of other charges lined up, too.'

'That's good.'

'Pity I couldn't do the arresting myself. The only thing he did in Cumbria was a bit of burglary. Never mind, I'll not miss his trial, even if I have to take some holiday leave. I bet Leanne doesn't go!'

'Revenge is best served cold?'

Ash laughed at the other end. 'Something like that. Anyway, have you got everything under control over there?'

'Yeah. Coping OK.'

'When this gets to trial, they'll want Carol over here to testify against Weatherley. Maybe you could come over with her.'

'I doubt it.'

'Oh.' The disappointment was obvious in his voice. 'So everything's fine?'

'Yes, everything's fine. Just one more thing to do.'

'Well, I'd better let you go.' He sounded reluctant to end the call.

'Thanks for calling, Kevin.'

'No problem.' He paused. 'Anita?'

'Yes?'

She could hear him clear his throat. 'Will you call me sometime? Other than about work, I mean.'

'Maybe I will.'

She allowed herself a smile as she put her phone away.

*

Friday night. Westermark hadn't felt this good for some time. He poured himself a second gin and tonic and turned the music up. It was ABBA. Now they were acceptable again, he didn't have to feel guilty or girlie about listening to them. He might go clubbing later. Find a hot woman, bring her back, put on some moody music and give her a good time. What better way to celebrate two great results? Björn Sundström had been fingered for Greta Jansson's killing and he, Karl Westermark, was a hero. The dramatic shoot-out at Ales Stenar was all over Sweden. The press had loved it. So, instead of Anita winning plaudits for discovering a murderous diamond robber whom everybody thought was dead, and solving the Graeme Todd case, he had stolen her thunder. He had stitched her up twice. Promotion was on the horizon and he would leave her in his wake.

He wandered out onto the balcony. He was wearing a new tan shirt. It wasn't designed to keep out the cold, yet he was in such an upbeat mood that he didn't feel the evening chill. As he always did, he marvelled at the view; the Öresund Bridge with its constant toing and froing of vehicle headlights and brightly lit trains; the orange glow above Copenhagen across the water reminding him of the skies depicted in the biblical illustrations he had been shown at school when he was a youngster. Maybe next weekend he would book himself into a hotel over there and trawl the bars and clubs for a bit of Danish skirt. He would have another holiday, too. Visit his little sister in Boston before Christmas. In his seedy world of selfish pleasure and one-night stands, he had never found a woman in whom he could confide, trust with his innermost thoughts, inspire loyalty. Only Sigyn. She'd always felt for her brother an unconditional love which made her blind to his shortcomings.

He was disturbed by the ringing of the doorbell. It was odd that the visitor hadn't buzzed from the apartment block entrance. Must be a neighbour. He was taken by surprise when he unlocked the door to find Anita Sundström standing in the corridor.

'Can I come in?'

Westermark smirked. 'Of course.'

He followed her into the living room. She was dressed all in black – short jacket, jersey and jeans. His hopes were suddenly raised. This could only be a social call. Anita scanned the room. Everything except the chestnut-brown wooden floor was in monochrome. The dining table and chairs in one corner were black, as were the sideboard, the lampshades and the thick surround of the enormous plasma television on the wall. The rest of the furniture was white and soulless. Black and white. That summed up Karl Westermark, Anita concluded. No grey areas in this man's life. All or nothing. There were a couple of modern ceramics and a range of DVDs on a shelf, but not a book in sight. That was telling, too. She sat down on the long, white sofa, clutching her keys on her lap.

'Drink?' Westermark offered.

'No thanks.'

Westermark shrugged and went over to a tray on the sideboard that was crammed with bottles. He freshened his gin. He didn't take a seat.

'And to what do I owe this visit?'

'I want you to come with me down to headquarters.'

Westermark took a swig.

'Why? It's Friday night and I'm going to have some fun.'

'I don't think so.'

There was something about the edge in her voice that alerted him. He could see she wasn't relaxed. He was immediately on his guard.

'If we've something on, why didn't you just ring?'

'Because, Karl, I'm here to arrest you.'

Westermark burst out laughing. 'Oh, just fuck off, Anita. I thought you might have come here to thank me for sorting out your case for you. But this? It's some kind of sick joke, right?'

Anita didn't move a muscle.

'I'm here to arrest you for the murder of Greta Jansson.'

Westermark paled. 'Oh, I see what this is. You're trying to get your pathetic ex off the hook. Won't wash Anita. He did it.'

'He didn't. You did. And it was Henrik Nordlund who found out. So you had to kill him, too.'

Westermark drained his glass. 'What are you on?'

'A wave of contempt for you. I knew you were rotten, but even I didn't think you'd go as far as murder.'

Westermark took a step towards her, and Anita thought he was going to strike her. He didn't, though for a moment he hovered menacingly over her. Then the old confidence returned. Even the self-satisfied smile.

'And how have you worked this out, exactly?'

'It wasn't me. It was Henrik. It all started with the interview you both conducted with Björn.'

'That was straightforward enough. The professor talked himself into a cell if I remember correctly.'

'I listened to it over and over again and, at first, I couldn't understand what Nordlund was on about. Then it struck me. The fingerprints.'

'Fingerprints?'

'They'd been a problem from the beginning. Why had Björn gone to so much trouble to get rid of prints in the bedroom and key areas where the rapist must have been, yet left others to be found elsewhere in the apartment? And you gave the clue to Henrik yourself. You described Björn as an "amateur".'

'He was.'

'I agree. But the person who cleaned up that apartment definitely wasn't. He knew exactly what he was doing. Thulin's findings confirmed that. It was a professional job by someone who knew what the forensics team would be looking for.'

'Big deal. So the professor was more thorough than I gave

him credit for. There's no link to me.'

'You're right. But that thoroughness was enough to get Henrik thinking – and double-checking. He possibly didn't have you in mind at that stage, but when he checked the CCTV footage and Jansson's call log, which only you handled, and found the footage for the Moosehead pub in Lilla Torg had mysteriously gone missing, he started to put two and two together. I've been doing the same digging, Karl, and I've come up with four as well.'

'You're talking crap – the CCTV was irrelevant.'

'Your photo wasn't. A helpful barman recognised you. He'd been chatting up Greta when she was waiting for her friend. So he remembered her really well – and the man who bought her several drinks later on. You.'

'Doesn't mean I killed her.'

'Not in itself. It was the call she made to you after Björn left her place.'

'You can't have found...'

'You doctored that too, of course. But your mobile call log was very revealing. I checked on that. You received a call from Greta Jansson at 11.47 on Friday night, September the twenty-eighth. The call lasted two minutes, nine seconds. Long enough to ask her new "friend", the one she had taunted Björn with, to come round and comfort her. She'd already had too much to drink after an evening spent with you. Too good an opportunity for you to miss. A drunken girl ringing up and inviting you round at that time of night – you must have assumed she was only after one thing. That's how your mind works, isn't it? You turn up and misread the signals. She'd have been upset after her row with Björn. For her, it would have been a traumatic experience. I suspect all she wanted was a shoulder to cry on. But to you that's an open invitation. After you raped her, you must have realised that this one might come back to haunt you. How many times has it happened before, Karl? Using your position as a cop to keep it all quiet? When this goes public, I expect a lot of women will emerge from the woodwork. Greta was different though, wasn't she? Brighter maybe? You had to do something to make sure she didn't blab. The state she was in, it must have been quite straightforward to get her into your car and down to the harbour. It was there that you killed her. How did that feel, Karl, strangling a helpless girl? I suppose if that storm hadn't thrown up Greta's body, you'd have been in the clear. Another week or so, and it would have been useless for forensic investigation. You must have been worried when a body was washed up outside here – and relieved when it turned out to be Graeme Todd's. Anyway, after killing Greta you go back to the apartment and clean up. It couldn't have worked out better for you when it later transpires that Björn had rolled up again and left his prints everywhere – or almost everywhere.'

'You're forgetting the earring. It was in the professor's car.'

'Of course it was. It was you who collected the car from Uppsala. The earring must have come off in that fancy Porsche of yours when you strangled the poor girl. All you had to do was drop it into Björn's car for forensics to find. It'll be interesting to see what turns up when Thulin's team takes your Porsche apart.'

'And Nordlund?' Westermark said matter-of-factly, his icy blue stare showing no glimmer of emotion.

'You realised something was up. He was continuing to dig, even though Björn seemed to be the perpetrator and the official investigation was as good as closed. You must have been worried because Henrik was always thorough. You started to follow him to find out what he was up to. He knew someone was watching him. It was no accident that I ran into you near his apartment that night I had dinner with him. What had he been telling me? Eventually, you were so concerned you had to act. I thought it odd he didn't want to meet at headquarters. Of course, he'd realised by this time the culprit was a fellow detective because of the evidence being tampered with. But you got to him just before I did. Again, Thulin said it was a "professional" job.'

'You've got it all worked out, haven't you?'

'Until that little slip of the tongue, you'd been so clever. Seemingly finding credible suspects in Fraser and Holm, while all the time manoeuvring Björn into the frame. You hijacked Henrik's investigation – and you so nearly pulled it off.'

Westermark turned his back on her.

'Where are you going?' she asked sharply.

'Some more ice for my drink,' he answered coolly, and sauntered into the kitchen.

Anita shifted in her seat nervously. It had taken great self-control to confront Westermark. And she still hadn't finished. She knew she must be calm and professionally detached, even though every fibre of her being wanted to scream out that this bastard had killed her friend and an innocent young woman. She had to play the game.

Westermark didn't return with his glass. Instead he was holding a regulation, police-issue Sig Sauer. It was pointing straight at her. Anita stiffened. She'd been naïve to think his pistol would be safely locked away at the polishus. He casually sat down in a white swivel chair and swayed gently back and forth. Eventually, he spoke.

'You think you're so fucking clever, Anita.'

Anita was mesmerised by the pistol. This was going to be difficult.

'Put that down, Karl.'

'You shouldn't have come on your own. Trying to be a heroine again. Sorry, it's hero in this fucking gender-equal world that we fanny about in, isn't it? Either way, you'll never be as good a cop as me. You're not tough enough. Not decisive enough. Too bloody emotional. Sucker for a sob story or a lost cause. Look at the Scottish prick you loved so much. I do things that need to be done.'

'Like killing Jansson and Nordlund?'

'Both necessary actions for different reasons.' Anita couldn't believe how unruffled and controlled Westermark was. That wasn't good. She wasn't sure what she had expected. Not this.

'But I have to hand it to you, Anita – your story's spot on. The Jansson bitch was whimpering on about reporting me. And Nordlund got too nosey. Why didn't he just leave it?' he said in a sudden burst of anguish. 'He was retiring in a couple of months. We had our murderer, for fuck's sake. If only he'd just let it lie.'

'He was a good policeman to the last.'

'Screw him! Screw you all!'

He leant forward and with the pistol he slowly began to make little circles in the air in front of Anita's face.

'Oh, Anita. We could have been so good together. I know you always wanted me. I would have been the best fuck you ever had. And now it's too late. Can't let you live.' In an instant he lost his temper. 'You've always had it in for me. Why?' he screamed. 'Why?'

Anita sat as passively as she could while he ranted. She was feeling sick, but she mustn't betray her fear. In a moment, the fury passed and he sat back in the chair, grinning.

'I always hated you for loving that journalist. It should have been me, not him.' He gave a slight guffaw. 'It was a pendant that gave Strachan away, remember? I thought planting the earring in your ex's car was a nice piece of irony. Well, I'm glad Strachan's dead. And as for Nordlund – why couldn't you show me the respect you showed him? That's what I wanted. That's what I deserved.'

'Not after our failure to arrest Dag Wollstad.'

He burst into a disconcerting giggle.

'I *knew* you knew. You were the only one who suspected I'd tipped him off.'

'How many pieces of silver did you get for that, Karl?'

'The Porsche, the apartment. Kristina paid me handsomely. I still get the cheques. Dag's somewhere in Bolivia, apparently.'

'And was she part of the deal?'

'Oh yeeesss. One night of passion with the delectable widow. She wouldn't let me have any more. It was worth it, though.'

'The force doesn't need people like you, Karl.'

He swivelled rhythmically in his chair.

'I'm a bloody good cop. Always will be. And when I've talked my way out of your disappearance, I will be again. I think another body in the Sound.'

He stopped moving the chair.

'Any last words, Anita?'

'Yes.' To Westermark's surprise, she held up her keys and spoke into the fob. 'Have you got all that?'

'Shit! You fucking—'

'Neat device. Video too. Moberg's watching this in an apartment down the corridor. There are police everywhere. Shooting me isn't going to save you, Karl. Give yourself up.'

She could see the panic spreading across Westermark's face as his mind frantically sifted through his diminishing options.

'We could have proved that you killed Greta Jansson, but we didn't have enough to get you for Henrik's murder. Until now.'

Then a calmness overcame him. Almost a look of serenity. There was a banging on the front door as his colleagues started to break it down.

He smiled again. That familiar, superior smirk that had been his trademark all the time they had served together.

'Well done, Anita. After all these years, you've outdone me at last.'

Karl Westermark poked his pistol into his mouth and pulled the trigger.

Other titles by the author

Meet me in Malmö is the first in the series of the best-selling crime mysteries featuring Inspector Anita Sundström.
Murder in Malmö and *Midnight in Malmö* are the second and fourth titles.

A British journalist is invited to Malmö to interview an old

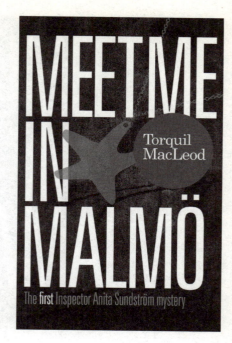

university friend who is now one of Sweden's leading film directors. When he discovers the directors glamorous film star wife dead in her apartment, the Skåne County Police are called in to solve the high-profile case. Among the investigating team is Inspector Anita Sundström, who soon finds the list of suspects growing. As Anita battles to discover the answers amid the antagonism of some of her colleagues, she even begins to think that the person she is becoming attracted to could be the murderer. This is the first in a series of the best-selling crime mysteries featuring Inspector Anita Sundström.

Other titles by the author

Murder in Malmö is the second in the series of the best-selling crime mysteries featuring Inspector Anita Sundström. *Meet me in Malmö* and *Midnight in Malmö* are the first and fourth titles.

A gunman is loose in Malmö and he's targeting immigrants.

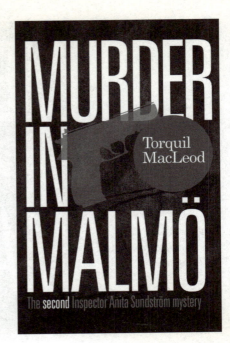

The charismatic head of an advertising agency is found dead in his shower. Inspector Anita Sundström wants to be involved in the murder investigations, but she is being sidelined by her antagonistic boss. She is assigned to find a stolen painting by a once-fashionable artist, as well as being lumbered with a new trainee assistant. She also has to do to restore her professional reputation after a deadly mix-up in a previous high-profile case. Then another prominent Malmö businessman is found murdered and Sundström finds herself back in the action and facing new dangers in the second Anita Sundström Malmö mystery.

Other titles by the author

Midnight in Malmö is the fourth in the series of the best-selling crime mysteries featuring Inspector Anita Sundström. *Meet me in Malmö* and *Murder in Malmö* are the first and second titles.

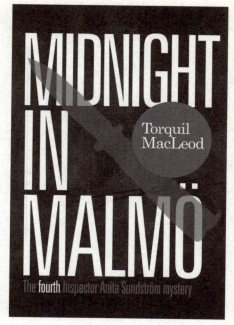

When a woman is stabbed to death while jogging in Malmö's main park, the Criminal Investigation Squad need to discover who she is before the case can properly get under way. Soon they realise the victim had flown in from Switzerland, and with links to important people in the city, she wasn't everything she seemed. Meanwhile, enjoying the hot summer away from Malmö, Anita Sundström is on her annual leave and is showing Kevin Ash the sights of Skåne. Their holiday is interrupted by the apparent suicide of a respected, retired diplomat. After a further death, Anita finds herself unofficially investigating a case that has its roots in the 1917 chance meeting of a Malmö waiter with the world's most famous revolutionary. All she knows is that the answers lie in Berlin. Two investigations that begin and end at *Midnight in Malmö* – the fourth Inspector Anita Sundström mystery.